She's Mine

She's Mine

A.A. Chaudhuri

hera

First published in the United Kingdom in 2021 by

Hera Books
28b Cricketfield Road
London, E5 8NS
United Kingdom

A CIP catalogue record for this book is available from the British Library.

Print ISBN 978 1 80032 607 1
Ebook ISBN 978 1 912973 73 6

Look for more great books at www.herabooks.com

Printed and bound in Great Britain by Clays Ltd, Elcograf S.p.A.

1

For my Family, the greatest gift in life

'In a child's eyes, a mother is a goddess. She can be glorious or terrible, benevolent or filled with wrath, but she commands love either way. I am convinced that this is the greatest power in the universe.'

N.K. Jemisin, *The Hundred Thousand Kingdoms*

Prologue

I walk into the room, and she turns to smile at me. But I don't smile back.

I know that behind that smile lies a monster.

A psychotic, self-serving monster whose only agenda is to destroy lives.

She reads this on my face. Sees the change in me. Displays a fear I have never seen before, yet at the same time, and what is most sickening, no remorse.

'Look, don't be dramatic, I can explain.'

She is poison. I act quick. Grabbing the nearest cushion before she has time to defend herself with yet more lies.

And with a force brewed from a rage I hadn't thought myself capable of, I press it hard against her face. Hard into the sockets of her eyes. Crushing the bullshit out of her deceitful lips.

It feels good. Cathartic. Satisfying. Harder and harder until she is still.

Those lips will lie no more.

Chapter One

Christine

Now

February 2019

This is my first visit. Not to a psychiatrist, but to this particular psychiatrist, Dr Freya Cousins, who, at this moment, is sitting just a few feet away from me. Unlike the other psychiatrists I've seen over the years, she works from her home off the Finchley Road and, conveniently, only two stops from where I live with Greg, my husband, in St John's Wood.

Before *it* happened, and my life, me, the person I was back then, changed forever, beyond all recognition, I had never imagined myself the type to visit a psychiatrist. In fact, should anyone have suggested it to me, I would have laughed in their face, considered it an insult to my highly educated, fully functional, supremely in-control self.

Back then, my opinion – which now makes me cringe with shame – was that psychiatrists were time-wasting money-grabbers. Failed medical doctors who preyed on weak-willed losers gullible and dumb enough to be fooled by their psychobabble, their incomprehensible jibber-jabber, designed purely to make them sound more intelligent than they really were, and which only ended up making their patients feel more depressed, more confused, more suicidal than before they started seeing them.

But then it happened. I lost *you*. And after that, I was never the same again. I went from being the most self-assured, rational person I knew, to a feeble, mentally unhinged nervous wreck who, for a year after, could barely pluck up the nerve to make a cup of tea, let alone leave the house and function anywhere like a normal person.

And suddenly, psychiatrists were the only people I felt able to talk to. Neutral players who would listen without judging me, and who, unlike my family and friends, I could look in the eye without feeling sick with guilt.

I lost you. *How the fuck could I have lost you?* This wasn't supposed to happen to someone like me. The worst nightmare imaginable for any parent shouldn't have happened to someone like me, so why in God's name did it? Why did I turn my back on you, walk away, prioritize a phone call over my precious child?

Why?!

I have tortured myself with these questions every day for the last twenty-three years, and it never gets any easier.

There are two reasons for this. The first is that we never got closure. You were never found, and so we don't know what happened to you. Whether you are still alive, or whether you died within hours, days, of being taken. And the not knowing, the not having closure, is torture. It haunts my dreams at night, plagues my waking thoughts, and there is no escape from it. I am its prisoner, and I fear that my sentence is infinite.

The second is that, although I have never told anyone this, not even the police, in my heart I know why it happened; why I turned away and failed to keep my eye on you as any mother should. And the reason is something I feel so ashamed of it's a wonder I am still alive and not destroyed by guilt. It's also why my relationship with Greg is dead.

You see, I was too cowardly to tell him the truth, even though he deserved to hear it. I couldn't bear to cause him further pain and so I consciously pushed him away because it was the easier thing to do.

3

The fact is, my darling, I let both of you down because I was selfish; too caught up in my own superficial needs and desires to think about the consequences of my actions. And that is why I find it hard to look Greg in the eye, let alone allow him to touch me, console me. I am simply not worthy of his love or compassion. Or anyone's, for that matter.

It is my fault, and mine alone, that you are gone.

I only had more children out of guilt, to please Greg, not because I wanted them. In fact, having your brother and sister made things worse rather than better. I despise myself for saying this, but it's the truth.

Greg, who has a heart of gold, thought having more children would help me get over losing you, help repair our relationship, bring us closer together again. But it didn't work like that. I could never let myself love them the way I loved you. I was too afraid that if I gave my heart and soul to them, if I truly immersed myself in them, and they were then, somehow, taken from me, I would never recover. I couldn't chance that; I couldn't possibly go through that again. And so, although I did all the functional things a mother is supposed to do, I did so dispassionately, and this has cost me dearly.

Now in their twenties, Ella and Daniel resent me. They eye me with a coldness that freezes me in my tracks every time I see them. But I cannot blame them. It is my own doing. They love Greg with a far greater tenderness than they love me; if, in fact, they love me at all – they've never actually told me so, at least, not since they were little. And even then, it was probably only because that's the kind of thing children say when they are small. It's automatic.

The fact is, I don't really know them; they are virtual strangers to me, as I am to them, and when they see me, they seem to look through me, perhaps because all they see is a hard, empty shell of a person. A mother that could have been, but never was. A mother in name only. Indifferent and self-absorbed.

'Don't be afraid, Christine.' Dr Cousins' soothing lilt stirs me from my thoughts. 'First of all, just tell me a bit about yourself – your background, where you live, your family.'

Like so many of her well-intentioned peers have done over the years, she is encouraging me to open up to her. Hoping the cathartic process of talking about myself, facing my demons head-on, will somehow make life more bearable. Help me to stop blaming myself every day of my life for your disappearance.

Help me to accept that you, my Heidi, my little girl, are gone and never coming back.

If only that were possible. Because the fact is, I can't stop blaming myself, and I cannot accept that you are gone. I will never accept that. So *why* am I here? If I don't want to get better, don't feel that I can, why am I talking to this woman?

It all comes back to the secret I've never dared tell anyone. A secret I kept even from my closest friends, Janine and Miranda. A secret so bad, so shameful, I don't deserve to be happy again, and I certainly don't deserve Greg – the best husband anyone could wish for.

But is Dr Cousins the one to whom I will, at last, unload the burden I've carried all these years? It's not just that I am afraid, it's also that I have never felt completely comfortable with any of my psychiatrists. Never felt that I could trust them with my deepest, darkest secrets. But perhaps she'll be different. Perhaps she's the one I'll finally feel able to trust.

I guess time will tell.

Chapter Two

Christine

Before

Your fingers tiptoe along the small of my back, making me quiver with pleasure; a calorific, insatiable pleasure that knows no bounds. They have traced this path countless times before, and others besides, but I never tire of your touch. It just makes me come back for more. You do something to me; have this hold, this power over me, a power that always makes your touch feel as exquisite as the first time. That delectable, heart-raising first touch at the start of an affair; a feeling which sends a rush of electricity through you, makes you heady, horny, as soft and light as a marshmallow. When you know that what you are doing is wrong and hurting those closest to you, but at the same time, you cannot stop yourself because nothing else in this world compares to that feeling.

You must know that it was never my intention to have an affair with you; to be smitten with a man who wasn't my husband. I have always been one to play by the book, the goody two shoes at school and beyond, the one to urge my flightier peers to exercise caution, to think before they act, to be careful not to let their heart rule their head. Such Mills & Boon sentiment is not in my nature, and I have never been one for clichés. I'll happily swear to that, even though my actions now suggest otherwise.

You – the one I am having an affair with behind my gentle, unsuspecting husband's back – aren't right for me. We would never work as husband and wife; we're too similar, and we would drive each other nuts. But there's this unquenchable carnal attraction between us that neither of us can resist; it sizzles through me, propels me towards you, and you to me. You are my cocaine. A drug that is bad for me, that will no doubt kill me eventually, but makes me feel so high at the time. You are the drug I simply can't get enough of.

My husband adores me. Which makes my adultery more unpardonable, my guilt so much worse. He has loved me from the first. His expression said as much the moment we first locked eyes. I remember there being such genuine warmth to his gaze, an earnestness that made me feel so secure, I instantly felt that I could trust him. And then, slowly but surely, I fell in love with him. He was the safe, sensible choice. Husband material. Father material.

But *you*? You are the opposite. You are selfish, power-driven, career-obsessed, and you have no doubt seduced more women than I would care to imagine. But that's what makes you so bloody irresistible. You make me weak, literally weak at the knees, and as I walk into the hotel lift with you right now, your fingers still skating across my back, I swallow my guilt and luxuriate in the moment.

Greg keeps me safe, and he will keep the child growing inside me safe, despite my uncertainty as to whether it is his. But our affair keeps me *alive*.

I cannot stop myself, despite my conscience telling me that someday I will be made to pay for my actions, and my perfect life will be no more.

Chapter Three

Heidi

Now

I am not dead.

I am alive, breathing, safe, intact. Physically intact, at least. Whether I am mentally is debatable. What's not debatable is that I am so much better off with *her* than I would have been with you.

Despite never being short of love or attention from her – who I'll always consider to be my real mother – when she told me the truth, it changed me. It rocked the very foundations of my existence. So you see, no matter how much love she showered me with, there's always been this underlying sense of discontent, betrayal, hurt, haunting my soul. It tugs at my insides, makes me feel bitter and vengeful.

Of course, I was too young to remember the day you abandoned me. The day you took your eye off the ball and lost me, all because you prioritized a call from your lover over watching your vulnerable two-year-old daughter. *How could you have done that?* A highly educated woman. Didn't it occur to you at the time that children get abducted every day? Didn't you read the papers, watch the news? For some reason, like my mother told me, you thought you were above all that, proving what a self-centred person you are. A person who stuffed her child's mouth with a dummy so that she could take the call in peace because it suited her.

Thank God my mother (again, not you, you're not my mother even though I have half your DNA), was watching. Thank God she saw how neglectful you were, took pity on me. Recognized that you were too wrapped up in your own selfish desires to be a fit mother. That you would starve me of love and attention the way you've since starved your other children. And she wanted to stop me from becoming a carbon copy of you: a vain, self-absorbed slut. A man-eater who seduces other women's men; men who should have stayed true to women who would have gone to the ends of the earth for them. She saved me while I was still young enough to be saved, before I became indoctrinated with your mindset, with your immoral lifestyle. The day she took me was the most fortunate day of my life, and I am so grateful to her. She raised me to be a kind and considerate person, despite her shitty childhood, and I respect her for that. She is someone who always wanted children, who always puts her family and friends first. Someone who'll do anything to protect them, loyal to the last. She is the best person I know, and I am so lucky that she is my mother, and not you.

When she told me what happened, what kind of a person you were – still are, in fact – it hurt badly, I won't lie. But I soon came to understand and appreciate why she told me. She didn't want to lie to me the way you have lied to so many people over the years. And I empathize with her desire to hurt you. Because I want to hurt you too. And that is why I am going to help her achieve that.

I really don't know how you can live with yourself. You've enlisted yet another shrink hoping somehow she'll be different. But the fact is, no amount of counselling can absolve you from what you did.

You need to learn your lesson, Christine. You might think you've suffered enough, but you haven't. You need to suffer more and you need to come clean so the world will finally see your true colours and justice can be served.

9

I am alive, but the most glorious part is that you have no idea. You will soon, though. And I can't wait to see the look on your face, Mummy dearest, when I reveal myself to you.

Chapter Four

Christine

Now

I lie flat on Dr Cousins' couch and try to relax my shoulders which are tense and knotted from anxiety, and the intensive weight training which, over the years since you disappeared, has rendered my body unrecognizable from how it was before. Of course, when I fell pregnant with Ella and Daniel I had to ease up. Which was tough. It didn't sit well with my need for control. But even then, I still hit the gym up to thirty weeks gone. It was selfish of me, and it stressed the hell out of Greg. But I didn't care. It was that or go insane. Gone are my fulsome breasts and generous curves, the rounded hips and loose tummy flesh which should serve as proud marks of childbirth. Instead, my arms are long and stringy, my biceps protrude through my close-fitting turtle-neck jumper like Cox's apples, my chest is flat like a prepubescent boy's, my hips are straight and bony, my stomach hard and steel-like, the result of one thousand crunches a day and relentless planks.

Transforming my body was a way of hiding from me; my real, disgraceful self. And so began an obsessive quest to make myself unrecognizable from the person I was before I lost you. The logic being that if I could somehow change my outward appearance, then perhaps I could fool myself into thinking I was no longer me, and therefore no longer the person who had lost you, who had behaved in the appalling way I had. It has become an addiction, I suppose. I seem to be prone to them. And like any addiction, it is dangerous and unhealthy. Both Miranda and Janine berate me for it. I have a feeling they talk about me on the phone. I'm not angry with them. It's not like they're conspiring against me. They'd never do such a thing. They're my friends, and it's only natural they'd worry about me and my obsessive nature which will probably prevent me from hitting old age. But what they can't seem to grasp is that I don't care. Why should I care about reaching old age when you, my darling baby girl, may have been denied the chance to reach adulthood because of my own selfishness?

You and I were in Peter Jones on the King's Road. It was an unusually hot late-summer's day and we'd ducked inside the air-conditioned department store to seek sanctuary from the heat. Like me, you were wearing a sleeveless cotton dress, only yours was dotted with pretty multicoloured butterflies, while mine was plain blue-and-white striped. I knew even then that you were a *girly girl*. You would giggle when I decorated your hair with ribbons and sparkly hairgrips, and you would always point to the pretty pastel-coloured dresses in the shops and in my glossy women's magazines, not to mention delight in opening my handbags, testing every cosmetic inside, often with very messy results. You would play for hours on end with your dolls, smoothing down their hair, giving them hugs when they were sad or scared, attempting to change their nappies, feeding them milk with your plastic baby bottle. And you would sit upright on my bed, watch me with fascinated eyes as I sat at my dressing table and applied my lipstick, or arranged my hair in the style I wanted for that day. You were my princess. But you were also a daddy's girl.

The joy on your face was priceless on the rare occasions Greg came home early from work and scooped you up in his arms, spinning you round until you were dizzy and showering you with kisses as you giggled uncontrollably. I can still remember your unaffected laughter, the way your face broke out into the broadest of smiles, the pure, natural elation of being loved. It is one of my fondest, yet most painful, memories.

That day – the day you were stolen from me – you had just turned two-and-a-half. That unbelievably cute age; chubby cheeks, chubby arms, chubby legs, loveable little phrases that would melt my heart. And when I looked at you, I'd have this urge to wrap you up in my arms and squeeze you tight, because you were just too goddamn gorgeous and it was almost hard to believe you were mine. You came from me, and I'd wonder how I had existed, truly lived, before you.

You had a delicious mop of chocolate-brown curls, just like your father, the dinkiest of milk teeth interspersed with a few adorable gaps, fat little legs that kicked about in the buggy as you took in your surroundings with glee, curious about everything, your big brown eyes filled with wonder, along with pure, unconditional love for the one with whom you felt most safe. The one person who attended to your every need. Who, more than anyone, you could trust to keep you safe.

If only that had been true.

Chapter Five

Christine

Before

August 1996

'What do you mean, you can't see me any more?'

I'm already feeling hot and flustered from getting on and off the bus in thirty-degree heat, not to mention all the added paraphernalia that goes with travelling with a toddler. The change mat, the baby wipes, the drinks, the snacks, the distraction toys, the whopping great Maclaren pram/pushchair contraption Greg insisted on buying that gets in everyone's way. I didn't drive because I resent paying the extortionate parking charges in and around Sloane Square, but now I'm sorely regretting taking the cheap option. Air con and a boot would have made life so much easier.

Heidi was getting crotchety on the bus, too, and I can't say I blame her, poor love, even though I lost my rag at one point and yelled at her to stop crying because Mummy was doing the bloody best she could. That made her scream even more, tears rolling down her plump, increasingly red cheeks, and I felt so bad, like the worst mother in the world, and it was as if everyone on the bus was looking at us as we manoeuvred our way off the number 22 onto Sloane Street. *What a bitch*, they must have thought, *shouting at her poor innocent child. Shouldn't bloody well have kids if she can't deal with them!* I'm certain such thoughts raced through their judgemental minds.

What they didn't know was that I'd been up half the night, trying to get her back to sleep – she's been having nightmares on and off for a week or so – and I'm dead beat. But it's so hot inside the house, I had to get out. I told all this to Miranda, who happened to call as I'd just boarded the bus. Not great timing, phone wedged under my ear as I attempted to haul the push-chair onboard with my right hand while showing the driver my travelcard with my left. The phone in itself drew enough of an audience, let alone my shouting. Greg's so protective of me and Heidi, he insisted on buying me the same model he uses for work, the Nokia 880, just in case I run into trouble. Even though I managed OK for the first two years of Heidi's life without one. It's typical of his caring nature, and I feel incredibly spoilt compared to other mum friends forced to rely on payphones. Not least because Greg's not the only one to have bought me a phone. You did, too. A different model, in case I mix them up. Just so it would be easier for us to contact one another, as you've just done. We've realized we can't be as spontaneous now that I'm a mother. It's registered in your name, though, to your work address. Obviously, I can't have bills being sent to my home in case Greg sees them. Even so, I'm constantly panicking he's going to find out, despite guarding the phone like a hawk.

Anyway, Miranda wasn't to know it was bad timing. She was just calling for a quick catch-up during her break from a client charity event she's attending today. Funnily enough, it's quite close to Sloane Square, at a hotel in South Kensington, and while she was on the phone she asked if I fancied meeting up later for a cocktail at The Berkeley, around eight-ish. Boy, how the other half live. How I would have loved to have said, *Yes, I'll be there, 8 p.m. sharp, wouldn't miss it for the world.* Just like the good old days. But I knew that by the time I'd finished up here, and made the arduous journey home, fed and bathed Heidi, not to mention phoned Greg to make sure he could race home in time to relieve me, all I'd want is to be able to put my feet up in front of the TV with a glass of wine and a take-out. Not exactly the rock and roll lifestyle I'd always imagined for myself, but in truth, I'm not complaining. I wouldn't trade my life with Heidi for my old life for the world, even though Miranda may not have believed it at the time, just because I kind of yelled at Heidi to be quiet so I could *bloody well talk to Auntie Miranda*. I hope she doesn't think I'm a bad mother. I hope she realizes I just said it in the heat of the moment. The last thing I want is to stir up bad memories from her own childhood for her. I can't imagine what it must have been like for her growing up without a mother; with only a father who treated her unkindly. The old codger's still alive, and as much of an arsehole as he was back then. She just about persuaded him to attend her wedding, but he refused to stay on afterwards for their reception. Claimed he had to get back for *Casualty*. Poor Miranda was devastated, although she did well to hold it together. Probably another reason she looked so glum for part of the speeches at my wedding. My father's speech – the wonderful things he said about me at our wedding breakfast – reduced me and everyone else to tears. But her father couldn't even be bothered to show up to hers. I'd feel resentful about that.

Anyway, thinking about it more deeply, I'm pretty sure Miranda doesn't consider me to be a bad mother. She's seen me enough times with Heidi to realize I'd go to the ends of the earth for her. Point is, she was fine about me passing up on her offer of a drink, probably expected me to, and made a light-hearted joke about how she'd much rather be shopping with me in Peter Jones than attending her boring client event with a bunch of tedious colleagues. I couldn't help but laugh when she said this, and it made me realize how much of my old life I don't miss. Then we rang off and agreed to touch base later.

There's another reason I ventured out today, besides needing to escape the heat of the house. I need something for Janine's surprise birthday party this Saturday. Mum and Dad are coming up to babysit, and although I adore my baby girl, I'm looking forward to an adults' night where I can let loose a bit, have a proper conversation without the fear of being interrupted. It's been hard keeping the party a secret. I've nearly let it slip on several occasions, but thankfully I caught myself in time.

In the short while we've been in Peter Jones, I've managed to find a dress. Heidi was very good actually, watching me try on several items as she played with her Care Bear, giving me gorgeous smiles and squeals of approval every now and again as I turned this way and that, checking out my bum, my boobs, making sure my mummy belly didn't protrude too much. It's been thirty months, and I've finally lost all the weight, and then some. I walk everywhere with the pushchair and am probably in better shape than I ever was, although that extra skin around my abdomen is never going to disappear completely without surgery, no matter how much walking, or how many crunches I do.

You said you don't mind, that you find it kind of sexy. Those were your exact words last week when we met after I told Mum I had a hairdresser's appointment and could she please watch Heidi for a few hours. Christ, I felt so bloody guilty, especially when Heidi started sobbing her eyes out as she watched me leave. But the guilt swiftly faded the minute you swept me up in your arms, kissed me long and hard, then threw me onto the bed and started ripping my clothes off. I love it when you're inside me, but you weren't letting me have my way, not at first. You stripped me to my bra and knickers, then slowly slid the bottoms off, teasingly, toying with me, before going down on me, making me arch my back with pleasure, making me come so bad it was like I was being electrocuted. And then you came up for air and kissed me, and I could taste myself on your lips. Later, I got my way, and when you came inside me, it was a real boost to my ego. Knowing that you still found me sexy and desirable, that I still turned you on.

I know it's unforgivable that we have continued our affair, but we can't stop ourselves. Or so I thought, until today.

Because now, out of the blue, just as I'm in the lingerie department picking out something naughty to wear for you, you've dropped this bombshell that we have to stop, and I feel sick, like my world has ended.

'We have no choice, don't you see?' you are saying. And although I do see, because you've just told me your reasons, reasons which are clear, logical and cannot be argued with, our passion was never clear or logical, it was bloody stupid, insane. But that's what made it so great, so addictive. All I can think is, *How can I possibly function without it?*

I almost can't breathe as the room starts to spin, your words playing on a loop in my head, making me deaf, dumb and blind to the world around me. I know you don't really want to end things, I can hear it in your voice, the underlying reticence, and that's some consolation. I just wish we could meet, talk things through face-to-face. Heidi has started to whimper, but I can't deal with that right now and so I do what I vowed never to do when she was born and stick a dummy in her mouth so we're not interrupted. She's far too old, it took us forever to wean her off them, but I still carry one around in case I get desperate.

I try to steady my breathing. Ask you again if you really mean it, suggest that perhaps we could meet and talk about it, just for old times' sake. But you are adamant and it's a crushing blow, and I wonder if you've gone off me after all. Maybe you're having an affair with someone else? I mean, I wouldn't put it past you, you've always been a bit of a cad. I am silent for a while, locked in my own turmoil. And then, as I look up to the ceiling, phone still pressed against my ear as I hear you say my name, ask me if I'm still there, it occurs to me that I have walked away as we talked as the signal wasn't so good where I'd been standing. But, without thinking, I have wandered further than I intended. I'm in a different department, and my chest is suddenly tight, my throat constricted as I look around and realize Heidi is not with me any more. In fact, she's nowhere to be seen.

And then I am saying, then crying, 'Heidi, oh fuck, where did I leave you, where are you, Heidi?'

And as I do, I vaguely hear you say my name, ask me what's wrong, but I let the phone drop to my side and start racing down the aisles, calling my daughter's name, but I can't find her, and I want to vomit as I realize that someone may have taken her, and I may never see her again.

Chapter Six

Christine

Now

Before you, I had been the consummate career girl; a high-flying litigation associate at a top City law firm. I was going places, the world was my oyster, and nothing and no one was going to stop me. Children didn't factor into my thinking, even when Greg and I got married. But all that changed the day you entered my world.

In my head, I have this romantic notion of you being a honeymoon baby, but I guess that's not strictly true. I cried when I discovered I was pregnant. Sitting on the toilet lid, staring at the third successive test I'd done, I'd bawled my eyes out. But they weren't tears of joy; they were tears of utter despair because all I could think was that you were going to ruin my precious career, my social life. My sex life. And I couldn't help wondering whose baby you were. I thought about not telling Greg, getting a discreet abortion, after which no one would have been the wiser; neither Greg, nor *him*. But in the end, I suppose what little conscience I had prevailed, and I reluctantly broke the 'happy' news to an ecstatic Greg.

So that's two reasons why I believe losing you was karma. Karma for the fact that I had an affair, and karma because I didn't want you at first. Whenever I mention the second to Greg (less so now, but I did so frequently in the early days of your disappearance) he tells me I'm being ridiculous, that karma is superstitious nonsense, that once you were born I changed completely and loved you with all my heart and soul. He's right, in that I did fall in love with you the moment you came out and were put to my breast. You were the most breathtaking thing I'd ever seen, and I was consumed by love and a desire to protect you, come what may. A love that was both thrilling and terrifying, I recognized that even then.

But how was I to know that, before your third birthday, I would experience a mother's love for her child at its most brutal? For surely there is no greater loss than the loss of a child. Only in my case, it's that much worse because losing you was of my own making, the result of my own self-indulgent weakness.

After taking a year's maternity leave, I gave up my job; something I could never have imagined doing before you were born. The six-figure salary and lavish lifestyle didn't come close to the time that could be spent with you. It was the easiest decision I'd ever made. I wanted to be around for every cuddle, every tear shed, every smile, that first step, first word, first tooth. I was the one person you'd be able to count on, the one who would love you with a fierce, burning love that would never peter out. A love so strong I would have given my own life for you, should it ever have come to that.

Greg – who worked even longer hours than me – supported my decision. Well on the partnership track, he made more than enough money for the both of us and leaving you with me every day took the worry and the guilt off him. The guilt of leaving you with a stranger, the worry of something bad happening to you in his absence. It was a comfort to him. At least, it should have been. But I failed him, like I failed you.

For a time, the various psychiatrists I saw over the years helped, I guess. Or perhaps it was the placebo effect – my head telling me I was paying these people a fortune to treat me, and therefore it had to be doing something, right? But the fact that I am sitting here with Dr Cousins is proof that none of it has worked. It's never long before I revert to my grief. A grief that's overwhelmed me lately, knowing you would have turned twenty-five this month, the day before yesterday, in fact; a day which I spent most of in bed. I'm always at my lowest around your birthday. I know it's been playing on Greg's mind, too, although, like most things, we haven't discussed it.

It's been nine months since I was last in therapy. Dr Montgomery was pleasant enough. We'd talk about my feelings, the pain of losing you, the toll it's taken on my marriage. But in the end, it was never going to cure me, because I hadn't unburdened myself completely. Hadn't told her what lies at the crux of my guilt. The reason I keep punishing myself, feel that I don't deserve peace.

—

'Try to relax, and just talk to me, Christine. Tell me about yourself, what you are feeling.'

The brown leather couch I am reclining on is so soft I have to fight the urge to fall asleep, and instead make a conscious effort to remain alert and focused. My best friend from uni, Janine, or Jani as I often call her, recommended Dr Cousins to me. Over the last few months, she has helped Janine deal with the death of her husband, Nate, whom she found hanging from the ceiling in his study. Pressure of work, they'd assumed. But that surprised me as I had never considered Nate, an ex-colleague of Greg and mine, the type to buckle under pressure. In fact, he'd always seemed to thrive on it.

He and Janine were married for twenty-seven years, twenty-three of those spent in the Far East, where Nate was posted to run the firm's Hong Kong office eight weeks after you disappeared. Fluent in Mandarin, and already a partner, he'd been the natural choice. It was devastating losing Janine so soon after losing you. The night before they left, we drank Chablis and cried like babies. I know she felt guilty, but it wasn't her fault; she had to go where Nate was sent. It was just the worst possible timing. We kept in touch over the years, of course. Phone calls, letters, email and, more recently, Skype. Would exchange photographs of our children – Janine and Nate adopted Sarah after discovering they couldn't have children of their own – but I could never summon up the impetus to fly out there, too locked in my own grief. France was about as far as we went when the kids were young. And after what happened to you, Janine was exceptionally protective of Sarah. Aside from Nate flying over for occasional meetings, they barely left Hong Kong, shunning social media as it became popular, lest it attracted unwanted attention. Greg and I were the same, despite it being less of a thing when our kids were growing up. Not just to protect Ella and Daniel, but because after the intrusiveness of the investigation, all we craved was anonymity. To this day you won't catch Ella and Daniel posting about their private lives. Greg instilled that in them. They know what the investigation, and all the exposure that went with it, did to us. It's another reason I never told the police my secret. The intrusiveness was bad enough without the addition of a sex scandal. I remember reporters camping outside our house. We were young, successful lawyers, ideal candidates for a juicy tabloid story. All I could think about was the damage it would do to the reputations of everyone involved. The hurt it would cause. I couldn't bear to lose the people I loved, even though, ironically, my guilt has caused me to push them away.

To be fair it was my other close friend, Greg's ex, Miranda, who brought Dr Cousins into our lives. Dr Cousins had been travelling to a work conference in Newcastle, where Miranda lives, when she accidentally slammed into the back of Miranda's car at a set of lights. According to Miranda, Dr Cousins was extremely apologetic. She'd been running late for a talk she was giving, her mind only half on the road, which was no excuse but there it was. Miranda had also felt partly to blame having braked hard at amber when she could have gone straight through. They'd swapped business cards and agreed to settle the matter privately. At the time, Janine who by then had moved back to the UK, unable to live amongst constant reminders of Nate, was severely depressed, and both Miranda and I feared she might do something desperate. Although Miranda's never been one for shrinks – for years she made a point of telling me I was wasting my time with them – there was clearly something about Dr Cousins that made her think otherwise. She'd passed on her details to Janine, and thank God she did because Dr Cousins has been instrumental in helping Janine get her life back on track.

–

Physically, Dr Cousins is very different from my previous psychiatrists. She looks like a movie star playing dress-up; Cameron Diaz or some other impossibly attractive female whom I wouldn't dare introduce to Greg. Although, having said that, do I really care? We never have sex. I lost interest around a decade ago, to be honest, although I succumbed occasionally, more out of duty than desire. Ironic really, considering my history. I'm not quite sure why we still share the same bed, although granted it's only been seven months since Ella moved out. I'm guessing she stayed that long out of loyalty to Greg, during which time we felt the need to keep up some sort of pretence for her benefit. And now that she's gone, perhaps subconsciously, we're both too afraid to take separate rooms. Knowing it would mark the beginning of the end. I'm not sure I'm ready for that, despite our remoteness. But maybe Greg feels differently. I wouldn't be surprised if he's strayed. He doesn't think I notice but I've caught him shooting daggers at me on those rare occasions when we happen to be seated on the same sofa. Three nights a week, he's out at some client dinner or work function. At least, that's what he tells me. The only time we sit down and have a proper meal together is on a Sunday, or if the children come round. We can't be in each other's company for long before it feels like someone's scratching their nails along the wall. The tension becomes excruciating, makes me want to scream 'Just say something or get the hell out!' at the top of my lungs. Not because he's done anything wrong as such, but because I know I am the cause of his estrangement.

There's something rather engaging about Dr Cousins working from home. She can't be more than thirty, but I like the fact that she's young and fresh. Not downtrodden by life and the depressive clients her vocation brings. My other shrinks were based in large, sterile hospitals or medical centres, but it's comforting, less intimidating, talking to someone in their own home. Makes me feel like less of an oddball than I usually do.

Dr Cousins has piercing blue eyes, ash-blonde hair and wide, full lips that speak warmth to a woman and seduction to a man. Her hair is held up by a simple black clip, making it impossible to determine its length, and her face is made up to perfection, yet still looks natural. She sits in her chair, dressed in a demure, navy blue skirt suit, her long legs crossed, and has a calm, patient expression that tells you, *It's OK, you can talk to me until the cows come home; I'll listen, no matter what, even when others might tell you to get a grip and move on with your life.*

Finally, I talk. And although I am lying down, I keep my eyes open. I tell her about my loving, secure upbringing, my parents who loved each other to pieces (still do, in fact), and my older brother, David. That I was a straight-A student, a consistently high achiever – head girl at my posh private girls' school, and hockey captain at university where I got a first in law and met Janine. That, having aced my law exams I got offers from three top-ten firms, plumping for Sheridans where I met Greg. Life was a breeze back then. I worked hard, played hard, and nothing could break me. But at that point, I hadn't known loss or pain. Hadn't known what it feels like to have your heart ripped out sending you insane with grief.

I tell her about Greg, the best man I know. About the day he caught my eye at a client function, about our first few dates, the day I realized I loved him, the day he proposed in Paris, on the Seine, and how happy we were initially. I tell her about our wedding day and then, nine months later, your arrival, the best day of our lives. About all the precious moments that followed as I watched you grow into an adorable toddler.

And then I stop. Because that's where the fairy tale ends and the nightmare begins. I expect her to finish there, to say, 'That's enough for today, we'll talk more next week.' But she doesn't.

'It's OK, Christine, tell me more. Tell me everything and try not to hold back.'

'But I've had my hour,' I protest. Not because I don't want to overstretch my stay, not because I'm worried about being charged more money; it's just an excuse to not talk about what followed. About my secret.

'It's OK. I don't work to a clock as such, not like the other psychiatrists you might have seen. I don't think that's fair to the patient. We will stop when I feel that a natural conclusion has arrived.'

There's something hypnotic, lullaby-ish, about her voice, and I find myself confiding in her (although not completely), even though it normally takes me at least two sessions to open up to a new therapist. The words just seem to escape my mouth without me really thinking.

'I was in Peter Jones, walked away, for maybe a few seconds, while I took a call—' a call I should have ignored, a call which I sensed would tell me something I didn't want to hear '—to get a better signal, and when I went back, she was gone.'

I pause, fleetingly wonder how it can still be so hard to relive that memory, all these years later, and after seeing so many therapists. I know why really, but I don't tell Dr Cousins. I'm too ashamed.

'Go on,' she says. 'Maybe it will help to close your eyes.'

I do as she suggests and feel calmer. 'I can still remember – still relive in microscopic detail – the gut-wrenching feeling of dread that took hold of me. It was like barbed wire wrapped around my waist, causing me unthinkable pain.'

Dr Cousins remains quiet. Lying down, I can't see her reaction, but I imagine her to be listening attentively, making notes every so often. I carry on, talk and talk until it becomes dark outside, and night sets in.

Chapter Seven

Greg

Now

I glance over at you, perched at the other end of the sofa, your stringy legs tucked underneath your bony bottom, and I feel nothing. I wouldn't say that I hate you, Chrissy, I certainly wouldn't wish you any ill, but I can't say that I love you. I haven't loved you for years. I stayed with you, not because you needed me, not because I feared what you might do if I left you, but because I didn't want our kids to be raised in a broken home. Not like I was.

My father, the CEO of a major investment bank, although good at his job, was a cocky shit who drank too much, and cheated on my mother repeatedly. She wasn't a pushover, though. She was strong, and she kicked him out, and later remarried. But at the time, it was hard being the kid whose parents weren't together. Even though it didn't seem to affect my younger sister, Meredith, as much as it did me. There were only a few of us like that at school – children of divorce – and somehow I always felt inadequate, a bit of a misfit. And I was jealous of my friends whose parents were still together. I didn't want Ella and Daniel to feel that way, even though, looking back, it often felt like I was a single dad.

Our kids were a distraction for twentysomething years. Christ, it's hard for me to say that, because it makes them sound like a convenient pastime, rather than the two joys of my life.

But the truth is, having them in the house meant we didn't need to work on us because they were our focus.

My job also helped in that regard. I worked long hours, I still do, which meant we only really saw each other on weekends or during family holidays, and even then, everything revolved around the kids. We 'functioned' as a family. Did our 'job' as parents. And we saw them through to adulthood. Something we failed at with Heidi.

But since they left home – Ella, who's twenty, is in her last year at fashion school with a part-time shop assistant's job, and Daniel, twenty-two, is currently on a graduate scheme with a firm of chartered accountants – and we've found ourselves alone, it's like living in a morgue. Our conversation is polite but strained, and we lead separate lives. Even sitting on the sofa with you, as I am tonight, is a rarity. It's torture. Aside from the occasional work function when you accompany me just to keep up appearances, we go out of our way to avoid spending time with each other. Frankly, I'm not quite sure how long we can go on like this.

The TV is on, showing reruns of *Game of Thrones*, but I'm not entirely certain you're watching it. You were surprised to see me walk through the door at just gone seven. To tell you the truth, I surprised myself, but we'd just closed a deal and I had no other excuse to stay away. My other form of distraction wasn't available, even though I could really have done with it tonight.

I know you've been to see yet another shrink today, someone who's helped Janine. Like me, you're always at your lowest at this time of year, although I'm better at hiding it. But I'm not hopeful she'll be able to snap you out of your misery. I don't want to hope, because in some ways you deserve to suffer. Also, unlike Janine, I don't think you want to be cured. I think you almost get a kick out of punishing yourself, a compulsion I find rather distasteful, self-indulgent even. Miranda agrees with me, although I've never told you that, just because I don't want to cause trouble between you. Trouble between you two means trouble for me. It took a while for Miranda to accept you. I was so relieved when you eventually bonded over a shared love of cheesy 80s music and Japanese food one Friday night at the pub after work. Despite Janine warning you to be on your guard because Miranda was my ex and couldn't be trusted. It's sweet that she's so protective of you, but sometimes her protectiveness borders on paranoia. Anyway, that's long in the past, and thankfully Janine overcame her misgivings. The three of you became as thick as thieves, with your fortnightly dinners and girly weekends away.

To give Miranda her credit, she often says I need to ease up on you, if only for the sake of the kids. Maybe she's right, I don't know. I have to say I was surprised at her keenness to recommend this Dr Cousins to Janine. She's always been so derogatory of shrinks, perhaps because of her difficult upbringing which forced her to grow up fast and fight her own battles. But, for some reason, she became convinced that this woman was the one to help Janine. And now you.

That aside, there's a big difference between Janine's case and yours. It's not Janine's fault she lost Nate, whereas it's your fault entirely that you lost our child. And that's why you torture yourself day and night. Why I almost find satisfaction in the fact that you do. Even though your martyrdom sometimes makes me want to place my hands around your scrawny neck and squeeze the life out of you. I'm not capable of that, though. *At least, I don't think I am?*

Miranda and I speak privately at least once a week on the phone. In your usual selfish way, you think you've overtaken me in her affections. But you haven't. She'll never choose you over me if faced with that choice. She was my friend before she was yours. My girlfriend, in fact. I know how much she loved me back then, perhaps still does. I can tell by the tone of her voice when we talk, by the way her eyes linger on me when she thinks I'm not looking. I know Janine's mentioned it to you, but you brushed it off as harmless. Which it is, in that I'm certain there's no malice behind it. Sometimes, I wish I'd stayed with her. Looking back, I didn't feel the need to be something I wasn't with her. Practical, unswervingly loyal, she gave me the stability I never had growing up. We dated for a year, but I never felt that 'spark' with her. At the time, I believed that in order to make a lifelong commitment to someone, there had to be that spark, that electricity – that feeling that you might die if you can't have them – and although things were nice with Miranda, they weren't exciting. But on reflection, maybe I was wrong to break up with her. But that's the benefit of hindsight, isn't it? When you get to my age, you realize that 'spark', 'passion', aren't everything. It's about companionship, trust. But I was young and reckless, ruled by my penis rather than my head, and I kept thinking there had to be someone better out there, someone who made my heart race, and when I met you, so beautiful, so intoxicating, I knew I'd found her. I'll never forget the look on Miranda's face when I ended things on our one-year anniversary. It was a shitty thing to do, I know that now – knew it then, in fact – and I still can't believe she forgave me, stayed friends with me, even became friends with you once she realized you and I were in it for the long haul. She's been a true friend through thick and thin. But above all, a shoulder to cry on when we lost Heidi, staying with us in the initial days of her disappearance, even when her own father had just passed away. A life raft of support to cling to when both of us were at risk of drowning.

And as much as I hate myself for thinking it, I can't imagine she'd ever lose her own child the way you did.

She deserves to be with someone better than Duncan. Granted, he was one of our richest clients, a bit of a hunk, in a greasy Latin kind of way. But he's always struck me as a player. Vain and self-absorbed. It puzzled me, back in the day, when you were always so quick to defend him. I mean, I know you worked closely with him on several matters, but didn't it bug you the way he continued to flirt with all the female staff after he and Miranda got together? You said it was harmless. That he was a good guy at heart, and made Miranda happy, which is all that mattered. God knows she fell for him hard and quick. But I'm sure he's the reason they never had kids. Despite Miranda insisting she never wanted them. Bullshit she never wanted them. I remember her cooing at babies back when we were dating. A look of longing, almost envy. She yearned to be the mother she never had.

It hit me hard when they moved to Newcastle, Duncan's hometown, six months after Heidi went missing. It just seemed so sudden. I was surprised Miranda didn't kick up more of a fuss, she'd always been such a quintessentially Southern girl. It made me wonder what they were running away from. And perhaps selfishly, it felt like she'd abandoned me. But maybe she craved a clean break after her father's death and Heidi's disappearance. I wouldn't blame her for wanting to bury bad memories. Looking back, perhaps that's what you and I should have done. Moved away, made a fresh start. But at the time, even getting out of bed was an effort for you. Plus, wherever we went, our grief would shadow us. Bricks and mortar wouldn't change that.

It's strange that Duncan never accompanies Miranda when she comes to stay with us. He always seems to be away on some business trip, or boys' weekend, or is off watching rugby, which he's fanatical about. And whenever I suggest visiting them it never seems to be a good time. Either Duncan's in a bad mood, or has friends staying, or too much work on. 'It's just easier if I come and see you' is Miranda's standard response. I might be imagining it, but it's like he's avoiding us for some reason, or Miranda's deliberately keeping him from us. *What are they hiding?*

It never seems to bother you as it does me, though. That puzzles me too. Before the darkness descended on our lives, you and he had always seemed to get on well. I'd assumed his absence would concern you, that you'd miss us socializing as a foursome.

But perhaps that's just it. That was before the darkness. When you were a different person. When life was a joy rather than a chore.

–

I am fifty-seven years old but I feel at least a decade older. Every day I rise at 6 a.m. and am at my desk by eight. As a banking partner at a Magic Circle law firm, I work a minimum twelve-hour day, often longer if there's a big deal on or I need to attend an important client function. It's the trade-off for the huge sums I make, which enabled us to put Ella and Daniel through private school and beyond. I was always a hard worker, but when you lost our child, I became someone I was once determined never to be – a workaholic. A slave to the City, just like my father. Not particularly because I get a thrill out of it but because expending all my energies at work allows me to temporarily discard the memory of our first child. Otherwise it would consume me, like a terminal disease, the way it has done you. I couldn't let that happen. One of us had to be strong.

–

I study the silhouette of your face, the lines of your emaciated body. Gone are your womanly curves. Your cheeks, once flushed and full, are pale and hollow, and from this angle, I can decipher a dark shadow under your right eye. On the rare occasions I happen to catch you naked, I am horrified by your skeletal frame. Your spine and ribs protrude from what little flesh you have, and there is an unusually large gap between your thighs.

Where has my Christine gone, once so beautiful, so full of life?

When I first set eyes on you at that client function all those years ago, you took my breath away. It was that classic lightning-bolt moment. I hadn't long joined Sheridans from Decker

Wyatt, where Miranda and I had both been associates. She and I moved together when our mentor at Deckers defected. You were speaking to a couple of portly, ruddy-nosed clients, classic City stereotypes. I could tell that you were bored stiff and trying to ignore the fact that every now and again their line of vision would venture to your open-neck blouse, the merest hint of cleavage on show, enough to titillate unsavoury types like them, well past their sell-by date and not getting any at home. I watched you laugh and smile, nod in all the right places, and at one point you threw back your head with fake laughter, then happened to glance my way. We exchanged shy smiles, and it was the most thrilling moment. For me, at least. And it suddenly made what had so far been a tedious evening worth the effort.

We didn't get the chance to speak until the end of the night when only a few clients remained and the room was full of empty glasses and one too many sozzled lawyers, seemingly oblivious to the fact that they were required to be back in the office, fully functional, the next morning.

Although I was popular at university, I'd always been more comfortable around my male friends. Women, particularly attractive women, had somewhat terrified me. Maybe that was why I'd felt so at ease with Miranda. I wasn't intimidated by her. I'm decent-looking, with an average five-ten frame, and a strong (not as slim as I used to be) build, and I've been told (you told me, in fact) that I have good bone structure and warm, friendly eyes. But I'm not drop-dead handsome, I know that. Although I tend to wear contact lenses these days (because I've been told by someone special to me that they make me look younger), back then I mostly wore glasses, giving me a studious, more-mature-than-my-years appearance. Funny how you always want to appear older when you're young, but will do anything to turn back time when you're past forty. It was a look that gained me many female friends, but not so many lovers. Until I met Miranda. She was fun, and easy to talk to. But she wasn't a sex kitten like you. I knew nothing about you as such, just that you were a four-year-qualified associate in litigation, but as if from nowhere, at the end of the evening I plucked up the nerve to approach you. It was like I had to, else I wouldn't be able to sleep that night, you got to me that much.

You'd just said goodbye to a client and were heading for the door when I made my move. 'How was your evening?' I asked. 'Just about bearable?' My heart had been going like the clappers as I came up behind you and almost made you jump in surprise. 'We should congratulate ourselves on being two of the last men standing,' I carried on.

You turned around, eyes full of surprise, and then, to my relief, you smiled.

'Well, the wine helped,' you said. 'Although I think I'm going to have a stinking hangover tomorrow. Not good.'

You flashed your beautiful smile, and my pulse went through the roof. Just like that, I was smitten. But I wasn't stupid; I knew you were out of my league.

After grabbing our coats, we shared a lift to the ground floor. The tension was almost unbearable; for me at least, I'm not sure it was like that for you. You seemed so calm, so at ease with yourself, and I guess you knew how gorgeous you were. Later, you confessed to me that you'd quite enjoyed watching me sweat. Although I'd tried to act cool, it was obvious from my body language how much I liked you. And I think that's what drew you to me. You were always a princess. You enjoyed being fussed over, wielding control. And because you were out of my league, you knew you could control me, unlike other, more handsome men, who were just as unattainable as you. Sometimes, I wonder if you ever really loved me, or simply loved the fact that I adored you. But perhaps I'm being unfair.

At first, we became friends. We saw each other at firm socials, and I always made a point of chatting to you. I could tell you were relaxed in my company. My best friend at the firm – Nate – noticed it too. He kept telling me to go for it, that life was too short to hold back. It was all right for him, though. Nate, God rest his soul, was a handsome bugger. In truth, I had envied him, had so wanted to hate him. But I couldn't. He was a bloody top guy, and I still can't believe he's gone. Just can't believe he killed himself, poor sod.

Anyway, if it wasn't for Nate, I wouldn't have asked you out. But he kept egging me on, and finally, after a few months of getting to know you, I plucked up the nerve to ask if you fancied grabbing dinner sometime. We were both working late, and your trainee had left for the evening. I poked my head around the half-open door, and you looked up from the chunky document you were working on. I'd been fit to burst with nerves, wondering how I was ever going to look you in the eye again if you turned me down.

But you didn't. You said, 'Sure, why not? That would be lovely', then smiled that smile, and it was a struggle not to exhale loudly with relief and punch the air for joy.

Thankfully, I managed not to embarrass myself. Gave a cool, 'Great,' in response, then left.

Turned out, dinner was a success. The conversation flowed, and I didn't want the night to end. You were so full of life back then, and I was captivated by you. Outside on the street, a cocktail and a bottle of wine later, we kissed for the first time, and then some more. Non-stop kissing like we were a couple of horny teenagers, and I thought I must have died and gone to heaven. That surely my luck had to run out at some point. That you'd come to your senses and realize that you were too good for me. But you didn't. We went out again, we became a thing, a couple, despite having to be careful in the early days – although relationships weren't strictly forbidden at our firm, they weren't exactly encouraged. But if anything, it cemented our love, proved how invested we were in each other. Before long, we were engaged, living together, then married, and not long after that, parents.

Now all of that seems like a lifetime ago. After *it* happened, I initially tried to comfort you, forgive you, but you pushed me away, became cold, punished me for something which, let's face it, was entirely your fault. You should have been grateful to me for giving you another chance – for not leaving you – but instead you wallowed in your own self-pity, as if my grief was secondary to yours. I tried to give you the benefit of the doubt, and I urged you to have more children. I thought it would help bring us closer together again, help repair the hole in our marriage.

But it didn't. You pushed me away even further, and the hole became an abyss. Janine sometimes admonishes me for being too harsh on you. But she doesn't have to live with you, does she? And I know Miranda's had to bite her lip on several occasions. Raised by a father whose heart turned to stone after losing his wife to cancer, she doesn't have much time for wallowers. Even wallowers who've lost a child.

What's more deplorable is that you weren't a proper mother to our other children. It was as if you resented them, something I have grown to resent you for almost as much as I resent you for losing our firstborn. How dare you push me away when it was *you* who lost our child? How dare you push our children away when they are equally blameless? You should have tried to do everything possible to make it up to me – you should have poured your love into Ella and Daniel – but instead you became distant and introverted. I couldn't understand this, I still can't; it just doesn't make any sense. All I can think is that there's something else that explains your unfeeling behaviour, something other than losing Heidi.

But if that's true, then surely I would have found out what it is by now?

Perhaps I don't want to face the truth, which is simply that it is all part of your innate arrogance. You were arrogant when we first met, thinking you could control me, hypnotize me, and you have been arrogant all these years in failing to admit your mistake and accept help from your loved ones.

Even though I am miserable, I won't be the one to leave first, nor even move out of our bed, as awkward as lying next to you makes me feel. I won't let you bulldoze me or make me out to be the loser in all of this. That's what allowing you to stay in this house – the house *I* kept afloat – while I'm forced to go elsewhere would feel like. Another win for you.

You must be the one to leave, but there's nothing to stop me pushing that along a little faster.

Chapter Eight

Miranda

Before

I watch you at the bar, Christine, getting a round of drinks. Greg at your side, fawning over your every move, hanging on your every word. I hate you for that, for taking him – the love of my life – away from me, even though I know deep inside that's a bit unfair because he'd already finished with me before you two started dating. When he broke things off, on our anniversary of all days, it was like a shard of glass had been thrust through my heart. Everything hurt and the pain was so intense that for a while I thought about killing myself so I would feel no more. Which is so unlike me.

I've never been the dramatic sort. My childhood ensured that. My mother, God rest her soul, died of cancer when I was two, and my father, who loved her more than life itself, became a stony-hearted bastard who, from that day forward, never hugged or kissed his only child, claiming that such displays of affection made people weak and unprepared for the shit life would unquestionably throw their way; the death of a family member being the prime example. *If you don't feel anything for anybody, if you don't open your heart to them, you can't miss them*, he'd say. *You'll be stronger as an adult, and you'll thank me for it.*

Well, turns out the old bastard – who I wasn't even allowed to call 'dad' because it was too touchy-feely – was right. I did open my heart to someone, and I ended up paying the price

39

for it, because when Greg ended things, it felt like someone had died. Before Greg, I'd never had a steady relationship. I'd had casual flings, the odd one-night stand, but never anything meaningful because Father's warning was so indoctrinated in me. And I guess that's why I never wanted marriage, a family. I saw what it did to Father, and I couldn't face that happening to me.

But then I met Greg when I joined Deckers, and everything changed. He was so kind, so warm, so easy to talk to, and we just clicked. I guess he was everything my father wasn't, and I suddenly realized what I'd missed out on for all those years. Couldn't resist baring my soul to him. And for a while things were good. Amazing, in fact. At least, they were for me. Already in our late twenties, I actually imagined being married to him, having his kids and showering our children with the singularly unique love only a mother can give. Greg had booked a swish Japanese restaurant in Mayfair for our anniversary. Somewhere I'd been dying to try. And I, with my head in the clouds, stupidly thought he was going to propose. But I knew something was wrong right from the moment we sat down. He seemed tense, his conversation stilted, his smiles forced, barely making eye contact with me. At first, I thought maybe he was nervous about proposing, but then, when things didn't improve and I started to feel more and more peed off with his attitude – for effectively ruining our special night – I asked him point blank what the hell was his problem. Why he was spoiling our anniversary.

And then he told me. Said he hadn't been happy for some time, that although he cared for me deeply, I wasn't the one he wanted to spend the rest of his life with, and he didn't think it fair to string me along. I could have killed him on the spot. I almost vomited up my £60-a-head meal, and it felt like the floor beneath me was folding in on itself, threatening to suck me into the underworld, even though I already felt like I was in hell. I asked him if there was someone else and he insisted there wasn't. Which was true, even though at the time I refused to believe him. I know he didn't want to hurt me, I could tell from his anguished expression. He's always been one of the good guys, would never intentionally make me suffer. And I'm not just saying that because I'm clutching at straws, forever making excuses for him. I just think that maybe the occasion got to him, and he wasn't thinking straight. But I did hate him for some time after that. Hated him, and yet couldn't stop thinking about him. He became a kind of obsession, I guess. Just because I loved him so much, and I couldn't bear the thought of not being with him.

We hardly talked for six months, even after we moved firms. But then, after we'd been at Sheridans a couple of months and I saw that he'd been telling the truth – he hadn't ditched me for someone else – I realized I missed him too much to cut him out of my life. And I know he missed me too, because he would text me every so often and tell me. So, one day I succumbed, picked up the phone and said I wanted to bury the hatchet, be friends again. He was so happy, and that touched my heart. It made me feel good that he still wanted me in his life, even gave me hope that one day he'd see the error of his ways and realize what he was missing; that I was the one after all.

But then you came along and messed up the plan. Messed up my chances of happiness with Greg. I don't really know you, but I can't help hating you because as much as I don't want to admit it, he never looked at me the way he looks at you. I see the longing in his eyes, the unabashed adoration, like he'd rip off your clothes and ravish you on the spot if you commanded it. You are smart, funny, and beautiful. What heterosexual man wouldn't want you? You are something I am not and can never be. But if I want to stay in Greg's life, I must become a part of yours. And so that's what I'm going to do.

Starting now.

Chapter Nine

Christine

Now

I stop talking and wait for Dr Cousins to speak. This is my second session with her, a few days on from my first. Although I wasn't brave enough then to tell her the secret that haunts me, I feel increasingly drawn to her, and I'm starting to believe that, with time, she's the one I will finally bare my soul to. Perhaps it's your recent twenty-fifth that's precipitated this. Or maybe it's purely the fact that she seems to get me in ways others haven't.

'Christine, do you want to sit up now, maybe come and sit down opposite me?'

I open my eyes, and they momentarily adjust to the natural light, having been encased in darkness these past twenty minutes or so. I haven't yet returned to the subject of *that day*. I just went into a bit more detail about my childhood, particularly my brother, David, who I was close to once, whereas now we hardly speak. I pushed everyone I loved (and who loved me) away after I lost you. Including my own parents. I could barely look my mother in the eye, knowing I'd lost her granddaughter. Knowing the reason why. And gradually we grew distant; more so once Ella and Daniel became teenagers. We speak, perhaps once every six weeks. Occasionally, I have this hankering to confess everything to Mum. Like I'm her little girl again, and she'll be able to make things better. But I know she can't. And I couldn't bear to see the disgust on her face.

I'm not quite ready to sit up. I feel safer, more relaxed, lying down, and I tell Dr Cousins this. She says that's fine, then continues, 'But deep down, you must know that you *do* deserve to be happy, Christine. In your heart, you know that you cannot continue to punish yourself for something that happened a long time ago.'

I appreciate her efforts, but if only it were that simple. She doesn't know the whole truth.

'I know that time's supposed to make things easier,' I say, 'everyone told me that it would. But it hasn't, not for me at least. And I know I'm not the only person to have suffered the loss of a child, and that others manage to get on with their lives. But the fact is, I haven't. I mean, yes, I got up every day, and I went on to have two more children, brought them up as best I could. But it was all very mechanical, routine-like. I hate myself for it, but it was the only way I felt able to cope.' I pause, then say, 'Have you ever seen that programme on TV, Channel 4, I think it is? The one about the synths.'

'*Humans*, you mean?'

'Yes, that's the one. Well, I suppose I acted like one of them. Not the special synths who have feelings, but the regular, emotionless ones. I raised my children, but without enthusiasm, without love; almost as if I was on autopilot.'

'So you admit now how selfish that was of you? How unkind it was to treat your own flesh and blood so coldly?'

Dr Cousins' sudden change of tone shocks me. There's a sharpness to her voice I hadn't expected, and it's completely at odds with her normal approach. She's not supposed to judge me, is she? None of my previous shrinks have done so. But then again, they haven't really helped. Maybe a kick in the teeth is what I need. Maybe there is no justification for the way I behaved, and I need to face up to that. I play back her words and feel a sharp pang of guilt. It's not as if I didn't know deep down that my behaviour was unkind, but this is the first time a stranger has told me so to my face. After a brief pause, I reply, 'Yes, I do. But it wasn't intentional.'

43

'Really? How can that be? Surely you knew at the time how badly you were treating them? You're an intelligent woman, after all.'

It's there again, the judging, the probing, the feeling that she is appalled by how I could have treated my own children so badly. But in a bizarre kind of way, it's refreshing. She's not allowing me to wallow in my self-pity, she's trying to snap me out of it, I see that now. Yes, that's her intention. It must be. She is what I need, what I've been searching for in my therapy all these years.

I sit up, feel the blood rush to my head, my line of vision a kaleidoscope of stars.

'Come and sit here.' Dr Cousins' voice is soft again as she beckons to the chair directly opposite her.

I do as she asks, then find my eyes wandering.

The first time I entered her room, I was struck by how homely it felt. Part of a two-bedroom flat occupying the second floor of an attractive semi-detached period building, she told me she'd only recently moved in and made it her office. Naturally, I've looked into her credentials. When she first told me how much Dr Cousins had helped her, Janine sent me the link to her website, which Miranda, being a typical lawyer, had researched thoroughly before recommending Dr Cousins to her. After completing her training, she decided hospital work wasn't for her, instead setting up her own practice from home, with a focus on grief counselling. Now that I've met her myself, I can see why Miranda was so taken with her. Despite her youth, she has a maturity beyond her years, and it's uncanny how well she seems to know me already.

Although she hasn't lived in her flat for long, it doesn't feel like that. There are two bookshelves, wall-to-wall with psychiatry-related textbooks, various autobiographies and a few novels, mainly psychological thrillers, which is hardly surprising, I guess, given her profession. On the wall behind her desk there is a framed certificate of her degree in medicine from

Imperial College. Her desk is polished and uncluttered, solid dark oak, with a few scattered dents embedded in the wood, suggesting it is second-hand. Various piles of paper are lined up either side of it, and in the middle sits her laptop – probably the newest item in her room – and to the right, a telephone. She has a couple of photographs, one of her as a child, sandwiched between a woman and a man (I'm guessing her parents), and one with a slightly younger boy – her brother, I presume, they have a similar look about them – but I don't feel comfortable asking her about them yet. I hope to at some point, though. Usually I'm not interested in my psychiatrists' personal lives because I'm there to talk about me, not them. Plus, like regular doctors, I'm aware that psychiatrists are duty-bound to adhere to a strictly professional relationship with their patients, which has always suited me fine because I think that if I were to see their human side, I might lose faith in their ability to cure me. But there's something about Dr Cousins I find intriguing, and it makes me want to know more about her. I like the fact that she cuts to the chase, doesn't sugar-coat my feelings, pander to my shortcomings. Rather, she wants me to face up to and accept them for what they are.

As I take a seat opposite her, she leans back in her leather swivel chair, her right elbow perched on one armrest as she taps her pen rhythmically against the side of her cheek. There's almost pin-drop silence as she scrutinizes my face. All that can be heard is the slightly muffled whirr of traffic outside, and occasional human voices. It's 11 a.m. on Monday, so well past rush hour. Children are in school, adults at work. But it's still London, and therefore never completely noiseless.

'So how do you feel right now?'

She continues to examine me with her electric-blue eyes which laser through her designer glasses. I can't quite tell if it's a look of concern or irritation, and therefore what she expects me to say. That thirty minutes spent talking to her has cured me of mourning you, and I can now finally move on with my life and forget it ever happened?

Because, of course, I can't forget. I will never forget. But I am glad I made another appointment to see her. I don't feel like it's been time wasted.

'OK, I guess. I mean, I already feel more comfortable talking to you than the other psychiatrists I've seen over the years, even though this is only our second meeting. Somehow, I feel more relaxed here.'

'Good. Why is that, do you think?'

I fidget in my seat, give a faint smile, and as I do, my stomach rumbles. But I ignore it – the way I always do – because I cannot reward myself with food. Not in an indulgent way. I eat to live, but I never give in to excess. Such behaviour would imply that I have forgiven myself, which I haven't.

I give a slight shrug of my shoulders, look around. 'Because we're not in some soulless medical centre, I suppose. This is your home, and it feels easier talking to you here. The other places I've tried didn't exactly invite openness, transparency. They just made me feel crazier than I already felt.'

She laughs, does the cheek-tapping thing with her pen again. 'Well, we certainly can't have that.'

I laugh too. She's so charismatic, I'm almost mesmerized by her. I try to explain further. 'Also, with the others, although I'm sure they meant well, it felt like they were going through the motions. They seemed dry, fatigued by years on the job. You seem fresher.'

'I'm glad you feel comfortable here. You came to me for help and I want to help. That's my job, and I wouldn't be doing it properly if I appeared disinterested.'

She smiles, revealing a perfect set of white teeth. I can't decide if they're natural or not. It doesn't matter; they suit her, and only add to her attractiveness.

'Although I take my profession very seriously, I believe it's crucial to make a patient feel at ease, especially when dealing with an issue like grief. That's why I decided to work from home. Plus, I enjoy being my own boss.'

It's hard not to admire her. She exudes such strength, and she reminds me of my younger self. I once had her optimism, her fighting spirit, but that now seems like a lifetime ago.

There's a brief pause. Then, looking at her watch, she says, 'Well, I think that's enough for today. You've made really good progress, but I get the feeling there's something you're not telling me.'

She looks back up and her gaze cuts through me, causing my muscles to tense, my deprived stomach now in knots.

'You're holding back,' she carries on.

I wriggle in my seat, and now I really need to get out of here because I'm not ready to tell her yet.

Thankfully, she doesn't press the issue. Just smiles and says, 'Same time, next week?'

I nod with relief. 'Yes, that would be great.'

Chapter Ten

Christine

Now

I insert the key into the front door and turn the lock. I can already tell from the open curtains that no one's in. Greg and I make a habit of closing the curtains when it's dark outside; a signal that one of us is home.

It's Thursday, just gone 6.30, and I'm gasping for a drink. Preferably a large glass of white wine. Although I wouldn't call myself an alcoholic (I don't carry around miniature bottles of gin in my handbag or pour vodka on my cereal or anything like that), I'd be lying if I said I can get through a day without booze. It's a reward, an incentive to get me through it. Every day is an effort for me, and so knowing I can reach for that bottle in the fridge when an acceptable hour arrives (six on a weekday, but any time after midday on a weekend) gives me the strength to plough on. It takes the edge off, helps me to sleep, despite so-called experts repeatedly lecturing us that alcohol is scientifically proven to disturb a person's sleep. I don't bloody care; it makes me feel better, blots out my pain, if only for a while, and it's therefore a friend I can't do without. It's not like I give two hoots about my vital organs anyway. So what if my liver packs up? So what if it kills me? So much the better. Although, I wonder what Dr Cousins would say to that? I haven't told her yet that I use alcohol as a crutch. I expect she wouldn't approve, would probably tell me to stop being so pathetic, that I don't need alcohol to get through life.

I enter the house, feel for the light switch on the wall, place my keys on the hook next to it, then remove my coat, which I hang on the rack Greg installed. He's good like that. A real handyman. I remember when we first started dating, my washing machine was playing up and he came and fixed it. Saved me a £200 call-out charge. *He* would never have done that. But *his* hands worked wonders in other ways. Mostly up my skirt and down my blouse, but I can't bear to go there now. Just thinking about what I did fills me with disgust.

There's a pile of post on the floor. I scoop it up, take it through to the kitchen, toss it on the sideboard and head straight for the fridge.

Three days on from my second session with Dr Cousins, I don't feel quite as empty and depressed as I usually do by the end of the week. It must be her who's making a difference because nothing else exceptional or different has happened to me since I got up this morning. I worked out in the gym for two hours, did some chores, went grocery shopping, the usual routine. I think it's her youthfulness that buoys me, and the fact that she's not afraid to be blunt with me. There's something so invigorating about that, along with her whole approach to my depression. Although I can't say I'm suddenly full of hope that life can be good again, I am looking forward to our third meeting on Monday.

I pour myself a large glass of chardonnay, take a big gulp, savour its delicious, reassuring taste and the instant feeling of relaxation that creeps over me like a second skin, then start flicking through the mail. Most of it's for Greg. Bills, bank statements, et cetera. But there are a couple of bits for me. The first is a letter inviting me for a mammogram. Great. I toss it aside. I ignored the last one, as well as the one about my overdue smear test, so why should I be bothered about this one? The next is a handwritten envelope. I don't recognize the handwriting, all in capitals. The postmark is Sunderland. Strange, as I don't know anyone who lives there. The only friend I have up north is Miranda, but she's in Newcastle and, like I said, the handwriting's unfamiliar. I'm curious to know who it's from and hastily run my thumb through the seal, before pulling out a single sheet of paper, folded once. I unfold it, read what's written, then everything after is blank.

Heidi isn't dead. She's alive and she is better off with me than with you.

Chapter Eleven

Greg

Now

I watch you sleeping peacefully in the hospital bed, the most peaceful I've seen you in a long time, Chrissy, and I feel a surge of guilt. If I'd been home, you might not have passed out, cracked the back of your head on the tiled floor and become unconscious. Luckily, the doctor who examined you has confirmed there's no internal bleeding, and that you're going to be fine. But they are keeping you in overnight, just to be on the safe side.

At first, when I walked into the kitchen and found you lying on your back and unresponsive, I was angry. I'd immediately spotted the wine glass on the sideboard (I know how much you drink despite not being home when you indulge yourself because I put the recycling out every week) and thought you'd finally done it. Your malnourished, over-exercised heart couldn't take any more and had finally given up. But as I felt for a pulse with one hand, and called for an ambulance with the other, I noticed the sheet of paper lying on the floor beside you. Waiting for the ambulance to arrive, I read what was written on it, and realized this had caused you to faint.

I think I might have passed out too, had I not already been sitting on the floor next to you. My fingers were trembling, my palms clammy, my heart pounding so erratically cardiac arrest felt like an imminent possibility. I mean, I'm a prime candidate for a heart attack. Late fifties, crazy work schedule, bad diet, not enough exercise.

I'd quickly unbuttoned my shirt collar, which was suddenly choking me, and then tried to wake you, shaking your bony shoulders, patting your hollow cheeks, willing you to come around, give me some sign you were still there. And that's when you began to mumble our first daughter's name, causing me to sigh with relief.

In the first six months following Heidi's disappearance, we and the police received hundreds of calls. All of which amounted to nothing. The police had warned us from the start to be sceptical, and not to get our hopes up. Not because they were heartless bastards, but because they knew the game, had seen it all before. The inspector leading the investigation – Detective Inspector Jack Grayson – was a good man. Forty-five at the time, married with two teenage kids, he was a quietly spoken straight-up sort of a fellow, with kind, sincere eyes and a full head of prematurely grey hair. He was just being honest, looking out for us, because he knew only too well that the situation we'd found ourselves in rarely ended well. But we didn't listen, or rather, we listened but ignored his advice. We felt cross with his scepticism, his apparent willingness to give in without a proper fight. In the early days, we survived on hope, clinging to any sign, any possibility that Heidi might still be alive and safely returned to us. But Grayson was right, of course. Every call, every possible sighting proved to be a dead end, a road to nowhere fast. As the weeks, months, years passed by, our hope faded, and we became resigned to the fact that Heidi was never coming home, despite the occasional blind lead or odd call from attention-seekers wanting their fifteen minutes of fame.

It's been ten years since someone got in contact claiming to have information on Heidi. So this letter comes as a bolt from the blue. The first claim in a decade that she isn't dead. Even so, I know the police will warn us not to get our hopes up, just as Grayson did back then. The fact that there've been no sightings of our child – or even of someone resembling her – clouds this ray of light before it's even had a chance to flicker with hope. The world is full of crazy people. Not just crazy people, but nasty, malicious types who'll say anything to gain notoriety, mess with people's minds. That's what the detective inspector I spoke to earlier on the phone said. But I didn't need him to tell me this. I learned my lesson twenty-three years ago.

But still, there's something about this note that sets it apart from all the others. For one, it's the first handwritten note we've received. And two, it's the first communication we've had from someone claiming to be the kidnapper. The others were mainly phone calls, or losers turning up at the police station claiming to have seen Heidi with the kidnapper, or to have information connected with her abduction. There was also the occasional email, as time went on.

But there's a different feel to this note, a personal touch that sends chills through me when I read it.

She is better off with me than with you.

I know it shouldn't have this effect on me. That I should view the note objectively. Penned by yet another crank who gets his or her kicks out of toying with people's emotions.

But I can't seem to. It creeps me out – the insinuation that Heidi's kidnapper wasn't some random stranger but someone who bore a grudge against you, who didn't consider you capable of being a good mother to Heidi. It begs the question, *why*? What does this person know that I don't? And why are they choosing to communicate now, after all these years? To make a statement around Heidi's twenty-fifth birthday? Or is that mere coincidence? It's as if our suffering hasn't been enough. As if they want us – or you at least – to suffer more.

While you were being attended to by the doctors, I rang Miranda and Janine to tell them what had happened. Both were shocked and terrified for us. I guess Miranda's like a comfort blanket for me, as Janine is for you. She knows me so well, in fact sometimes I think she understands me better than you. She has this level-headed way of speaking that always calms me down. Like Janine, despite her initial shock, Miranda told me not to panic, to take things one step at a time and not jump to any conclusions before the police have looked into it. But she did say I should have a frank talk with you once you've recovered. Ask you straight out why you think the sender might have written those words. Whether there's any truth to them? Whether there's something you're not telling me? I don't for a second believe Miranda's trying to make trouble between us. I mean, why should she – she's been married to Duncan longer than we have to each other, and she's your friend as well as mine. Besides, I've always had the feeling you've been hiding something from me. And I think that something has stopped you from moving on with your life after losing our daughter. A secret that has caused you to isolate yourself from those closest to you.

You can't be OK with that. Isolation will drive the sanest of people out of their minds. Eventually.

I don't know what I'm going to say to you when you wake up, or how the hell we're going to deal with this. We've been strangers for so long, talking about the note is going to be hard. But we can't hide from it, we have to face it, like Miranda said. Whether it will finally sink us for good or wake us from our apathy and force us to work together remains to be seen.

At least I got home in time. At least my conscience is appeased by the fact that before I did, I was actually at work, rather than screwing my mistress's brains out. That's what I'm really doing half the time when I call you to say I've been delayed at the office and therefore please don't wait up. I never thought I'd turn into my father. When I married you, I could never have imagined cheating on you. And before Heidi was taken, I'd often pinch myself, because I couldn't believe how lucky I was to have you. Would tell myself that I'd be damned and go to hell if I ever did anything to jeopardize what we had.

But then you lost our daughter, and piece by piece, my fairy-tale princess disappeared, and in her place remains a shadow of her former self. I've tried to be patient with you, but you didn't make it any easier for me by lounging in your grief, rather than snapping out of it for the sake of our children, if not for me. Seeing the way you raised Ella and Daniel, the way you kept them at arm's length, leaving me to endow them with the love you never gave them, made me so angry. And it made me fall out of love with you, because I couldn't believe a mother could behave that way towards her own children. I mean, what if I'd been weak and selfish like you? Our children would have been more screwed up than they already are. They wouldn't have had a hope.

Daniel's got your looks, but he can't hold on to a girl because he has trust issues. You let him down, the primary woman in his life. He doesn't trust you, and if he can't trust his own mother, how can he trust another woman? He can't, and he won't, and he's scared of getting close to a woman for fear of being let down by her, the way you let him down. And that's why he drinks too much, why he's taken hard drugs in the past, ended up in hospital having his stomach pumped. I'm worried he'll never find contentment in life, because he's not content with himself.

Ella's the same; forever trying to escape her past, who she is. Donning that fake mockney accent around her fashion-school friends like some pretentious pop star. You were never there to guide her when she needed you most. When her hormones were raging and she needed advice on girls' stuff like boys and make-up and periods. You have no idea who she's slept with, what her first time was like, whether her heart's ever been broken, whether she's ever taken drugs like Daniel or got in with the wrong crowd – normal things I know my sister's gone through with my niece – because you were too afraid of getting your own heart broken. I can never forgive you for how selfish you've been. And, of course, she's never opened up to me about any of those things because you don't talk to your dad about stuff like that. Even though I've spent many sleepless nights wondering what she's been up to, whether she's safe and being treated OK. Like Daniel, she has trust issues and I worry that she'll never be a mother herself because of the way you were with her.

The woman I've been sleeping with for the last six months is called Amber. She is young, single and incredibly hot, and I get hard at the mere sight of her naked body. She turns me on like you used to, but she's also dirtier, more risqué than you ever were. And that excites a man of my age beyond belief. There's something mysterious, almost wicked about her, and I can't stop myself from going back for more. We meet at the same hotel and have mind-blowing sex; sometimes we don't even make it to the bed, just go at it against the door or the wall. And when I am inside her, I forget everything. All the pain and sorrow that has amassed in me these past twenty-three gruelling years. It's exhilarating, a fantastic, heady release, and I tell myself I've earned it because *you* lost our child, because *you* couldn't be a proper mother to our remaining children. Because *you* threw it all away.

That's my excuse, even though, when I think about what I read just a few hours ago, my excuse feels less watertight.

You'll probably be cross with me for talking to the police without talking to you first. But there it is, I've gone and done it now, so there's no turning back. Right now, DI Phillips is on his way here. We can't handle this alone; we need help from those with the expertise to determine whether the note might be genuine, and therefore give us reason to hope.

I deserve to have hope, don't I? Despite the fact that I've been screwing a woman half my age behind your back. Wake up, God damn you, we need to talk.

Chapter Twelve

Amber

Now

The first time I saw you, Greg, I felt nothing but contempt. You were the ultimate cliché. Middle-aged man with a receding hairline. Boring navy striped shirt. Dull matching blue tie loosened at the collar. Hand clasped around a beer with a whisky chaser on the side as you sat at the bar of a familiar City haunt filled with clones of you. Washed-out, sex-starved losers, whose only solace at the end of a dog-eat-dog day lies in enough booze to give them the courage to face yet another one tomorrow.

You were prime meat. A target I couldn't possibly fail to hit. I love a challenge, and you were almost too easy.

The bar was located near Liverpool Street Station, not far from your office, and as I walked in, loud pop music was playing. So loud, it made any kind of conversation hard, particularly for strangers like us. But I was prepared for this. I'd done my research. I had a game plan. I hovered a while at the door, just to make sure you were alone, and then I went for it. Strode up to the heaving counter and waited behind a couple of smug-looking City traders dressed all too predictably in pinstripe suits, with too much gel caking their hair and already too much alcohol in their overtaxed systems. I looked hot, I knew that, because that's the look I was going for. It was August, so I could get away with a white skirt suit, its single-buttoned blazer accentuating my tiny waist and tight-fitting blouse, the skirt resting mid-thigh and showing off my slim, toned legs to perfection. My hair was styled in loose tumbling curls and I'd gone for a deep red lipstick that emphasized my full lips and oozed sex. The look was completed with two coats of black mascara and neutral eyeshadow, because it was all about the lips, and I was aiming for the sexy, domineering look, rather than cheap and tarty.

It wasn't long before the traders, standing beside you as they ordered a round of beers, noticed me. No surprise there. I virtually felt their dicks harden as they did.

One of them leered at me over his left shoulder, and within seconds his friend predictably followed suit. 'Sorry, we're in your way; just waiting on our beers,' the first one said. 'Can we order you something while we're here?'

He followed this up with a cheesy grin that turned my insides, as did his beer-laced breath, but I kept it together, smiled politely and said, 'No need to apologize. That's very kind of you, but I'm fine, thanks.'

But the twat persisted. 'You sure? We've got a table over there.' He gestured with his eyes to the back of the bar, but I didn't bother to follow his gaze. The last thing I wanted was to lead him to believe that I might be remotely interested in spending time with him.

You still hadn't looked up from your drink while all this was happening, and I couldn't help but feel a little affronted. I mean, every straight guy in the bar had surely noticed me by this point. But I guess you were so caught up in your sad little life, so lacking in confidence where women were concerned – because of her and the way she'd treated you for so many years – you'd become blind to the opposite sex.

I gave both twats – who, amazingly, still seemed to think they were in with a chance – a steely look and repeated, politely, but with a palpable tartness to my voice, 'Really, I'm fine.'

Just then, their beers arrived. *Finally, thank God*, I thought. Looking sorely put out, they grabbed them and left (although

I heard one of them mumble 'Stuck-up bitch' under his vile breath), allowing me space to reach the counter and make eye contact with the dishy bartender. Very fuckable, but sadly I wasn't there for my own pleasure. I was there on a mission, and nothing was going to stop me from keeping my eye on the prize. I ordered a gin and tonic and inched a few centimetres to the right where you were sitting, my hip almost touching yours, your hand gripping your shot glass.

Finally, you noticed me. I caught your gaze in the mirror behind the bar, watched it veer left, first down to my hip, then up to my face. My chance had arrived. I reached inside my handbag to retrieve my purse to pay for my drink, then 'accidentally' dropped the purse on the floor, just by the leg of your stool. I made to pick it up, but you were already there, having pushed back your stool, and you said, 'Allow me.' So polite, so harmless, and so very pitiful. You bent down to pick up my purse, and then I watched your gaze travel up my leg as you rose to a standing position.

'Thank you,' I gushed, my intense coffee eyes penetrating yours. You blushed like a pubescent schoolboy, and again I pitied you. Not out of sympathy, but out of scorn, because I knew all about you – who you were, what you'd done, or rather, had failed to do, despite having had every opportunity.

I still pity you, but the nature of my pity has changed. Now I do feel sorry for you. You don't deserve all that you've suffered over the years. You are a victim. And when I screw you, I do so partly because I feel something for you, and I want to help you bury your pain, block it out, if only for a short time, before you wake up the next day and it's there again. Relentless. Interminable. But mainly, I screw you to hurt her. Because when she finds out, it will hurt her, and it will be payback for what she did.

You said it was no problem, then smiled and sat back down again. The stool on the other side of you was free, and so I took my chance, said, 'I'm Amber. Mind if I sit down?'

The look on your face was priceless. As if I'd asked whether you fancied a blow job. There was the same intense blush, and I could tell that your heart rate was off the wall. I also knew there was no chance of you giving me a straight no; you were too polite, too *English*, but I did worry that you might bail on me out of fear, perhaps use the excuse that you were late for dinner or had a train to catch. But you didn't.

'Sure,' you said, your face a picture of bewilderment, and inwardly I sighed with relief.

I sat down, took a sip of my drink, told you I'd been stood up. You gave me an incredulous look, as if you didn't believe me.

'All I can say is that you've had a lucky escape,' you finally stammered, 'because whoever he is, he must be insane to have done such a thing.'

It was sweet, in a pathetic sort of way, and so I smiled coyly, then enquired what you did for a living, even though I knew exactly what you did. In fact, I knew your whole life history. But you told me readily. And gradually, you started to relax, and I could tell what a release it was for you, being able to talk about yourself for once. How invigorating it was for someone to take an interest in *your* life, because nobody had done so for such a long time. Because that's human psychology, isn't it? We're a naturally conceited species. We like to talk about ourselves, we like to feel special, valued, that we have a point, otherwise what *is* the fucking point? Before long, you bought us another round of drinks, and then I told you I was in marketing, which was bullshit, of course. By then you'd removed your jacket, and so had I, and we proceeded to talk about all manner of things. All except one crucial subject. A glaringly obvious one.

Your wife, together with the tragedy that had hung like a heavy black cloud over much of your adult life. You never attempted to hide your ring; why bother? It had been sitting on your finger when I walked in, and a hasty removal would have looked too obvious. Also, sad, desperate. But it clearly bothered you, and I could tell that you wished you weren't wearing it from the way you kept twiddling it between your thumb and forefinger.

In no time at all, the alcohol had well and truly loosened your inhibitions, and the barman was calling last orders. Your glazed eyes lingered on me as you said, 'I have to go. It's late, and I have an early morning meeting.'

'OK,' I replied, holding your gaze and undressing you with mine. 'What station are you headed for?'

As it turned out, we were both headed for Liverpool Street. Go figure. You helped me with my jacket from behind, and I knew what you were thinking at that moment. You were a lonely, sex-starved male in your fifties, and I was in no doubt that you badly wanted to fuck me. It was the only thought running through your mind: my young, hot body and what it would feel like to run your hands between my legs, thrust your neglected dick inside me, and release all that pent-up sexual frustration that festered in you like a malignant disease. There was no time like the present. I just needed to take advantage of that, engineer the right moment.

We ventured outside, into the chilly night air, although after the heat of the bar, it was refreshing. 'I know a quick way to the station,' I said with a twinkle in my eye, taking your hand, our first physical contact. 'Follow me.'

I didn't give you time to protest, even though I knew you couldn't say no to me. We practically skipped into a backstreet, and you chuckled like a carefree teenage boy.

'Where are you taking me?' you asked. And then I stopped to catch my breath against a wall, tossing my hair back, bending my knee ever so slightly so that more flesh was on show, tracing my index finger across my chest, hot from our exertions. There wasn't a soul about. I watched your eyes, hungry and animated, travel over me, emboldened by alcohol and the bond we had forged in the bar.

And then you couldn't help yourself. You came over and pressed yourself against me, then closer still, pressing me into the wall so that there was nowhere for me to go. I felt the heat, the desire radiating off you, saw the excitement in your eyes. You were gagging for it, gasping for it, I knew that from the hardness of you as you pressed tighter still. I could tell you'd never done anything like this before, that it wasn't in your nature, and that's what made it so arousing for you. I grabbed your hand and guided it up between my thighs, and although I didn't fancy you, because I am a highly sexual person the heat of the moment made me wet. I steered your fingers underneath my panties, running them up and down me, and then you took over, rubbing me faster and faster until I came, and my pants were soaked.

We were motionless for a while, recovering our breath, but then, with your face still buried in my neck, you said, 'When can I see you again?'

And that was the start. You still can't get enough of me. We have sex at the same hotel two, maybe three times a week. You told me you're married, unhappily, but not why. You will tell me soon, though, because you need me. You can't hold off much longer, especially in light of recent events.

I am your release, your addiction, and I pity you because you really don't deserve what's coming to you. It's not your fault, but you are a necessary instrument in the game of torture I am playing with your wife. A game I intend to win.

Chapter Thirteen

Christine

Now

Greg opens the front door as I hover behind him in the biting February air, cold, tired and groggy from the pain medication the hospital gave me. My head still aches from the fall, despite the co-codamol the doctor prescribed for me. I fell hard and caught the edge of a tile, cutting my head open quite deeply. They used glue stitches to seal it, an ingenious invention I am familiar with because Daniel needed them a couple of times, once when he was six and fell off a climbing frame, gashing his forehead badly, another when he was playing rugby and split his knee open. Greg took him to hospital on both occasions. He was much better at comforting Daniel than I was. Even now, I am amazed how a thin strip of glue can seal the deepest of cuts, leaving minimal scarring, and without the pain of stitches. Daniel is quite proud of his war wounds, but mine won't even show, covered by my hair. Not that I really care about my appearance these days.

Right now, all I can think about is the note. When I read it, it was like being knocked out by a tidal wave. For so long, although my heart didn't want to believe it (it still doesn't), the rational side of me accepted that you were gone. Although the police file on you was never closed, as the days, weeks, months, years passed, my hopes of ever seeing you again faded to nothing, despite the occasional trouble-stirrers claiming to have seen you. But now we get this, twenty-three years after you went missing, and from someone claiming to be the kidnapper. Why?

We'd always assumed it was a random abduction. There'd been nothing to suggest otherwise in the previous leads we'd followed, the police having questioned and eliminated friends, family, colleagues. But this note suggests otherwise. It feels personal. Like the sender knows about my past – what I've done – and therefore took you out of spite, to teach me a lesson. But who is he or she? There's only one person I can think of, but I bought her off years ago, and my instinct tells me it can't be her. Or can it? Perhaps buying her off wasn't enough? After all, she was infatuated.

The thought of what I did back then coming out terrifies me. I should have told Greg the truth long ago, but now too much time has passed, and it's too late for that.

–

When I woke up in the hospital around eleven last night, Greg was sitting by my bed, staring at me. Still in his suit, no tie, he looked dead beat. He told me what he thought had happened, and I nodded.

'Is this really happening?' I asked him. 'Can we really have reason to hope after all this time?'

'I don't know,' he said gently, shaking his head. 'It could just be another sicko stirring up trouble.'

'But it might not,' I said. 'Somehow, this feels different.'

'I know what you mean. But we still need to take things one step at a time. There's a police inspector on his way right now, Detective Inspector Ryan Phillips. I told him about the note, and he wants to have a chat about it.'

Greg rushed this last bit, as if afraid I was going to cut him off mid-flow. Cross that he'd gone to the police without consulting me first. But I didn't cut him off. I knew I'd given him enough grief over the years, and in any event, he'd done the right thing.

We *need* the police. We don't have a hope of tracing the note's author without them. But there's also a part of me that's afraid of them doing so, lest my secret should come out. I can't bear to think about how many people it will hurt.

Finding you, or keeping my secret? The choice should be simple, but it's not.

–

It's 10.30 a.m., and the temperature has dropped well below double figures; punishing weather for my skeletal frame. As I enter the house, I feel frozen from head to toe. Last night, I told Greg it would be no problem for me to get a taxi home from the hospital. But he insisted on picking me up, and as we pulled up in front of the house, he announced that he intended to work from home today. It's sweet of him, the kind of selfless gesture I'd expect from Greg, but I would much rather be alone. I'm used to my own space, especially in the daytime, and I don't want him to feel that he has to check up on me every few hours like some kind of carer. How sad is that, that I should feel so uncomfortable about my own husband looking after me?

Once inside the house, Greg says he'll make us some tea. I say thanks and ask him to crank up the heating too. He says no problem, although I'm sure this irritates him. He never feels the cold, used to comment how I wouldn't feel it so much if I had a bit more meat on me. He's long since given up trying to convince me of that, though.

I head upstairs to grab a thicker jumper as Greg shuffles around the kitchen, opening cupboards, filling the kettle, humming to himself as he often does.

I know how fortunate I am to live in such an affluent area of London. We bought our house the year before we were married, back when residential property was more affordable and we both earned large salaries. We'd previously owned separate flats in North-West London, although Greg's was worth more than mine, and mortgage free. His parents – who, in the last year have passed away within months of each other – were loaded owing to his father's CEO status. By the time he hit fifty, he was able to buy properties outright in North-West London for both Greg and his younger sister, Meredith. Because of this, and because of the money Greg made on his flat, our mortgage for this house was tiny, and has now been paid off in full.

It's a lovely three-storey town house on a quiet residential road, with a south-west-facing garden, four bedrooms, a spacious reception and separate dining room. It's close to the Tube and the main high street adorned with cafes, restaurants, boutiques and trinket shops.

As I pull out a thick cashmere sweater from my wardrobe, I think about our conversation with DI Phillips last night. He's very different to DI Grayson. Much younger than Grayson was at the time, he's tall and slim, with jet-black hair and a clear, articulate voice. More like a Cambridge professor than your average police inspector. Although maybe that's me being close-minded. Or perhaps forgetting how times have changed. It was obvious he'd done his homework on our case. Wasn't unfriendly, just pragmatic and to the point. Told us exactly what we'd expected to hear: 'Don't get your hopes up, this could very well come to nothing. Just some mischief-maker who chanced upon your case, perhaps twigged your daughter's birthday was coming up and saw it is as an opportune moment to create a stir.' In this respect, he was much like Grayson.

'I understand—' I nodded, as did Greg '—but even so, what are you going to do about it?'

Phillips told us not to worry, that he'd get on the phone to Sunderland Police, see if they'd be able to trace the postmark to the sender. Right now, the postmark is all they have to go on, he said, besides possible prints. In the meantime, both Greg and I are to keep our eyes out for anything or anyone suspicious, and certainly refrain from taking matters into our own hands. I should have told him about my secret then, about the person who could be behind this. But how could I tell him in front of Greg? My husband will know that I've lied to him all these years.

I enter the living room. It's wide and spacious, with solid oak flooring fitted with underfloor heating which I insisted on around ten years ago. I love the feeling of warmth bathing my feet as I pad around barefoot. At the time, Greg commented that it would be a hell of a lot cheaper for me to just buy a pair of slippers. As usual, like most men, he missed the point. He's sitting on the sofa when I walk in, two mugs of tea resting on coasters on the glass-topped coffee table in front of him, a thin trail of steam rising from each.

'Thanks for the tea,' I say as I sit down on the same sofa as Greg, but not too close. Similar to the way we keep our distance in bed. We've led separate lives for so long, it doesn't feel right; it feels too intimate. My fault entirely.

I study him for a while. I don't pay much attention to his appearance these days, but looking at him now, I'm sure he's lost a bit of weight. He's definitely trimmer, and I wonder if he's on a diet or gone back to the gym. And it's not just his physique. His face somehow looks younger, less worn down by life. It makes me wonder if he's having an affair. I wouldn't blame him; I've been such a misery to live with. Even so, I feel a twinge of jealousy, and I wonder how long we can go on like this. Perhaps this note will make or break us for good.

Now is not the time to discuss our relationship, though. First and foremost, we need to talk about the note. I know it's on his mind as much as it's on mine, and for the first time in ages, I feel like we have something to talk about. A common interest. Despite knowing in my heart that talking is pointless if I don't tell him what I've been hiding all these years. I'm about to kick off the conversation when my mobile phone rings. I left it on the hall table when we got in.

'Be back in a sec,' I say to Greg. He nods, almost looks relieved, and fishes out his own phone at the same time, the way men always do when they're left alone at a table in a restaurant, or in a bar.

Whoever's calling, they're persistent, and I smile when I see from the caller ID that it's Janine. I know when Greg rang her from the hospital explaining what had happened, she was desperate to come and see me. But I told him to tell her not to worry, and that she should pop over later today once I was home.

I'm so relieved she's back from the Far East. Better still, setting herself up in a lovely two-bedroom terraced house one stop from us in Swiss Cottage. I just hope she's happy. I keep telling her to sign up for a creative writing course – she always had such a good imagination – but she insists she's content with her charity work and pottering around the garden. I'm not convinced she is content, though. Sarah stayed on in Hong Kong, having landed some high-powered job, and now Janine's all alone. I know she misses Nate terribly. He'd been her world. It was me who set them up after she'd caught her good-for-nothing boyfriend cheating on her. Nate was charming, handsome and funny, the complete package. Understandably Janine had been wary at first, but I knew they'd be good for each other. Turns out, I was right. Engaged after four months, they got hitched on a beach in Mexico six months before Greg and I tied the knot.

'Hey, Jani,' I say as brightly as possible. 'You OK?'

'Am *I* OK?' she repeats. 'I'm fine, but what about you? I was so worried when Greg called and told me what happened. Bloody nutters – why can't they leave well alone? Why do they have to start all that shit up again? You could have died, Chrissy. I mean, what if Greg hadn't come home and found you, or you'd had internal bleeding, started haemorrhaging, it… it just doesn't bear—'

'Stop it, Jani, you're getting carried away. I'm fine, and that's all that matters. Why think about stuff that hasn't happened?'

But that's exactly how Janine works. She constantly worries about stuff, the possibility of something bad happening or something going wrong, even when there's no good reason to think it might. I blame her mother; a cold woman who ruined the first twenty or so years of her life, while her father, who played around, was weak and never stood up for her. Small wonder she distrusts people. They died before she and Nate got married. Not that she missed their presence.

When all is said and done, she has a good heart, and that's why Nate loved her. Why I became friends with her at uni. So many of the girls at my school had been cliquey, pretentious types, and I never completely trusted them not to stab me in the back. But Janine was different. She wasn't the most beautiful or confident, but she was kind and sincere, and we'd clicked from the moment we got talking in the dinner queue in halls.

'I know, I know, I'm a worrier,' Janine admits. 'Anyway, I'd love to come by and see you. I've made scones.'

'Scones?' I arch my brows in surprise. For one, I can't remember Janine ever baking, she's more of a main-course person, and two, I don't think I've touched, let alone eaten, a cake in years. But I don't want to upset her, so I say, 'Yes, of course you should. Greg's working from home today, but he'll be locked in his study. Come by around three-ish. I think I might need a nap before then; the painkillers have made me feel really drowsy.'

This is a lie. In truth, I feel wide awake now, but I really need to talk to Greg first.

'Of course, sweetheart,' she says. 'I'll let you rest. See you around three.'

We say our goodbyes and I return to the living room where Greg is tapping away furiously on his iPhone. I sit back down on the sofa and pick up my mug of now-lukewarm tea.

'Janine?' Greg says.

'Yes,' I nod. 'She's popping round at three. You don't mind, do you?'

Greg shakes his head. 'No. In fact, I was thinking, and seeing as you'll now have company anyway, I might go into work after all.'

He gets up and looks at me expectantly, like a teenager asking for permission to be out late. I feel a pang of disappointment, even anger at his change of heart, despite originally not wanting him around. My churlish side coming out, I guess.

He can tell by my face what I'm thinking. 'Something rather urgent's come up on a deal, you see,' he mumbles. 'Otherwise, I'd stay. You understand, don't you?'

'We need to talk about the note, Greg,' I say sternly. 'We can't shy away from it, we need to face it head-on.' I give him a hard look, and immediately see the frustration on his face. I don't know why I'm forcing the issue, since whoever wrote the note has implied that they know about my past. Surely that's not something I want to draw attention to? I guess it's the little voice inside my head telling me I must if we're ever to get to the bottom of things.

'I know that,' he snaps, 'but someone's got to earn the money.'

That old chestnut. But I can't really argue with him. I lived that life once; I know how demanding it is. I also don't have the energy to argue. It's just not worth it. 'OK, sorry. You go, then.'

His face softens.

'But promise me we'll discuss this later?'

'Of course,' he says more gently. 'But for now, we need to be patient, see what the police come up with.' He bends down and kisses the top of my head. The most affectionate he's been with me in months. 'I'll see you later. Get some rest before Janine comes over. Find out what she thinks. She's always sensible, always has good advice. And eat something, for Christ's sake, you're all skin and bones.'

He leaves the room. I hear the rattle of keys, and then the front door opening and closing.

I suppose he's right; there is nothing we can do until whoever sent the note makes contact again, or the police find something relevant, which I'm not too hopeful about.

All we can do for now is wait.

Chapter Fourteen

Greg

Now

'Sorry for the short notice, I just had to see you. I was feeling so claustrophobic in there.'

Amber is standing in the doorway of the hotel bedroom, looking as gorgeous as ever. When I texted her, asking if we could meet at our usual place, she was working from home, like I had planned to do before it all got too much and I knew I couldn't spend the entire day around Chrissy, as guilty as that made me feel. For so long, I've been the strong, dependable one – for her, for the kids, at work, keeping us financially stable – but this note has taken the wind out of my sails, and suddenly I feel like I'm drifting off course, with no idea how to navigate my way going forward.

The only time I feel free these days is when I'm with Amber. She is my Valium. She helps me to escape the pressure, the tension, all the shit life's thrown at me, if only for a few hours. A few hours when I can block it all out, pretend everything's just fine. Blissful, even.

She pulls me close and kisses me long and hard. She tastes sweet, smells like honey and cinnamon; the same exotic scent she always wears. Even in jeans and a V-neck jumper she looks incredible. She could have been a model, and not for the first time, I wonder what the hell she's doing with me. Although, maybe I'm being naive in thinking I'm the only man she screws.

We've not had that conversation, and regardless, I'm married; what right have I to pass judgement on her? Even though the mere thought of another man touching her consumes me with envy.

For a moment, I wonder if I'd feel that way if I discovered Chrissy was cheating on me. Twenty-three years ago, I wouldn't even have had to ponder that question. I loved her with such passion the thought of her sleeping with someone else would have driven me insane with jealousy. She was so vivacious, so beautiful back then and, of course, I'd notice the looks we'd get. She turned heads wherever she went. And secretly, I loved that. Revelled in it. Because she was mine. It was an ego boost, and I felt so bloody proud to have her on my arm. But in some ways, it was also a burden, because there was always this lingering fear at the back of my mind that she'd meet someone else, leave me for someone as good-looking as her. Or, at least, give in to temptation and sleep with another man in the heat of the moment. I mean, it happens all the time. Look at me, for Christ's sake, and I'm nothing special. In fact, I remember Miranda asking me whether I was sure Chrissy was marriage material after I told her we were engaged. Whether I might be rushing into things and ought to give it a bit more time. I don't think she asked it out of jealousy. She'd come to terms with our relationship by then. Duncan had already proposed, and she and Chrissy got on fine. In fact, we'd double date occasionally, even though Duncan got on my nerves. I just think, being one of my best friends, she was genuinely concerned for my happiness and, with Chrissy being an exceptionally beautiful woman, was afraid of her straying and me getting hurt.

But Chrissy never gave me cause to doubt her loyalty. She was a wonderful wife and mother until the day she lost our child. And then the woman I'd known and adored had gradually disappeared. And now that version of her feels more like a vivid dream I once had than reality.

Amber asks me if I want a drink. A hard one from the minibar. It's a bit early, but I say what the heck, because the truth is, I'm dying for one. She grabs two miniature vodkas, fixes them neat, and we sit next to one another on the bed.

'What is it?' she asks, stroking the top of my thigh with her hand.

I can't keep it from her any longer. She knows I have a wife, grown-up kids. But no names, no details. For the first time, I tell her about Chrissy, about what happened to us, to our family. Amber doesn't say much – she's a good listener – but I can tell from her face that she's shocked. Hadn't expected me to have such a tragic past.

And then I tell her about last night. Finding Chrissy on the floor, the note, the awkwardness between us before I left to come here. She listens patiently, never interrupts, waiting for me to finish. I pray that I haven't scared her off, that she'll still want to see me, despite my sorry tale. Right now, I need her. I don't think I could handle all this without her.

Finally, when I'm done, she comes closer and caresses the side of my face. 'You poor darling, I'm not surprised you need one of these.' She gestures to our glasses. 'Dredging all that up again. Do you think the note's genuine?'

'Who knows,' I sigh, relieved she hasn't told me to fuck the hell out of her straightforward life; a life that doesn't need this kind of complication. 'When Heidi first went missing, we had hundreds of calls from people claiming to have seen her or pretending to know something about her disappearance. But they all came to nothing. And like DI Phillips said, this note might not be any different. The sender could well be just another troublemaker who happened to read about Heidi's kidnapping and wanted to cause a stir.'

'Maybe, but it happened a long time ago. How would the sender have heard about it now? Plus, you said this note *feels* different.'

I nod. 'It does. It feels personal.'

'Because it said your daughter was better off with her kidnapper than with your wife?'

I nod again. 'That bugs me. Another reason I had to get away from Chrissy. I wanted to ask her about it, but I bottled out.'

I pause, at which point Amber leans in closer and looks at me with heartfelt eyes. 'You can't hide from it, you have to bring it up with her.'

'I know I do. And I will. But the thing is, unless this person chooses to give us anything more, we aren't any closer to finding Heidi. I didn't want to say this to Chrissy, but despite what DI Phillips says, I'm pretty sure the police up north won't have a snowball's chance in hell of tracing the postmark. And I'm betting the sender wore gloves.'

'That's probably true,' Amber nods sympathetically. Then, looking thoughtful, she asks, 'Do you want to know the truth, after all this time?'

I don't answer immediately. It's a question I wrestled with for much of the night. For so long, I've dreamed about being reunited with my daughter. Just being able to see her face, hold her, kiss her, hug her, tell her how much I love her. But now, the thought of seeing her scares me, because I will be a stranger to her. Dead to her, even. No more her father than the next man on the street. The idea that she might resent me, want nothing to do with me – even though it's not my fault that she was taken – doesn't just upset me, it terrifies me.

'I don't know,' I reply. 'Or rather, I'm not sure. For ages, I'd resigned myself to her being dead. So I'm not sure I'm really prepared for her being alive. I mean, Chrissy and I would be strangers to her.'

'Why do you think Chrissy pushed you away after Heidi disappeared? I mean, if it were me, I would have needed you more; begged for your forgiveness.'

I know this is my chance to lash out at Chrissy, but for some reason, I try and make excuses for her. 'Because she felt guilty, I guess. Guilty for losing Heidi. She was ashamed, and I suppose closing herself off from me, rather than seeking my help, was a defence mechanism of sorts. She's always been a bit stubborn; dare I say it, arrogant. That's why she's seen so many shrinks over the years. They don't judge her, they have no emotional investment in her. She's nothing but a patient to them and they'll listen to her talk until she's blue in the face.'

Despite attempting to defend Chrissy's behaviour to Amber, I still resent her for pushing me away. I mean, I was hurting like crazy, I needed her love and support more than ever during that time, but she didn't give it to me, didn't appear to consider my feelings. She just shut herself off, and that still pisses me the hell off. Especially in light of what Amber's just said; that she would have needed me more, begged for my forgiveness. The reaction of a normal, humbler person.

Amber takes a slug of vodka, then slides her slender fingers through her lustrous hair. You can just make out her roots, but there's no question that blonde suits her. 'Well, I hate shrinks,' she says. 'I don't trust them. There's something unnatural about the whole thing. My view is, when you're in a bad place – when you've hit rock bottom – what you need most is family, those who love you most. I think I would find it weird talking to a stranger about something so personal.'

I love her for saying this. She's the opposite of Chrissy. Warm and loving, not cold and aloof. She nestles up to me so that our hips are touching, holds my gaze and says, 'Are you sure she's not hiding something from you? Something she's ashamed of, but never had the nerve to tell you about? Maybe that's what whoever sent the note was getting at?'

I feel my muscles tighten as she offers up this possibility, because she's said out loud what I've been wondering ever since reading the note.

She carries on. 'You need to ask her, you deserve to know the truth.'

She looks at me with her doe eyes, and I thank my lucky stars I walked into that bar six months ago. Thank God I didn't chicken out when she asked if she could join me. I was so tempted to – she was so young and intoxicating, so bloody sexy, everything I didn't look or feel. But I didn't, and it was the best decision I'd made in a long time. She keeps me sane, and she's more than a good screw. She's special, one in a million, and I can't lose her. Not yet, at least.

Amber places her left palm on my chest, then runs her painted nails down my shirt buttons until they reach my fly, which she slowly unbuttons before delving inside. I tingle all over, hardening immediately.

'You need to let some tension out; it's not good for a man your age.' She grins suggestively, and I instantly feel the stress subside.

I watch her slide off the bed, kneel on the floor, and lower her head. And then, knowing what's about to happen, I lie back and forget everything, and tell myself how lucky I am to have found Amber.

Chapter Fifteen

Christine

Now

Janine and I embrace in the hallway. She's warm and fleshy, and I immediately relax, reassured by her familiar, friendly touch. She stands back, looks me up and down, and says with a frown, 'Jesus, woman, you look awful.'

I smile at her almost comical frankness. 'Thanks,' I say.

One thing I can rely on with Janine is that she'll always tell me the truth, even if I'm not going to like it. I like that about her. Like the fact that with her, what you see is what you get. I can trust her not to tiptoe around my feelings like my other so-called friends do. No niceties for the sake of it, no games. Miranda's the other exception. She'll tell me straight if I'm talking shit. But I also wonder if that's Duncan's influence, being a straight-talking Northerner. He used to make me laugh with his blunt dry humour. But that was a long time ago, when I was somebody else. I expect he was too.

Anyway, on this occasion, Janine's absolutely right. I do look bloody awful.

After Greg left, I took a long, hot shower in our en-suite bathroom. As I stood there – the shower's powerful jets making my skeletal body feel quite sore – his comment about my figure plagued my mind, and as I gazed down at my body, at my flat, mannish boobs, my stick-insect legs, my washboard stomach, I felt repulsed. Clearly, I repulsed him. *Sooner or later, the excessive exercising and bird-like eating is going to catch up with me*, I told myself, *but I can't let that happen if there's any chance of you still being out there, Heidi. I need to keep strong in mind and body*. In short, I realized that I needed to take better care of myself, and at that moment I promised myself that I would.

'Well, I'm sorry, but you do,' Janine says, heading straight for the kitchen. She goes over to the table and sets down the cake tin she's holding before opening the lid. 'Scones and clotted cream,' she announces proudly. 'Hope you have butter and jam.' She winks. 'Now get the flipping kettle on, so we can tuck in.'

Ten minutes later, we're sitting at the table, munching on scones, which are – to my surprise – bloody good. Or maybe they're just average, and it's merely the fact that I've denied myself for so long, anything would taste good. Anything with sugar, fat, a bit of substance. I couldn't quite bring myself to add any of the clotted cream, but I did apply a thin layer of butter and jam. A real achievement for me.

There's a roguish glint in Janine's eye as she grins widely and says, 'Good, aren't they?'

I grin back. 'Yes, bloody good.'

'Save some for Greg, though.' She smiles again, then pricks up her ears. 'It's very quiet. I expected to hear his footsteps pacing the floor, or him ranting down the phone.'

Being a law widow, Janine knows the drill all too well. Knows how stressful life can be for a City lawyer, and often lonely for their spouse.

I chew and swallow the last of my scone, thinking it will keep me full until at least dinner time, possibly breakfast. In fact, I feel mildly queasy because I'm not used to anything remotely stodgy, and it's a shock to my system. I push my plate away. 'He went into work after all. Said something urgent came up.'

Janine sits back, looks unimpressed. 'You're joking? After what happened, he just abandoned you? How can you stand for that?' She frowns, almost looks fit to burst.

I don't want to be angry with Greg, but I can't help thinking she's right. Even so, I make a half-baked attempt to defend him, perhaps because I feel it would be hypocritical of me to criticize him. After all, it was only when he announced that he was leaving that I realized I wanted him to stay.

'Calm down, Jani, he knew you were coming over, and I said I'd be OK.'

Janine's eyes narrow. '*Are* you OK?'

She has me. She knows me so well.

I sigh. 'Not really.'

'The note?'

I nod. 'It was just such a shock. After all this time, trying to come to terms with the fact that she's gone… I just don't know what to think.'

Janine reaches for my hand and squeezes it gently. 'Can I see the note?'

'Sure.' I'd always planned to show it to her, but I'm glad she's expressed interest without me offering it up. Makes me feel like less of a burden. It's a wonder she's not bored of it all. Like Miranda, she's had to listen to the same stuff repeatedly for the last two decades. I go and retrieve the note which I locked in a drawer in the study last night before going to bed, then return to the kitchen. I hand it to Janine, watch her read it in silence.

'Fuck,' she says when she's finished, looking up at me with wide eyes. Exactly the reaction I'd expected.

'It's killing me, Jani. I mean, do I even dare to have hope? Or do I tell myself it's just another prankster?'

'You can always hope, love, there's nothing wrong with that. But you must also be prepared for it to amount to nothing. I'm sure the police said the same?'

'Yes. He's nice, DI Phillips, but predictably cynical.' I inhale deeply, then let out a big sigh. 'I know you're both right. It's… it's just that somehow this note…'

'Feels different?'

'Yes. For one, it's handwritten, and two, it feels like it's come from someone I know, or knew.'

'Because of the last sentence?' Janine looks at me intently, and I feel my cheeks redden. A sure sign I am hiding something.

79

But she doesn't probe. Says, 'Just because the tone is personal, it doesn't necessarily mean the sender knows you. It could just be part of some sick mind game he or she is playing with you.'

Logically, this makes sense. But there's something to be said for trusting your gut, and my gut tells me otherwise. But I don't labour the point, just say with a faint smile, 'I know.'

Janine leans forward, looks at me earnestly. 'Can you think of anyone who might bear a grudge against you for something you did, either to them, or to someone they knew or loved, back then? Or perhaps someone who was jealous of you?'

I shake my head. 'No one springs to mind.'

Liar.

'What are you hiding from me, Chrissy?'

Janine's gaze penetrates me so deeply, I have to look away. I'm too afraid, too ashamed to tell her the truth, and so I get up from my chair, move to the window, and say, with my back to her, 'Nothing, it's nothing. Like you said, probably part of some sick mind game the sender is playing with me.'

Janine doesn't respond. I don't like the silence, so I turn around and meet her gaze again. To my relief, she doesn't press the issue further. Just shakes her head and says, 'Well, all we can do for now is wait. See what the police come up with, see if the sender gets in contact again. But you need to keep your head. You can't let this drive you mad.'

I nod gratefully. 'I know.'

There's a short pause before she asks, 'How are things going with Dr Cousins?'

'Good,' I say brightly, 'I really like her.'

'I knew you would.'

'She's quite unconventional, surprisingly harsh at times, but I think that's what I like about her. She does the unexpected, keeps me on my toes.'

Janine nods enthusiastically. 'Yes, exactly. It's a bit of a shock at first, but sometimes you need to be shocked out of a bad situation, don't you think? I mean, she didn't allow me to wallow in my grief for Nate. Don't get me wrong: in our first couple of sessions, she just listened and let me sob and whinge about how bloody unfair it was, but then she told me to get real, get on with it, because, quite frankly, what was the point in moaning, endlessly grieving? Nate was dead and never coming back. In fact, she said I could either snap out of it and get on with my life, or I might as well put a bullet through my head.'

I gasp in shock. 'She actually said that?'

'Well, no, not those *exact* words,' Janine admits with a wry smile, 'but that was the gist of it.' She pauses, then says, 'Bit of a weird thing to say, I know, but I'm sort of glad Dr Cousins crashed into Miranda's car that day. I mean, we'd never have known her otherwise. It's like fate drove them together, literally.' She smiles again. 'It's ironic when you think about it.'

'How do you mean?' I ask.

'Well, Miranda used to be so disparaging of shrinks. I remember her saying she'd never touch one with a bargepole. But she completely changed her attitude when she met Dr Cousins.'

It's a good point. Greg said the same. But I guess that just goes to show how special Dr Cousins is.

Janine hesitates.

'What?' I ask.

'She also gave me some pills.'

'Pills? What, like antidepressants?' I had a brief spell on diazepam, but I didn't like the way they made me feel lethargic, spaced out. The gym is my tranquillizer. The gym and wine.

'Sort of.'

I shake my head. 'Sort of? How do you mean? You know I don't like pills, Jani.'

'I know, neither do I. And I didn't want to take them at first. Felt almost cross that she appeared to be advocating them as a solution. But I felt so desperate, I agreed. And they really helped. Whatever was in them, they did the trick. Made me feel calmer, but never like a zombie. I know that's what you don't like, right?'

I nod.

'I don't either, but these ones actually made me feel more in control, able to function better.'

'But you're off them now, right?'

Janine nods. 'Oh yes, completely off them. All I'm saying is, if this thing starts up again, and you're feeling a bit overwhelmed, you might want to ask her to prescribe what she gave me. Just to get you through it.'

'OK, maybe,' I say.

Just then, my phone, which is lying on the table, vibrates. I pick it up, check the message. It's a total shock, and that must show on my face because Janine immediately asks me what's wrong.

I look up, still knocked for six. 'It's Daniel,' I mumble.

'Is he all right?' Janine asks anxiously.

'Yes,' I say. 'He's engaged, apparently. And he wants to introduce me and Greg to his fiancée over lunch this Sunday.'

Chapter Sixteen

Daniel

Now

It's Saturday, and I wake up with a clear head, rather than feeling like it's being pummelled from every angle. It's still a pretty novel sensation for me, feeling so alive on a weekend morning, but at the same time, it's bloody fantastic. The sound of birds tweeting, children playing, traffic droning doesn't grate at my throbbing head like it used to, and I don't have that hideous choppy sensation in the pit of my stomach that tells me I'm going to spew at any moment.

I'm ready to face the day. Enjoy it, rather than battle it. Enjoy life, just being in the moment. And it's all because of *you*.

I turn and prop myself up on my left side, then gaze down at you, locked in a deep sleep. My sleeping beauty. I desperately want to kiss you, but I can't bear to wake you, you look so peaceful.

I could watch you forever. Your profile is exquisite. Your dainty nose, your ridiculously long eyelashes, the curve of your lips. And then there are your soft, golden locks which, right now, caress your slender shoulders and back. You excite me, fulfil me in ways I never thought possible, having virtually given up on the female sex. You've been such a good influence on me, you are so *good* for me, full stop, and I thank God for the day you walked into my life. I still can't believe my luck, because I never thought such incredible fortune could happen to someone like me. You are almost too good to be true, and I can't help wondering when the blissful bubble I am living in might burst. The thought of it doing so terrifies me.

Before you came along, I would binge-drink several times a week – mainly beer, but also spirits like vodka or Bacardi – rising to dangerous levels on weekends. I also took drugs, hard stuff like coke and heroin, ate crap, but didn't give a fuck what I was doing to myself. And I could never maintain a relationship. I thought it was all my fault; that I was too screwed up to ever be able to trust and fully commit myself to someone. In some ways it was true, because I *was* screwed up. But you unscrewed me. You helped me see that I could change, that I could commit. I was merely waiting for the right girl to come along. You.

It's very easy for me to lay the blame on my childhood. Although I grew up in a home that wanted for nothing materially, it was devoid of the one thing my sister Ella and I craved above all else.

A mother's love.

I've never told Mum or Dad this, but there've been times when I've found myself loathing my older – most probably dead – sister. I think I was seven and Ella was five when Dad sat us down and tried to tell us about her. Her disappearance destroyed my parents' relationship, destroyed my (and Ella's) childhood before it had even begun. She has been the bane of our lives right from when we were foetuses in our mother's womb, even though we didn't know it at the time. I realize that sounds insane, that it's in no way Heidi's fault, but I can't help thinking this way.

Dad did his best, poor sod. But there are times when a child just needs his or her mother, especially when you have a dad like ours who works insane hours and you don't get to see him much, except on weekends. And even then, he was always on his frigging BlackBerry, as smartphones were back then. Mum was never consciously cruel to us – she didn't hit us or call us horrid names – but she performed her motherly duties in a cold fashion. And it always felt like she was a million miles away, rather than in the here-and-now with us.

Ella and I weren't stupid. Just because we were kids, we weren't blind to our parents' unhappy relationship, to their negative body language and clipped conversation. We noticed how Mum was just as frigid with Dad as she was with us. Witnessing any affection between them was rare, and although I don't like making excuses for myself, there's no doubt in my mind that Mum's coldness towards me and Dad had a harmful bearing on my behaviour towards women in general.

But you are different from other women. From the start you seemed to get me so well, and you helped me see that it's not my fault, that I don't have to be unhappy all my life – that my mother's actions needn't shape my future, or Ella's. You penetrated the stone veil that previously enveloped my heart.

Just now, you stir, do that funny scrunchy thing you do with your nose, and I can't resist. I kiss your shoulder tenderly. You smile, your eyes still closed, and murmur, 'What time is it?'

'Just gone nine,' I say, then follow up with another kiss, this time on your back. But I don't stop. I keep going, my lips travelling lower and lower down the small of your back, making your body jerk with pleasure, my head now completely under the covers, my right hand wandering between your thighs until I reach the most delicious thing in the world.

I don't stop there. Hearing you moan excites me. I love that sound. And then you shake uncontrollably, and I am in paradise. Your pleasure is all mine.

You, my new fiancée, saved me. And I will do anything to keep you happy.

Anything, Freya, anything at all.

Chapter Seventeen

Heidi

Before

'Heidi, darling, there's something I need to tell you; something that's going to be hard for you to hear at first, but I believe it's for the best.'

I look at my mother with inquisitive eyes. It's unusually warm today, and we're sitting in the shadiest part of our garden, on a swinging chair under a sprawling maple tree. I loved rocking on this chair when I was little; my very own personal swing, no need for a trip to the park. I still do, in truth, even though tomorrow I become a teenager, and must surely put away childish whims.

I'm very mature for my age, apparently. I've heard some of the older ladies at the club Mother goes to whisper as much to her. 'She's so well behaved, so well spoken, you could take her anywhere. If only all children of her age had such impeccable manners.'

I suppose that comes from being an only child. Ever since I can remember, I've gone everywhere with my mother or childminder. In fact, when I'm not at school, she hardly ever lets me out of her — or the childminder's — sight. Once in a while, she lets me go over to a friend's house, but she always gives me strict instructions never to leave the premises under any circumstances, until it's time to go home.

Until I was eleven, I had a tutor called Mrs Bates. There were times when I resented being cooped up inside with her, when I knew other children my age were busy mixing with each other, running riot in the playground, forming solid friendships, getting invited to birthday parties. But it wasn't all bad. Mrs Bates was a lovely woman. Willowy, dark-haired, with feline green eyes and porcelain skin, she was strict and earnestly religious, but also kind and fair, and she made lessons interesting and fun. Once I asked her why she thought Mother had chosen to have me home-schooled, rather than attend a normal primary school like other children my age. She said my mother had been through a lot and was right to be wary of the dangers out there. That I was very lucky to have a mother who loved me as much as she did, and that I mustn't resent her for wanting to protect me. Every so often, Mother goes away for the weekend, to where I don't know, and I don't ask. But when she does, she leaves me with Mrs Bates, who she knows she can trust to keep me safe.

'There are a lot of bad people out there, and your mother just wants to protect you. Always remember that.'

Put that way to a six-year-old, it all made perfect sense. And I did remember. I never forgot. I love my mother with all my heart, and it's the most wonderful feeling knowing that I am completely and utterly loved by her. She told me what an unhappy childhood she'd had. Like me, an only child, but lacking in maternal love. No cuddles, no one to tuck her up in bed with a tender kiss and a fond goodnight. No soothing words after a terrifying nightmare. I feel so sad when she tells me these stories because I can't imagine how horrible that must have been for her growing up. My mother is the kindest person I know, and she deserved to be loved. She told me how it made her heart sing to be the mother to me she never had, and just hearing her say that meant the world to me. When I'm with her, I always feel safe. She's the one person who will never let me down. Whom I can rely on come what may.

When I turned eleven, Mother decided it was time for me to go to school. I was old enough to be trusted, to be aware of the dangers out there. Although it was a big change for both me and her, it was a change I welcomed with open arms. Don't get me wrong, I love spending time with my mother. She's my best friend (on weekends we bake, watch movies, go for strolls in the park, play tennis), but I also need to spend time with kids my own age. It's only natural.

My school is great. The teachers are brilliant, the timetable varied and stimulating, and I already have a good idea of what I want to do with my life.

Although there are a few unfriendly types, that's just normal, and most of the girls in my class are lovely. I also have a massive crush on this boy in the year above, and I think he might like me too (we exchange shy smiles in the corridors regularly), but I daren't tell Mother. She's so protective.

At times, I find her love somewhat smothering. Feel like telling her to loosen the cord and let me be a normal teenager. But when I feel like I'm on the verge of lashing out at her possessiveness, I remember what Mrs Bates said, remind myself how lucky I am to have her, and my frustration immediately thaws.

Father's quite protective, too, but he's not as intense as Mother. Perhaps because he knows what good care she takes of me, and because he doesn't have time on his hands to constantly worry about me. He works long hours, frequently goes away on business trips, and I only ever see him properly at weekends. Even then, he works until lunchtime on a Saturday, or is off playing rugby.

He and Mother seem to have a good relationship, although I wouldn't say they're particularly affectionate with one another. I'm too young and inexperienced to know if this is normal, and I don't see enough of my friends' parents together to know what's typical after years of marriage. Plus, we never have anyone come to stay with us. I can only assume that it is. The point is, I hardly ever hear them argue, and Father is always pretty amenable to whatever Mother wants. Not that she's high maintenance, she just likes to run the house in a certain way, and he seems happy to leave all the domestic stuff to her. In fact, I've never heard him argue against anything she suggests, almost like she's got something on him. Although maybe that's just my imagination getting carried away.

Just then, a butterfly flutters past my line of vision. It's so beautiful, and I almost want to reach out and capture it, keep it in my room, just so I can admire it every day. But I know how cruel that would be, and I don't want to be cruel, I want to be a good person. Like us –

the pinnacle of Creation – God's lesser creatures also deserve to run wild, fly free, rather than be caged for someone else's pleasure. That's what Mrs Bates used to say. Not that I am comparing myself to a butterfly or anything. I'm just saying, is all.

'Heidi.' My mother's voice brings me back to reality and I remember why we are here. She has something important to tell me. I haven't a clue what she's about to say, but there's an uncharacteristic edge to her voice, and I experience a feeling of dread that frightens the life out of me. I'm terrified she's going to announce that she or Father is sick, or that they're splitting up. Being my mother, my flesh and blood, she can read my mind, sense my unease.

'It's OK, sweet girl. Your father and I are fine. We're not ill and we're not splitting up.'

Relief washes over me like a new lease of life, and my face breaks into a wide smile. 'What is it then, Mother?'

I watch her inhale deeply. If it's not illness or divorce, what can it possibly be that's troubling her so much?

She cups my cheeks with her soft, comforting hands, looks into my eyes, her own eyes filling with tears, although there's also a wildness to them which unnerves me, then says softly, 'Heidi, darling, I am not your real mother.'

Chapter Eighteen

Janine

Now

'Janine, it's Miranda.'

I've just got off the phone with my daughter. Another draining conversation. Although she's much more self-assured than I was at her age – probably because, unlike my own mother, who never gave a fig about me, I've always been there for her – I know she hates the fact that she's adopted. I constantly tell her it doesn't matter that she's not my flesh and blood, that I have loved her from the first day she entered my and Nate's world. But I suppose it's only natural for her to feel insecure, to always have that nagging feeling at the back of her mind that she wasn't good enough for her real parents. I've discussed her insecurity with Chrissy over the years, who's always at pains to point out that, *Sarah is probably a lot more secure than Ella and Daniel, despite them being my own flesh and blood, so what does that tell you?!* She's right, I guess.

Anyway, right now my incredibly smart daughter is having a hard time at work. There's this project she's been assigned to, and it's taking its toll. I told her repeatedly that she's doing fine, that I'm certain she'll be brilliant, and everything will work out in the end. And I think she felt reassured by the end of our conversation, which made me feel better. But no sooner had I put down the phone, than you, Miranda, called.

I could really do without talking to you at this moment. I always end our conversations, which invariably revolve around

Chrissy and Greg – after all, they're the common denominator that links us – feeling exhausted because you don't let me get a word in edgeways. You've been this way for as long as I can remember. Overpowering, a bit of a motor mouth, although I guess I shouldn't be surprised. You're a corporate lawyer, after all, and Nate always said they were the worst. Which is a bit contradictory coming from him, seeing as he was one too. Perhaps that's why you married Duncan. He's another one who loves the sound of his own voice.

At first, I thought maybe you talked too much out of nerves. Because you were apprehensive about entering Chrissy's world, being Greg's ex, and therefore keen to make a good impression. People often do that to ingratiate themselves with others, don't they? They think if they're quiet, it'll make them appear standoffish. But I'm always suspicious of people who talk too much. And I won't lie, I *was* suspicious of you to begin with. I mean, it hadn't seemed natural for you to want to become friends with your ex's new girlfriend, especially when it was obvious that you were still madly in love with him. I could tell by the way you'd talk about him, still do, in fact. And I can't begin to count the number of times I've caught you gazing at him wistfully. Like at their wedding, and Heidi's christening. It was as plain as the nose on your face that you wished more than anything it was you standing beside Greg on both occasions; two of the happiest days of his life. You thought no one was watching, but I was. You looked like you were in pain, and I can't say I blame you entirely for that. I know what it feels like to love someone so much you feel like you might die if you can't have them. That's how I felt about Nate. And although I think you were genuinely upset for Greg when Heidi went missing, I also think a part of you enjoyed seeing Chrissy suffer. Maybe you saw it as *kismet*, I don't know. I do know what a crappy childhood you had, with no mother and a father as hard as nails. And although you claim neither you nor Duncan wanted kids, I secretly think you pined for them. None of us know the full story there, I'm sure of it. Not even Greg. But you're hiding something. Of that, I'm certain.

I take a laboured breath, summon up the strength to speak to you.

'Hi, Miranda, what's up?'

'It's Chrissy, that's what's up. Obviously, you know about what happened?'

No *hi, how are you doing?* Just straight in there like a bull in a china shop.

I feel like saying, *Yes, of course I do, I was her friend long before you came on the scene, plus I only live down the sodding road, unlike you nearly 300 bloody miles away.* But I don't say any of that. Just breathe deeply again, say as calmly as possible, 'Yes, I saw her yesterday. She was very shaken up, which is completely understandable considering what the note said.'

A second's pause and I wonder what's coming next. 'That's just it,' you say.

'What's just it?'

'I think she's hiding something from us. I think she has been for some time now, and whoever sent that note knows it too. Listen, I like Chrissy – you know I do – but I'm really worried about Greg. She has you to look out for her, but who does he have? I'm wondering whether I should come down and make sure he's OK? What do you think?'

You devious cow. I just can't believe it. Are you seriously trying to sidle your way back into Greg's affections at a time like this? You know that their marriage is hanging by a thread; maybe you think the note will be the nail in the coffin and cause him to go running back into your arms. I have to admit, in some ways, I admire your tenacity where winning back Greg's affections are concerned. But I also find your desperation somewhat loathsome.

You carry on without giving me a chance to reply, a Machiavellian tone to your voice. 'You know, after Heidi went missing, I always thought Chrissy was hiding something. Just by the way she shut herself off from us all, Greg especially. I hate to say this, but the fact is, Janine, you view Chrissy through rose-tinted glasses, but I'm not sure she's as innocent as you like to make out. Let's face it, the way she raised Daniel and Ella was unforgivable. I mean, they bloody hate her!'

'Why are you trying to stir up trouble?' I say angrily. 'You're meant to be her friend. Is there something you're not telling me about Duncan? Have you two split up? Is that why we never see him?'

Silence.

'Well?' I persist.

'Duncan and I have been living separate lives for a long time now.'

Knew it!

'Have you told Greg?'

'No, I didn't want to burden him with my problems.'

How considerate of you.

'Tell me straight, Miranda. Is it your aim to get back with Greg? Are you trying to make trouble between him and Chrissy?'

'How dare you!'

'It's a reasonable question to ask. Everyone knows you're still in love with him. And now you're calling me saying Chrissy's hiding something, that you and Duncan aren't together any more, that you want to come down here and comfort Greg – what else am I supposed to think?'

'Don't tell me the same thought hasn't occurred to you, based on what the note says, the way Chrissy's always so reticent when it comes to talking about that day, the way she treated Ella and Daniel growing up.'

'She lost a child! What do you think that does to a person?'

There's a pause, then you say, 'OK, I'm just worried about Greg, that's all. I really don't want to split them up, I just want him to be happy. But if you think me coming down will do more harm than good, I won't. OK?'

'Sure, OK,' I say.

'Please don't tell Chrissy about our conversation. I know that you want to protect her, and I'm really not out to get her. I sincerely want the best for her and Greg, but until we know what the sender of that note was getting at, I don't think they'll be able to have peace.'

You're right on that score. It'll be like a millstone around their necks, driving them to distraction, not knowing who sent the note, whether it's just another crackpot or someone they know, someone who has reason to bear a grudge.

'You're probably right,' I concede. 'And I won't tell Chrissy about our conversation. But like I said, I'm not sure they need a house guest right now. They need to work this through together. At any rate, I'm just around the corner if they need a friend.'

We say our goodbyes and I put down the phone, exhausted as predicted.

Chapter Nineteen

Christine

Before

My jaw is aching with all the smiling, and I worry about the new lines and crow's feet that must surely be developing around my eyes. Just because I am vain like that.

Everyone warned me this would happen. It's not just the official photographer who wants to take a gazillion photos of the bride and groom on their special day; there are also the well-wishers, the guests, even passers-by, keen to get snaps of the happy couple, particularly the bride. Even if she's not particularly beautiful, or is looking as grumpy as hell, they want a photo. Snaps that will be shared around like a pack of cards. Bandied about for a week, maybe two, then never looked at again, except, perhaps, by the bride and groom on anniversaries, and to prove to their future children that they were once young and in love.

I do the same at other people's weddings. There's nothing like a wedding to put people in a good mood. Like the birth of a child, it's an uplifting occasion. It's about having a purpose, a meaning in life. A wedding is something to celebrate, look forward to, because it signifies the greatest thing in life: *love*. And because it marks the beginning, rather than the end, of something. And isn't that what we humans fear the most? The end of something? The end of a relationship, the end of child-hood and, most of all, the end of life?

It's not just the bride and groom who look incredible on their big day. The bridesmaids, the best man, the ushers also look amazing. As do the guests. A wedding is the perfect excuse for that new dress, new pair of shoes, new hat, new hairdo. A licence to spoil ourselves and spend stupid amounts of money.

It's a beautiful day, aesthetically and spiritually. A day filled with merriment, dancing, food and too much booze. And today, at my own wedding, despite feeling rather exhausted from all the posing, I am happy, simply because I know how fortunate I am to be marrying a good man. A man who truly loves me. And, without question, I love him too.

Why, then, when I look at *you*, do I get this insatiable urge to tear your clothes off and shag you senseless? I have everything I could ever want. A fantastic career, an amazing house, supportive parents, a wonderful older brother, and a kind, intelligent, thoughtful new husband who I know would take a bullet for me. And to top it all off, once this day is over, Greg and I will be jetting off to the Maldives for a fortnight. Two weeks of uninterrupted bliss on a heavenly island.

Why, then, do I imagine myself committing adultery with you on that island, rather than my husband making love to me? Why do I imagine us stripped naked, entwined on a deserted beach, sand clinging to our bronzed, sweaty bodies, our tongues exploring each other's mouths as you thrust yourself into me and I moan with pleasure and experience the most amazing orgasm? I can't seem to shake the vision as I smile, then smile again, and pretend the only thoughts I have right now are of my husband and how happy I am that this day has finally arrived and I am Mrs Greg Donovan.

'Chrissy, over here!' I turn my head and see Giles, a friend from uni, gesturing to his camera, wanting me to pose for him.

'Can't we just escape upstairs to our room?' Greg whispers in my ear, squeezing the bodice of my dress as he does so.

'I wish,' I whisper through clenched teeth. 'Smile for the camera.'

I look in Giles' direction, and then I spot you, standing not too far from him. You look incredible. Like a movie star. The midnight-blue suit – offset by a crisp white shirt and dark blue tie – really sits well with your tanned complexion. You've recently had a haircut, and I can tell there's a smattering of gel keeping it perfectly in place, and as it's a sunny day, you're wearing sunglasses. You look hot, and you make me hot. Why can't Greg be enough? Why can't I get past this shallow adolescent fantasy of you? Why, when I see you, do you have this effect on me? I'm not a teenager, for pity's sake; it's laughable. Even so, it's there, this irresistible urge, and it's both frustrating and exhilarating.

We've only had sex twice, but it could easily have been more often. The first time was in your house, when your wife was away, and I'd popped round to get something I'd left behind on another occasion. You took me on your desk in your study, my legs wrapped around your waist after you stripped off my panties and nearly brought me to orgasm with your tongue. You made me feel like the star of some X-rated movie, and when I finally left, I found myself wanting more.

The second time was in some back alley in the City. I felt so filthy afterwards, no better than a prostitute, but that was what had made it so hot, so exciting. It's the thrill of it. You love that, like me. It's addictive. Seductive. Makes me feel euphoric. I felt terrible for cheating on Greg, and when I went home to him and he asked me how my day had been, commenting that I looked tired, a bit flushed – was I coming down with something? Could he get me a glass of wine? Run me a bath – I felt even worse. I couldn't face him, and so I said yes, a bath would be nice, thanks, just so I could get away from him and stop feeling so guilty. But when I got in it, I thought of you and started rubbing myself, imagining it was your hands all over me.

I can't seem to get enough of you, and I hate myself for it. I wish we'd never acted on the attraction we'd felt for so long, because once you take a bite of the apple, you want more.

'Chrissy, smile.' Giles' chirpy voice brings me back to the here and now, and I perform for the cameras once again.

It's gone 2 p.m. and I hear my stomach groan. I've been starving myself for six months. I hate dieting. It's not in my nature, I love food too much. But the dress I chose – after a month of shopping around London with Janine – is not forgiving even to an ounce of flesh, particularly around the arms and back. So aside from my hen weekend, it's been months of cutting out carbs, virtually no alcohol, plenty of protein, veg and water, and regular, punishing gym workouts. Something I also hate because, quite frankly, I can think of better things to do with my spare time than sweat in a stinky gym with a bunch of narcissists. Like getting some sleep or a manicure. I've had lots of those too, not to mention regular facials and deep-tissue massages. It's paid off, though, I have to say, because I look a million dollars. My strapless dress, lace all over, is close-fitting down to my knees where it fans out in a spectacular fishtail. My bodice is fastened with a multitude of fiddly buttons running up the back, so tight I can scarcely breathe. Like a true hypocrite, I wore a veil, front and back, but after the ceremony – during which I promised to love, cherish and be faithful to Greg for as long as we both shall live – I only kept the back veil on, fastened with a clip into my hair which is arranged in an elegant chignon, and further accessorized with a silver diamanté tiara.

I saw the look on Greg's face as I walked down the aisle of the same church I was baptised in. It was the same look he gave me the first time we locked eyes. A look of lust, love and devotion.

How lucky am I?

From the church, we and our guests moved on to the reception venue, one of Surrey's most impressive country estate hotels. The grounds are breathtaking, while the house itself dates back to the seventeenth century, with an attractive mix of original features and twentieth-century luxury. It's where Greg took me to celebrate our first anniversary of being together, a place I instantly fell in love with and knew, the moment I said yes to Greg's marriage proposal, was where I wanted to celebrate our day.

We're standing in front of a striking water feature. The weather is perfect. Twenty-two degrees, not too hot, with cloudy and sunny intervals and no wind. A bride couldn't hope for a better day. I was offered a glass of champagne when we first pulled up to the hotel in our classic royal blue Bentley. Having been practically teetotal and on a near-starvation diet for the last six months, it's made me feel rather dizzy, and what I really need is something to eat, but the fizz has made my bodice feel even tighter, and I'm worried I won't be able to breathe if my stomach expands even a few millimetres more.

Finally, the guests start to disappear back in the direction of the main house, and a member of staff asks us to follow him that way as the wedding breakfast will shortly be served. Janine asks if I'm OK as we watch our guests walk off.

'Yes, just a tad woozy. The champagne's gone to my head. Guess it's to be expected after six months of hardly any booze to speak of.'

She eyes me with concern. Looks really lovely today. Her dress is a tasteful gold, straight, with spaghetti straps and an elegant empire line. Like me, she made a conscious effort to lose weight for my big day, having been on the plump side ever since I've known her. Although, admittedly, she did lose a few pounds for her own wedding. She has light brown shoulder-length hair, hazel eyes, and what I can only describe as a warm, friendly face. She's not beautiful like me, something she's said to my face on numerous occasions, and which makes me feel decidedly awkward and yet, rather strangely, doesn't seem to bother her. It's almost as if she enjoys having a more glamorous friend, not to mention a glamorous friend who genuinely likes her.

After we became friends at uni, she told me she was never popular at school, never chosen for plays or sports teams or suchlike, that the pretty girls would deliberately ignore her. So I suppose she and I becoming best friends came as something of a surprise to her. It's something she's grateful for. As am I.

I would never say this to her face, but I'm secretly glad she's not exceptionally pretty or popular. It would be so tiring having to keep up with someone like that. The same is true of Miranda. If she were a stunner, I'd see her as more of a threat to my relationship with Greg, even though they are no longer together and she's with someone else. It makes life so much simpler. And, selfishly, better for me.

Although I have several close female friends who are here today, including Miranda, I only wanted Janine for my brides-maid because she's my oldest friend. There's only one thing I can't tell her. But keeping it from her is nearly killing me. Just as it's nearly killing me keeping it from Miranda. I mean, Miranda's tried so hard to be my friend – letting me into her sad childhood – yet here I am concealing something so huge from her. I feel like I'm betraying our friendship, lying to her face, but I can't bear for her to hate me, for all the good work to be undone. I also can't bear for you and I to stop.

I briefly considered asking Miranda to be a bridesmaid. But then thought better of it. Just because it might have been a bit awkward, what with her and Greg having dated. I didn't want her to think I was rubbing her face in it, despite the fact that they broke up a long time ago and she's been married for two months now. I told her I'd thought about it, though. I didn't want her to think I hadn't considered her and therefore get her back up. But she hadn't seemed bothered. Even though, every so often – on my hen do, for example – when Janine and I got talking about our dress fittings and general wedding-related stuff, it was pretty obvious she wanted us to shift away from that particular topic. Like it was getting on her nerves. She seems fine today, though. Laughing and joking with her new husband. I was relieved when she started dating again because it took the heat off me, even though I thought her choice slightly odd; the complete opposite to Greg. But perhaps that was the point.

I've told Greg repeatedly that he needs to be happy for Miranda, pleased that she's found someone else to love. But he can't seem to be at peace with her choice, and that unsettles me.

Janine is seated at the top table with me, Greg, Greg's parents, my parents, and the best man, Tom, Greg's oldest school friend. I smile at Janine, reassure her again that I'm fine. She looks so happy, and I only wish I could be as content as her, in the arms of the man she loves with all her heart. Completely and unconditionally, no strings attached.

Just then, Greg comes up and grabs me by the waist. 'Ready, Mrs Donovan?' He pulls me to him, kisses me on the lips. Then breaks away and smiles. I smile back.

'Ready,' I say.

–

'To the happy couple!'

Tom has just delivered the best man's speech. As expected, he suitably embarrassed Greg, but without too many cringeworthy moments or awkward silences. He was genuinely funny, drawing raucous laughter all round. Even Miranda was in fits. Which relieved me somewhat, because I couldn't help but notice her pinched expression when Greg was talking about me. Although maybe I'm overthinking things. Perhaps because of my own guilty conscience.

I look again at the sea of faces – happy, smiling and flushed with booze. And as I do, I see *you*. Momentarily, we lock eyes; not so long as to draw attention to ourselves and arouse suspicion, but long enough for us to share a mutual understanding. And at this point, I cannot resist. Can't help myself. I know it's wrong, and I'm not thinking straight with all the alcohol in my system, but I'll go crazy, literally crazy, if I don't get a moment alone with you. And I can tell you're thinking the same thing.

'Darling,' I lean to my left and say into Greg's ear, 'I need the loo.'

He looks at me lovingly. 'You OK?'

'Yes,' I assure him, 'just had a bit too much liquid, and now I'm bursting. I may be some time, owing to this dress.' I chuckle lightly, and he chuckles too. I am such a bad person. A liar and a cheat, and I don't deserve him. I deserve to be struck down by God and sent to hell.

I get up, and make sure I tell everyone quite loudly that I'm off to the ladies'.

'Need any help?' Janine offers.

I bend down and whisper another lie into her ear. 'Bit of a dicky tummy. I'm going to my room for some privacy. I'll be back as soon as I can.'

Then I smile and kiss her tenderly on the top of her head, despite feeling like a total charlatan inside. Janine still looks concerned and again offers to go with me, but I insist that I am fine and will get word to her should I need her.

As I leave the room, I make eye contact with you. You hold my gaze, you understand, and I can't get out of there fast enough. Instead of heading for the ladies' downstairs, I creep up the sweeping staircase to the bedrooms. Greg and I have a suite for the night. A member of staff passes me en route, and I give him some excuse about needing to get something from my room. Not that he cares. It's just my guilt complex talking.

Upstairs, I remove the room key from my purse and insert it into the lock. Again, my urgency is so great, I can't turn it fast enough, and my hands are literally shaking with fear and excitement. I know what I'm about to do is immoral, of course I do, but it's like I'm some junkie needing her hit.

I'm in, and I wait, but not too long. Within a minute, there's a knock on the door. I go to open it, but before I can even utter a word, you're pushing me inside and closing the door behind you, which you lock. You don't say a word. I say something meaningless about this being wrong, but what's the fucking point, I'm going to do it anyway. You spin me round roughly, virtually push my face against the wall, hoist my arms above my head and trap them there with your left hand. And then you kiss the side of my neck and I am tingling all over with desire as you place your free hand under my dress and allow it to leisurely make its way up my thigh, until you reach the crotch of my satin thong, which you caress gently, sensually, until the material is wet, and then you suddenly break away. A cruel and delicious move. You are wicked, toying with me, whipping me into a frenzy, and I almost can't bear it. But then you fall to your knees and this time you pull my thong down to my ankles and your head is under my dress as I instinctively part my legs allowing your tongue easy access flicking left and right until I am ready to come, but somehow I manage not to because I want you to be fully inside me, and we don't have time for both. You emerge from under my dress, rise up and I can feel the hardness of you pressing into my buttocks. And then slowly, one by one, you undo the buttons on my corset, a relief in itself. But I hardly notice that at all; all I want is for you to be inside me. It's so dangerous – so indisputably bad – but that's what makes it so good, so irresistible. And then my dress is on the floor, and your hands are cupping my breasts, making my nipples erect, as you thrust yourself inside me – and what comes next must remain a secret forever.

Chapter Twenty

Christine

Now

'It's good of you to see me again at such short notice.'

I'm back on Dr Cousins' couch. It's Saturday afternoon, the day after I was discharged from hospital. I feel terrible, encroaching on her weekend, but the note is playing on my mind and I simply can't wait until Monday to see her. The note, along with Daniel's announcement that he's engaged, although surely that's something I should feel happy about rather than worried? I guess it all seems a bit hasty. After all, neither Greg nor I have met the girl and, as I understand things, they've not been dating long.

I can't sleep or think clearly. Last night, I woke up in a cold sweat, panicky and disorientated. All I could see was your face, Heidi, and you kept saying the same thing, over and over: *Why did you abandon me? Why did you leave me to a stranger?*

I woke poor Greg. Bless him, he was very understanding as I sat up, panting. He admitted he hasn't been sleeping well either. He stroked my back, fetched me some water, tried to get me to relax. After I drank the water, he made me lie down again, then shushed me to sleep like a baby, smoothing my hair as he did so. Apart from the kiss on my head when he left for work yesterday, it was the most loving he's been with me in what seems like forever, and it felt wonderful. But I was glad my back was facing him so that he couldn't see the tears pouring down my cheeks.

This morning, while Greg was in the shower, I rang Miranda and told her about my bad night, about seeing you in my dreams. I didn't want to bother Janine again. I know she's had her hands tied with Sarah who's been under the cosh at work. Plus, I thought it might be good to get someone else's perspective. Janine's only recently been through a traumatic time herself, while Miranda, as far as I know, has a stable enough relationship with Duncan, and always seems reasonably together. I could tell from her voice that she was worried about Greg, though. I know she's my friend, but I'm also under no illusions – despite what Greg might think – that if he and I were to divorce and she had to choose between us, she'd choose him. Even so, I'm certain she'd never do anything deliberately malicious to hurt me, because she'd be too afraid of Greg's reaction were he to find out. The fact that she made such an effort with me proves how much she'd rather have him in her life as a friend than not at all. And so, when I rang to tell her about my dreams, I trusted her to give me a sensible response. And she did. She immediately suggested I ring Dr Cousins and ask if she could fit me in today.

'It'll do you good to talk to someone objective. It'll help clear your head, get a grip on things.'

'I can't call her on a Saturday,' I said. 'That would be over-stepping the mark.'

'Sure you can,' Miranda assured me. 'I know Janine did. She told me so. Told me Dr Cousins doesn't seem so concerned about strict rules. She cares deeply for her patients, treats them like family.'

Miranda's always been a voice of reason, and because of this I need to trust her judgement. So, I put my misgivings to one side and called Dr Cousins. Naturally, she sounded surprised to hear from me, but then, when I explained what had happened, she was so kind, so understanding, I felt less guilty and she said of course we could bring our meeting forward, and how did 2 p.m. sound?

Dr Cousins says, 'Of course, don't mention it. Janine must have told you that I don't believe in strict rules and guidelines. People don't work like that – life doesn't work like that – so why should psychiatrists?'

She's quite something. She makes so much sense. Makes me feel less guilty for imposing on her weekend time, and I instantly feel the tension inside me ebb away. When I first stepped into her hallway, I was hit by the smell of eggs, toast and coffee. It seemed she'd enjoyed a late breakfast, and I wondered if she'd had a man here with her, despite it being none of my business. She's so attractive and smart, she must have men knocking down her door. In fact, although it may sound arrogant, she reminds me of me when I was her age. Although I'm guessing her profession might put some men off. I mean, men are generally so bad at talking about their emotions, some might feel intimidated and steer clear.

Evidently, I need to work on my poker face, because she read my mind, and explained with a smile, 'Only just got rid of my boyfriend. We had a bit of a late night, and breakfast sort of turned into brunch.'

I felt my cheeks burn at being caught out, but then I smiled, remembering my younger, carefree self. No major responsibilities, full of youthful optimism.

'He's gone to watch Spurs with a mate this afternoon,' Dr Cousins elaborated.

'Ah,' I said, 'just like my son. Also a Spurs fan.'

'Really?' she said. 'Well, I imagine there are a lot of them out there. My father wasn't into football, he was more of a cricket man.'

'Each to their own I guess,' I commented.

Now Dr Cousins asks me to talk through the events of Thursday night, even though I already explained all that on the phone. Again, I tell her about coming home to find a load of post on the doormat, opening the note, reading it, then waking up in hospital having passed out. And that last night I barely slept.

'Why did you faint?'

'From the shock,' I say without hesitating, at the same time thinking this should be obvious. 'Despite DI Phillips warning us not to get ahead of ourselves, it's the first ray of hope we've had in a long time that Heidi might still be alive. I hadn't expected it.' I pause, then come clean. 'It didn't help, of course, that I'd already taken a sizeable gulp of wine on an empty stomach, but that's really by the by. It really was just shock.'

'Are you sure it was just shock?'

No, it wasn't. It was largely because of what was written: *she is better off with me than with you*. I can't stop thinking about those words. Whether it was just a throwaway comment, written by some lowlife who doesn't know me from Adam, or whether it actually holds far greater significance, written by someone who knows me, knows what I've done. Bears me ill will.

Do I tell her this? Is it safe? Will I be opening a can of worms I'll never be able to contain?

'It's OK,' she reassures me. 'What you tell me will not leave this room.'

A bit more hesitation on my part, and then, just because it's itching to get out, I say, 'OK, well, it's the wording. *Better off with me than with you*. It feels personal, which makes me think the note could be genuine.'

For now, she ignores the wording, which I find a bit odd. Instead, she asks, 'How does that make you feel? Knowing she could still be alive?'

I hesitate, then say, 'Well, I know I should feel happy. Relieved.'

'But you don't feel either of those?'

I shake my head. 'It's been so long, and I've been miserable pretty much all of that time; I just don't know how to be happy any more. I don't know how to hope. Also…'

'What? Is it the wording? *Better off with me than with you?* Is that what you're worried about? You're wondering whether the author of the note is right?'

Finally, she gets to the nitty-gritty, and I can feel the tears forming in my eyes, just as rain starts to pelt the windows. 'Yes.'

'Why? Why would that bother you? It shouldn't; why let it? After all, you're a good person, it's just your own insecurity telling you this person is right. But they're messing with your mind, and you need to block it out. Block out the other voice in your head telling you that you failed Heidi.'

The tears are flowing fast and furiously now. I badly want to confess, tell her what I did, who I was speaking to when you were taken from me, but I just can't bring myself to. I like Dr Cousins, and it's as if I don't want to let her down, make her think any less of me. She's not dumb, and I'm sure she knows I'm keeping something from her, but her job is as much about being patient as anything, and so she doesn't press the point.

'What does Greg say?'

'Not a lot. I wanted to have a proper conversation about it yesterday, but he ducked out. Said he was snowed under at work, and that we'd talk later.' I sigh. 'I've been hell to live with, though, so why should he even give me the time of day?'

'Because this is not about you, or him, it's about Heidi. It's much bigger than you as a couple; it's about the daughter you lost.'

'I know, but…' I want to say what's really bugging me, but I hesitate.

She senses this. 'But what?'

'Well, a part of me wonders if he suspects I've done some-thing wrong.'

'Wrong? Why would he think that? Because of what the note insinuates? We've already been over that. Don't let it get to you.'

'Yes, but, I mean, it was more than an insinuation. It was a judgement, written with conviction. As if the person knows me.'

'So that's what's *really* troubling you: what Greg is thinking?'

'Well, yes.'

'But if you know it's untrue, why should it? You know what kind of person you are, what kind of mother you were to Heidi. If you did nothing wrong, why punish yourself? Unless, that is, there is some truth to it?'

There's a harsh silence. My heart kicks, and I'm about to speak, but she doesn't let me.

'Then again, Greg doesn't know what's going on in your head. He only knows what he sees, what he reads. And so, looking at things from his perspective, it's only natural that he should wonder why the author wrote those words. Plus, you admitted in our last session that you weren't a great mother to your other children, that you feel you let them down, and that the damage is irreparable...'

I didn't exactly say that, but thinking about it now, she's right: the damage is done, and we can never be close, the way a mother and her children should be.

'...that Greg resents you for not being the mother they needed as children. So, bearing all that in mind, he'd have every right to identify with what the note is implying, wouldn't he?'

'Yes,' I say faintly, feeling like the worst person alive, but also seeing the situation I am facing with more clarity than before I arrived here today.

'And that's probably why,' she continues, 'he's so far avoided discussing the note. He doesn't want to start up an argument and is perhaps a little scared of facing the truth.'

She's right, I see that. But now I'm petrified of talking to him about the note, because what if he asks me outright why I think the author said what they did? I'd either have to tell him the truth or lie to his face. *Again.* The more I think about it, the more the note creeps me out. Whoever took you, my baby girl, wasn't some random weirdo off the street. He or she knew me, was watching us that day, waiting to strike.

And now, by coming back into our lives, perhaps this person's aim is to finish me off. Destroy what's left of my sanity, my marriage.

Drive the wedge even deeper between Greg and me.

'Christine, you've gone quiet. Are you OK?'

'Yes, just a bit overwhelmed with it all.'

'That's understandable. Would you like me to prescribe something for your nerves?'

I think about what Janine said; that Dr Cousins gave her some pills which really helped. But do I really want to go down that route? Surely I need a clear head, for now at least?

'No, no, I'm fine, thank you.'

'OK, fair enough. But please know there's no shame in taking something short term. Sometimes you just need a little extra help to get through a particularly trying time. It doesn't make you weak, or an addict.'

'Thanks,' I say. 'I'll see how things go.'

I leave Dr Cousins feeling somewhat lighter, having further unburdened myself. But, paradoxically, weighed down by my guilt for having failed Ella and Daniel.

As for the note, I fear the dark path it's taking me down.

Chapter Twenty-One

Heidi

Before

A month has passed since Mother told me she's not my real mother. At first, it was like time had stopped and there was this deafening silence, so loud I wanted to cover my ears with my hands, shut my eyes and pretend nothing existed. That I didn't exist.

There was this girl at school who was adopted. She's left now. She seemed perfectly normal, perfectly happy, but I always felt sad for her when I saw her. As if she had somehow been let down in life, was less loved, less normal than the rest of us; almost like she had a disease or a long-term illness meaning she required special attention or consideration where her feelings or shortcomings were concerned.

But then I learned that I was just like her. Someone to be pitied. My mother insisted I was special, that it didn't matter one jot that her blood wasn't running through my veins. All that mattered was that she loved me with all her heart, and weren't the last eleven years proof of that? After all, there'd been no obligation on her part to raise me as her daughter.

I didn't see it that way at first. When I realized she wasn't joking, I felt sick. Sick with shock and disbelief. It was like my entire life until then had been a lie, and the person I loved most in this world was suddenly a stranger to me. In the space of a few seconds, my whole world was turned upside down, and I no longer knew who I was or where I came from. I remember the vomit creeping up my throat, the feeling of isolation, shame, confusion.

'Heidi, it's OK, I know this is hard to take,' she said with tears in her eyes. 'But you need to calm down, hear me out.'

'Are you serious?!' I screamed, leaping off the swinging chair. 'You tell me you're not my real mother and you want me to calm down?!'

I didn't give her time to explain. Just ran back into the house, straight up the stairs and into my room, slamming the door behind me. Flinging myself face down on my bed, I sobbed and sobbed into my pillow until it was soaked. It was the first time I'd felt real anger. A horrible feeling that scared me. Released a side of me I didn't like. Of course, it wasn't long before Mother came knocking on my door, asking me if I was all right, pleading with me to hear her out.

But I wasn't ready. Not yet, at least. Four hours went by before I allowed her in, just because I knew locking myself in my room wasn't doing me any good. What's more, I was curious. Curious to know my background, what happened to my birth parents, whether they were dead or alive, in this country or elsewhere, and the biggest question of all: why didn't they want me?

My mother came in, her face cloaked with worry, and I could see how much she was hurting, how painful this was for her. Father wasn't around at the time, and I wondered why she'd chosen to tell me without him there. I desperately wanted to run to her, allow her to take me in her arms and embrace me fiercely, the way she'd done a thousand times before. But I held back to begin with. We sat side by side on the edge of my bed, and then I grudgingly let her hold my hand in hers and talk.

'I am still the same person, sweetheart: your mother, who loves you more than life itself.'

I kept my head bowed, but she placed the tip of her forefinger under my chin and raised it up gently so I was looking at her.

'You know that, don't you? You can tell from my face?'

I could. I could feel the unconditional love springing from her, the love that flows like a natural spring from mother to child and never dries up. And so I nodded.

'Good.' She smiled with relief. 'So now I am going to tell you a story, and you must listen carefully, because it's very important that you don't miss a thing. Some of it will be hard to hear, but you need to hear it, so you understand why I had to rescue you.'

Once again I nodded, intrigued by the idea of me needing to be rescued. It made me wonder if my birth parents were drug addicts or had physically abused me, and the sick sensation I'd felt earlier returned with a vengeance. 'Why?' I asked faintly.

'Because your mother never wanted you. You were a mistake, and you ruined her life.'

Chapter Twenty-Two

Ella

Now

My parents don't know I'm a lesbian. Although, to be honest, I'm not even sure myself that I am one. Not a fully fledged one, at least. I mean, it's not like I haven't had boyfriends in the past. Because I have. And not because I was forced into having one because it's expected of a babe like me. No, it was because I fancied those boys and I wanted to kiss and shag them. So I guess that makes me *bi*. But the fact is, none of my shags turned into anything lasting, and I wasn't fussed when I split up with them, even if it was the bloke who did the dumping. But then I met you, and we clicked so perfectly, both physically and spiritually, almost like you could see into my mind, read my thoughts, worries, hopes, fears, and I just knew that I wanted to be with you.

Later, you told me your secret and although at first I felt a little used, I realized the way we'd met had been the only way, and that ultimately, all you've ever wanted to do was help me.

I can't imagine Dad's reaction. Poor guy, he certainly doesn't need this complication in his life after all he's been through, but it's hardly my fault, and I'm not gonna toss aside my chance for happiness because he might disapprove. Although, come to think of it, he was a lot chirpier the last time I saw him, which makes me think he's getting some, and it's obviously not from Mum because they're as miserable as sin. They make a lame attempt to act 'normal' around Dan and me, but they're fucking deluding themselves if they think we're fooled. Every time I visit them I can't wait to get out of the house. It'd be OK if it was just Dad, but it's *her* who makes things so bloody awkward. Frigid, selfish cow. She deserves exactly what's coming to her. Deserves to go nuts, end up in some loony bin being fed pureed food from a plastic spoon.

I really couldn't give a shit that she'll be upset about my sexuality. She's no right to an opinion on my life. In fact, I can't wait to see the look on her face when I tell her we're together. Once we've pushed her to breaking point, that is.

I remember the day you walked into the fashion store where I work part time, just off Oxford Street. You'd recently moved back to England from France where you worked as an au pair for a few years. It was pissing down with rain – you'd clearly been caught up in the worst of it, looking like a drowned rat, and I thought you only came into the shop to escape the weather. A simple twist of fate. My colleague, Liza, a snooty cow, gave you an unimpressed look as you dripped near a stupidly expensive rail of tops. You asked her what her problem was, your eyes ablaze, and things got a bit lairy until I stepped in and told both of you to calm down, aware that your little spat was driving customers out the door. I steered Liza towards a customer who was waiting impatiently at the counter clutching several hundred pounds' worth of clothing, then turned my attention to you. You still looked livid, but your eyes were also sad and I couldn't help feeling sorry for you.

'You OK?' I asked.

'No, not really,' you replied through clenched teeth. I noticed how perfect they were. In fact, you had a perfect face; that completely symmetrical look models have. 'My boyfriend dumped me this morning by text, the job I was hoping for has fallen through, I'm behind with my rent, and to top it all off, it's pissing down with rain even though it's supposed to be frigging summer, and I have no sodding umbrella.' You paused, then declared, 'Basically, I have no job, no boyfriend, no money, no umbrella and I'm not sure how to deal with all of that.'

Your eyes welled up as you bit your lip in a vain attempt to stop the tears from falling, but then one did, and you hastily wiped it away, as if you couldn't bear to be seen crying in front of a stranger, even though you'd just made a scene in front of a roomful of strangers. I felt so sorry for you at that moment; in fact, I felt like I could almost relate to you, that feeling of being abandoned and alone. We locked eyes and it was as if you recognized that. Having learned that your name was Robyn, I was hit by this incredible urge to ask if you fancied going for a drink when my day was over in just under an hour. Your eyes lit up, and I told you I'd meet you at All Bar One on Regent Street.

When I arrived, you were seated in a corner of the bar, which was busy, but not overly so because of the shite weather. You agreed to share a bottle of Sancerre, and although it should have been awkward because we didn't know the first thing about each other, it wasn't. You told me about your childhood growing up in Esher, that you studied languages at Warwick University, and spent two years in France trying to earn some dosh as an au pair and figure out what you wanted to do with your life. You'd come back having met Mr Right in Lyon who was English and on a gap year, and had recently landed himself a job in finance in the City. He claimed he couldn't bear to be apart from you and wanted you to shack up together.

'So what happened?' I asked.

'He's fallen for some floozy in his office. Bastard said he was sorry, but he's realized now that he's too young to be tied down and should never have forced me to come back with him. But no hard feelings, eh? Fucking arsehole. How could I have been so stupid?'

'And he dumped you by text?'

'Yep, can you sodding believe it? Men – I don't think I'll ever be able to trust one again.'

'Don't say that,' I said. 'They're not all like that.'

'Aren't they?'

'No, I don't think so. I know my dad isn't.'

You gave me a searching look. 'Really? How do you know?'

'I just know,' I shrugged, wondering how much to divulge, and whether I was perhaps being too open with a relative stranger. But then I thought, what the hell, you'd been so open with me, it was only fair I do the same. And so I told you about my parents, about Mum losing Heidi, and how Dad had stayed with her despite her being a total bitch to him ever since.

'Jeez, that's so tough,' you said. 'Makes me realize how lucky I am with my mum.'

All at once, I felt a ripple of jealousy. 'I take it she's a good mum?'

'The best. Tough when she needs to be, but she also has a warm, loving side. Despite what happened to her.'

'What do you mean?' I asked.

You hesitated at that point, almost like you didn't want to upset me. It was decent of you, and as I searched your eyes, I felt increasingly drawn to you.

'It's OK,' I pressed, 'you can tell me. I want to know.'

You looked down, then up again, took a large gulp of your second glass of wine, then said, 'My five-year-old brother drowned when we were on holiday.'

I felt my stomach lurch. 'Jesus, that's awful.' At the same time, I couldn't believe you'd lost a sibling just as I had. It was like fate that our paths had crossed. 'How did it happen?' I asked shyly.

'It was early August, and my parents had rented a villa in Spain. I was only two, so I don't remember a thing, but apparently it was in this remote Spanish coastal town. Really beautiful, with gorgeous scenery, and the villa had a pool out the back overlooking the sea.'

My stomach heaved again, because I knew what was coming.

'Dad had gone out to buy a few groceries, and Mum and Sam – that was my big brother's name – were lying on adjacent sun loungers while I slept in my buggy. I hadn't been sleeping well at all and poor Mum had been up half the night with me, trying to get me to settle down.' You paused again before continuing. 'It was hot, she was dog-tired, and she fell asleep, so she didn't hear my brother, who couldn't swim properly, when he snuck off and started playing with the beach ball which had been wedged under her lounger. Police later presumed that he must have kicked it into the water and fallen in trying to reach out and get it.' There was a catch in your voice, but you kept going, so bravely, I thought, despite the tears streaming down your face. 'It was my dad's voice screaming Sam's name that woke Mum. He dived in, fished Sam out of the water, frantically performed mouth-to-mouth, but it was too late. He was dead.'

It was such a sad story, and I felt so bad for you, despite barely knowing you.

'I'm so sorry,' I said. What more could I say?

'Mum was in a bad way for some time. Of course, she blamed herself, and at one point I think the family was worried she might kill herself.'

'So what happened?'

'Well, for one, she turned to the church and I think that helped. And…'

'And?'

'And she still had me. Really, she could have gone one of two ways: either shut herself off from me completely, or throw her heart and soul into me. Luckily for me, she went with option two. We did everything together, and I still consider her to be my best friend.'

That searing envy was there again, and I felt so guilty for it. But I couldn't help myself; couldn't help but compare her mum to mine. All I could think was, why couldn't my mum have done the same when she had me and Dan? Why were we never enough, why did she bloody well have us in the first place if she had no intention of loving us?

'And how is your parents' relationship now?' I asked.

'Dad died recently.'

'Oh, no, I'm really sorry to hear that.'

'Thanks. But in answer to your question, they were never quite the same again. Still, they stuck together, and they got through it, made sure I had a happy childhood.'

The opposite of mine, I thought. And I suddenly resented Mum even more. Hated her, in fact. God, how I hated her. Wished she wasn't my mum.

'So, you and your mum aren't close, I take it?' you asked.

'No, not at all,' I replied harshly. 'She's a cold-hearted cow, and hearing your story, I envy you. I wouldn't worry about your ex, though, he was obviously bad news, and there are plenty more fish in the sea.'

And then you winked at me, reached out and put your hand on top of mine, making my insides flip with excitement. 'Yes, I realize that now,' you smiled.

That was six months ago. The start of you and me.

But you hadn't told me the truth then. That came later, and that's when the fun really began.

Chapter Twenty-Three

Heidi

Before

Some day, I'm going to get my revenge on you. You, who didn't want me from the start. From the moment you saw those two blue lines.

I'm eighteen now, and it's been five years since Mother told me the truth. That you'd never wanted children and when you found out you were carrying me, you were desperate for an abortion. But you couldn't go through with it in the end. Not because your conscience couldn't take it, not because you grew soft and suddenly warmed to the idea of having children, but because your husband found the pregnancy test in the bathroom bin and there was no getting out of it if you wanted him to stay with you. He wanted me, even though you didn't. You grudgingly carried me for nine months with a sourpuss face, like some bitter pill you were finding hard to keep down, disgusted by your rounder cheeks, your ever-expanding belly, the fact that you could no longer see your feet when you looked down in the shower. And later, you reluctantly pushed me out into the world, all the while resenting me because it would affect your precious career and social life, not to mention your sordid affair.

My mother showed me photos of you with him. Sneaking into some tawdry hotel when you thought you weren't being watched. Although, that just goes to show how arrogant you are – you weren't exactly discreet, snogging him in the car park before you'd even entered the building. But even more disgusting, she told me how you'd fucked him at your own wedding. No thought given to your new husband, a good kind man whose only crime was to love you, or your lover's poor wife. I mean, what kind of a person does something like that on their own wedding day? A sick, narcissistic person, that's who. And the worrying thing is, knowing what you are – that you, my birth mother, are a heartless bitch – is turning me into a heartless bitch too.

For much of the time, all I feel is bitter and angry. When I hear how you refused to breastfeed me because you couldn't stand me sucking on your nipples, didn't want me ruining their shape so that your lover would still fancy you, how you never got up in the night to feed me, would make your poor husband do it because you needed your beauty sleep even though he had to go to work the next morning, how you palmed me off on a childminder half the time because playgroups and the park bored you senseless, and how you secretly wished I'd been a boy because you dreaded having an attractive daughter who, in time, would make you look old and frumpy and draw the male attention you craved... When I hear all this, I am filled with anger and resentment, and I am so grateful to my mother for rescuing me from you. It was a lucky escape. Even so, your actions have made me wary of everyone I meet, suspicious of their motives. Ensured that whenever someone tries to get close to me, I push them away. I don't trust men because it was a man who cheated on my mother – a man who disappointed her as a father – and I don't trust women because I'm always afraid they'll turn out to be like you. I am consumed by thoughts of revenge, of wanting to hurt you, even though, right now, I'm not exactly sure how I'm going to do that.

Sometimes, I resent Mother for telling me the truth, for her brutal frankness, because if she hadn't, I'd be living in blissful ignorance, and I wouldn't be so fucked up in the head. I mean,

I was getting on fine before she told me, and there's a good chance I would have grown up happy and content, without all these trust issues, without this constant feeling of emptiness.

But then, when I think about it, I understand her reasons for telling me. She lived in constant fear that one day I might discover the truth from someone else, and it was therefore better I heard it from her than a stranger. At least she's got guts, unlike you.

At least *she* wanted me.

Chapter Twenty-Four

Miranda

Before

As I look at you, Chrissy, sitting like a princess at the top table with Greg, I can't help wishing it was me by his side, not you. Despite the fact that I now have Duncan. I've tried so hard to like you, be your friend, but there's something about you that grates on my nerves. And I know my new husband fancies the pants off you, even though he emphatically denies it. You're like this compulsive irritation. I know it's not your fault that you're beautiful, but there's an unmistakable arrogance about you I find decidedly repulsive. Don't get me wrong, when we're out on the town, having a girls' night, I always have fun with you, because you can be amusing, especially when we've all had too much wine. Janine included. Although, in all honesty, I still find her tiresome. I mean, she's so bloody defensive of your friendship, and I could tell she resented me entering the fold, saw me as some kind of threat to your cosy little twosome.

What she doesn't realize is that I have no intention of replacing her as your best friend. I'm only friends with you because I don't want to lose Greg. Being close to you ensures I stay close to him, and I guess there was always this little part of me that hoped you'd ditch him and he'd come running back to me. But that didn't happen, and now I'm sitting here getting plastered as I watch the love of my life coo about you, because getting hammered is the only way I can get through the night.

I probably shouldn't have married Duncan so quickly, but when it became clear that you and Greg were serious and Duncan started flirting with me – later confiding in me that he too was hung up on someone he couldn't have – I guess I enjoyed feeling desired again. And I needed that affirmation in writing that someone else loved me. I mean, I'm sure he does love me, in his own way. And the sex is always good. Plus, he's as dishy as hell. He looks so hot today in his suit and tie and I know we'll have great sex later. But I do wonder if we'll last. Especially as I know he's not keen on having kids. And because I probably chose him out of spite; because he was the male version of you, and I wanted to show Greg that two could play at that game. That aside, now that I've finally watched you both go through with your vows, I know that I need to move on, stop brooding over the past. But it's so bloody hard. I can't seem to rid myself of this toxic jealousy that infests my veins every time I see you with him. I don't trust you entirely to be faithful to him either. I've seen the way you flirt with other men at the firm, even though you think you're being discreet. Sometimes I think you don't even realize you're doing it, it's so ingrained in your make-up. I worry you won't be a good wife to Greg, and I definitely can't see you as mother material. But that's a good thing. It's bad enough seeing you married to Greg. To see you bear his child will be intolerable.

Greg gazes down at you adoringly, then whispers something in your ear, and I feel my stomach burn with envy. You survey the room, smiling, and we lock eyes, and I don't have time to gather myself, force a smile, and I'm certain you sense my unease. I scold myself inside for failing to conceal my feelings, because so far I've done a damn good job in fooling you that I am completely fine with you marrying Greg.

I really need to get a grip on my emotions, else I'll risk losing him completely.

Chapter Twenty-Five

Christine

Now

It's Sunday, midday, and Daniel and his fiancée are coming over at one o'clock. Although I'm keen to meet her, I'm also dreading it. Largely because Greg isn't going to be around. He's in the bloody office. Again. His current deal exploded on Friday – *apparently* – and so it's all systems go for him and his team. He didn't come home until midnight last night. I was still up, and I had a bit of a hissy fit when he told me he had to go in at nine this morning and didn't anticipate being back this evening before eight at the earliest. I know it's not his fault, that it's the nature of the job, but of all the weekends for it to happen, it had to be this one, didn't it?

Ella can't make it either. Having promised to come, she rang me at ten to say the store's short on Sunday staff, so her boss asked if she could come in for eleven. She was very apologetic. Although I'm wondering whether she made the whole thing up just to get out of it. Sounds paranoid, I know, but she and Greg chat all the time. So maybe she bailed after hearing he wouldn't be there. Granted, I don't particularly get on with either of my children, but my relationship with Ella is worse. Strained to near breaking point best describes it. It feels like she resents me more than Daniel does, although maybe he just hides it better than her. After all, women tend to wear their hearts on their sleeves, while men generally do all they can to conceal their feelings.

So, with no Greg, no Ella – even Janine isn't free – it'll be up to me, and me alone, to make conversation with this girl, decide if she's suitable for Daniel. And even if she doesn't make the grade in my eyes, I'll still have to be polite to her, get through lunch and possibly beyond, with no support from Greg, no chance to take a breather, listen and observe while Greg does some of the talking. I feel tired just thinking about it.

I'm serving roast chicken for main, apple crumble for pudding. Simple, reliable, homely. The opposite of me. My stomach is so shrivelled, I know I won't manage much of it, but I am trying to eat better – because of the note, and because I know I need to keep my strength up in case Heidi is still out there and needs me.

I try to imagine what this girl will look like. I have in mind someone slim and petite, with dark hair and a sparkly personality. That's generally the way Daniel's previous girlfriends have been, although none of them lasted more than a few months, so perhaps this girl is the total opposite. I'm glad he's finally found 'the one'. He deserves to be happy after I failed him as a mother, even though I think he's too young for marriage. She must be special for him to have popped the question, though. Perhaps, rather selfishly, it will appease my guilt, allay my fears that I might have messed him up for life, ruined his chances of finding lasting happiness.

I try to forget about the note for a few hours, and for once focus on my son. Greg and I decided not to tell our children about the note for now. Nor my parents. Just because it may come to nothing, in which case there's no point treading old ground and stressing them out unnecessarily.

I lay the table, put some flowers I bought locally first thing this morning in a vase in the centre, open a bottle of red and set it down next to the vase. I'm about to pour myself some wine when the doorbell rings. My pulse quickens as I realize the moment of truth has arrived.

I take a deep breath, put on my best smile, go to the front door and open it.

And then I get my second biggest shock in less than three days.

Chapter Twenty-Six

Christine

Before

'What are you thinking?'

I'm lying next to my lover in bed, sweaty and slightly out of breath, because we've just had sex. He always lights a cigarette as soon as we're done and – in line with what has become an unspoken ritual – we pass it back and forth until it's burned down. Usually I'm beaming with satisfaction at this point. But not today. He picks up on this, he's not stupid. He senses something's wrong – can tell from my expression – from the fact that when we were doing it, my mind was only half there. I want to tell him what's up, but I'm afraid that if I do he'll end things between us. A bit rich, really, because I'm fully aware that what we're doing is cruel and wrong, and this should give us the perfect excuse to stop hurting our loved ones. But I can't seem to exist without him; he's a temptation I can't bear to say no to.

It's Saturday afternoon and we're in some back-of-beyond hotel in Stepney Green, miles away from our respective homes. A deliberate ploy, of course. His wife is at a day spa in Knights-bridge, using the extortionately priced pampering package he bought her for Valentine's Day (no doubt out of guilt), while I told Greg that I needed a new pair of boots and was off to Oxford Street and expected to be a good few hours, especially if I got waylaid at the champagne bar in Selfridges as I often do.

He knows how long I take going round the shops, so it was a very believable lie. And besides, he wasn't much bothered. In fact, he might even have been relieved as there was a Tottenham game showing on Sky and my absence gave him the chance to watch it without feeling guilty.

It's amazing how easy lying gets if you do it often enough. It's like any skill, I suppose. Practise it regularly, and it becomes second nature. Greg and I have been married for three months now, and in that time, I have continued to be unfaithful.

We meet once, maybe twice a week, if we can manage it, and we never tire of each other. The carnal attraction we felt from the first is as potent as ever. We probably wouldn't feel this way if we were a proper couple. It's the thrill of it, the risk involved, that's what turns us on, what we can't resist.

I give a heavy sigh, still gazing up at the ceiling, then check my watch. It's 5 p.m. and I need to make my way home within the next half hour. Which means taking a quick shower first in the room's dingy bathroom, to wash your smell off me.

'Chrissy, tell me what's wrong.'

I turn my head left to look at my lover, who's now rolled onto his side, and is tracing the side of my face with his forefinger. Even though we can never be together, I know he cares for me, that he's genuinely concerned, and this somehow assuages my guilt.

There's no getting away from it. I need to tell him.

My belly churns as I say, 'I'm pregnant, and I don't know who the father is.'

Chapter Twenty-Seven

Christine

Now

'Mum, what's wrong? You look like you've seen a ghost.'

My son eyes me with a mixture of curiosity and irritation as I stare at his fiancée in astonishment. Needless to say, this isn't the reaction he'd been expecting, or indeed hoping for. He's probably thinking, *Why can't the bloody woman act normally just for once? Why does she have to fuck everything up in my life?*

But I am not alone in my reaction. His fiancée looks equally shocked. Something Daniel also notices. 'In fact, you do too, hon,' he says to her. 'What's up? Do you know each other or something?'

'Dr Cousins,' I just about find my voice. 'This is rather awkward.'

Dr Cousins is Daniel's fiancée? I'm flabbergasted, and I feel like I must be dreaming because it's just too bizarre, the most surreal coincidence ever. But I'm not dreaming. She's standing there in the flesh, looking as lovely as ever, but different. No suit, no immaculately pinned-up hair. She's wearing jeans, ankle boots and a cream puffer jacket; her blonde hair is loose and wavy, her eyes spectacle free. Almost like a fresh-faced teenage girl, rather than a sophisticated professional woman.

'So you two *do* know each other?' Poor Daniel, still out of the loop, must be wondering what the hell is going on.

Finally, Dr Cousins turns to him and says, 'Your mother is one of my patients, Dan. I had no idea.' She turns back to me, holds my gaze. 'Really, I didn't.'

'And I obviously had no idea you were dating my son.' I look at Daniel. 'Didn't you tell Dr Cousins—'

'Please,' Dr Cousins interjects before I can finish my sentence, 'we're not in a session; you can call me Freya.'

'OK,' I say, now wishing more than ever that Greg was here. I also realize she must be a good seven or eight years older than Daniel. How will that work? Perhaps he thinks she'll give him the emotional stability he never got from me. I turn back to Daniel and say, 'Didn't you tell Freya about your family? About me, about our past?'

I feel cross with my son, even though I probably don't have the right to be. Cross that he's clearly so ashamed of me – of our family, of what we've been through – that he's deliberately kept who we are from the person he intends to spend the rest of his life with. I'm cross because, instead of being able to applaud him for his choice of wife (because, let's face it, he's managed to hook himself the woman who has it all – looks, brains, a good job), I'm angry with him for not being upfront with her from the beginning. If he had been, we'd have saved ourselves this awkwardness. And obviously I can't be angry with Dr Cousins because, being the consummate professional she is, she won't have discussed me with Daniel. I hate being angry with him, but I am, and he can tell this from the look I give him as the three of us continue to linger uneasily on the doorstep.

'Well, can we come in at least?' Daniel barks. 'I'd like a drink before explaining why I don't particularly enjoy airing our dirty laundry to other people.'

I catch Dr Cousins' reaction to Daniel's comment. She looks hurt, and I can't say I blame her. Her fiancé has just referred to her as *other people*. Completely tactless. 'Is that all I am to you?' she asks, with a wobble in her voice I've not heard before. '*Other people?*'

I feel sorry for her, and am suddenly filled with the urge to comfort the person whose job is to comfort me. And then I think about Janine, what she'll make of all this. She'll be as gobsmacked as me. As will Miranda.

Daniel looks horrified with himself. He immediately pulls Dr Cousins towards him, kisses her forcefully on the cheek, at the same time cutting me an evil look. 'No, no, of course you aren't. It's just that you're so out of my league, and I fell so head-over-heels in love with you the first time we met, I guess I was frightened of scaring you off. Plus, you deal with crazy people—' (*Thanks, son, that's actually quite offensive*) '—all day, for God's sake. The last thing you need is to come home to more craziness. I didn't want to burden you with all that. I wanted to seem normal.'

Guilt hits me like a punch to my guts. My son doesn't consider himself normal, and it's all my fault. What kind of a mother causes her son to feel abnormal? Still, it baffles me how he ever imagined he could keep the truth from his fiancée. Perhaps it was a case of getting her to say yes first, before he aired our *dirty laundry*.

I put him on the spot. 'But she was bound to find out the truth sooner or later, Daniel. You couldn't have hidden our past forever.'

'Yeah, thanks, Mum, I know that. Look, it's cold, I'm freezing my bollocks off, can we please come in?'

I let my guests inside, still not quite over my shock. And then I remember the tempting smell of coffee and eggs in Dr Cousins' flat yesterday afternoon, her explanation that she and her boyfriend had had a late breakfast. And I realize it was my son who'd been there with her.

Five minutes later, I've poured each of us a glass of wine and we're sitting in the living room, me on an armchair, Freya – it still feels odd calling her by her Christian name, but she insisted again when I automatically called her Dr Cousins – and Daniel side by side on the sofa. Poor Freya sits there looking awkward, still as much in shock as I am. I feel frustrated because it felt like our sessions were doing me good, but now I wonder how we can possibly continue them, now that I know she's sleeping with my son. Surely, that would be ethically wrong.

'Can I use your bathroom?' Freya asks, breaking the painful silence.

'Of course,' I say. 'You can use the main one upstairs if you like? First on the left.'

She smiles, says thanks, leaves the room and I am alone with my son.

'Well, this is awkward, isn't it, Mum?' Daniel says cuttingly. He glares at me as if it's all my fault. I'm not angry with him for meeting Dr Cousins – I can't be, he wasn't to know – but equally, I am not to blame for the awkwardness he's just referred to.

'Janine recommended Dr Cousins to me,' I say, keeping my voice down. The last thing I want is to come across as defensive, simply because I've done nothing wrong. I explain Miranda's chance meeting with Freya, how she passed on her details to Janine. 'She helped Janine deal with Nate's death,' I say, 'and, very kindly, Janine thought she might be able to help me.'

Daniel tuts and rolls his eyes, then says under his breath, 'You're beyond help, Mum.'

His words wound me. So bitter, so full of contempt. I want to be mad at him, but I don't have the right. His contempt is warranted. My heart is suddenly thumping hard inside my chest, but again, I manage to keep my voice even. 'I don't blame you for thinking that way, Daniel, but Dr Cousins is different to my other psychiatrists. There's something about her and her methods that gives me hope that I can finally overcome my issues.'

He looks up, raises an eyebrow. 'Twenty-odd years too late, though, isn't it, Mum?'

I look at my son, my heart full of sadness as I think about what I have done to him. Resentful and cynical at the grand old age of twenty-two. Thank goodness for Freya, though. Even in this short time I've seen them together, it's obvious to me how different he is around her; the way he looks at her, touches her, shows a soft side I've never seen before. Perhaps the age gap's no bad thing.

'No, I don't think it's too late,' I say. 'There is still so much we can look forward to as a family. You and Ella getting married, you both having kids. I may have failed you as a mother, but I can try and make it up to you now, by being a good grand-mother.'

Even as I say the words, I know I am being deceitful, trying to smooth things over just so we can have a peaceful lunch. Because how can I freely look forward to their futures, when I know Heidi might still be out there? When I have the note hanging over me? And it's only now that I realize it would be wrong to keep the note from my children; I must tell them because I cannot lie to them any more. Even so, I want Greg to be at my side when I do.

A hint of a smile, or is it a smirk, creeps across Daniel's face, and he's about to reply when Freya walks back into the room.

'What have I missed?' she asks brightly.

'Nothing much,' I say. 'Let's eat.'

Chapter Twenty-Eight

Christine

Before

We both know who the father of my unborn child is. You agreed to take a test just to put us out of our misery. I'm not sure getting an answer has helped, though. Whichever way it went, it was never going to make us happy; never going to make things OK. We're still cheating on our partners, and neither of us wants to stop, despite our guilt.

Greg is so excited about the baby, getting the nursery ready, baby-proofing the house. I'm only twenty weeks gone, but we've already bought a pram, Moses basket, cot, baby bath – the list seems to be never-ending and I'm feeling quite overwhelmed by it all. This baby is taking over our lives even before it's arrived, and although I hate myself for thinking it, I find myself disliking it more and more by the day.

Which already makes me a bad mother, right?

I'm looking a bit podgy around the hips and bum, and my face is rounder, my waist gradually disappearing. I hate being this way. I'm scared you won't find me attractive any more, even though you tell me that you love my bigger boobs. I'd die if you went off me. You help me feel more like myself, rather than the mother Greg wants me to be. He already looks at me like I'm a different person. A sort of 'aww' look, rather than a 'phwoar' look, and I hate him for that. It's infuriating, and I don't feel the least bit attracted to him right now. In fact,

I find him downright irritating to be around. The one good thing is that I can use the 'I don't want to hurt the baby' excuse whenever he tries to initiate sex. He falls for it every time, even though the midwife told me there's no reason for us to stop having sex. Thank heavens for that. She didn't realize I was asking on *our* behalf rather than mine and Greg's.

A big plus about being pregnant is that I feel incredibly horny much of the time, and experience the most intense orgasms, especially when I go on top. The downside is having to slow down generally. I've never been one to sit around, take it easy. But these days, all Greg can say is 'Put your feet up', 'What can I get you?', 'Don't overdo things.' Jesus, it's driving me fucking crazy! I ranted to you about it the other day, and when I was done I worried you were going to walk out the door and never come back because who wants to be with a pregnant psycho bitch, right? But you didn't. You said my rant turned you on, and you unhooked my bra to reveal my swelling breasts, sucked them as if you were dying of thirst, then roughly turned me onto all fours and entered me from behind, cupping my boobs at the same time, driving me insane with pleasure.

I'll be damned if I'm going to ditch all I've worked for, for the sake of this child. All those years of study, all those shitty jobs as a trainee, working all-nighters, I can't bear for them to go to waste. I love my independence, I love having my own income, not being dependent on a man for money. All that puts me on a level playing field with Greg, and no baby is going to change that. As soon as the first six months are over, I'll be back in my suit and handing the child over to a full-time nanny, no shadow of a doubt.

Nothing is going to change.

Chapter Twenty-Nine

Miranda

Before

You've been in such a foul mood since falling pregnant, Chrissy, and I can't help but feel sorry for Greg. I was green with envy when he told me you were going to have a baby. What made things worse, more painful, is that I'd only just suffered a miscarriage myself. I mean, you're so lucky to be carrying Greg's child. It should be the happiest time of your life. But you seem more concerned about your weight gain, about not being able to fit into your tight pencil skirts, about not being able to put in the same outrageous hours at the firm, than your precious unborn child. Every time I see you you're snappish with me, and it pisses me off. You're so bloody ungrateful. Not only are you married to a wonderful man, in a few months' time you'll give birth to his baby. If it were me, I'd be on cloud nine.

I had a word with Janine about you last night but as usual she took your side. Said I needed to give you a break. That you had a whole host of hormones raging around inside your body, and as neither of us have ever been pregnant we didn't have the right to judge you. She doesn't know that's not true, though; that I've also felt those crazy emotions which are often heightened in the first trimester. But she's the last person I'd tell about my miscarriage. I don't want her fake tears. Having said that, she's probably right that I need to cut you some slack. It's just that you seem to have it all, but don't actually realize it.

I haven't told you, but Duncan came round to the idea of having a baby several months ago. Hence, the miscarriage. I think he's mellowing with age, wants something of him left in this world when he departs it. Either that, or he's harbouring a guilty conscience about something. Trouble is, I've completely lost interest in having sex with him because I'm certain he's cheating on me. I keep imagining how my life might have been different had I married Greg and had children with him. Mini Gregs with his unique looks and mannerisms. A distinctive part of him that belonged to me. But maybe I'm not destined to have children? Perhaps my body doesn't work like yours?

Just thinking about that heartbreaking possibility makes me even madder when I catch you sulking about your 'condition' as if you've got some kind of disease. Your unborn child isn't a fucking cancer! I just feel so sorry for it. I know what it's like not to be loved as a child, not to feel wanted, and it's taken every morsel of effort for me not to have a go at you and tell you to grow up and start acting like a mother; to actually put someone else's needs above yours for a change. It strikes me that you just don't seem happy with Greg, and I'm convinced you've played around behind his back, even though I can't prove it. I almost mentioned it to Janine last night on the phone, but then thought better of it. She's so ferociously protective of you, she'd probably tell you, and I can't risk that. Can't risk you ditching me as a friend, because then Greg might be forced to cut me out of his life and I can't cope with that.

I have to be patient, more subtle about things. Even so, your attitude really ticks me off. To bring a child into this world but not love it is downright evil as far as I'm concerned. Sometimes I think an unloved child would be better off dead than be forced to endure an unhappy childhood that scars them for life and turns them into fucked-up adults. It may sound harsh – a bit unhinged, even – but I don't think I'm being cruel or irrational.

If anything, I'm being kind. I just hope you change your attitude once the baby is born. Else it'll be nigh on impossible for me to stand by and do nothing about it.

I just won't stand for it.

Chapter Thirty

Christine

Before

No words can describe the pain of childbirth to someone who hasn't gone through it. It's simply impossible to comprehend. That feeling as though your entire body is being ripped apart, that your pelvic area is about to explode. But on the flip side, it's the best kind of pain; the most fulfilling, uplifting kind of pain. In fact, looking back, it was the most exhilarating thirty hours of my life. I have never felt so empowered, never felt such an overwhelming sense of achievement, invincibility, self-worth, as I did after giving birth to you. Nothing compares to it. Nothing compares to you. And everything has changed now that you are here.

You were ten days late, and I went in overnight to be induced the next morning. But at 4 a.m. I started contracting spontaneously, and no induction was necessary. The pain was so bad so quickly, I felt sure you would make an appearance sooner rather than later. But, can you believe it, my waters hadn't broken, and twenty hours of excruciating contractions later, I was still only two centimetres dilated. I was cranking up my TENS machine to the max, inhaling gas until I was blue in the face, but neither did anything to alleviate the pain. Although I kept begging for an epidural, all the anaesthetists were busy with caesareans, and I thought I couldn't go on. But, of course, stopping isn't an option when you're giving birth, and somehow, I soldiered on until finally, after twenty-seven hours, I got my epidural and was suddenly floating on air.

Six hours later, I pushed you out, and within seconds I heard you cry before they put you to my breast. All at once my indifferent heart melted, my selfish desires faded into obscurity, and you became the most important thing in the world to me. It was as if the person I was before you appeared had never existed. I couldn't believe you were mine – you were just so perfect, with your tiny fingers and toes, and your nails so small they seemed like a miracle of creation, which they were, of course. And that tiny rosebud mouth, cute snub nose, eyes that barely opened, you were so full of sleep. As I lay there, I marvelled at the way you immediately latched onto my breast; such a wonderful feeling that I, and only I, could sustain you, nourish you, help you grow into a healthy human being. I remember the overwhelming love in Greg's eyes as he edged closer and gazed down at you cushioned snugly in my arms. He looked so content, so amazed at me and you, and said, 'You are amazing, our daughter is perfect. I am so proud of you.'

And at that moment, I didn't think about *him* and what we had done, the lies we had told, the people we had hurt and continued to hurt. I didn't want to think about all that. So I parked that sinful side of my life at the back of my mind, as if the person I was with *him* was a separate being from the person I was with you and Greg right then in the hospital.

I didn't want this perfect, pure moment to be sullied by lies and deceit, by gratuitous human folly. You didn't deserve that, and neither did Greg, who had been such a pillar of strength throughout my labour. I don't think I've ever been as content with life as I was in the few hours after giving birth, all the pain I had endured swiftly fading to insignificance because I knew you had changed my life forever.

Chapter Thirty-One

Greg

Now

It's 3 a.m. and I can't sleep. I'm lying on my back staring into darkness, thinking about how tired you looked, Chrissy, when I came home last night. It was clear you'd had too much wine, but I didn't admonish you on this occasion. You had good reason, and now I feel bad for not being at your side when Daniel and his fiancée came round for lunch. But at least I was telling the truth for once. I *was* working, not off banging my mistress. Even though I could have been. She called me Sunday morning, asking if I was free to meet up. But I wasn't; I told her I had no choice but to go into the office. So really, I shouldn't feel bad. But I do.

At least before the note, we were plodding along a reasonably straight line; the same line we'd been walking for years. Dull, yes, but at least we knew what we were doing, what to expect. But in the space of a few days, there's been the note, and now the surprise that Daniel's engaged to your psychiatrist. It's unsettling, makes me wonder what other surprises await us. And I feel bad for you because lately, your mood has seemed better. This particular shrink is obviously helping you, but now, understandably, you feel unnerved because you don't know if you can look at her in the same way. It's an odd, downright uncomfortable situation to be in even though she assured you over and over that things don't have to change until they are married (at which point she will be related to you and therefore unable to treat you), that there's no reason why you can't keep your private and professional lives separate in the meantime.

Logically, I guess that makes sense. But these things are easier said than done. I mean, it must feel strange knowing that your future daughter-in-law has an insight into your thoughts, fears, failings. Your daily purgatory. Your secrets. How vulnerable you must feel. Above all, mothers-in-law want to feel strong, in control, be sounding boards for their children and their spouses, but you must feel weak, exposed, and I feel bad that I can't help you with that, even though, for so long, I've resented you, almost enjoyed seeing you suffer after you lost our child and pushed me away.

I admitted this to Miranda one night, a long time ago now, whilst we were having a late-night call and I'd had one too many whiskies. As usual, she took my side, said it was a perfectly normal reaction to have and that I shouldn't feel guilty about it. That I had every reason to resent you. I also had a feeling that she'd discovered something about you, something I wasn't going to like. I didn't ask her what it was, though. I wasn't strong enough for more bad news. I know she was trying to be kind, that I should have been grateful for her support, but when she said all that, it riled me somewhat. She can be so blinkered about me, it makes me wonder if she just says things to please me. It also struck me as double standards that she appeared to have no qualms about badmouthing you behind your back, but at the same time be your friend to your face.

I think she picked up on my disapproval because then she backed down, said it couldn't have been easy on either of us and that maybe you and I needed a break. She was probably right about that. I perhaps should have moved out for a bit, given us space, but by then, we'd had Daniel and I didn't want to leave him alone with you. I wanted to make sure he was safe and loved. By me, at least. Thinking about it, I wonder if that's why he's getting married so young, and to someone older. Symptomatic of his inherent need to be loved, cared for.

I can't lie here any more. You are sleeping, though not entirely peacefully, because every now and again, you give a little whimper, jerk your shoulders, as if you're having an unpleasant dream. But it's not that which causes my insomnia; it's my guilt. Not just because I wasn't there for you today, but also for being repeatedly unfaithful to you, even though, until today, I told myself that it served you right, that I have nothing to feel guilty about after the way you treated me and the kids.

Recently, you've seemed warmer, more approachable, like you're making an effort to open up to me, get closer to me. But is it too late, I wonder? Truth is, I'm torn between breaking things off with Amber and trying again with you – particularly in light of the note and the possibility that Heidi might still be alive – and staying with Amber and her intoxicating elixir for life. Her amazing body, her ability to make me feel young and attractive and optimistic, even though I know how shitty and cruel life can be. I know that if I continue to see her, it can only end badly. But she's like a magnet I can't – don't want to – repel; an exciting temptation I don't want to be led away from because it gives me so much pleasure, and I want to feel pleasure, I deserve it after all I've been through.

But again, I feel guilty for even thinking this, and I know I cannot lie next to you a second longer because the guilt is killing me. I get up, feel my way downstairs in the dark and head for the study, where I turn on the light, then sit down at my desk, thinking I might as well check my emails because I'm not going to get much chance later with completion meetings and so forth.

I have 200 new emails, some of them important, some of them junk, which I automatically bin. But then something catches my eye. It's from an address I don't recognize, with no subject heading, but there is an attachment. The email itself is blank. It's probably spam and my head says don't open it because it's doubtless some hacker and opening it will unleash a whole host of problems. But my heart says otherwise, and I cannot resist. Feeling wide awake now, I double-click on the attachment and see five words typed in capital letters:

YOUR WIFE IS A WHORE.

Chapter Thirty-Two

Heidi

Now

It's been fun watching your movements recently. Watching you come and go, enter and leave your psychiatrist's home, reliant on yet another quack to untwist that twisted mind of yours, still failing to accept that only you, and you alone, can do that, by taking responsibility for your own actions. But that's always been your biggest problem. You've been so used to getting your own way all your life, you think you're immune to judgement. Even now, after twenty-three years of guilt eating away at you, reducing you to a deplorable scrawny wretch of a woman, whose own family resents her, you refuse to come clean.

That's what my mother says. That's what she despises most about you, the fact that you won't own up, and the fact that you've always acted so entitled, never really appreciated how goddamn lucky you are to have the life you have with Greg. And despite what the note says – accusing you of being an unfit mother – you're still too chicken to tell your nearest and dearest the truth. A cowardly part of you clinging to the hope it's just another creep who doesn't have a clue what he or she is talking about and so with time it will all blow over.

I wonder how you can live with yourself. All these people who have loved you: Janine, Miranda, Greg, you owe them the truth. But it seems that your selfishness knows no bounds. And that's why I won't let up until your deceit is laid bare and you lose everyone who made the mistake of ever loving you.

Chapter Thirty-Three

Christine

Now

I didn't see Greg this morning. It wasn't as if I got up late. I woke at 7 a.m., but he was already gone. Usually I stir when he unwraps himself from our duvet, so the fact that I didn't on this occasion makes me think he got up in the middle of the night and didn't come back to bed. The study door was open when I went downstairs, but I'm certain I closed it when we retired for the night, so perhaps he couldn't sleep and decided to check his emails and go in early.

It irritates me, because he knows what a shock I had yesterday, and he'd seemed genuinely apologetic about not making it home for lunch with Daniel and Dr Cousins, or Freya as I should probably get used to calling her when we're not having a session. He hasn't even bothered to leave me a note or send me a text to explain his early departure and check that I'm OK. It's my own fault. I pushed him away for so long, how can I now expect him to treat me with kid gloves on the basis of recent events?

I'm seeing Dr Cousins/Freya a little later, at eleven. Despite only seeing her on Saturday, we decided to keep our appointment scheduled for today. She's so nice. Yesterday, when Daniel went to the bathroom, I didn't even have to raise the question as to whether it was wise for us to carry on our sessions, because she read my mind – which I suppose isn't surprising as it's her job to read people's minds – and assured me repeatedly that things didn't, and shouldn't, have to change between us on a professional level, just because she's marrying my son. She said I shouldn't think of her as my future daughter-in-law when she is being my psychiatrist, and that she certainly won't treat me any differently during our sessions just because I'm her fiancé's mother.

And so I am going to be rational about it, give it a go, because it felt like our sessions were helping and I don't want to stop unnecessarily. Daniel didn't mention the note and so I'm certain he's still in the dark about that, which only goes to show how professional Freya is, and that my secrets are safe with her.

Greg and I must tell him and Ella soon, though. It's just a case of finding the right moment.

Chapter Thirty-Four

Greg

Now

We don't usually meet in public, but I really needed to see you, Amber. When I called, you weren't at home; you were just coming out of the gym, having done an early morning spin class. You spin at your local gym three times a week, and it shows. Unlike Chrissy, you look fit and healthy. Not too skinny, but slim and toned with curves in all the right places. You look slightly flushed as you walk into Deco's – a trendy cafe fashioned in the Art Deco style – and spot me at a table for two at the back, trying not to look conspicuous, even though it feels like I'm on some reality show and the whole world is watching me, waiting to catch me and my infidelity out.

But I don't care. I can't get the email out of my head; the accusation that my wife is a whore is too shocking to discount, to keep bottled up inside me. And I can't help wondering whether it was sent by the same person who sent Chrissy the note. It just seems like too much of a coincidence, in which case, I should probably tell Chrissy about it, and we should both tell the police. But I can't quite bring myself to do that. Not before I've spoken to someone about it. Someone neutral and uncomplicated. Someone like you.

You approach the table, wearing Lycra leggings and a purple zip-up top, pulled down just enough to reveal the top of your cleavage. There's still a faint line of sweat on your chest, and your face has a glow about it, while your hair is pulled up in a high ponytail. You look so young dressed as you are, with no make-up, and again it makes me question what on earth you are doing with me. I suddenly feel ashamed of my behaviour, like I'm some dirty old man. Then again, you're probably off screwing guys your own age on the nights you don't see me. I mean, who am I kidding, that's what young, attractive, single girls like you should be doing. Although, of course, the rules are different for my daughter. I shudder at the thought of Ella doing such a thing.

I've already ordered you a skinny latte, your favourite, while I've gone for a large, full-fat version. Slyly scanning the other patrons as you sit down opposite me, you smile faintly, and look nearly as nervous as I feel, which is hardly surprising because it occurs to me how panicked I must have sounded on the phone, and you must surely be wondering what was so urgent that I needed to see you at 8 a.m. on a Monday morning.

'Thanks for this,' you say, gesturing to your latte, before you coolly bring the mug to your lips and take a sip.

I say it's nothing, then take a sip of my own drink, before setting it down on the table, at which point I start tapping the side of my mug with my forefinger.

'What is it, Greg?' you ask, eyeing me with concern – or is it irritation, I can't quite tell? Or maybe I'm just imagining things?

I don't dither. I pull out a folded piece of paper from my jacket pocket and hand it to you.

You look at it with a puzzled expression, then ask, 'What's this?'

'Open it,' I say, my heart beating frantically.

You look nervous again; you're probably asking yourself what the hell you've got yourself into, thinking that perhaps you should never have given a washed-out middle-aged man like me the time of day. But then you slowly unfold the paper and read the words, frowning, before looking up at me with quizzical eyes. 'Where did you get this?'

'It was sent to my email account last night.'

'From who?'

'I don't know.'

'You don't recognize the address?'

'No.'

'Do you know what the sender's getting at?'

This strikes me as a rather superfluous question, because it seems pretty obvious what the sender is getting at. He or she is insinuating that my wife has cheated on me, perhaps many times. I repeat my thoughts to you, whereupon you redden slightly, and I feel bad for laying this on you because, of course, it isn't your problem. You didn't sign up to be my agony aunt.

'And do you think it's come from the same person who sent the note?' you ask, doing your best to look interested and concerned.

'It has to be the same person, don't you think? It's too much of a coincidence, and if you remember me saying, the note claimed that Heidi was better off with her kidnapper than with Chrissy – this email appears to be telling us why.'

'You mean because Chrissy slept around, and therefore wasn't fit to be a mother to Heidi?'

'That's the implication, yes.'

'Did you ever have any inkling that Chrissy might have cheated on you?'

'No, none at all.' *And that's the God's honest truth.*

'Are you going to show it to Chrissy?'

I sit back and sigh. 'I think I have to. I just can't ignore it, and who knows what other messages we'll get? We need to be on the same page. The police also need to know. They may be able to trace the email, spot a pattern.'

'I'm no expert, but unless this person wants to be found, I'm sure they've done everything possible to ensure the email can't be traced back to them.'

I smile wryly, thinking you're not just a pretty face. 'Yes, you're probably right, but I have to try at least.'

You smile back, reach for my hand and take it in yours, and we stay locked in that moment for some time, smiling at one another. But then, as I happen to glance past your shoulder, I see the door open, and a new customer walks in.

My heart drops to my stomach. This surely can't be happening.

It's Janine.

She spots me, as if she has a cheat antenna attached to her head. And even though you have your back to her, she sees that I am not alone, that I am holding hands with a woman who isn't Chrissy.

She sees that her best friend's husband is an adulterer.

Chapter Thirty-Five

Christine

Now

It's just gone 10 a.m. I plan to head out in half an hour, but before I do, I'm going to call Janine. I've not had a chance to respond to the text she sent me late last night. She asked how lunch had gone and was keen to know what I made of Daniel's fiancée, but I had a lot of clearing up to do after they left around five, and then Greg came home and that conversation took a while. By the time we were done talking, I was beat, and just wanted my bed. I can't imagine her reaction when I tell her Daniel is marrying our shrink. Or Miranda's for that matter. After all, she was the one who brought Dr Cousins into our lives.

Apparently, they met at a festival last summer. Freya was in the row behind Daniel watching some band or other. They made eye contact, got talking, went for a drink, and things just went from there. One of those instances where two people gel immediately, although – and I'm really not trying to belittle Daniel in any way because he's a bright, good-looking boy – Freya could have her pick of men and I would have pictured her with some smart, dashing doctor.

It's obvious what Daniel saw in her, though. She's stunning, intelligent, has a lovely personality (I saw a warm, funny side to her at lunch, very different from the serious, professional persona she adopts in our sessions, making the age gap less noticeable), and Daniel must know he's hit the jackpot. So really, I should be over the moon for him as he's not exactly had a great track record when it comes to relationships.

I pick up the phone and dial Janine's number. She'll know it's me because we have special ringtones programmed in for each other. But it takes eight rings for her to pick up.

'Hi.' It's not a bright and breezy 'hi'. It's almost reticent, like she's on edge about something and reluctant to speak to me.

I wonder what's wrong, whether I've done something to upset her. My stomach feels uneasy as I say, 'Hi, Jani. What's up, you OK? You don't sound right.'

There's hesitation at her end.

'What is it?' I press, really starting to worry. 'Listen, I have to go out soon, I've got a session with Dr Cousins, so whatever it is, tell me, please.'

'OK, but I think you should sit down.'

My stomach is now in knots and I feel rather light-headed, wondering what the hell she's going to say. All sorts of morbid thoughts filter through my mind, like she's got cancer, or someone close to me has died or been involved in a serious accident.

I perch on the bottom step of the hall stairs, phone pressed against my ear, and say nervously, 'OK, I'm sitting, so what is it?'

'OK, so…' I hear her inhale deeply, like she needs the extra air to get the words out. 'So I went for a swim this morning, like I often do, at Swiss Cottage gym, and afterwards, I fancied a coffee, and so I popped into Deco's to grab one to go…' Another pause, and I haven't the foggiest what's coming but I also feel relieved that she's clearly not about to tell me she's dying.

'And?' I probe.

'And I saw Greg with another woman.' She rushes this last sentence, as if she's ingesting a bitter-tasting medicine she knows she must take quickly if she's ever going to keep it down.

I'm stunned. It's so not what I expected. 'What time was that?' I just about get the words out, feeling foolish for assuming he must have headed to the office early.

'Around eight-fifteen.'

'Perhaps it was a business meeting?' Even as I suggest this, I know how far-fetched it is. Why would he be having a business meeting in Swiss Cottage? It just wouldn't happen.

'I don't think so,' Janine says cagily, like she feels bad for not confirming my hope.

'What did she look like? Old, young? Did it seem like they knew each other well?'

More hesitation. Then, 'Perhaps I should come over?'

This gets my goat, and I lose patience, even though I know I am being unfair because Janine is just trying to protect me, soften the blow. 'No, I don't have time, I told you I have a session at eleven, so just answer the bloody question, will you?'

Another pause, then, 'It was hard to tell, she had her back to me. She was blonde, had a ponytail, was possibly wearing some sort of gym top. I couldn't be sure, of course, but I got the feeling she was quite young.'

Nausea washes over me, and it's a good job I'm sitting down because I sense there's more. 'And what else?'

'Greg was leaning in towards her. I think they were holding hands.'

So that's it, then. He's having an affair. I guess I shouldn't be surprised. But I am surprised she's young. One thing I've always considered Greg to be is dignified. Also cautious, timid, where women are concerned. I mean, he took bloody long enough to ask me out and we were practically the same age. But carrying on with some peroxide gym bunny? That I didn't expect.

It's hard to take, especially right now, what with all that's happened lately; it's suddenly all getting on top of me. I wonder, all those nights Greg was *supposedly* working late in the office, even yesterday when he missed lunch because he was *supposedly* closing a deal, was he actually off banging his mistress, playing me for a fool? What the hell will Miranda think? She'll be furious, that's for sure. Jealous, too. She just about accepted me. But some dollybird? I can't help thinking this will prove too much for her.

'Chrissy, you still there?'

I wonder if I am. I feel like I've left my body and am looking down at this pitiful, scraggy woman who not only lost her child, but has now lost her husband. Doubtless it's payback for my affair. An affair I should have stopped when Heidi was born, but didn't, all because I was too selfish. I am suddenly appalled by myself. What right do I have to be angry with Greg? I asked for this.

'Yes, yes, I'm still here. Did he see you?'

'Yes. We just stared at each other for a few seconds. Part of me wanted to march straight up to their table and ask him what the hell was going on. But I panicked, bottled it, I'm ashamed to say. I turned around and walked straight out.' Janine pauses, then says, 'I'm so sorry, Chrissy. Of all things, I never pegged Greg for a cheat. I always thought of him as one of the good ones. And the cheek of meeting her in public like that, and so close to where you live – I mean, it's just so… it's just so bloody brazen! I'm so angry with him. How could he do this to you? It's unforgivable.'

I appreciate Janine standing up for me. She probably expects me to rant and rave in response to this startling news. But I am not entitled to rant and rave. That would make me a hypocrite, although she's not to know that. So, I take a deep breath, try and stay calm, and say, 'I can hardly blame him, after the way I've treated him.'

But Janine is right about the brazen bit. That was pretty dumb of him, to risk being seen out in public with her, in the area where we live. And why was he meeting her so early? Was he unloading his problems onto her, telling her how we'd rowed the night before about him not being around for lunch, asking for her advice on whether he should leave me?

'Infidelity is still inexcusable,' Janine insists.

Jesus, how I envy her and her simplistic way of looking at things. Sometimes, I think I would have been much happier had I been ordinary like her. Less driven. And I don't mean that in a nasty way. It's just that when you're pretty and ambitious, your expectations are so much higher, and you find it hard to be content with the mundane, simple things in life. I constantly wanted more, and I wasted the opportunities life threw at me to be happy, with Heidi and with Greg, all for the sake of sex. I've been shallow and stupid, and it may be too late for second chances.

But I don't argue, just say, 'How the hell do I deal with this, Jani? What do I say to him? He'll assume you've told me.'

'I'd give him hell.'

'Really? Rather than give him the chance to own up first?'

'No, why should you? You need to go on the offensive, show him you're not a pushover. Confront him when he comes home tonight. And if he has a problem with that, tell him he can go to hell.'

I guess I shouldn't be surprised by Janine's tough stance; she's my best friend and she's only sticking up for me, trying to protect me from further heartache, which is what best friends do. I'd do the same for her. As I know Miranda would for Greg. When Heidi went missing, and Miranda saw what it did to him, she was a tower of strength. At first coming to stay with us, and then later, when she and Duncan moved up North, at the end of the phone, ready to lend an ear in his darkest moments. She put me to shame, really. And I suspect she secretly resents me for pushing Greg away when what he needed most from his wife was comfort. I mean, she has lost it with me on a couple of occasions.

'OK,' I say, 'I will.'

Just then, I realize I haven't told her about Dr Cousins being Daniel's fiancée; the reason I called her in the first place. I check my watch; it's 10.30. I need to leave soon.

'Jani, there's something I need to tell you. Something you're not going to believe.'

'Oh God, I don't think I can take any more surprises. Go on then, hit me.'

'Daniel's fiancée is Dr Cousins.'

No response. I don't blame her for being lost for words.

'You're joking, right?' she finally says.

'No. I nearly fell over when I opened the door and saw her standing there.'

'Unbelievable. You're sure? Absolutely sure?'

'Course I'm sure.'

'How did she react? Did she know?'

'No, she had no idea. Daniel had barely mentioned me to her, which just goes to show how much he hates me. I guess he didn't want to put her off by telling her about his crazy mother.'

'He doesn't hate you.'

'OK, so maybe "hate" is too strong a word, but he doesn't like me, he thinks I'm nuts. So why would he tell the woman he's in love with that his mother's a basket case? You wouldn't, would you?'

'She's a shrink, she should be more understanding than most. Plus, she's older, less fickle. I'm guessing that's what drew him to her.'

'Yes, but surely the last thing she wants to do is talk shop when she's not working. That should be her escape time.'

'So why did he bring her round for lunch?'

'Well, he probably had no option, having got engaged. I mean, he had to introduce her to me and Greg at some point, whether he liked it or not. And maybe she thought it strange he hadn't done so yet? Maybe she forced his hand.'

'Has Daniel met her parents?'

'Her mother died of cancer when she was a teenager and her father lives in the US with his second wife. I guess we'll meet him at some point, though. Along with her brother, who's here in London, apparently.'

'That's so sad, I had no idea,' Janine murmurs.

I remember Freya's woeful expression when she told me about her mother. It made me feel guilty for burdening her with my problems when she herself – through no fault of her own – had such a sad family history. A history I had hitherto been oblivious to, but that perhaps explained her focus on grief therapy. And it made me think, still makes me think, how can I continue to see her when I know she has problems of her own?

'So you're still going to see her, despite all this?' Janine asks. 'Isn't that unethical? Have you told Miranda?'

'Technically, it's not against the law until we're related. So I will continue for now. Freya tried her best to reassure me that it shouldn't change things until she and Daniel are married. I'm not so sure, but let's see. And no, I've not yet mentioned it to Miranda. I'm sure she'll be as shocked as the rest of us.'

'Give it a go, at least. It'd be a shame to stop seeing Dr Cousins when you think her sessions are doing you good. Why don't you give Miranda a call, see what she thinks?'

Truth be told, I'm not sure I can have a conversation with Miranda about Freya without spilling the beans on Greg's affair at the same time. Janine's reaction was bad enough, goodness knows what Miranda's will be. I can't have her laying into Greg before I've confronted him myself. So, I chicken out, pass the buck to Janine.

'Would you mind telling Miranda about Freya for me?' I ask.

'Me?' Janine sounds briefly confused, before twigging. 'Ah, I see. You don't want her knowing about Greg's affair just yet. Right?'

'Yes.'

'No problem,' she says.

I smile, grateful that despite the mess my life has become, my friends remain the one constant I can rely on. 'Thanks. And I will continue seeing Dr Cousins for now. As you say, I can only give it a go.'

Chapter Thirty-Six

Greg

Now

I'm at the office, sitting at my desk trying to work, but it's a struggle. I can't seem to focus on anything. I'm too full of panic, wondering what the hell I'm going to do now that Janine's seen me with Amber. OK, so she didn't see her face, but she did see that I was holding hands with another woman, so all in all it's not looking good for me. She didn't even give me the chance to concoct some false explanation. Just glared at me – a look that said, *How could you, you cheating swine?* – then turned around and walked out the door.

I wonder if you know already, Chrissy. Whether, the second Janine left the café, she whipped out her phone and called you to let you know that your husband is an adulterer. I dare not call or text you, even though I know I'm probably already in the doghouse for shooting off early this morning, without bothering to leave you a note or send you a message checking that you're OK after our argument last night. I also wonder if Miranda knows. She's the only other person Janine might ring and tell, perhaps to teach me a lesson, cause me to lose the only true friend I have left in this world. As far as I'm aware, she doesn't know. I think if she did, she'd have rung me up straight away and given me hell. She'd be jealous, but more so, disappointed. Wondering how the man she loved could sink so low, become such a cliché?

Clearly, I'm getting my just desserts for cheating on you. What a fool I've been for thinking I could get away with my affair without you finding out. But then again, perhaps deep down, I wanted to get found out. Perhaps Janine seeing me with Amber is my ticket to freedom, my way out of our shambolic marriage. Maybe it's your way out too? Only, unlike me, you'll have the moral high ground and feel entitled to kick me out first because I'm the one who cheated.

Then again, *will* you? After all, the reason I met up with Amber this morning was because I needed to talk to someone about the email. The email that alleges you're not so squeaky clean yourself. That you slept around behind my back, quite possibly when we were still happily married and had Heidi in our lives. I focus on this, and in doing so, feel less anxious about you confronting me about Amber.

I just hope Amber doesn't begrudge me for using her as a sounding board, for bringing my problems into her life. Right now, I need her.

Right now, she's the only thing keeping me sane.

Chapter Thirty-Seven

Christine

Now

'Please try not to feel awkward, Christine. At this moment, I'm not thinking of you as my future mother-in-law. I see you as my patient and nothing else. Rest assured that nothing you say to me will leave these four walls. I have never discussed your issues with Daniel, and I never will. He knows how seriously I take my work, and therefore not to ask questions.'

I appreciate Dr Cousins' assurances, but Daniel is the least of my worries. By not even mentioning your disappearance to her – nor how it affected us all, particularly me – it just goes to show how he's tried to blank all of that out and couldn't give a monkey's how I feel or what I say to my shrinks in private. All he sees is a rotten mother who deserves to be miserable.

No, it's my own awkwardness that concerns me. Whether I can come to terms with my future daughter-in-law knowing my innermost thoughts, my murkiest secrets. After all, she doesn't know the whole story yet; she doesn't know the worst part, and if I tell her everything, what will she think of me? How will she be able to sit in a room with me, Greg and our children, without telling them what I've done, what I am?

An adulterer and a fraud.

But despite my misgivings, I stay. There's just something about her that calms me. 'OK,' I say, 'let's see how it goes.'

She smiles, then says, 'So, I get the impression there's something you want to get off your chest. Something that's been burdening you for some time now, something related to Heidi's disappearance.'

She's too sharp. I want to tell her, I really do, and before I spoke to Janine earlier, I thought today might be the day. But Janine's revelation has put a spanner in the works. All I can think about is Greg's adultery.

Right now, I'm lying on Dr Cousins' couch. If I was going to tell her about my affair, I would have stayed in this position because I wouldn't have had the courage to look her in the eye. But instead, I'm going to tell her about Greg's affair, and for that, I feel the urge to face her square-on. 'Do you mind if I come and sit opposite you?' I ask. 'I think I'd prefer that.'

'Of course not.' She smiles and waits patiently for me to get off the couch and park myself in the tan leather chair facing her. It's strange seeing her in a suit again. Her hair pinned up with the same black clip, glasses on, perfect make-up. Almost like a different person. I'm glad of it. It helps me separate 'Dr Cousins' from 'Freya'.

Once seated, my insides burn with trepidation as I work up the nerve to tell her. She's not even met Greg, but perhaps it's a good thing that she can't put a face to the name. It will allow her to view him in a detached manner. Her eyes fix on mine, willing me to confide in her. And then I go for it.

'Before I came here today, I found out that Greg is most probably cheating on me.'

Not a hint of emotion. No reaction at all. As it should be. I'm encouraged by this.

'I see. How did you discover that?'

'Janine told me.'

Obviously, she knows I am here on Janine's recommendation, that Janine and I are best friends, and therefore I can trust my source implicitly.

'How did Janine find out?'

'She saw them together this morning. They were having coffee in Deco's on the Finchley Road.'

163

'That's not proof he's having an affair.'

I swallow hard. 'They were holding hands.'

A slight flicker of the eyes, then, 'Still, he might have been comforting her about something.'

She's trying to rationalize the situation, which is her job, of course. And I'd like to think that her possible explanation is a viable one. But one, judging by the blonde hair, ponytail, gym top, it's likely this girl's young and attractive; two, I don't have a clue who she is – Greg has never mentioned her to me, which proves he's been hiding her from me deliberately; and three, why sneak off to meet her at 8 a.m. before work? It smells bad to me. I tell all this to Dr Cousins.

'OK, so, granted, that doesn't look great.' She pauses, then says sharply, 'But are you surprised? After all the years you've neglected him, it can't come as a shock to you that he's having an affair. Men have affairs all the time, and I would have thought he's more justified than most.'

Her sudden brusqueness catches me off guard. That same shock treatment she initiated last time. And when I look into her eyes, they are no longer soft and sympathetic, but hard and accusatory. It's almost a look of disgust.

'No,' I stammer, 'I'm not surprised; I've been a terrible wife, and a terrible mother.' I can barely look her in the eye as I say this, but I brave it and see that her expression has softened again. It's a little unsettling. She gives me a faint smile.

'That's good. Good that you are admitting your mistakes; that's all part of the healing process. The question now is, what are you going to do with this information?'

'I don't know.'

It's true, I don't. Part of me wants to hurl abuse at him. But the other part knows I am a fraud; an even worse liar than him. So what right do I have to take him to task?

'You can't let it fester, Christine,' she says. 'It will eat you alive. You must confront him about it.'

Rationally speaking, she's right, but she doesn't know what's stopping me. Do I tell her now? This is the perfect moment;

164

I'll never be able to make proper progress before I confess to what I consider to be responsible for my life descending into total wretchedness.

I hesitate.

'Don't hold back, Christine,' she urges, 'it's what I'm here for. You can trust me, tell me anything. I'm not here to judge you. I'm the one person who won't judge you.'

She sounds so sincere, and I'm about to explode with longing to tell her, get it out of my system once and for all, but I still can't bring myself to tell her everything. So instead, I tell her half the story.

'This is very difficult for me,' I say rather lamely.

'I know,' she says gently. 'But from small steps, we can make great strides. Just tell me. Think of it as a horrid medicine you know you must take to feel better.'

I inhale deeply. 'OK.' A brief pause, then, 'I had an affair.'

Fuck. It's out. After twenty-three years of suppressed guilt, I've told someone and it's like the biggest sense of release ever. In fact, I feel a bit light-headed, causing me to grip the armrests of my chair just to steady myself.

She notices this. Tilts her head, asks, 'You OK?'

'Yes. It's just that, after keeping it to myself for so long, it feels like quite a big deal telling someone. It's a relief, though.'

'I understand. When did this affair happen?'

I'm sure she assumes it was before you disappeared, which explains my guilt, but she obviously has to ask the question. Even so, I feel terrible as I reply, 'A long time ago. When Greg and I were only just married.' I swallow hard, then say, 'Actually, it started before we were married.'

I study her face for a reaction, but it remains impassive, so I wait for her next question.

'And it continued after you had Heidi?'

I nod like a shamefaced child. 'Yes.' I can hardly hear my voice, it's so pitiful.

She sits back in her chair and taps her pen between her pristine teeth. Jesus, I think to myself, my future daughter-in-law must think I'm a slut. She promised she wouldn't tell Daniel anything I discuss in confidence with her, but I wonder, is this new information just too juicy for her to keep to herself? I'm not sure I could keep such a secret.

'Who was he?'

'Someone I met through the firm.'

'Married?'

'Yes.'

'And were you with him when Heidi disappeared?'

I shake my head. 'No, I wasn't with him, but I was talking to him on the phone.'

'You had a phone? Back in, what was it—?'

'Nineteen ninety-six.' I explain how I had two. Courtesy of the two successful men in my life who'd wanted to keep me close at hand.

'And you got distracted?'

'Yes.'

'Why?'

'Because he said he wanted to end things between us.'

'Why?'

'He said it was too dangerous to carry on. That he was worried about being caught. About others getting hurt if we were.'

'And his decision surprised you?'

'Yes. We'd been sneaking around for three years, and in all that time, he never gave any indication that this was worrying him. In fact, he enjoyed the sneaking around, that was part of the thrill.' I pause, remembering what we were like back then. 'He was like that. Reckless, like me. A thrill seeker, addicted to pleasure, excitement.'

I pause and look at Dr Cousins. Is she sickened by my explanation? By my irresponsible attitude, my total disregard for my husband's feelings, or the feelings of my lover's wife?

Probably, and I don't blame her. Now that I am older and wiser, I'm sickened by it myself.

'And you told me at our first meeting that you were in Peter Jones at the time?'

'Yes.'

'Where exactly?'

'In the lingerie department.' My cheeks burn as I remember a sexy black lace basque I spotted as I simultaneously hummed a nursery rhyme to you. I remember imagining the look on his face when he saw me in it; him going hard with excitement, something that always excited me. But now all I feel is shame; utterly repulsed by my shallow thoughts. I should have been there for you, not imagining dirty romps with my married lover.

'Were you buying something to wear for him?' Dr Cousins' question catches me unawares. I'm not surprised she read my thoughts, but I am surprised that she chose to ask the question out loud. It feels unnecessary.

Still, I can't lie. 'Yes.'

'And Heidi was in her buggy while you were on the phone to your lover?' She says the word 'lover' with some emphasis, making my actions – the whole situation – sound so crass, and the word seems to ring in the air like a thunderous echo.

'Yes. But as I said before, I couldn't quite hear him properly, the signal was bad, and so I moved away to try and get a better signal.'

'You just walked away and left the buggy where it was? You left your child to fend for herself?'

Her tone is incredulous, almost vicious, and again, I feel like the worst person alive. The worst mother. Someone who had no right to be a mother.

'Yes. I just wasn't thinking straight. It was a boiling hot day, I was feeling tired and flustered, and then he called and dropped this bombshell on me and I… I lost my head.'

Pathetic, pathetic, woman.

'Did she cry?'

I falter again. Then admit, 'She had a dummy in her mouth.'

There it is again, the same laser look.

How many times have I replayed this sequence of events in my head? Too many to count. How could I have failed to keep you with me? What on earth possessed me to leave you stranded alone in your buggy? How could I have been so caught up in myself, had such flagrant disregard for your safety?

'Do you remember seeing anyone about at the time?'

'The department was quiet, virtually empty. I don't remember seeing anyone, aside from a shop assistant. It was a weekday and still early. Hot, too, as I said.'

'And the shop assistant didn't see anyone?'

Why does this suddenly feel like a police interrogation, rather than a session with my psychiatrist? Or is this what I deserve? What did I expect? A hug and cup of cocoa?

'No, I think we concluded that she'd gone out back to check on something around the time Heidi was taken. A call had come through from the stockroom or something.'

'And did anyone know you went shopping at Peter Jones that day?'

I think. Remember my call with Miranda. 'Besides my mother, only Miranda, who you know, of course. She was attending a client event in Kensington at the time. She called me when I was on the bus with Heidi.'

'Miranda seems like a good person. Devoted to you and Greg. Does she have children?'

This seems like a strange digression, but maybe it's part of her unique approach? So I go along with it. 'No, no she doesn't.'

'That's a shame, it sounds like she would have made a great mother.'

She's right, she would have. She wouldn't have lost you. She wouldn't have cheated on Greg. She wouldn't have been cold towards Daniel and Ella, treated them more like lodgers than her own children.

'Yes,' I nod sheepishly. 'I think she would.'

'Who was your lover, Christine?'

The question hits me cold. I say nothing.

'You won't name him?' she persists.

'I'm not ready for that.'

'Why do you think Greg wasn't enough for you?'

My shoulders drop, and I don't answer at once. It's a question I've agonized over for a long time. Why wasn't he enough? He was gentle, loving, a great father and an attentive husband. Not exceptionally handsome, but nice-looking. Why wasn't that good enough? After all, I wasn't some glamorous movie star, some impossibly beautiful supermodel. I was just a lawyer, like him. No one special. What gave me the right to be so full of myself?

'Because it wasn't hot with Greg,' I say bluntly, knowing how superficial that sounds. 'We couldn't help being attracted to each other. He did something to me, made me sizzle all over, made me feel like the sexiest woman alive. He had this naughty glint in his eye, a certain charisma, arrogance I found irresistible. Greg's never been like that. He's safe. He's father material. That's the only way I can explain it.'

Christ, it's a double-edged sword saying this out loud. On the one hand, it's liberating after repressing the truth for so long, on the other it only intensifies my shame, the feeling that I deserved to lose you.

'But you didn't think to stop once you had Heidi?'

It's a good question.

'I wanted to. I really did. At least, I did in my head, because in my head I knew it was wrong. In fact, I thought about stopping the moment I realized I was pregnant. And then again, a couple of months later. But then something happened to change my mind. Both our minds.'

'What?'

I can't answer that right now. It's too much, too soon. Just like telling her my lover's identity is too soon. 'Not yet. I can't, I'm not quite ready.'

169

I make out a slight heave of her chest as I say this, while her lips are slightly pursed. Is she angry with me? Feeling impatient with me? I can't quite tell. But then she smiles and nods her head.

'That's OK, I understand. We've made good progress today, don't you think?'

'Yes,' I nod. 'I guess so.'

'We're nearly at the end of our session, but I think we should talk about one more thing.'

I'm instantly on edge. 'What's that?'

'How did you leave things with your lover? Did he realize Heidi had been taken?'

Chrissy, what is it? Why have you gone so quiet? Did you hear me? We need to stop, it's too dangerous; we have to think of others, not just ourselves. You have to think of Heidi, her future.

I can still hear his words, as if he only said them yesterday. Even though my mind was only half there, frozen with fear at not being able to see you, my precious baby girl.

'Christine, did you hear my question?'

I repeat my lover's words to Dr Cousins, then say, 'At this point I'd realized I'd wandered into a different department without thinking, and when I returned to where I'd left her, she was gone. I was frantic. A choking, frenzied fear I'd never felt before. And then *he* was suddenly unimportant, and I remember hanging up, running up and down the aisles as I screamed her name, looking for her everywhere, but she'd just vanished, and it didn't make any sense to me that she could have just disappeared without a trace. And then suddenly there were people around me, shop assistants, customers, asking me what was wrong, what or who I had lost, what she was wearing, how old she was, her hair colour, eye colour, type of pushchair, did she have a toy with her, could she talk, and then those reassuring words along the lines of "Don't worry, we'll find her; just you wait and see, she'll turn up." Meaningless words that are far from true, but people say them anyway to be kind and comforting even though you know there is nothing they can say or do that can possibly comfort you, short of knowing where your child is, and telling you that they know for sure that she is safe and well.'

I pause, and there are tears streaming down my face. Dr Cousins looks as distraught as me, which I find endearing, and makes me forget her earlier harshness. It's clear to me that my story has touched her, even though she's supposed to be rational and detached. I like that about her. And I realize that's what Janine must have liked about her too. Her natural empathy, the fact that she feels personally affected by her patients' suffering; an impulse perhaps borne from her mother's untimely death. It may not be normal, even advisable in her line of work, but I don't care, it works for me, makes me feel I can trust her, makes me want to confide in her more.

'I can tell that was extremely difficult for you to relive,' she says, a slight tremor in her voice.

'It always is,' I nod. 'Although that's the first time I've told anyone I was on the phone to my lover when Heidi disappeared.'

'You didn't tell the police?'

Guilt and panic swell in me. I wonder, if the police discovered the truth now, would I be in trouble, despite so much time having passed? I'd like to think not. I mean, what difference would it have made, telling them? It wouldn't have changed the fact that you were kidnapped while I was on the phone. It wouldn't have changed the fact that I wandered off without thinking.

'I did tell them I was on the phone at the time,' I say, 'but on the Nokia Greg bought me, which I always carried around with me. I said it was just some random cold caller, and that I'd walked away to get a better signal. I never told them I had two phones, it raised too many questions.'

That's perverting the course of justice, isn't it? A blanket lie. I brush the thought off.

'I see. And as the other phone was registered in your lover's name, they'd never have reason to doubt your story?'

'No, why would they? I wasn't under suspicion. At no point was I under suspicion.'

I'm lying, of course. Parents are always under suspicion in the case of a missing child and the police obviously did what they needed to do to eliminate Greg and me from their enquiries. That included checking our phone records, which verified the cold call made to my Nokia. The same phone everyone, bar *him*, called me on.

Thank heavens for the individual who called me around the same time. Whoever it was, helped me to preserve my shameful secret. Even so, a burst of anger shoots through me. I mean, I'm not sure what Dr Cousins is trying to achieve with this line of questioning, but she doesn't apologize, just says, 'OK, let's leave it at that for now.'

Chapter Thirty-Eight

Miranda

Before

It pained me, Chrissy, to hear the way you shouted at that poor child as we spoke on the phone. Reminiscent of my father, who had little patience for me. No parent should treat their child like that, especially one so young. After all, she doesn't want to be lugged around London on a stiflingly hot day like today. As usual, you're putting your own needs above hers, just as you do above Greg's. He can't see it, he's so blind to your selfishness because somehow you cast this spell over him, made him worship you like an angel sent from above. But I see your true self, even if no one else does. Least of all Janine, who likewise seems to idolize you like a saint. But you're no saint, and you're certainly no angel. Unless you include the Devil in that category. After all, people forget he's also an angel. Albeit a fallen one.

No one will miss me at the hotel. They're all so full of themselves. Most of them beer-swilling bores who love the sound of their own voices. A bit like Duncan. I instantly said yes when he proposed because it made me feel wanted, gave me something to focus on other than you and Greg. Although it helped that he was so bloody gorgeous. And then, after Greg proposed to you, I convinced Duncan that we should move in together, bring the wedding forward, just so I could get another one up on you, get that wedding band on my finger before you.

He's been such a disappointment, though. Caused me so much pain by his thoughtless behaviour and complete disregard for my feelings. I mean, I knew when I married him he was a bit of a lothario, but I thought that perhaps, with time, he'd settle down, mature. But he hasn't.

In fact, he's got worse. I found text messages on his phone. Only it wasn't his usual business phone, it was a different phone I'd never seen before, which I found in one of his jacket pockets when I was searching for some loose change. I've no idea who they're from, because the sender was programmed in as anonymous. But whoever sent them, they're pretty filthy. How cliché is that? I so hate clichés. He says it's my fault we're not happy. That I pushed him away after my miscarriages. I can't believe how bloody selfish he is. I mean, how the hell can he know what it feels like to carry the child you've yearned for all your life, and then have it taken away from you. Not once, not twice, but three times. The pain is excruciating, without equal. Even losing Greg doesn't compare.

Neither you nor Greg know about the miscarriages. I never told anyone about the pregnancies because I didn't want to jinx things. But it turns out my superstition was a load of old crock because I lost all three before hitting the magic twelve-week mark. I wanted to be pleased for you and your pregnancy – for Greg especially – but when I saw how irritable you seemed to be, how obviously not happy with the idea, despite putting on a show for Greg, it made my blood boil. I wanted to yell at you how bloody lucky you were, but somehow I controlled myself.

I'll admit that when you first had Heidi, I saw a change in you; saw that you loved her, finally recognized what a gift it was to be a mother. And that should have pleased me. But I still couldn't find it in myself to be happy for you. Especially when I watched you at her christening. Lapping up the attention like always. Your husband's doting eyes locked on you. I felt strangled by envy. Envious of you and your perfect face, perfect figure, perfect husband, perfect child. Envious of the way even

Duncan appeared to covet your picture-perfect family. I wasn't blind, I saw the way his gaze fell upon the three of you. Seems he yearned for a child after all. What was it I had done to be cursed with no mother, no father to speak of, no husband I really loved the way I'd loved Greg? No child of my own to cherish. Why is it some women have it all? And why is it that they don't even realize it, aren't even fucking grateful for it?

Hearing you yell at Heidi on the bus this afternoon was the last straw. And that's why I'm here, at the entrance to Peter Jones. I'm not entirely sure what my plan is, but I do know you need a wake-up call. You need to realize just how much you've failed to appreciate all your privileged life.

The fact is, it's only when you lose someone you love that you realize how much you took them for granted. I know that more than anyone. And now you will too.

Chapter Thirty-Nine

Heidi

Before

I watch you, Father, and I try to love you, but I can't. Not like I used to.

Before Mother told me the truth, you were my hero. No guy could compete with you, and I never imagined you could do any wrong. But then Mother told me everything, and I discovered what kind of man you really are: a selfish, vain, shallow man, and my perfect image of you was tarnished for good. There's nothing you can do to change that, no matter how hard you try to be a good father to me. Every time I see you, my hatred, my disgust for you and what you did, for the fact that you knowingly and repeatedly hurt all the people you supposedly loved, grows stronger. Mother says she's learned to deal with it; that having me to love and care for helped her overcome the pain you caused her, made her stronger. But I know that not a day goes by when she doesn't think about your betrayal. With a woman who'd made a habit out of stealing men from decent women. Which is why she can never be content with just taking me from *her*. She needs to make *her* suffer more. And I am going to help her do that.

I take comfort from the fact that you don't seem happy, that you always have this troubled, faraway look on your face. As if you're expecting your past indiscretions to catch up with you. You've done the same job for thirtysomething years, and you exist in a sexless marriage, although now I know what you're really like, I wouldn't be surprised if you seek your thrills elsewhere. I've been tempted to follow you on several occasions, but I know that I wouldn't be able to stop myself from telling Mother if I saw you with another woman, and the last thing I want is to cause her more pain. It's probably better for both Mother and I to live in ignorance where your extracurricular activities are concerned.

After Mother told me the truth, and I finally calmed down, she called the three of us together in the sitting room and told you I was no longer ignorant of my past. You went as white as a sheet, like you were about to throw up, no doubt with shame. You didn't say much, just looked at me with apologetic, almost pitiful eyes, slightly dumbfounded, I suppose. I don't think Mother had previously filled you in on her plan to tell me everything – where I came from and who my real mother was. I remember the incredulous look you gave her, followed by an icy glare that said you wanted to kill her. Then you told me to leave the room and go upstairs to my bedroom.

At first, I stayed put; waited for Mother to give me the OK because I wasn't taking orders from you any more. She said it was OK, that I should go, and so I left. But I didn't go to my room. I hid at the top of the stairs, trying to make out what you and Mother were saying, but I only caught snippets of your conversation. It was clear you didn't want me to hear because you kept your voice low, even though you must have been dying to scream blue murder at Mother.

'…How could you tell her?

'…Why wasn't that enough for you?

'…Why go to such lengths? Are you so heartless, so blinded by revenge that you'd use your own daughter to make *her* suffer more? You're sick, you know that, don't you?

'…Why can't you just move on, be happy for once?'

Those were your words. And then there were Mother's:

'...You cheated on me repeatedly, and if you don't keep your mouth shut and go along with the plan, I'll tell the world who and what you really are, and how you helped me take Heidi.'

I heard the anguish in her voice, understood just how much pain you and *she* had caused her, and at that moment I vowed to help Mother destroy the woman who destroyed her life.

I can never forget how *she* wanted to get rid of me, that she would have murdered me had her husband not found the test in the bin. That's what Mother told me. How she was sickened by me feeding from her breast, how she left me with either his mother or hers so she could shag you, my slimy, sex-crazed father.

She is just as cold to her other children. She has ruined them, just as she would have ruined me. She doesn't deserve to be a mother, the greatest gift of life, and the suffering she has endured after losing me is not enough.

She needs to suffer more.

Chapter Forty

Greg

Now

For once, I am home before you. It's only 6 p.m., and I'm guessing you've either gone to the gym after your session with Dr Cousins or stopped off to see Janine. I'm not aware of anything else you do to fill your time, but then again, the email has unsettled me, made me question whether I know the real you. Whether you're actually full of secrets, have another side to you I am ignorant of. *Tell me, Chrissy, have I been a fool all these years for believing my unqualified devotion was enough for you?*

I pour myself a stiff drink and sit with it on the sofa, switch on the TV and stare at the moving images but take none of them in, my mind occupied by other thoughts. I wonder if whoever has accused you of being a whore also knows I am cheating on you? Whether our every move is being watched? The thought makes me shiver, and I decide I must tell the police about the email as soon as possible, but not before I have spoken to you. It's only fair, and I am certain that we'll be stronger together, even though I get the feeling that whoever is behind all this wants to drive us further apart.

My phone receives a message. A text from Ella saying she was in the neighbourhood earlier and knocked to see if either of us was in. But we weren't, of course. She says she feels bad for missing lunch yesterday, but between us, she couldn't face it without me being there to act as a buffer. How sad is that?

When I married you, I imagined we'd have this perfect family – this solid unit of sublime happiness – but we're not even close to that. We're poles apart from each other and our children have serious issues, although I think Ella has suffered more than Daniel. Forever in the shadow of her older sister. You weren't there for her when she needed you most, and I wonder if she'll ever recover from that, whether your indifference, your neglect, has ruined her for life. She says she's met someone, but who knows if it'll last or whether this chap is good enough for her?

Having said that, I wonder if any bloke will ever be up to scratch for my darling girl. Fathers are – for the most part – fiercely protective of their daughters, but losing Heidi made me more so, to the point where I'm not sure it's entirely healthy on my part. But I can't help it.

I hear the faint jingle-jangle of keys, then one being turned in the lock, and I realize you're finally home. I chuck back my drink, but my heart is racing and I'm dreading what I know is going to be a difficult conversation. I'm almost certain that by now Janine will have told you she saw me with Amber; she's too good a friend to have kept it from you this long. She'd never want you to live in ignorance, to be made a fool of by your traitorous husband.

But she doesn't have the whole story. She hasn't seen the email accusing you of being a whore, a printout of which is tucked inside my trouser pocket. Like a gun in a holster, it is primed ammunition I intend to whip out to counter your accusations of infidelity.

You'll know I'm home because I've drawn the curtains, our signal to each other that one of us is in. You don't call out to me; the only sounds are the shuffling of footsteps, keys being thrown on the hall table, shoes being removed, coat being hung. You prolong my agony by going to the kitchen, no doubt to get your daily dose of wine, but to my surprise I hear the tap being turned on, then the sound of a tumbler being filled with water. Are you torturing me with your protracted avoidance of the living room, where you must know I am because the door is slightly ajar, the light on?

I refuse to leave this sofa; you need to come to me if you want an explanation and, having stuck to my guns, I finally hear your footsteps approach, and then the door swings open.

But it's not you. It's Daniel.

Chapter Forty-One

Christine

Before

I don't want to see you. I can't even bear to look at you, even though practicalities make that impossible. Losing Heidi has killed my passion for you. I'd never have thought it possible, to go from feeling like I couldn't live without you, to never wanting to see your face again. It's like a switch has been flicked from on to off, the electricity between us extinguished like a blown fuse, and it's hard to imagine the intense feelings I once had for you. I might even grow to hate you if my baby girl is never found, even though I know that's unfair because the blame lies squarely on my shoulders.

Six weeks have passed since Heidi was taken, and the police are no nearer to finding her, or her kidnapper. Every call or possible sighting turns out to be a dead end or – even more soul-destroying – the work of some crackpot or heartless trouble-maker. Whoever took her was very quick and very smart. Watching me with her that day. Seizing that small window of opportunity, as if he or she knew it was coming. Knowing which route to take out of the department store so as to draw the least attention to themselves and Heidi.

I feel numb from head to toe, consumed by grief and guilt. I find no joy in anything. I dread waking up in the morning; everything is a hassle and a burden, even putting one foot in front of the other is an effort, and my usually healthy appetite has vanished completely. After spending a month doing press conferences, helping the police with their enquiries and field searches, I am fast losing hope. I've not left the house for three days.

Greg went back to the office yesterday. Although they told him to take all the time he needed, I don't think he could stand being cooped up in here with me any longer. And, to be honest, I'm glad he went back, because I can't look him in the eye. Every time I look at him, I think about the lies I have told him and the fact that I am still lying to him. I can't bear for him to touch me because I am not worthy of his kisses or his cuddles or his sympathy. I am a vile human being who is getting her rightful punishment, but it is beyond unfair that Heidi should have to suffer for my sins.

Gone is the vivacious go-getter. In her place stands the carcass of the woman I once was. I reject even those closest to me, those who are trying their hardest to comfort me, like Janine (obviously her surprise birthday party was called off as no one was in the mood to celebrate, and she will shortly be off to Hong Kong), my brother, my parents, and Miranda. Poor Miranda. Having to deal with her father's heart attack the same afternoon Heidi was taken. She rang to tell us that she had no choice but to go to his bedside. As much as she resented him, he was her only remaining flesh and blood after all. It really was the most ill-fated day, and she felt so bad about not being there for us. But what could she do? She had to be there for her father. Even though, when we spoke that first week on the phone, it didn't sound like she was in the hospital. It sounded too quiet, echoey. Suspicious, even. It's sad he didn't pull through. I'll always be grateful to her for coming to stay with us so soon after he died, even though at the time all I wanted was to be left alone.

Although he hasn't said so to my face, I know Greg blames me, and I don't resent him for this, because if the roles were reversed, I'd probably do the same. But that's all hypothetical, isn't it? Because it *was* me who lost our daughter, all because I was too busy talking to you, worrying about myself, about losing you; something Greg would never have done, because he's the opposite of me.

You have tried calling me several times, left messages saying how sorry you are, and if there's anything you can do to help, just say the word. You always sound genuine, almost as distraught as me, which I guess shouldn't surprise me because of what only you and I know. I dare say you blame yourself for calling me, for trying to end things while I was out and about with Heidi, and that guilt must be devouring you.

But you know as well as I do that unless you have the capability to turn back time –

unless you can find Heidi for me – nothing can put this right. Nothing.

Chapter Forty-Two

Greg

Now

'Dan, what are you doing here?' I get up from the sofa and walk over to our son, who's loitering in the doorway.

'Nice to see you too, Dad.' Daniel's tone is caustic, and I see his eyes flit to my empty whisky tumbler. 'Bit early for the hard stuff, isn't it? You turning into a lush like Mum?'

There's clearly something very wrong. Daniel hardly ever speaks to me that way. Such sarcasm is usually reserved for you, Chrissy.

'Sorry, son, it's not that I'm not pleased to see you, I just wasn't expecting you.'

I study our son intently, still wondering what's up. After berating me for missing lunch, you told me you'd never seen him looking so content, so I am both puzzled and unnerved by his moroseness.

'What's wrong, Dan? Something's up, I can tell.'

Daniel ventures further into the room, moves past me. As he does, I catch a whiff of alcohol, and it's clear he's had a few himself. He comes to a standstill in front of our fake fireplace, spends a few seconds examining the family photos lined up on the mantelpiece. Some of them were taken when he and Ella were small, some of them as teenagers. A stranger to our family would never guess that behind these happy, smiling faces was a highly dysfunctional family.

185

Daniel echoes my thoughts out loud. 'What a joke,' he sniggers, but doesn't turn around.

I move closer to him, conscious that you're still not home. *Where are you?*

I place my hand on his shoulder. 'What's wrong? Mum said you seemed the happiest she's ever seen you. Is it to do with Freya being her psychiatrist? I'm sure that must have come as quite a shock to you. I know I was taken aback when your mother told me.'

Daniel turns around, and there are tears in his eyes. 'It was a shock, Dad, but after the three of us talked it over, they both seemed fine about it.'

'So, has something happened since, son?'

'Freya's called off the engagement.'

My heart stops. I watch a tear roll down Daniel's cheek. He wipes it away angrily, like he's embarrassed to cry in front of his old man.

'Why?' I ask.

'It's *her*. She fucks everything up, she always does. She's so bloody selfish, such a deranged, twisted bitch who only ever thinks of herself. She fucked me and Ella up as kids, and now she's fucking up any chance of us being happy as adults. What's wrong with the stupid cow?'

I look at our son, in such pain, and my heart bleeds for him. I feel so angry with you, almost like I want to kill you, just so you'd be out of our lives, and there'd no longer be any risk of you messing things up for us. Daniel and Ella would be happy, and I could run off into the sunset with Amber. But I manage to calm myself, tell myself I don't know the full story yet.

'How do you know Mum did anything?'

'Why are you always defending her?' Daniel rages. 'She treats you like shit; why didn't you leave her long ago, Dad?'

It's a question I've asked myself many times. And now, looking back, maybe I should have left you, married someone else. Someone who would have been a proper mother to our children. But I guess I was determined not to be my parents.

'Life's not always that straightforward, Daniel. Maybe I should have, but we can all wish we'd said or done things differently. That's the beauty of hindsight. If we had that luxury, we'd all be living perfect lives.'

He doesn't argue, but he's still full of rage. I can't stand seeing him like this.

'Freya said she could tell Mum's massively uncomfortable with us being a couple while she's seeing her as a patient. She said she thought she could separate our relationship from her professional relationship with Mum, but apparently Mum said some stuff to her today which makes that impossible. She said there's too much of a conflict of interest for us to carry on as a couple.'

'What stuff?' I mutter. I wonder if this has any connection to the email? A copy of which is still tucked away safely in my pocket, and which I have no intention of burdening poor Daniel with.

'Obviously she didn't say.' Daniel glowers at me. 'She's too professional. Which is why she's ended things.'

'Tell your mother to stop seeing her,' I say. 'No, sod that – I'll bloody well tell her.'

Daniel shakes his head. 'It's too late for that. Whatever she told Freya, it freaked her out. She says she knows too much for things to ever work between us.'

Daniel ruffles his hair in frustration, looks up to the ceiling as if seeking help from some higher entity. 'After all this time being miserable, I finally thought I could be happy.' He lowers his eyes, still wet with tears, and meets my gaze straight on. 'I was happy, Dad. But now I've lost Freya, I don't think I'll ever be happy again.'

He makes to leave, but I put out my hand and catch his arm. 'Where are you going?'

'Home. To get wasted.'

'Let me come with you,' I protest, fearing he might do something stupid. I think about his history of drug abuse and worry he'll fall back into his old habits.

'No.' His expression is fixed. Our son is stubborn, and I realize he won't budge. 'Don't worry, Dad, I'm not going to top myself, if that's what you're worried about. Not today, at least.'

Feeling mildly relieved, I let him go, but make one last attempt to try and persuade him to stay. 'Stay, wait for your mother. We can talk this through. Perhaps she can have a word with Freya?'

'No.' His tone is adamant. 'I don't want to see her, and I don't want her help. She can go to hell for all I care.'

I follow him to the hall where I watch him throw on his jacket, open the front door and leave without saying another word.

Chapter Forty-Three

Christine

Now

When I left Dr Cousins' place, I went for a long run on the treadmill at the gym. Too wired from our session to go straight home.

I still can't believe I told her about my affair after keeping it to myself all these years. OK, so I've not told her *everything*, but it's still a massive step, and I feel like I've come further with her in the few sessions we've had than I did with any of my other psychiatrists.

Why did I feel able to tell her? I thought about this as I ran, cranking up the pace every ten minutes until sweat poured off me and my heart rate climbed to near-dangerous levels. Was it just a question of timing? Just the fact that after all these years, I could no longer keep it inside me, simply had to tell someone and, if not her, it would have been some other equally qualified psychiatrist? Was it the note that pushed me, warning me that I need to be truthful with myself and with others if I want to discover the truth behind your disappearance? Was it Janine seeing Greg with another woman this morning that made me feel less guilty about my own infidelity, and therefore less scared about coming clean? Or is it simply that I've finally found the right psychiatrist who's able to draw it out of me, perhaps because of her unusual approach – caring one moment, disapproving the next? Whatever the case, both Janine and I have a lot to thank Miranda for. If it wasn't for her, we'd never have met Dr Cousins.

After the gym, I had a drink in the members' bar to reward myself for the progress I made today. Besides my own good fortune, I also think how lucky Daniel is to have found Dr Cousins. Maybe life is finally looking up for me and my family. If only the police could make some progress with the note, that would be something, but my guess is that they're not even close to identifying the sender. It's a nigh on impossible job tracing untracked mail.

It's 7.30 by the time I arrive at my front door. I see that Greg's beaten me to it because the curtains are drawn and the hall light is on. High from my run and buoyed by my large glass of Chablis, I feel ready to confront him about his mistress even though I know I'm a hypocrite and should be confessing to my own infidelity. But when I open the door, remove my coat, and find him pacing the living-room floor, I am not prepared for the onslaught that awaits me.

'Where the hell have you been?' he says.

Chapter Forty-Four

Ella

Now

It's just gone 7.30 and you and I are enjoying a quiet night in. Recently, we've both been so busy, with work, college and other stuff, we've not had a proper chance to catch up. The pizza's just arrived, and we're in the middle of tucking into our first slices, having cracked open a couple of beers, when my mobile rings. Seeing Dan's number come up, I grimace.

I'm pretty sure I know what it's about. Women troubles. He only ever calls me when he needs my advice on the opposite sex. He thinks I enjoy listening to him offload on me, that I get a kick out of playing the Good Samaritan to my big bro.

But that's where he's wrong. And where, although he doesn't realize it, he and Mum are so alike, in that they're both supremely selfish. So full of their own problems, they are totally blind to other people's.

When I was fourteen, I remember being ditched by a boy I thought was all that. I was crushed, and what I needed more than anything was a sympathetic ear, someone who'd say, 'It's OK, fuck that tosser, you'll find someone better.' But when I told Dan, he just laughed in my face, told me to get over it. Obviously, I couldn't tell *her*. She couldn't have cared less.

And then there was this other time, when the fashion college I was desperate to go to rejected me. Instead of consoling me, Dan told me to stop being such a drama queen, and that if

I'd only worked harder, I might have got better grades and been accepted. It was such a cold, spiteful thing to say, and it reminded me of Mum, the way she'd tell me to stop making a fuss about trivial things. The way she'd constantly remind me that life was hard, and that I needed to be tough because you never knew what might be thrown at you unexpectedly. She told me that feelings, emotions, going with your heart rather than your head, got you nowhere in life.

I knew all of this stemmed from losing Heidi, but that was hardly my frigging fault, was it? I mean, just because it happened to her, did that mean it should apply to me? No, I don't think so.

Dan always has an angle. He never asks me about my life, never calls just for the hell of it. After a vague, half-hearted, 'You OK?' to which I say yes because I know there's no point saying otherwise, he'll launch into his problems. And today is no different.

Although you've never met him, I've described him to you in detail – namely, that he's a replica of our mum – and I'm certain that you already dislike him almost as much as I do. I show you the caller ID and you whisper, 'Take it. See what he has to say.'

I hesitate, but then you smile kindly at me, softly stroke the side of my face, whisper again, 'Answer it,' and I obey without protest because you always know best, Robyn.

'Dan, what's up?'

'She's finished with me, and it's all because of our bloody screwed-up mother.'

'What? Why?'

Dan proceeds to tell me everything. The fact that his fiancée – or rather, ex-fiancée (whom he's waffled on about before, but whom I've never met) – also happens to be Mum's latest shrink (I nearly laugh out loud, it's so hilarious, I mean, what are the odds?), the awkward lunch (I'm so glad you convinced me not to go, that it would just have stressed me out without

Dad being there for moral support, even though, of course, I gave Mum some bullshit story about the store being short-staffed), and the fact that something Mum said during her last session caused his fiancée to dump him. I should feel sorry for him, but hearing his voice, so desperate and feeble, makes me smile. Cruel, somewhat sadistic, I know, but it feels like payback for all the times he told me to grow up and stop being a wuss. Now he knows what it feels like to be hurt badly. But I keep this to myself, especially because you are mouthing, *Be nice*, and I know it won't do me any good to lower myself to Dan's level.

So I act all sympathetic. 'I'm really sorry, Dan. Do you know what Mum said to her?'

'Not a clue, but it must have been something bad. Something so awful Freya doesn't even feel able to look me in the eye. I mean, I get how important her job is to her, how tricky the situation is, but surely if you love someone, those kinds of obstacles shouldn't be insurmountable.'

Fuck, I've never heard anything so philosophical come out of my brother's mouth. He's a changed man. But I fear it's too late for that.

'We need to find out what it is,' I say. Not because I want to help Dan, but because I suspect I know what Mum told her shrink, and I want Dan to learn the vile truth too. 'We can't let her keep her lies to herself. I've always had a feeling she's been hiding something from us all these years, and I reckon whatever that something is, she's gone and told Freya.'

Silence at the other end, and I wonder what Dan is thinking. Finally, he says, 'Don't worry, I reckon Dad'll do the job for us.'

'You've spoken to him?'

'Just come from their place. I told him exactly what I told you. He was angry with Mum, really angry.'

Excellent. That means he's read the email I sent. Obviously, I couldn't ask for a read receipt. Too dangerous, despite it being encrypted.

'OK, let me call him in the morning. Actually, maybe I'll suggest dinner, see what I can find out then.'

'I'll wait to hear from you, then.'

Typical – no 'thank you'. *Selfish prick.*

'Yep. I'll call you as soon as I know anything. Now open a beer and watch some porn.'

He gives a vague grunt. 'OK, bye then.'

'Bye.'

I lean over and kiss you on the lips, then we clink our beer bottles in triumph.

Chapter Forty-Five

Christine

Now

You're pacing the floor with a whisky glass in your hand. I'm not sure how much you've had, Greg, but evidently, it's quite a bit. Clearly, you think I know about your mistress, and therefore you are preparing yourself for a showdown.

But I am surprised by your tone of voice. It pisses me off. If anything, you should be treading carefully, asking me if I'm OK, pouring me a drink, kissing my frigging feet. But instead, you're glaring at me, as if I'm the guilty one, and it makes me nervous. Makes me wonder what's happened. What you know.

'Where have you been?' you repeat, slurring your words.

'For a run, then a drink.'

'Ah, how predictable, how nice for you. It's good you feel able to do whatever suits you, without giving a second's thought to anyone else. Even your own family. But then again, why break the habit of a lifetime? Miranda was so right about you. You're incapable of give and take, of committing yourself to others, of putting their needs above yours. I should have listened better when she asked me if I was sure I was doing the right thing in marrying you!'

Anger flares up in me. You may not know it, but today has been a good day for me, and now you've gone and ruined it. I'm also livid with Miranda. She's always been so supportive to my face, but turns out Janine's suspicions about her still being in love with you were right. And, from the sounds of things, it seems she's been trying to turn you against me for the whole time we've known each other. I feel wronged on so many levels, and I just can't hold it in any longer.

'So who's your bit on the side, then? A client's daughter? Janine got the feeling she's quite young, although it was hard to tell from behind. Someone you picked up on one of your supposed "work"—' I do the air-quotes thing, something I hate with a passion but do anyway in this instance '—nights out?'

You are momentarily caught off guard. Maybe you didn't think I'd have the nerve to confront you about it so soon, and when you're so obviously in a filthy mood. Maybe you think I've become too weak. But that's where you're wrong; I am stronger than you think.

'She's twenty-six and we met in a bar.'

I throw my head back and laugh, clap my hands, mimicking you. 'Oh, Greg, how *predictable* you are. Poor overworked, unloved man, sitting alone in a bar, looking sad and sorry for himself. Prime meat for some young, slutty, money-grabbing social climber.'

This makes you angry, your face suddenly red and twisted with rage. 'It wasn't like that.'

'Yeah, course it wasn't,' I mock. 'What was it like, then? Love at first sight? You finally going to leave me, like you've wanted to since Heidi was taken? Is the plan to marry her, escape to the Caymans, leave your sorry, boring life behind you?'

'Don't be stupid,' you mutter, but I can tell it's crossed your mind. Some far-flung middle-aged fantasy of yours. I imagine Miranda's reaction to this. She'd spontaneously combust with jealousy. The thought makes me smile inside. And then you get up, move closer to me, and for the first time ever in our marriage, I feel scared of you. Your eyes are wild, and I almost think you're going to hit me. Something you've never done; not even come close to doing because it's not in your nature.

And then you say, 'Dan was here earlier. Freya broke up with him.'

Your words hit me like ice-cold water, and I wonder if I heard right. 'That can't be true,' I murmur. 'I only saw her today, and she said nothing about breaking up with Daniel.'

'She ended things this afternoon, after you saw her.'

I'm confused by the timing. So soon, right after our session? It makes no sense. 'But she insisted at the beginning of my appointment that I shouldn't view her any differently just because she's with Daniel. She assured me we'd be able to keep our personal and professional lives separate.'

You frown. 'Yes, well, that was before you told her whatever it was that made her think differently.'

I freeze as you continue. 'She texted Dan, told him it was too complicated, that there was too much of a conflict of interest. She also said you couldn't deal with them going out while she was your shrink.'

Outrage burns through me. 'That's not fair, that's a blatant lie. How could she do this to Daniel? How could she lie like that? They were so happy, I don't understand how she could be so ruthless.'

I know I'm gabbling, but all I can think is that it makes no sense. I mean, I saw the way she looked at Daniel. It's obvious she adores him. And I never said I couldn't deal with the situation. All I did was express my concerns, which she bent over backwards to allay.

'Ha!' You shake your head. 'There you go again, always blaming others. Why don't you shoulder some of the blame for once? And as for calling Freya ruthless, have you taken a long, hard look in the mirror recently?'

Your words wound me. Not because they are cruel and said with such conviction, but because I know that they are true.

'OK, I accept my failings, I do,' I nod. 'I may not have done so in the past, it's true, but I feel different lately. And it's all because of Dr Cousins. I finally feel like I'm making headway with her. Some real progress.'

'Twenty years too late!'

'Yes, maybe, but that's the way it is, OK?!' I felt so calm and relaxed on the journey home, but I'm suddenly as tense as ever.

'So what was it you told her that changed her mind?' Your foot is still on the pedal, and with this final acceleration, you're pushing me into a tight spot from which I have nowhere to go, except straight into a wall.

What do I say? The truth? But I don't get much chance to think about it, because with your next move, you have me. Checkmate.

'Was it something to do with this?'

You reach into your pocket and pull out a folded piece of paper which you offer to me. I take it, perplexed, a feeling of trepidation rising in me as I unfold it. I read the words and feel sick. Although I realize any number of people could have been spying on me and my lover, there's only one person I can think of who knew about our affair for sure. The same person I should have told DI Phillips about at the hospital. I daren't look up and meet your gaze.

'Look at me, God damn you!' you demand.

Slowly, I raise my head and I know there's no hiding from the truth any more. 'Greg, I—'

'Were you having an affair around the time Heidi was taken?' You don't raise your voice, but your tone is frosty, which I find more disturbing. And then, when I fail to answer, you lose patience and shout, 'Answer me, woman!'

Right now, I wish the ground was made of quicksand. You're right in front of me and I know that if I so much as dare to move, you'll block my path. I have no choice but to stand here and answer your question.

I swallow hard and say, 'Yes.'

You barely move, but I notice the tendons in your neck flex. Your eyes are watery, and you're clearly hurting badly. 'And that's what you told Freya?'

'Yes.'

'Was it just the one affair?'

'Yes.'

Don't ask me any more questions. I can't answer them yet.

'Who was he? Do I know him? How long did it last?'

I don't respond.

You come for me, shake my shoulders violently, and for the second time since I arrived home I feel frightened of you. You are not a violent man, but I have made you one, and I hate myself for that.

'I didn't tell Dr Cousins who it was,' I reply.

'That's not an answer.'

'It's the answer you're getting.'

'You selfish woman, still trying to get your own way.'

'It won't help us, though, will it? I was having an affair, OK, and I was talking to my lover—' you flinch at this term '—on the phone when I took my eye off Heidi and she was taken.'

'What phone? The phone I bought you? How can that be? The police only found…' I hold your gaze, see the realization sweeping your face. 'You had another phone. One registered in his name so I'd never know.'

I nod. Tears flood my eyes, and I am hot all over with shame and guilt. 'It's all my fault she's gone, and not a day has passed since it happened that I don't blame myself.'

'Good,' you growl. 'Was he married?'

'Yes.'

'It's no wonder Freya feels uncomfortable continuing her relationship with Dan, is it, Chrissy?'

Now I think about it, no, it isn't. Even if I stop seeing her, it won't change the fact that she knows. It's not something she can extinguish from her mind. She's only human, after all. Once again, I've ruined everything, and that chink of light I was beginning to see has faded in the short time I've been speaking to you.

I look down at the piece of paper. 'How did you get this anyway?'

'It was emailed to me. That's why I met Amber this morning.'

Amber. That's her name.

'Because I needed to talk to someone about it,' you go on. 'Why, Chrissy? Why were you having an affair? Why wasn't I good enough? I thought we were happy?'

'We were happy.'

'Yeah, right, and that's why you were screwing another man behind my back? Jesus, we'd barely been married five minutes. We were supposedly still in the honeymoon period, so why did you cheat?'

It breaks my heart to see you like this. Hurt, humiliated, confused. But the truth will hurt you even more. What do I say? That he was like a drug I couldn't do without? That we couldn't keep our hands off each other? How is that going to make you feel any better?

'I can't explain it,' I say weakly.

'Great.' You briefly look down in frustration, then return your gaze to me, your eyes narrowing, as if a slow realization has hit you. 'Were you seeing him before you got pregnant?'

I know where this is going. I can't dodge the question. 'Yes.'

And then comes the killer: 'Is Heidi mine?'

I note your use of the present tense. Like me, the note has given you hope that she might still be alive. I don't hesitate. 'Yes.'

'How do you know?'

'I do, OK?'

'How?!' Your eyes are determined, and I can tell you're not going to budge, and I can't bear to hurt you any more.

'Because I made him take a test, OK?'

Your shoulders relax a little. But then you snigger. 'I feel like such a fool. All this going on behind my back, and I hadn't a clue. I loved you, Chrissy, with all my heart. I knew you were vain, a bit high maintenance, but I never took you for a cold-hearted, cheating bitch. No wonder you've been such a misery all these years. You deserve to be miserable for all fucking eternity.'

I am in hell. I hate myself more than ever, and I feel like I'm losing it. I need something to take the edge off. I need some of those pills Janine recommended; booze just isn't going to cut it, even though I don't know if I can be civil with Dr Cousins when I see her.

'Are you going to show the email to the police?' I ask nervously.

'Yes. We need to try and find out whether it's the same person who sent you the note.'

'Do you think it is?'

'Yes. It's too much of a coincidence. Both are written by someone who has it in for you, and both insinuate you weren't fit to be a mother to Heidi.'

You're right, and I'm scared. Whoever it is must have been watching my every move at the time.

'The police have access to special decryption techniques. They can trace IP addresses,' you say. 'But before we go ahead and show them the email, tell me, do you have any idea who might have sent it?'

It's a long shot, but there is one person who springs to mind.

'Yes,' I say. 'Now I think about it, there's a possibility it could be someone I used to work with. You might remember her. Julia Keel.'

Chapter Forty-Six

Christine

Before

There's this mature trainee at work called Julia. She used to teach maths, but after fifteen years in the classroom, decided to retrain as a lawyer. She's single as far as I know, a bit weird, a bit nerdy, but a diligent worker and not afraid to speak her mind, both of which count for a lot in the City.

At my firm, trainees sit in four different departments (or 'seats') over their two-year training period, and those who are adventurous and lucky enough to be selected have the chance to spend six months abroad in their second year. Julia's nearly at the end of her second seat – my department, litigation; one of the compulsory seats. She did a lot of work for me in the first three months, on one case in particular, a case which regularly kept us late at the office.

Before our falling out, Julia never complained. In fact, she was eager to the point of being nauseating. Poking her head through my office door every twenty minutes, asking if she could do this or that. Offering to carry my case, my files, even when she was loaded down with her own. Fetching me coffee, biscuits, et cetera. I think she would have wiped my bottom had I asked her to. But before long, things started to get uncomfortable. It started to feel like she was stalking me. I would notice her staring at me. Not just a fleeting glance, but proper staring. I knew I wasn't imagining it. Even my colleagues noticed. They'd joke about my trainee having a lesbian crush on me. I'd laugh, tell them to shut up, stop being so stupid, but in my mind, I wondered if they were right.

One night, around a month before Greg and I were married, Julia and I were working late, and by the time it got to eleven, it was just the two of us left on the floor. I remember she was sitting across from me at my desk as I scanned a bundle of documents she'd put together for a hearing the following day. But then, out of nowhere, she started asking intimate questions, mainly about Greg and me. How long had we been dating? Did we live together? Was he really the one? Greg's a very lucky man, she hoped he knew that. Caught by surprise, I tried to keep my answers short, not wanting to give the impression that I was enjoying our conversation, which, of course, I wasn't. I was feeling bloody uncomfortable. I think she realized this, because she then made a point of apologizing, said I was one of the nicest associates she'd worked for, and she had simply thought we'd struck up a bond, having worked together so closely for the past few months. Again, this made me feel uneasy because I certainly hadn't seen things that way. She may have been older than me, but she was still my trainee and we weren't bosom buddies. But then, before I had time to blink, she reached across my desk and placed her hand on mine. It was so unexpected, and I automatically snatched my hand away in disgust.

'What are you doing?!' I said. I've never been interested in women, and the thought that I'd given her reason to think I might be interested in her appalled me. I realized I needed to nip things in the bud before the situation really got out of hand.

'I just thought we'd made a connection,' she stammered, going red in the face.

'Well, you're wrong,' I snapped. 'We're not friends, you're my trainee, and if you want to stay at this firm, you need to act professionally. I don't care what you like doing in your own time, but please don't try and include me in it.'

I remember her face, brimming with hurt and humiliation. I realized then that she probably didn't have many friends, or much of a life outside work, and regretted my tone. I was going to apologize, but she didn't give me time. Just said, all flustered, 'Yes, of course. Sorry, forget it. Look, if you think the file's OK, I'll head off home.'

Awkward to say the least. Even if I had wanted her help with something else, I wouldn't have asked her to stay. I would have done anything to extricate myself from the unpleasant situation I'd found myself in. And so I didn't hesitate to respond, 'Yes, of course, it's very late,' upon which she was off like a shot.

After that, she did her best to avoid me – in the corridors, in the cafe, at client events – and generally did as little work as possible for me. Although I initially felt bad for snapping at her, I was glad to have made my position clear before things got out of control. She needed to know her place.

But something bad happened last night – nearly three months on from our awkward exchange – and now it feels like I'm the one who's been put in her place.

There was this big client do at the firm. Held in the top-floor client function room. We had a massive turnout, with no expense spared. As usual, the booze flowed freely, and I was pretty pissed after a couple of hours. As were *you*. Greg was in Paris at the time, pitching to potential new clients. He got back this morning, but after I'd left for work, and so I haven't seen him yet.

I always find these events rather tedious, and with Miranda off sick there was no one about to tag-team with and it felt more tiresome than ever. All night we tried our best to ignore each other, just a few brief glances across the room, but the point arrived when neither of us could stand it any longer. Not long after, I casually walked past you while you were speaking to a couple of associates, and held your gaze, a signal that only you understood. A signal to wait a few minutes before following me out of the room in the direction of the ladies'.

I sauntered down the corridor and then, just before reaching the ladies', turned right and waited in a tiny alcove where I believed we could shelter from prying eyes. A few minutes later, you appeared and, checking that no one was around, you pushed me up against the wall and kissed me hungrily. I could feel the lust dripping off you as it did off me. Although we knew we were taking a big risk, we couldn't help ourselves, our inhibitions loosened by too much wine. We carried on kissing as your hand wandered up my skirt and around to my thigh, and we were so lost in ourselves and each other we didn't hear footsteps approach. But just as we broke apart for air, Julia appeared in my eyeline, and I nearly screamed in shock.

You immediately spun round to see what was wrong, and when you saw her staring at us, your face turned ashen. The guilt was written on both our faces as we stared back at her, unable to speak, but suddenly a lot more sober.

No one said a word. And then, after a few seconds – although it felt like hours – she turned around and walked off out of sight, leaving you and me alone, still standing there, thunderstruck. It certainly killed the mood. It was so reckless, so stupid of us, and I chastised myself for being so weak, imagining all the terrible things that might happen if she talked. The end of my career at the firm, the end of Greg and me, my reputation blown to pieces. Even though that's probably what I deserve.

I flew into a panic and vented my fears out loud to you. You already knew about my falling out with Julia, how I'd upset her, and now she had the ammunition to make my life and yours a living hell. You told me to calm down, think straight. That I should speak to her first thing in the morning, but for now just pray she kept her mouth shut.

–

Last night I couldn't sleep, and when I left home at seven this morning, I did so with a raging hangover and a sense of foreboding as to what awaited me at the office.

I'm now at my desk, summoning up the courage to dial Julia's extension. She's usually in by 8.15, so I'm hoping to catch her for a quiet word before the floor gets busy. I look at my watch. It's just on 8.20. I dread picking up the phone, but I do. I reluctantly punch in her number, then wait for her to pick up, which she does after three rings. I keep my voice steady and politely ask her if she wouldn't mind popping into my office. She says no problem, and within thirty seconds she appears at my door. I make a feeble attempt at a smile and ask her to shut the door and take a seat. She does as instructed, and my insides are turning over because I'm not sure how to start.

But I don't need to; she pipes up first, her eyes sly. 'I know why you called me in here.'

I swallow hard. 'Look, about last night—'

She raises an eyebrow. 'You mean the moment I caught you red-handed with a man who isn't your husband? Your face stuck to his, his hands all over your crotch? I assume that's what you're referring to?'

Her tone is steely, while her eyes shimmer with delight, as if she's enjoying every moment of my discomfort. I want to scream at her for her disgusting behaviour, but all the balls are in her court and it's imperative that I keep her onside.

'It was nothing, a big mistake,' I say. 'I had too much to drink, that's all. A one-time thing only. Please can you just forget about it, forget you ever saw us? Innocent people will get hurt.'

'People like your husband and *his* wife, you mean? Why didn't you think of that before you decided to ram your tongue down his throat? No wonder you don't like being asked personal questions. You have a lot to hide.'

She's really enjoying this. *Bitch.*

'It was a one-off, please believe me.'

'Really? Other people at this firm might be stupid, but I'm not. I've been watching you closely; I've seen the looks that pass between the two of you.'

I'm suddenly hot and angry. And a bit scared. '*Why* have you been watching me closely? You shouldn't be – that's borderline stalking.'

'Don't get angry, Christine,' she snarls. 'You're in no position to.' She grins smugly.

I always thought she was a bit odd, but now I realize she's more than that. She's fucking bonkers, and I need to tread very carefully. I need to bargain for her silence.

'What is it you want?' I ask.

She sighs, sinking back into her chair. 'I want guaranteed qualification and six months in the New York office.'

My heart drops.

'I don't have the power to make those decisions,' I say. 'I'm not a partner, there's no way I can guarantee either of your requests.'

'I know that. But *he* can. His voice matters. He helps keep the coffers full. And that's what counts.'

She's halfway through her training contract, and applications for internships abroad have already been submitted. 'Have you applied for New York?' I ask.

'Yes, but we all know it's the most popular seat. And despite it being a clear case of age discrimination, it's no secret the partners would prefer to send a twentysomething trainee to the Big Apple than an oldie like me.' She pauses, then, 'That's why I could do with some help.'

Another smirk. I want to strangle her.

I take a deep breath, then say, 'I'll see what I can do.'

'Thanks,' she says with a wide grin. 'Give me what I want, and your secret is safe with me.'

Then she gets up and leaves without either of us saying another word.

Chapter Forty-Seven

Christine

Now

Greg looks at me, astounded. Despite promising myself there'd be no more lies, I still couldn't pluck up the courage to tell him the whole truth and name names, principally because I'm not sure he could handle that right now. In fact, I think it would break him. Plus, there are other people's feelings at stake, not just his. All I told him was that Julia had some kind of fixation with me and turned nasty when I didn't reciprocate her advances, and that later, when she saw me with my lover, she threatened to talk if I didn't agree to her demands.

'So you spoke to the partners about her?'

'Just Graham Small.' Another lie. Small was the senior partner at the time, but I never talked to him.

'And he agreed to Julia's terms?' Greg is right to sound amazed.

'Yes,' I nod, swallowing hard. Swallowing away my lies, my seemingly endless deceit.

Of course, it was *you* who spoke in confidence with Small because your voice mattered. He wouldn't have listened to me, a lowly associate. You told him Julia had some serious scandal on you and had threatened to go public with it if she didn't get a job at the end of her training contract. You never told him what she had on you – didn't mention my name, thank God – but you did say if word got out it could seriously hurt the firm's reputation.

'And you kept this from the police?' Greg asks.

He looks at me like he doesn't know me, and he has every right. I'm not even sure I know myself any more. The fact is, I didn't tell the police because I didn't want our affair to get out.

I explain this to Greg, who's appalled. As am I, looking back. I know I should have told them everything, but in my defence, I genuinely didn't think Julia had anything to do with Heidi's disappearance, on the basis that she got what she wanted, and seemed content with that. What's more, I didn't want to chance pissing her off again.

'You should have told me and the police about her,' Greg says. 'It could have been relevant. That counts as perverting the course of justice, you know that, don't you?'

'I know, but I honestly didn't think it could have been her. I mean, she stayed on at the firm after she qualified. Surely she wouldn't have done that if she'd kidnapped Heidi?'

'Who knows? She might have done, especially if she killed her.'

I shudder at this suggestion.

'That's what psychopaths do. They kill, yet happily maintain normal lives. How do we know she didn't murder Heidi and get rid of her body? You're less likely to suspect someone who's right under your nose, aren't you?'

He's right, of course, but his brutal frankness is hard to take. I look at his face, distorted with hurt and anger, and I realize all he must see in me is a liar and a cheat. I wouldn't blame him for never forgiving me, for hating me with every fibre of his being. Truth is, with every passing minute, I hate myself more and more.

'I don't recall the woman,' he continues. 'If she was a mature trainee, then she must be retired by now.'

'There's no reason why you should remember her. And yes, she must be in her mid-sixties now.'

'So why have you bothered to tell me about her now if you don't think she had anything to do with Heidi's kidnapping?'

'I don't know,' I say, pacing the room. 'I guess because of the email. And because I'm desperate for any clue as to who's trying to mess with us. Even if it wasn't her who took Heidi, maybe she told someone else about my affair.'

'Which explains why the email referred to you as a whore?'

Greg's tone shocks me. It feels like an unnecessary comment, but I don't react, because he's obviously hurting. I just say calmly, 'Yes. I can't think of anyone else who saw me with him, so she's the only one who could have gossiped.'

'So where do we go from here?' he asks.

'I need to find her and question her.'

'You? Don't you mean the police?'

'No. It needs to be me. I need to look her in the eye, hear it from her own lips.'

I expect Greg to protest, but he doesn't, perhaps because he's given up on us being able to make decisions together.

'Greg, I never wanted to hurt you,' I say, edging towards him. I try to place my hand on his shoulder, but he shrugs me off and looks at me with cold, mistrustful eyes.

'I'm not sure we can ever come back from this, Chrissy. All I know is that I can't be around you right now. I'm going to see if Dan can put me up for a few days.'

I open my mouth to speak, but he leaves the room without giving me a chance to say anything. Half an hour later, he's gone, and I have never felt so unloved and so alone.

Chapter Forty-Eight

Greg

Now

In the end, I didn't ask Daniel if I could stay at his. I figured he needs to be on his own right now, not have his old man encroaching on his space. I went to see him, though, just to make sure he hadn't slit his wrists. Thankfully, he seems to be holding it together. I didn't tell him about your affair, Chrissy. I couldn't bring myself to, not yet. I will, of course. I just need a few days to come to terms with it myself before breaking the news to our son.

I found a hotel near work – costs a small fortune, but it's only until I find a place to rent. I just can't be around you. You've told so many lies over the years, I'm finding it hard to believe anything you say, and now there's this anger inside me that scares me. I'm not a violent man, but I felt like hitting you when you owned up to your affair. The meaning of the note suddenly ringing loud and clear. You've ruined my life, and I'm not even sure if I want to find Heidi any more. If she's alive, she's probably much happier without us than she'd ever have been with us. Why spoil that? Why inflict her real, screwed-up parents and their screwed-up lives on her? Lives tainted by lies, pain and misery.

More depressing is that I haven't been able to get hold of Amber since we had coffee. I've sent her texts, left voicemails, but got no response. I'm worried our being spotted by Janine has scared her off, and I just pray Janine doesn't track her down and give her an earful. She's always the first to defend you so I wouldn't put it past her. I remember, not long after Heidi was taken, I had a go at you for losing her, and Janine slapped me across the face. She made me feel so ashamed of my behaviour at the time. But I don't feel ashamed any more, because now it's clear that both Janine and I have been fooled by you all these years. I'm certain you've never told her about your affair because she idolizes you, and you wouldn't be able to stand losing her respect. The same is true of Miranda, only in her case because she idolizes me and would have told me straight away. You don't have any other friends you could have confessed to as far as I know.

Despite fearing her reaction towards Amber, I'm still tempted to call Miranda to tell her about your affair. Just for the sympathy vote, I guess. But in the end I don't. Because that would be childish. Plus, I'm afraid she might play the *I-told-you-so-all-those-years-ago* card. She warned me you might be trouble, break my heart. But I didn't listen. I was blinded by love. Blind to your faults. And now I, and our children, are paying the price.

I'm having dinner with Ella tonight. Daniel told her about his break-up with Freya, and the fact that he blames you for it. And now I expect Ella is acting as his go-between, wanting to know if I can shed any light on Freya's decision. Depending on how the conversation goes, I might tell her about your affair because she's even more reproachful of you than Daniel, and therefore won't be as shocked by your behaviour. Whether I do or not, I am going to tell her about Amber. I'm sick of all the lying and sneaking around, and now that you know about Amber, our children should know. And if Amber will have me, I'm going to ask her if she wants to get serious.

You and I have no future, we're finished. And if there's any chance of me being happy in the last third of my life (assuming I don't keel over from stress), I'm going to grab it.

Chapter Forty-Nine

Christine

Now

Greg's been gone three days now, and in all that time I haven't left the house. Not even to exercise or get some fresh air. My home feels toxic with all the lies and deceit, but it's only right that I choke on its fumes after the hurt I've caused.

I've tried searching for Julia on the internet, but without success. She must be retired, and probably ex-directory. I'm not sure why I thought I'd be able to find her alone. Maybe that was just me talking big in the heat of the moment, trying to prove to Greg how sorry I am, how I'm prepared to do everything in my power to make things right and find out who's behind the note and the email. But realistically speaking, it looks like I'll have to bring the police in after all – unless I hire a private investigator, of course, but that seems unnecessary when it would be just as easy to get DI Phillips on the case. It does mean I'll have to tell him about my affair, though. Julia is bound to mention it if he turns up on her doorstep asking if she had anything to do with your disappearance.

Christ, what a mess I've got myself into. I feel so tired, and I just wish it would all go away.

It's 9 p.m. and Janine's coming over any minute. As far as I'm aware, she still doesn't know about my affair, or that Greg's left me, but I am going to have to tell her something; word's bound to reach her sooner or later.

The main reason I called her was for company. If I don't talk to someone, I fear I'll do something stupid. Or maybe it won't be stupid? If it wasn't for that shred of hope that you might still be alive, I wonder whether downing a bottle of pills and going to sleep forever might be the best solution to everyone's problems? Greg hates me, my children hate me, and I hate me. So what's the point? Janine is the only one who doesn't hate me. But like them, she's too good for me. Always has been. And as for Miranda – after what Greg said – I feel like our friendship's been a lie all along. I so want to call and have it out with her for trying to poison Greg's mind against me; tell her how her perfect man's been screwing a woman half his age. But I don't. I mean, what good would it do? Give me a brief sense of triumph, allow me to score some petty victory before I'd go back to feeling as worthless as before?

I haven't made another appointment with Dr Cousins. I just can't bring myself to, despite wanting some of those pills she prescribed for Janine. Truth is, although I'm still cross with her for breaking up with Daniel and making out that I couldn't deal with them being in a relationship while I was her patient, I'm more cross with myself. I told her about my affair, and so it's my fault they're no longer together. How, then, can I possibly continue to see her when my son remains heartbroken and miserable? It would be unforgivably selfish of me – even though a part of me wants to talk to her face-to-face, ask her if there's any chance she might reconsider her decision and get back with Daniel.

The doorbell rings and, thinking it's Janine, I move the fastest I've moved in three days. But it isn't Janine. There's no one there. Just a package lying on the doormat. I step outside, and the porch light automatically comes on. I look left and right, but there's no sign of anyone. I'm frightened, and I don't linger a second longer, just pick up the brown Jiffy bag and close the door behind me.

I take it through to the kitchen, place it on the table and stare at it for a moment or two. It's blank, no address or markings on it, and whatever's inside is soft and light.

Satisfied it's not a bomb, curiosity gets the better of me and I tear open the package, before pulling the contents out. When I realize what it is I can barely breathe, and I blink three times just to make sure my eyes aren't deceiving me.

Your butterfly dress from the day you disappeared.

Chapter Fifty

Greg

Now

'Sorry I'm late, Dad, bloody signal failure. Christ, you look like shit.'

Our daughter comes bounding up to the table, slightly out of breath, yet full of youthful exuberance and the kind of energy I can only dream of. It's just turned 9.30 and she's half an hour late for our dinner at a restaurant near my hotel. Luckily, the restaurant's not busy, so I've passed the time with two beers and by checking the BBC sports pages. Distraction in any form is what I need right now. Amber still isn't picking up my messages, and although I can't bear to think about it, I fear it's over between us, and my dreams of a future with her are swiftly evaporating. I feel like I'm losing my grip on things, and the only thing that's keeping my head above water is the need to be around for our children.

I'm hardly sleeping and I'm drinking too much. It's killing me not knowing who you had an affair with, Chrissy, but I realize I can't force you to tell me. It does make me think that it must be someone I know, though, otherwise you'd have nothing to lose by telling me. Unless, that is, you think I plan on confronting the bastard (to be honest, I'm too old for fist fights), who, incidentally, must be alive, otherwise why wouldn't you tell me his identity? It makes no sense for you to keep quiet about a dead man.

All things considered, it's no wonder Ella tells me I look like shit, because she's right, I do, and I feel about ninety.

She looks well, though, I'm pleased to say. Whoever she's dating, he clearly makes her happy, and I'm pleased for her. At least one person in our family appears to have got her life on track. Although the cynical side of me worries that something bad is lurking around the corner for her, just because our family seems to be jinxed.

Ella orders a white wine, then quickly scans the menu before the waiter comes to take our food order. Once he's gone, she places her elbows on the table, leans forward and asks bluntly, 'So what the hell did Mum tell Dan's fiancée to make her dump him?'

I didn't expect her to be so direct, and I find myself caught on the back foot. I can literally feel my face burning and imagine that it has turned scarlet, a sure sign that I know something. Unlike Dan, who can be a bit slow on the uptake, Ella's very perceptive. Nothing gets past her.

'Dad?' she persists.

I reach for my beer, which unfortunately is nearly empty, and waste a bit of time by taking a drawn-out sip. There's no point in beating about the bush, I guess, it will come out eventually. But so will other stuff, because Ella will ask me what made you confess to your affair after all this time, and I shall have to tell her about the note and the email, and the possibility that Heidi is still alive out there somewhere.

Ella doesn't take her eyes off me as I lean in and say in a low voice, 'She admitted to having an affair.'

Our daughter doesn't move a muscle or even look that surprised. 'Right. When?' Her tone is matter-of-fact.

'A long time ago. Before we were married.'

'And did the affair continue after you were married?'

I swallow hard, feeling ashamed, even though I shouldn't because you're the one who's to blame here. It's a male pride thing, I suppose. 'Yes. It carried on after we had Heidi, and it seems your mother was on the phone to her lover when Heidi was taken. She's admitted to getting distracted by his call and wandering away from Heidi while she was talking.'

Now Ella looks horrified. 'How could she? How could she have kept something so huge from us? Who was he?'

I shake my head. 'I don't know, she won't say.'

'Why?'

'I don't know.'

'That's a bit sus, isn't it? It must be someone you know.'

'Yes, that occurred to me too. And he must still be alive, else why wouldn't she tell me his identity? Makes no sense.'

'Not necessarily. You must make her tell you, Dad.'

'I can't. I can't *make* her do anything.'

Ella takes a swig of wine, her expression one of disgust. 'I hate her even more now. Didn't think that was possible, but I do. She's so bloody selfish. No wonder she's been such a misery all these years. She's swimming in guilt. Well, I'm glad she's miserable; anything else is too good for her.'

Like Ella, I now realize why – unlike me, and despite so much time having passed – you've not been able to get on with your life since Heidi's disappearance. It's not just a mother's grief for her missing child; it's because you know what you did at the time was wrong, and so your addiction to exercise and near starvation, not to mention keeping your family at a distance, is a form of self-punishment.

But in doing this, you've hurt others. You were selfish before Heidi was taken, but just as selfish after. Don't you see that?

Still, I'm shocked by Ella's tone. Only now does it dawn on me: the scale of her contempt for you. 'Do you hate her that much?' I ask. 'I know she wasn't the best mother, but she always took care of you.'

'The way a childminder takes care of her charges, yes,' she retorts, as if prepped for my remark. 'But I didn't need her for that. Children need their parents' love. Parents who'll hug and kiss them good night, soothe them when they have a bad dream or get made fun of at school. She never did any of those things; she simply didn't want to know. She'd tell me to stop being silly, toughen up, go to sleep. What kind of mother does that? I'll tell you, Dad. A cold, hard-hearted one. So why should I feel sorry for her now? And why should I love her? She did nothing to win my love.'

I'm not sure I've ever heard Ella talk like this. For so long she's projected this tough, street-smart image, but that's all stripped bare now.

My eyes well up, and I am heartbroken by our daughter's words. She goes on.

'And she was the same with Dan. No wonder he's so selfish, so fucked up. He's more like her than he realizes.'

'You think?'

'Yep. He only ever phones me when he wants something. He's always been completely self-absorbed. He never gave his little sister the time of day when she needed a shoulder to cry on, some brotherly advice. Like Mum, he didn't want to know.'

'You could have come to me, Ella.' I look at our daughter earnestly. I love her so much, and it kills me that she felt so alone during her childhood. I feel like such a failure.

'You were hardly ever around, Dad,' she says, her tone softer, almost apologetic. 'You were always at the office. Don't get me wrong, you were a good dad, the best you could be under the circumstances, and I don't blame you for how things were. Now that I'm an adult, I realize that throwing yourself into your work was your way of dealing with your grief and Mum's behaviour. But if Mum had let you in more, been more affectionate, I don't think you'd have stayed away as much. She made our home life suffocating for us all, and you needed a release from that. I get that, Dad.'

She's spot on. You made our home so joyless, the office was an escape. More recently, Amber has been my escape. Even so, now Ella has told me how alone she felt growing up, I feel like a coward for doing whatever made my life easier at the time.

After all, parents are supposed to make sacrifices for their kids, no matter how tough that makes things for them. I wonder, do I tell Ella about Amber, now that you and I have come clean to each other? How can I possibly keep my affair from our daughter, now that she knows about yours?

'So is Dan going to speak to Mum?' I ask.

'He doesn't want to see her, he's too mad. Can you blame him?'

'No, I can't. Although...'

'What?'

'Well, something niggles me. I mean, if Freya was in love with Dan, ready to marry him, how could she have called off their engagement so quickly? It's a very harsh, impulsive reaction, don't you think? One minute they're engaged, the next she calls it off because of your mother's confession, despite having assured them both that she'd be able to keep her personal and professional lives separate. I mean, it's not like Dan's the one who had an affair.'

The waiter arrives with our mains, and we wait for him to place them down and disappear before continuing the conversation.

'Maybe,' Ella says, picking up her cutlery, 'but Mum confessing to an affair is still pretty huge.'

'Yes, but it's not insurmountable. I don't know, it just seems a bit hasty to me. And to not even tell Daniel face-to-face, I find that rather odd. Don't get me wrong, I'm unbelievably angry with your mother right now, she's hurt me more than I could ever imagine, but I could tell she was genuinely horrified by Freya's decision and that, given the chance, she'd stop seeing her as a patient if it meant Dan and Freya could get back together.'

Ella takes a bite of her steak. 'Hmm, I'm not so sure. Your problem, Dad, is that you're too nice. Miranda always says that. She says you always see the best in people, which is quite unusual for a lawyer.'

I smile to myself. Good old Miranda. I really missed a trick there. Ella appears to read my thoughts. 'Miranda would have been a good wife to you, Dad.'

I smile. A smile as if to say *I know*.

'I reckon she has her secrets though.'

I cock my head, my interest piqued. 'How do you mean?'

'Well, in all the years I've known her, I don't think Duncan's ever been down to visit with her. There was always some excuse that he was off on some business trip or boys' weekend. And it was never a convenient time for us to visit them. Like she was consciously hiding something from us.'

Ella's right. I've had the same thoughts. But Duncan and I never bonded, so it wasn't like his absence bothered me. Even so, I must pin Miranda down on that one day.

'Anyway, probably nothing in it,' Ella says. She pauses, then gives me a puzzled look.

'What is it?' I ask.

'What I don't get is why Mum owned up now. Did something happen to trigger her confession?'

As I expected, Ella's mind is one step ahead. She never takes things at face value; she's naturally suspicious, like her lawyer parents. I've not got the go-ahead from you to tell our children about the note and the email, but sod it, I don't need your permission. You lost that right when you admitted to cheating on me.

I tell Ella about both. Again, she doesn't look that surprised. Perhaps it's got to the point where nothing surprises her any more.

'So there's someone else out there who knows about the affair? Someone who may or may not be my sister's kidnapper?'

'Yes.'

'Any idea who?'

I tell Ella about Julia Keel.

'And Mum's going to try and find this woman?'

'Yes, apparently. Although I'm not sure how.'

'Should I tell Dan all this?'

'Do you think it will help?'

'At least it'll give him more context.'

'Yes, OK, good point. You speak to him. Let me know how it goes.'

Ella nods. 'Of course.'

There's a lull in the conversation as we focus on our food, but soon I reach the point where I can't hold it in any longer.

'Ella?'

'Yes, Dad?'

'I've been seeing someone.'

She stops short, mid-chew, then grins. 'Really?' There's a twinkle in her eye, almost like she's pleased for me, and I immediately relax.

'Yes.'

'Since when?'

'Oh, it's been going on for about six months now. I didn't set out for it to happen, just sort of stumbled into it.' I don't look our daughter in the eye as I say this. It feels weird, embarrassing, talking to her about my mistress. Still, I'm relieved she doesn't seem angry.

'Where'd you meet?'

'In a bar.' God, it sounds so clichéd, said out loud. You were right about that.

Ella grins again. 'Original, Dad. Your age? Younger? Older?'

'Younger,' I say, almost in a whisper.

Ella stares at me intently. 'How much younger?'

'A fair bit younger,' I mumble. My cheeks are burning now.

'My age?'

'A *bit* older. Twenty-six.'

Now she's grinning broadly. 'Dad! You sly old fox.'

I should be happy she's taking it so well, as opposed to being sickened by the fact that her fifty-seven-year-old father is sleeping with someone young enough to be his daughter. But

I actually find her reaction a little disturbing. Abnormal, even. 'Aren't you cross?' I ask.

She frowns. 'Cross? Why should I be cross? I'm stoked for you, Dad. Jesus, one thing we should all have learned from Heidi's kidnapping is that life's bloody cruel. If you find happiness, I say hold on to it, make the most of it. I certainly plan to live by that motto.'

'Even though your mother and I are still married?'

'Dad, all that joins you two is a piece of paper. She's made you miserable for years. Isn't that why you strayed in the first place? Because I'm certain you're not the philandering type. She pushed you to the limit, and you've earned a bit of happiness. And now you know she had an affair herself, why should you be sorry? Does she know, by the way?'

'About Amber?' Christ, I hadn't meant to blurt her name out.

'Amber, eh? Sounds exotic.'

'Yes, she does. Janine saw us in a coffee shop together.'

Ella's eyes widen. 'Shock horror, coffee! Saucy stuff.'

'We were holding hands,' I explain.

'Ah. And she told Mum, I take it?'

'Yes.'

'Jesus, she's so holier-than-thou.'

'Don't be hard on Janine. She's a good woman, and she's been a faithful friend to your mother all these years.'

Ella rolls her eyes. 'Yeah, I guess. Plus, I suppose she has a lot of time on her hands now her husband's dead.'

I think of Nate. His suicide really knocked the wind out of my sails. He was the kind of bloke I expected to live to a hundred. Always fit and healthy, sporty, loved his job. His death still doesn't make sense to me. We were close once, before he got posted to Hong Kong. I wish we could have kept up the friendship.

'Nate was a good friend too,' I say. 'They were a lovely couple, and we had some good times together.'

'Yeah, whatever. So, moving on, what did Mum say?'

'She had a go at me at first, but obviously the tables were turned when I showed her the email and she confessed to having an affair of her own.'

Ella's eyes are gleaming again. 'Leave her, Dad.'

'Really? Not sure there's much point now. Since Janine saw me with Amber, Amber's gone silent. I'm not sure she wants to see me any more. She hasn't responded to my voicemails or texts. I think it freaked her out.'

'Sorry to hear that, but it doesn't matter. There'll be another Amber. Point is, you can't stay with Mum a second longer. Leave her, be a free man. She won't give a crap, I'm certain about that.'

Again, although I'm furious with you, I feel saddened by Ella's attitude towards you. And anyhow, it's not that simple. Life never is when you get to my age.

I change the subject by switching to Ella's love life. 'So, who's this new man you've been seeing? You seem very happy.'

'I am,' Ella beams. 'But I don't want to say too much yet. All in good time, Dad.'

'What, not even a name?'

She tells me.

'Robin. OK. Got a photo?'

'Not any good ones.'

I smile, wondering what our daughter is hiding; why she is being so secretive about this guy.

'So when will I get to meet him?' I ask.

Her eyes sparkle like stars. 'All in good time, Dad. All in good time.'

Chapter Fifty-One

Miranda

Now

I cannot believe what I'm hearing. It just can't be true. Surely, she saw wrong, surely it's some ghastly mistake.

'You're wrong,' I say, the receiver shaking in my hand.

'No, I'm not wrong,' Janine says. I can tell she's angry, from the clipped tone to her voice. 'I saw them together, and he's admitted it to poor Chrissy.'

Poor Chrissy. How I'm sick of hearing those words. What about *poor Miranda*? It's your bloody fault you're in the state you are, Chrissy. You shouldn't have been such a terrible mother, neglected your child, pushed your husband and your other children away. You deserved all that was coming to you; deserved to have your child taken from you, to be cheated on. But I deserve better. I've been loyal to Greg all these years. Loyal and patient. Watching, hoping from afar. Ever since that day. The day I did something I'm ashamed of –

but in doing so, only ever had the child's best interests at heart.

Duncan and I have lived separate lives for years now, so it was never a question of choosing between him and Greg. I've been biding my time, still pretending to be your friend, just so I could stay close to Greg. Waiting for the day when your marriage would eventually fizzle out and he'd come running back to me. And with Duncan no longer in the picture, how easy would that have been? I didn't tell you we'd separated because I couldn't bear to have you feeling sorry for me. Didn't want you thinking that, once again, I couldn't hold onto a man.

How could Greg do this to me? How could he turn out to be such a cliché? I feel broken, my patience all these years wasted on a man who's turned out to be as shallow and untrustworthy as Duncan.

'Why are you telling me this?' I say faintly. 'Did Chrissy ask you to? Just to rub my face in it?'

At the beginning of our conversation, Janine told me about Freya being Dan's fiancée, no doubt thinking I was going to be shocked. I wasn't, though. Which surprised her. But I am shocked by her latest revelation.

'No, Chrissy's too nice for that. But I thought you needed to know; needed to wake up and recognize Greg's not the knight-in-shining-armour you've made him out to be all these years. I want you to realize he's a shit, like all men, when it comes down to it. I mean you – of all people – should know that, with the father you had.'

It's a cruel thing to say, but she's right. I should have known better based on my own dismal childhood.

'I know you've been angling for them to break up all these years,' Janine continues.

I can't speak.

'Tell me it's not true.'

My silence speaks volumes.

'Well, there's no need now. I think that particular fate's been well and truly sealed, although not by your hand.'

I feel weak, and it's a good job I'm sitting down as I continue to hold the phone to my ear.

'Yes, it seems so.'

'It's not that I want to hurt you, Miranda…'

Bullshit.

'…I just want you to have the full picture. I think you have a right to know.'

'Will you tell Chrissy we spoke about it?'

'No, but maybe you can give her a call at some point, ask her how she's doing? Allow her to tell you off her own back. I'm sure she'd appreciate that.'

I'd rather choke on my own vomit.

'Yes, maybe.'

We say our goodbyes and I hang up.

I tolerated Janine before, but now I truly loathe her. What a load of tosh she thought I had a right to know. She's always been so possessive of you, paranoid I was trying to steal you away from her. And now, with Greg's affair, she's like the cat who's got the cream. Gloating in her self-righteousness, in my dismay.

Maybe this is me getting my comeuppance for what I did all those years ago. For the wicked thoughts I had, for the trouble I stirred, for the heartache I caused. Just to get closer to the man I loved.

Just to get back at you.

Chapter Fifty-Two

Christine

Now

I clutch your dress like a lifeline, raise it to my nostrils and inhale deeply, trying to make out your childish scent. But it's long since faded. It's yours all right, though. The stain where you spilled strawberry yoghurt that fateful morning is still there, although the sweet strawberry aroma has faded to nothing. I wonder, did you fade to nothing also?

When I realized it was your dress, a strange mixture of horror and elation shot through me. The realization that this might be confirmation that you are dead, but equally, that you might be alive, fills me with simultaneous hope and despair. I desperately want to know which it is, but perhaps that's the sender's intention. To torture me, toy with me, raise my hopes, only to confound them at the same time.

I need Janine. It's 10 p.m. and she's late – why is she late? She's never late. I hope nothing bad's happened. I feel afraid, unstable. Greg's gone, Dan's not speaking to me, I can't get hold of Ella, and now this. Someone put this dress on my doorstep, very possibly the kidnapper, and I am all alone. Scared and vulnerable.

Although I've been miserable for years, at least I've always been in control, with my diet, my exercise, my regular therapy sessions. I've lived an ordered, regimented life since you were taken from me. But now all of that is unravelling fast because someone else is calling the shots, making me live in fear as to what further surprises await me.

I place your dress on the kitchen table, spread it out like a fan, run my hands over the fabric, and remember your chubby frame filling it. How sweet, how gorgeous you looked in it. And as I do, it feels like a knife is being twisted inside my guts. You should have been my sole focus. I should have ended things with him as soon as I found out I was pregnant. *If only, if only* – the words pinball round my head until I feel dizzy and sick with remorse. If you knew what I did, how I neglected you for *him*, I'm certain you would hate me. And you'd have every reason to. I would hate my own mother if she'd done the same.

Locked in my guilt, I jump at the sound of my mobile phone ringing. I pick it up. It's Janine. 'Jani, where are you? You're late.'

'I know, and I'm sorry, but Sarah called. Boyfriend troubles. I couldn't exactly tell her to get lost. What's wrong? You don't sound right.'

I love the way Janine always manages to read my thoughts, gauge my mood by the sound of my voice. Sometimes I think she gets me better than Greg.

'I'm not all right, Jani. The kidnapper's been in contact again.'

'What do you mean?'

'I received a package tonight.'

'A package?'

'Yes. It was Heidi's dress.' I can't stop the tears from flowing now.

'Oh my God, are you sure?'

'Yes, I'm sure!' I snap.

She's quiet, and I realize I've offended her. Again. Some friend I am.

I quickly try and make amends. After all, if I lose Janine, I'll have no one. She's all I have left. Now that I know Miranda's a fraud. Although, what right have I to call her that? Considering the lies I've told, the secret I've kept from her all these years.

'Sorry, I really didn't mean to snap. Yes, I'm sure. It still has the yoghurt stain I told you about.'

'Jesus, does Greg know?'

'No, you're the first person I've told. It only came tonight. Someone left it on the doorstep.'

'You need to call the police.'

'Now? At this hour?'

'So what? They're the police, it's their job. And you could be in danger. Call them now. I'm coming right over.'

I look at my watch. It's gone 10.15. 'Are you sure you still want to? It's getting late.'

'Don't be silly. You'd do the same for me, wouldn't you?'

'Of course I would.'

'Well then, there's no more to be said on the matter. Now hang up, call the police and I'll see you shortly.'

Ever grateful for Janine's support, I hang up the phone, then pour myself a large brandy. I rarely touch the stuff, but I need something stronger than wine. My hand shakes as I put the glass to my lips, and it's as if I am steadily going mad. After taking a big slug, I find DI Phillips' card and call his number.

He picks up after several rings. 'DI Phillips.'

'Yes, it's Christine Donovan, I'm sorry to bother you at this time.'

If he's irritated by my late call, he doesn't let on. Asks pleasantly, 'Not at all, what can I do for you?' Trained to pick up on these things, I'm sure he detects the panic in my voice. 'Have you received another note?'

Plied with sufficient brandy, I tell him about the email sent to Greg and the package left on my doorstep tonight. It's clear that Greg still hasn't told him about the email.

'And it's definitely Heidi's dress?' he asks.

'Yes.'

'Christine, you should have contacted me sooner about the email.'

In truth, I thought Greg was doing that, and I wonder why he hasn't. I don't put the blame on him, though. Just say, 'I know, I'm sorry.'

'It's not a nice question to ask, but I need to ask it. Why do you think whoever sent the email called you a whore?'

I realize I can no longer hide the truth from him. 'Because I had an affair.'

'When?'

'It started before Greg and I were married and continued after Heidi was born.'

'And you were still seeing this man – I'm assuming it was a man – when she was taken?'

'Yes.'

'And you didn't think to tell the investigating officers at the time?' There's a trace of irritation, almost disdain in his voice. Not unexpected.

'No.'

'Why not? It could have been relevant.'

'For one, I was afraid of the scandal. And two, I couldn't bear to hurt Greg. He'd just lost his daughter. To find out I was cheating on him might well have killed him. And as time went on, it became harder to tell him, even though it's preyed on my mind every day since.'

'And when did the affair end?'

'The same day I lost Heidi.'

'At your instigation?'

I don't give him a direct answer, because there isn't one. It's more complicated than that. 'I was on the phone to my lover when Heidi was taken. He said we needed to end things because it was too risky for us to continue and people might get hurt. I was upset. I walked away to get a better signal and, in the process, took my eye off Heidi.'

Silence. DI Phillips has probably gone from pitying me to loathing me.

Eventually, he asks, 'Christine, did anyone ever see you with your lover?'

I tell him about Julia, not mentioning my lover's name, but how I didn't think it could be her who took you because we gave her what she wanted, and she continued to work at the firm.

'I see,' he says. 'Well, we still need to find her and question her. Rule her out, if nothing else.' A pause, then, 'Is your husband there?'

I hesitate, then say quietly, 'No, he moved out a few days ago.'

'Because of your affair?'

'Yes.'

'Have you told him who your lover was?'

'No, and he can't know.'

'Why? Who was it, Christine? *I* need to know.'

I've told too many lies, kept too much from the police all these years, and I know that needs to stop if we're ever going to find out what happened to you.

'Please don't tell Greg, he can't ever know.'

'Tell me, Christine.'

I take a deep breath and feel slightly nauseous as I say my lover's name.

Chapter Fifty-Three

Ella

Now

I got home from my dinner with Dad around ten minutes ago. Since then, I've told you what he and I discussed. As ever, Robyn, you listened patiently.

'So, you were right about him getting laid,' you say. 'Why's he so glum, then? Shouldn't the fact that he's managed to hook some hot babe soften the blow of his wife's affair?'

'It should. But apparently, this Amber's not responding to his messages. He thinks it's over between them, that she freaked out after Janine saw them together.'

'Who cares? There are plenty more Ambers out there. You need to tell him that.'

'I did.'

'And stop looking so blue yourself,' you say. 'The whole point is for your mum to suffer – to be alone – and now with your dad moving out, you're finally getting what you wanted. Him having an affair must be a giant blow to her ego.'

'Yeah, but I don't want Dad getting hurt any more. He's innocent in all this. I want him to be happy.' I pause, then say what's been playing on my mind. 'To be honest, I'm surprised Mum told Freya about her affair. I mean, sure, the note must have freaked her out, but it can't only have been that which forced her hand. She didn't even know about the email at the time.'

You shrug your shoulders. 'She's obviously bagged herself a good shrink who managed to prise it out of her, although I think you're underestimating the impact of our note. Plus, she probably didn't feel so bad confessing to her own affair, having found out about your dad's. Maybe she thought it put them on a level playing field. It doesn't, of course.'

'No, it doesn't. Dad would never have strayed if she'd been a proper wife to him.'

There's a brief pause, then you say, 'And about your dad – he will be happy. Once he's completely free of her. Stupid man should have left her long ago.'

'Don't call him stupid. He's a good bloke, his heart's just too big.'

'He's been weak.'

'Don't say that.' I rarely get shirty with you, but I don't like you being unkind about Dad. He doesn't deserve that. Kindness doesn't equal weakness. Kindness equals strength. My mother is the weak one. Weak and self-centred.

'OK, I'm sorry,' you say, edging closer and kissing me softly on the lips. You break away, then say gently, 'I know it's hard for you, seeing your dad suffer, but he had to find out sooner or later about your mum's affair, and the email was the best way to provoke that.'

'I know.'

'She must really be bricking it now, after receiving her surprise package.'

You grin, and although I love you, sometimes you terrify me; I'm not sure I trust you entirely. After all, you lied to me when we first met. It took you two months before you told me the truth: that my mum had an affair with your dad; something your mum told you after he died. That you were devastated to learn how she'd suffered this, as well as the loss of a child, and how she never got over his betrayal, but kept up a brave face for your sake, something my mum would never have done. It made me hate Mum even more. As someone who had also lost

234

a child, she, more than most, should have empathized with your mum. How could she have caused her more pain by shagging her husband?

You came to London seeking revenge against the woman who broke your mum's heart and viewed seducing me as a stepping-stone to achieving that. It hadn't been chance that you walked into the store that day. You deliberately sought me out, to see if I could be of use, but then the unexpected happened. You fell for me, as I fell for you, and now we are in this together. Although I know what we're doing is wrong, plus I have a feeling you're keeping something from me – that's the beauty of it. And yeah, I know I must be a bit fucked up in the head to see it this way, but I can't help it. There's something irresistibly alluring about our scheme, the opposite of my grim, loveless upbringing. I no longer feel fragile, directionless, because you have brought meaning to my life, made me feel whole. You listen to me, take an interest in me, the way she never did, and so I must do what you say or risk losing you and being broken once more.

'Yes, she must be,' I reply, enjoying the thought of my mother suffering. 'As long as she believes it's Heidi's dress.'

'Of course she does. It's an exact match, yoghurt stain and all.'

'I'm still amazed by how you managed to get hold of the same dress and make it look so authentic.'

'Wonders of the internet. You can find anything these days, if you look hard enough.'

You're so smart, and it turns me on. I reach for you and pull your head towards me, kiss you feverishly. 'Tell me again what *you* want from this.' Of course, I know already, but I just like hearing you say it. It's comforting. Empowering.

'I just want to humiliate her. She's kept her affair to herself all these years, made herself out to be some kind of victim. But she's no victim, my mother was the victim, and the world needs to know that. You see that, don't you?'

'Yes,' I say. 'I want her to face up to her actions just as much as you do. I want her to admit she lost Heidi because she cheated on Dad, that she was a shit mum to me and Dan, and that she fucked us up; fucked Dad's life up. And I want Dad to leave her for good. I want him to be free from her clutches, to finally be happy.'

'Well then, let's make that happen.'

My insides froth with a nervous excitement. Finally, I have the chance to make my mother pay, and I mustn't fail.

Chapter Fifty-Four

Robyn

Now

I'm wide awake, staring at your face as you sleep. You're quite pretty, although your unhappy childhood has given you a hardness not befitting your twenty years. I can't believe how easy it's been, getting you to torment your own mother, but perhaps that's just indicative of the extent to which she fucked you and your brother up. You act tough, but inside you are scared and vulnerable. And needy. So needy. You've been let down so many times in the past. By your mother, your father, your brother, boyfriends.

I was like a breath of fresh air coming into your life. You loved the fact that I seemed to get you so well from the start. The way no one else ever has. And when I had done enough to earn your trust (telling you some sob story that wasn't strictly true but resonated with you in so many ways), made you feel like you couldn't exist without me, that's when I made my move. Told you about your mother's affair with my father. Gave you another reason to hate her. Someone who, it now appears, has hurt not only her immediate family all these years, but also others, including me, and a woman who had lost a child, like her. All because of her intrinsic selfishness; her barefaced disregard for other people's feelings. And so, you couldn't be angry with me for long, and you agreed to help me get my revenge.

I don't love you, even though you believe with all your heart that I do. But I do pity you. More than I pity your brother, who, like you said, is more like her than he realizes. You think you know me, but you don't. You don't know the half of it, but my plan was never going to work if you did. My initial strategy was to lure you into my bed purely to piss your mother off. But when I realized the extent of your hatred for her, I saw that you could be useful to me.

Poor Ella. You are just another pawn in the game I am playing. And when the game is over, and the pawns have been brought together – having been driven to near distraction – I will enjoy seeing the looks on all your faces. And I won't care that I might be forced to account for my actions.

The only thing that matters is destroying *our* mother.

Chapter Fifty-Five

Christine

Now

I didn't expect to be sitting here again. And yet, here I am. Last night, after the police came round (they took your dress for forensic testing), I finally told Janine that I'd had an affair. It was excruciating telling her after all these years, harder than you could possibly imagine. I felt so ashamed, so guilt-ridden. But I also felt I had no choice; that having told Greg and DI Phillips, there was every chance she'd find out.

She was shocked, of course. Said she'd never have believed me capable of hurting Greg, and was hugely disappointed in me, especially as I hadn't uttered a word after she told me about Greg's affair. Her eyes were unusually hard as she said this, made me feel like such a hypocrite – which I am, of course – and now I feel even worse about myself. I just pray this doesn't change things between us. She asked me who it was, but I couldn't bring myself to tell her, and this also seemed to upset her, although she didn't press the issue further. I begged her not to tell Miranda, just because I'm not ready to face that one yet. I know she'll ask me the same question, and I won't be able to hide the shame on my face when she does. Janine did suggest I make another appointment with Dr Cousins, though. Insisted that I still need help, and that although it might upset Daniel, I'm better off seeking it from the one person who finally seems to be making strides with me.

But now, as I sit across from Dr Cousins, I feel like I'm betraying Daniel. And although she was perfectly pleasant when she opened the door to me, the tension between us is unmistakable. Even so, I know I won't be able to carry on if I don't say what's on my mind.

So I do.

'I wish you hadn't broken up with Daniel. I would never have told you about my affair if I'd known it would lead to that. He's devastated. And why did you tell him I couldn't deal with you and him being engaged while I was your patient? You were the one who convinced me it shouldn't matter.'

Instead of giving me a straight answer, she says, 'Are you trying to blame me, Christine, when you're the one who had the affair? You chose to tell me about it; I didn't force you.'

Her eyes are hard, her tone accusatory. I expected her to be more conciliatory. Say something along the lines of, 'I know, I'm sorry, I just felt very uncomfortable myself, and laying the blame on you was just me being cowardly.' But there's none of that, and her comments make me feel both childish and foolish. But is that fair? I've said it before, and I'll say it again – she's the one who insisted we'd be able to keep our private and professional lives separate, no matter what I told her in confidence. So I stand my ground and remind her of this.

'That was before I knew you'd done something wrong,' she says, 'before I knew you'd betrayed your husband, hurt others. Before then, I was just trying to help you get over your daughter's disappearance. But your confession changed things. You were at fault when she was taken. You neglected her because you were talking to your lover. All this explains your guilt, your inability to come to terms with her disappearance all these years later, as well as your inability to love your other children. You don't feel that you have a right to be happy, to love, to be a mother. Not because you lost her, but because you lied to them all. Isn't that right, Christine?'

I'm shocked by how cruel she's being. It almost feels like she's enjoying my pain. She's right, though. Cutting myself off from my nearest and dearest was a form of self-punishment. I knew it was hurting them too, of course I did, but I couldn't bear to relinquish that one bit of control I had over my life. Even so, does she have to get so personal? It's unprofessional, surely? Perhaps her break-up with Daniel has coloured her judgement?

'Has something else happened?' she asks. 'It feels like you're holding back.'

She's remarkably perceptive, I'll give her that. I guess that's why I keep coming back here, in spite of her cutting comments.

I tell her about your dress.

'Are you sure it's hers?' she asks.

'Yes.'

'Because of the stain?'

'Yes, I...' I stop short. Realize I never told her about the yoghurt stain. I'm certain of it. I scrutinize her face. 'I never told you it had a stain on it.'

'Yes, you did,' she replies quickly, almost defensively. 'In our first session, when you described the day you lost Heidi. You went into a lot of detail, don't you remember?'

Why does she always refer to it like that? *The day I lost you.* Like she enjoys rubbing salt into my wounds, emphasizing what a rubbish mother I am. Surely, *the day Heidi went missing* would have been the more appropriate – not to mention kinder – thing to say? Suddenly, I'm beginning to have serious doubts about Dr Cousins. She has a dark side to her, a malicious streak I find disquieting, and I wonder if she ever showed this side of her personality to Janine.

Plus I'm still convinced I never told her about the stain on your dress. No matter what she says.

'I really don't remember telling you about the stain,' I say.

'Look,' she says more amicably, 'you're not yourself, you're upset, you've had a lot to deal with in a short space of a time – it's no wonder you're confused, not thinking straight. Are you sleeping OK?'

I'm not, actually. The only night I've slept well was the night I spent in hospital, and that was because of all the drugs they gave me.

'Lack of sleep can really mess with your brain,' she continues. 'It can cause memory loss, hallucinations, have all sorts of unpleasant effects. Would you like me to prescribe something for you?'

Although I'm warier of Dr Cousins, her offer is tempting. Truth is, I'm shattered, and I suppose it's possible that my fatigue is impairing my memory. I long for a good night's sleep – a night not spent tossing and turning, having nightmares, wishing I could click my fingers and magically make things right. And so I say, 'Yes, OK then – nothing too strong, just enough to calm my nerves, help me sleep.'

She smiles, gets up and walks over to a cabinet positioned to the right of her desk. As she opens it, she says, 'Luckily, I already have something to hand. No need to trouble yourself with going to the chemist.'

'What is it?'

'Just a mild relaxant. You can take up to three a day.'

'I only need something for the night, I don't want to be a zombie in the daytime,' I say as she hands me the brown plastic pill bottle. On the front is written *Lithobid*. 'Is this what you gave Janine?' I ask.

'Yes,' she says. 'It worked wonders for her. Hopefully it'll work like a charm for you and have you feeling better in no time.'

–

After leaving Dr Cousins' flat, I stop by the gym and do a 10K run on the treadmill. I want to tire myself out, so that I can sleep without the aid of the pills she gave me. I want them to be a last resort.

But my mind is still racing when I get home around 4 p.m. I wonder how long I can keep my lover's identity from Greg.

He can't force me to tell him, but how can I not? It'll always be the elephant in the room, and I can't have that if there's any chance of saving our marriage. It's taken Greg's affair to make me realize it's worth salvaging. He's always been my rock, the one stable influence in my life. Having said that, I wonder if it's already too late. Greg's not been in touch since he moved out. And I can't forget the look on his face just before he left – of pure disgust and contempt for everything I've done to him and to others.

It's dark as I stand on my doorstep and rummage inside my handbag for my keys. Eventually, I find them and let myself in. There's a mound of post on the doormat, and I am filled with trepidation, wondering whether there are any more messages from the person who's trying to torment me amongst it. I turn on the hall light, pick up the mail, take it through to the kitchen, then go through the envelopes one by one. Nothing as far as I can tell. Feeling relieved, I grab a quick glass of water, then go upstairs to shower.

But as soon as I enter my bedroom, my attention is caught by a large brown envelope lying on my pillow. I shudder at the thought of how it got there. There's nothing written on it, and I feel queasy with the realization that someone's been in the house even though, as yet, I've spotted no signs of a break-in. My eyes dart left and right as I wonder if whoever it was is still here, lying in wait for me.

Since Greg moved out, I've kept a knife in my bedside drawer in case of intruders. I quickly pull it out, then start patrolling my bedroom, checking in the wardrobes, under the bed, in the en-suite bathroom, making sure I am alone. Satisfied there's no one here, I lock my bedroom door, then go and sit on the bed and place the knife beside me. My hands are shaking as I pick up the envelope and tentatively unseal the flap. They continue to shake as my fingertips ease their way inside, then pull out two large glossy photographs and a note.

The photos are of me and my lover kissing in an underground car park. The note says:

> *Show these to the police, you filthy slut, and you'll never*
> *see Heidi again.*

Chapter Fifty-Six

Greg

Now

I'm so relieved you texted, Amber. I really thought we were done, but your message gives me fresh hope.

> Sorry for the radio silence, but been super busy at work. Also had some family issues to deal with. Come by my place tonight, I'll cook. 39 Acol Road, NW6. x

I've never been to your place – you've always preferred us to meet somewhere neutral – so I take this invitation as a good sign. Surely it means you want to get more serious with me, rather than end things? Now that I'm living in a hotel, I feel lonelier than ever, and I crave your vibrant company.

It's 6.30, and I left work early to be here on time. I go up to the front entrance and press your buzzer. After a few seconds, you let me in and tell me to come straight up to your flat on the second floor.

It's one of four flats in a converted white Edwardian house in North-West London. A bit close to home, being only a few stops from Chrissy, but who cares now that our affair is out in the open. You're there to greet me, and we share a brief kiss before you lead me inside and close the door behind you.

Your place is nice, and before we sit down I ask you if you'll give me a quick tour. You happily oblige, and before long, I've seen most of it. Contemporary furnishings, wooden flooring throughout, a decent-sized open-plan kitchen/diner, a spacious living room, and two double bedrooms. You also have a balcony, which you say is big enough for you to sit outside on with a glass of wine in the summer. I fleetingly imagine us doing this together in a few months' time when the weather improves. There's just one room I haven't seen, to the left of the hallway as you walk in. But the door is shut, and you say it's just your study, where you work from home when you need to. When you're not working, you like to keep it shut, which is fair enough – who wants to be reminded of work? But it's still a bit weird that you won't let me have a peek inside. I brush it off, think no more of it, and soon we're sitting on the sofa in the living room, drinking wine.

'So, how have you been?' you ask.

Where to begin? I want to tell you everything, pour out my heart and soul to you; it feels like so much has gone on since Janine spotted us together. There's Chrissy's affair, Dan's broken engagement, Heidi's dress – which, incidentally, I only found out about from DI Phillips. I haven't spoken to Chrissy since I left her, and I realize that might be overly harsh of me because getting our daughter's dress in the post is no small matter and she must be freaking out big time, it certainly freaked *me* out. But I'm still not ready to have a civil conversation with her.

Assuming the dress is the genuine article, though, which Chrissy apparently believes it is (forensics have yet to come back with their findings), this is surely confirmation that the note and the email weren't sent by some random attention-seeker. Whoever took Heidi must have sent all three, but we're still no closer to knowing who that is, or whether Heidi is alive or dead. And so, the torture continues.

But despite wanting to unburden myself on you, I don't want to scare you away. You're the one normal thing in my life right now; the one person who takes me away from the mess my life has become.

Even so, you take my hand and urge me to say what's on my mind. 'It's OK, I won't be put off,' you say. 'Tell me everything.'

I smile, grateful for your kindness. And then I go ahead and tell you all that's happened. By the time I've finished, I have tears in my eyes.

You pull me close, take me in your arms and soothe me the way a mother soothes her baby. But then, once you're satisfied that I am calmer, you break away, look me in the eye and say wickedly, 'Let's go have sex.'

Chapter Fifty-Seven

Christine

Now

Someone was watching us all those years ago. All those times when we believed we were being careful. It must have been Heidi's kidnapper who took those photos, the same person who sent the note, the email and the dress. But why? What does he or she want from me now? Why not stay silent, having got away with it all these years? What is the plan? To terrorize me? Taunt me with the possibility that Heidi might still be alive; destroy my marriage, my reputation, for good? Is that the intention? To break up what's left of my splintered family? Scare me witless, drive me insane, to the point of no return?

If that is the plan, then it's working, because I feel like I'm losing my mind. And what really nags me is that – although it's probably a coincidence – all this seems to have started soon after I began seeing Dr Cousins.

There's been an intruder in my house, and I want to tell DI Phillips, but I can't, because there's a chance Heidi is still alive, and I might be risking her safety. That's what the note implies, at least, even though it might not be true, and she might well be dead. But how can I take that risk? I can't. Even if it's a slim one, the chance to see her again is something I cannot jeopardize.

I wonder about Julia Keel, whether it could be her. DI Phillips left a message on my phone while I was on the Tube home, to say they'd traced her to an address in Chichester, and that he was sending two officers to interview her first thing in the morning. My sixth sense still tells me she has nothing to do with Heidi's disappearance. If hurting me had been her intention, she would have done it by exposing our affair twenty-five years ago. She wouldn't have waited all this time. And besides, I kept to my end of the bargain; she got what she wanted.

It's times like this when I have this urge to talk to you. You were always so good at keeping your cool, at knowing how to play things. You were even more pragmatic than me. That's why you were OK with what we were doing – as was I. We felt able to separate our affair from our everyday lives, as if it existed in some fantasy realm, distinct from the real world. We weren't in love. We were in lust with each other, obsessed with having sex with each other, being dirty, being naughty, and that is how our rational minds justified what we were doing even though – when I look back now – there is no justification for what we did, or the hurt we will cause should the truth come out.

I go downstairs armed with my knife, check every room, then bolt the front door. I then go to the kitchen, grab the half-empty bottle of wine from the fridge and pour a large glass, before taking it upstairs to my bedroom. I badly want to call Janine, but I know I can't. This is something I must brave alone.

I should eat something after my long run, but I don't feel hungry. I am incredibly tired, though, and yet, at the same time, I don't think I'll be able to sleep, knowing that the kidnapper has probably been in my house; knowing that there are photos of me and you together, but not knowing whether the kidnapper plans to send them to Greg and your wife.

But I must sleep. I need sleep badly. A deep, restful sleep. I realize there is only one solution. I go to my handbag and fish out the pills Dr Cousins gave me. Without hesitating, I unscrew the cap, tip one out and swallow it with a generous slug of wine. I pause, then down the rest of the wine and, in no time at all, I am asleep.

Chapter Fifty-Eight

Greg

Now

You're dead to the world, Amber, when I wake with a start at 3 a.m. We're both naked and your bed is infused with the smell of sex. You're lying flat on your stomach, your blonde tresses sheathing your shoulders and back, and when I see you like this, it's hard to believe how rough you can be in bed. You were rougher than ever last night. I could feel your nails digging into my back when I went on top, and when you went down on me I was worried you might bite my penis off. But you didn't, of course, and my climax was out of this world. But now you look so innocent, and I feel somewhat mortified to be lying naked next to you. Perhaps that's why my sleep is disturbed?

In truth, I know it's not just that. Chrissy's affair is always there, chewing away at the back of my mind. I'm desperate to know who she slept with. I just want to see the bloke; understand what it was about him that excited her more than I could.

My mouth is dry, and I badly need water. I creep out of bed, pull on my boxers, then –

with one last look over my shoulder to make sure I haven't disturbed you – I gently open the door and slink out into the hallway and head for the kitchen.

There's a jug of filtered water in your fridge. I grab a tumbler and drink two glasses in quick succession. My mouth refreshed,

I realize I'm starving because we fell asleep after having sex, having had no dinner. I find some cold leftover pasta and eat it straight from the plastic tub. I'd prefer it warmed up, but I don't want to wake you with the microwave – it still tastes pretty good and satisfies my growling belly. Wide awake now, I decide there's no point in going back to bed just yet. I'd be better off finding a book or watching some TV, and hope that one of these distractions makes me sleepy.

I head for your living room, pick up the remote control lying on the coffee table and switch on the TV but keep the volume down. Nothing grabs me. I switch it off, get up and look around for a book, but all you have are women's magazines. I'm guessing you keep all your books in your study, but it's the one room you didn't want to show me, and so I respect your wishes and refrain from going to look in there.

Still restless, it occurs to me that a smoke might help. Since meeting you, I've been smoking on and off. I used to smoke but gave it up when Chrissy and I got together because I knew it was bad for me. But there's nothing like a cigarette after sex, and it's become a kind of tradition for us. I know you sometimes keep a pack in your coat pocket, and I'm sure you won't mind me checking if you have any. I go to the hallway and find several coats hanging on the rack attached to the wall. I try a couple of pockets with no luck, then your plaid overcoat, hoping to strike lucky in there. And I do. I pull out a packet of Marlboros, but also something else.

A business card for Dr Freya Cousins. Chrissy's psychiatrist and Dan's ex-fiancée. Strange. I suddenly get a sinking feeling in the pit of my stomach as I wonder, are you in therapy too? If so, why haven't you mentioned this to me? Especially as you know Chrissy's been seeing Dr Cousins, who was also dating my son. It makes me wonder what else you are hiding. And although I feel like I'm betraying your trust, something urges me to check out your study. A feeling that I might find some answers in there.

Although the door is shut, thankfully it's not locked. You hadn't banked on me getting up in the middle of the night to snoop around. I quietly go inside and close the door behind me. There are bookshelves to the left and right, a desk with a laptop, phone and assorted bits of stationery, various filing cabinets and a poster of the human brain – which strikes me as a little odd – on the wall. There's no debating it's kitted out as an office. But then I spot something rather alarming: a reclining couch to the left of the desk. A psychiatrist's couch. I scan the bookshelves, stacked with various titles on the mind, psychology and psychiatry, along with a few novels, all psychological thrillers.

And then I spy confirmation of what I was most dreading. Pinned to the wall just behind the desk is a degree in medicine from Imperial College awarded to Dr Freya Cousins.

The ghastly truth hits me like a slap across the face. I've been sleeping with my wife's shrink, and even worse, my son's fiancée. But why are you pretending to be someone else with me?

Why are you playing this sick game with me and my family?

And who are you, really?

Chapter Fifty-Nine

Christine

Now

Jesus, I feel sick. Sick, dizzy and dry-mouthed. And my head is killing me. I've just woken up and can see from the time showing on my bedside clock that I've been asleep for fifteen hours. I didn't wake once in the night; exactly what I wanted. So why don't I feel refreshed? Why do I feel like I've got the biggest hangover ever, when I drank no more than one glass of wine last night?

I ease myself off the bed, my head still feeling like it's being stabbed by a thousand needles, while my stomach is churning so violently I virtually have to crawl to the bathroom to pee. And then, sitting on the loo, I remember taking one of Dr Cousins' pills, and why I took it. The photographs of me and you kissing; the note warning me not to show them to the police.

I still can't understand how the intruder got in. There was no visible sign of a break-in, and the only people apart from me who have keys to the house are Greg, Daniel, Ella, Janine and Miranda. And it can't be any of them.

Can it?

Downstairs, I drink a pint of water, make some strong coffee, and slowly begin to feel better. It was absolute bliss to sleep through the night, but I'm not sure I can face feeling like this every morning. I wonder if the pills affected Janine this badly? Maybe they can't be mixed with any alcohol? But surely Dr

Cousins would have warned me if that was the case? I'm about to call Janine to ask if she can shed any light on this when the doorbell rings. It's 9 a.m., too early for the postman. Feeling on edge after last night, I go to the window to check who it is.

It's Daniel. I'm shocked to see him standing there, not just because it's early but because Greg said he was refusing to see or speak to me. Plus he invariably lets himself in with his own keys. No doubt he's here to lash out at me. It's the last thing I need, but I can't turn him away. I've done that enough times over the years, and I know how badly he must be hurting.

I'm not dressed, but I can't possibly go to the door in my dressing gown; he'll respect me even less. I call out, 'Hang on,' then rush upstairs and throw on some joggers and a sweatshirt, before racing back down and unbolting the front door.

He looks awful. Sunken eyes, blotchy face, as if he's been drinking too much, and his hair is greasy and unkempt. 'What took you so long?' he snarls. 'I was about to let myself in, but thought it only polite to knock first. Even though you don't deserve it.'

'Come in,' I say, ignoring his remark. There's no point in getting into a meaningless argument.

He comes in without taking his coat off, then heads straight for the living room. I follow him there and we sit down on opposite sofas. The atmosphere is stifling as I wait for him to speak. Finally, he says, 'So you had an affair behind Dad's back, and that's why Freya feels uncomfortable being my fiancée and your shrink at the same time. You managed to make things so awkward for her, she's ended our engagement. Tell me, Mum, why do you do it? Why do you seem to enjoy making me miserable?'

I'm crushed by his words because what he's accusing me of isn't true. Causing him further unhappiness is the last thing I wanted. But I understand why he sees it that way.

'I don't enjoy making you miserable, and it was certainly never my intention to break you and Freya up,' I say. I yearn to go over to him and place my hand on his, but I know he'll snatch it away so there's no point. I wasn't a good mother to him as a child, so why would he welcome my affections now?

'Why confess to your affair now, after all these years you've kept quiet, lied to me, to Ella, to Dad? Was it purely because of the note, the email?'

I realize Greg must have told him about those. 'No – I mean, I don't know,' I say. 'I wasn't even aware of the email when I told Freya. She was very persuasive. She encouraged me to be honest with her in a way that others hadn't before. And there was something so soothing, so engaging about her, it just felt right to tell her. Yes, the note played a part in my decision, but so did hearing about your father's affair, which I assume you now know about?'

Daniel nods.

'I guess it made me less afraid to tell her.'

'I see. An eye for an eye, right, Mum?'

'No,' I protest, although he's probably not entirely off the mark. I certainly felt less guilty telling Dr Cousins about my affair after finding out about Greg's.

'And what about the email calling you a whore? How does that make you feel, Mother? Not good, I bet.' Daniel's eyes are scornful and it's obvious he enjoyed saying that word, making me feel cheap, making my cheeks prickle with shame.

'No,' I reply, 'not good at all.'

'Can't you try and change her mind?' Daniel pleads. Scorn is replaced by despair, and my son looks about ten again. 'Won't you at least do that for me? Ella says you're too self-absorbed to do such a selfless thing – that you always put your own needs first and there's no chance of you changing now – but is she right, Mum?'

'Ella knows about my affair?'

'Yes, of course. She's the one who told me about it; along with the note and the email. She knows about Dad's affair, too. He told her when they met up for dinner.'

It feels like my entire family is ganging up on me. 'Your father said you didn't want my help.' I look at Daniel, hoping for a reaction, but he remains poker-faced. 'Despite that, I tried to help. I asked Freya yesterday to rethink her decision.'

'You did?' Daniel's eyes are suddenly anxious.

'Yes.'

'What did she say?'

'She said it was too late, that she knew too much.'

I watch his shoulders slump. 'I don't get it. It's not like *I've* lied to her. And it can't be our age difference. It's never felt like an issue. It's you, all you!'

'Daniel...' I say, rising from the sofa to go and comfort him, but he anticipates my move and leaps up before I can get to him. 'I can try again,' I offer. 'She might still change her mind now that you know the truth. She won't be keeping anything from you any more.'

Daniel looks up, mutters, 'Yeah, OK, whatever.'

'Do you want me to or not?' I say more sternly.

'Yeah, I said yes.'

'OK then, I will.'

Daniel's face relaxes a little as he offers a grudging, 'Thanks.'

There's an uneasy pause, and I hate the fact that there should be such awkwardness between me and my own child. But there it is, it's all my doing, and I need to accept it.

'Who was he, Mum?' Daniel's question breaks the quiet. I'd half expected him to ask, but I still don't feel prepared for it. I answer the only way I'm able to.

'It's not important. What's done is done. It happened a long time ago, and not a day's gone by since Heidi was taken when I haven't regretted it.'

'Still not being honest, even after causing all this heartache.' He grimaces, before making for the door.

'Please, Daniel, I'm not keeping quiet for my sake. Other people's feelings are at stake, and I'm thinking of them, not me.'

'Yeah, right, you're such a saint,' he sneers, before leaving and slamming the door behind him.

Chapter Sixty

Ella

Now

I've not seen or heard from you in some time, Robyn, and I'm starting to worry. OK, so you've always been secretive. I mean, I've never even seen your flat because you say it's safer for you to come to mine, which is probably true because I know you live in North London and so there's every chance of us being spotted together by Mum or someone she knows, and I'm still not ready to tell her I'm into women.

But still, I'm beginning to wonder what you're hiding from me. Why you go off for days on end, fail to return my messages, almost vanish into thin air. *Are you seeing someone else?* The very idea makes me feel ill. I can't bear the thought of you being with another woman. Or a man.

Dan's gone to have it out with Mum today. I told him all about my dinner with Dad; what he said about the note, the email (omitting the fact that we sent them, of course), and the fact that Dad's having an affair. Dan almost seemed jealous of Dad, perhaps because he and Freya have split up and – in his usual selfish way – he's finding it hard to be happy for someone else who's found a bit of joy in life. And he didn't even seem bothered about the possibility of Heidi being out there. He said she's like a bad penny: always turns up and manages to ruin our lives, even after all this time. He said there's no getting away from her, that he wishes they'd find her body and we could be rid of her for good.

And for once, I agree with my brother.

Chapter Sixty-One

Christine

Now

It's midday, and I'm with Dr Cousins again. When I turned up without an appointment, she looked very surprised to see me. In fact, I thought I detected a hint of anger in her demeanour, despite telling me before she doesn't believe in strict rules. Perhaps she thinks I'm becoming obsessed. Stalkerish. But after leaving me in her office for five minutes while she sorted herself out, she was all smiles and back to her usual composed self when she returned.

'So why are you here, Christine?'

'Well, firstly, I took one of those pills you gave me.'

'And? Did it work?'

'Well, yes and no,' I say.

She frowns.

'Yes, in that I slept through the night, but no, in that I woke with what felt like a raging hangover. The absolute worst. And my mouth was so dry. Is that normal?'

'Did you have a glass of wine at the same time?'

I feel myself blush, give a feeble, 'Yes.'

'Ah, that's the reason then. Sorry, I should have made that clear. They're perfectly safe provided you don't combine them with alcohol and aren't dehydrated. Did you at least take the pill with water?'

No wonder I felt like death. Not only did I take the pill with wine, I must have been massively dehydrated from my run at the gym. I meant to drink the water I took upstairs with me after I got home, but the photos distracted me. I tell her about my oversight (but not about the photos), feeling relieved that there's a rational explanation, but also annoyed with her for not warning me of the possible side effects. It feels slack, irresponsible, and not what I'd expect of a professional.

'And the other thing?' she says. 'Has something happened since yesterday?'

As usual, she reads my mind. Like she knows something's happened to upset me since we last met. But how can I tell her about the photos, let her into my life again, when the main reason I'm here is to try and convince her to get back with Daniel? It's the opposite of what I should be doing. I'm not here for me, I'm here for him.

So I lie, say no, nothing's happened since our last session. She seems surprised, but lets it go. I then tell her how unhappy Daniel is.

'Won't you reconsider? Surely you still love him? You can't have fallen out of love with him so quickly because of me? And now he knows about my affair, what does it matter? It's all out in the open.'

'Please don't tell me how I should be feeling, Christine.' She doesn't raise her voice, but there's an acidity to it which unnerves me.

'I'm not,' I protest. 'It's just that I feel guilty for breaking you two up. I feel responsible for Daniel's unhappiness.'

'Daniel's a grown man, he'll get over it. Besides, you've been responsible for his unhappiness his whole life, why change old habits?'

Her vindictive words stun me, but before I can say anything in response, she says, 'I can tell something's troubling you, Christine. Something other than Daniel. Tell me what it is.'

Her voice is determined, as is her gaze – it's as if she's desperate to know. My mind wrestles with the idea of telling her, knowing it would be counter-intuitive to any chance of her and Daniel getting back together. But despite being annoyed with her – despite being here for Daniel – I find myself wanting to tell her. Truth is, I *need* to tell someone, because keeping it to myself is killing me. And despite the note warning me not to tell the police, I think to myself, what harm can there be in telling her? She's a professional, and I know whatever I say in this room is confidential. So how will the sender ever know?

'OK, you're right,' I sigh. 'When I got home last night, there was an envelope on my pillow. Inside it were two photographs of me with my lover, taken not long before Heidi was kidnapped.'

For once, she looks amazed. 'Are you sure?'

'Am I sure? Of course I'm sure. I saw them with my own two eyes, held them in my own two hands.'

'Have you told the police?'

'No.' I tell her about the accompanying note.

'What have you done with them?'

'I hid them in my underwear drawer.'

'Look, this is serious, Christine, and out of my remit. You need to tell the police.'

'But what if Heidi's alive? How can I risk telling them? The sender might kill her.'

'Whoever sent the photos is messing with your mind. They're playing a game, and right now, they're winning. They want to make you sweat and suffer.'

'But why all these years later? Surely they must know I've suffered enough?'

'Do you think? Whoever's been sending you this stuff clearly doesn't agree. He or she knows you've kept your affair to yourself all this time, but presumably doesn't know you've finally confessed. All they're focusing on is you being so caught up in your affair you took your eye off your child. Which is probably why they never returned her. They didn't think you could be trusted with her. That's what the first note implies, anyway.'

Once again, her cold analysis stings me like salt on an open graze. It's almost like she sympathizes with the kidnapper. But

I guess she's right. The photos are a reminder of all that. The fact that I failed my child because I was obsessed with *him*. And it dawns on me, how could I possibly explain this to Heidi if I ever saw her again? There's nothing I could say that would make things right. She would only see it as me choosing him over her, no matter how sorry I am now.

Something else occurs to me. Something that should have triggered alarm bells when Dr Cousins previously asked me if I'd told anyone I was going shopping at Peter Jones the day I lost Heidi. Aside from my mother, the only other person who knew I was going there was Miranda. We spoke when I was on the bus, when Heidi and I were on our way to Sloane Square. It suddenly hits me that Miranda's been secretly jealous of me for years, no doubt hates me for having Greg's children. And Greg's only recently admitted how she'd warned him he was making a mistake marrying me and that I couldn't be trusted. And now I wonder, was she so driven by jealousy, by the desire for revenge, that she felt compelled to rob me of the single most important person in my life?

Could she have taken Heidi?

'Call the police now,' Dr Cousins says. 'I'll make myself scarce.'

She leaves the room, and I fish out my phone from my handbag. I dial DI Phillips' number, and when he picks up I tell him about the photos. He instructs me to go home and wait for him there, he'll be over ASAP.

I put my phone away, then go and find Dr Cousins in her kitchen, making tea for us both. She offers me one of the mugs.

'Oh, that's kind of you,' I say, 'but I've just spoken to DI Phillips and he told me to head home straight away. He's going to meet me there shortly.'

'OK, no worries.' She smiles, going over to the sink and throwing my tea down the plughole.

'Thanks for listening,' I say.

'Not at all. Telling the police is the right thing to do,' she assures me. 'You just needed a little push, and that's what I'm here for. To help you every step of the way.'

Once more, I go from feeling cross with Dr Cousins to appreciating her. I remind myself that her harshness is purely a tactic designed to wake me from my passiveness, make me do the right thing.

In the hallway, I put on my coat. But then, just as I'm about to leave, I spot something on the window ledge. A Jack Daniels cigarette lighter. It occurs to me that Greg had one just like it when he used to smoke. But then I realize they must be pretty common and leave without thinking any more of it.

Chapter Sixty-Two

Greg

Now

This morning, when you woke, Amber, I think you suspected something was up because I didn't want to have sex. I tried to act normally, but it was a real struggle, so I faked a stomach bug and took off before breakfast. You texted not long ago to tell me I'd left my Zippo at your place, but I said it was OK, I had others (a lie), just keep it till next time.

Not that I'm sure there'll be a next time.

I know I should have been a man about it and confronted you there and then. Asked you what the hell kind of game you're playing with me and my family, because you're obviously up to something. But I was too much in shock. The fact that you happened to be my son's fiancée and my wife's shrink without either of them realizing this until you came round for lunch is coincidence enough. (Come to think of it, I'm wondering if that's why you called me that morning; to make sure I wouldn't be able to make lunch, thereby enabling you to keep up your charade).

But picking me up in a bar doesn't feel like coincidence. It feels planned. And it's especially alarming because you go by a different name with me. I don't know what you're up to, but I intend to find out – although I first need to make sure you are who I think you are before I do anything rash. After all, Freya Cousins could be your secret room-mate, or your sister, although I realize I'm clutching at straws, desperate for this to be the case when I know how unlikely that is. There's a website for a Dr Freya Cousins who specializes in bereavement counselling, but no photo. That's not particularly unusual. Some people prefer not to have their photo on show to the world. But now I'm wondering if there's a more unsavoury reason at root.

I press Dan's door buzzer and pray to God he's home. When I texted him earlier, he said he would be. Although it's a weekday afternoon, he's pulled a sickie because he said he can't face work, what with all that's transpired. Before long, I receive an unenthusiastic grunt, the door clicks open, and he's there to greet me. He looks terrible, and I feel bad for what I'm about to do but it can't be helped.

'I saw Mum,' he says.

'Oh?'

'She said she'd try and make Freya come round. Try and convince her to get back with me, now that her affair is out in the open.'

Poor boy. He's smitten with Freya. The way I was smitten with you, Amber. But are you one and the same person?

'But you've heard nothing from her yet?'

'No. It'll probably come to nothing.'

I inhale deeply, say, 'Son, you never showed me a photo of Freya. Do you have one?'

He looks at me questioningly, then shrugs his shoulders and says, 'Sure, I was waiting to introduce you to her in person, but obviously that's not going to happen now.'

He pulls out his phone and scrolls through his photos. The entire time he's scrolling, my insides are churning, and all I can do is pray that I'm wrong.

But I'm not. My worst fears are confirmed when he shows me a photo of a stunning blonde. It's you, Amber. Or rather, Freya. Except that in this photo you have striking blue eyes. Contact lenses? I wonder.

'Dad, what's up? You've gone white. Are you feeling unwell?'

'Yes, actually I don't feel so good, son.'

I excuse myself to the bathroom and throw up.

Chapter Sixty-Three

Christine

Now

DI Phillips is waiting for me on my front doorstep when I get home from seeing Dr Cousins. He comes in and explains that earlier two of his officers spoke at length with Julia Keel and concluded that there is nothing to indicate that she's behind all this. She admitted to catching me with my lover shortly after Greg and I were married, and to blackmailing me, but insisted she'd been horrified to hear about Heidi's abduction, and would never in a million years have wished such a thing on me. The officers – both highly experienced – believed her story and I have no reason to doubt their judgement. In any case, she was visiting a client's offices in the West Midlands when Heidi was taken. I don't feel disappointed; it's what I expected.

There, in the back of my mind, I keep seeing Miranda's face. The only person I can think of, aside from my mother, who knew I was there that day and had motive. I wonder, do I mention this to DI Phillips now? Maybe not just yet. First, I need to deal with the photos.

'I've kept them in one of my bedroom drawers,' I explain.

As I lead the way upstairs, I feel grateful to Dr Cousins for convincing me to contact DI Phillips. The photos are too big a deal to keep from him, and I'll feel safer knowing the police are keeping a watchful eye over me. We enter my bedroom and I go over to the relevant drawer. But when I open it and feel for the envelope underneath my bras and pants, it's not there.

'That's odd,' I say, looking over my shoulder at my visitor.

'What?'

'They're not here.'

'You sure you didn't put them in another drawer?'

'Yes, quite sure.' But just in case, I look in all my drawers, but the envelope's nowhere to be found.

I feel both angry and embarrassed, and as I run my hands through my hair in frustration, I realize Heidi's kidnapper has been here again.

DI Phillips looks at me strangely, then his gaze flits to the pill bottle beside my bed. I should probably just ignore it, but I feel the need to explain.

'I've not been sleeping well. They're just to help me nod off.'

'I see,' he says with a doubtful look.

I can see it on his face. He thinks I imagined the photos. That I was so high on pills, I was delirious. But he's seen the note, the email, the dress, with his own eyes. He knows I wasn't imagining them.

'Maybe you should lie down, Christine,' he says.

Jesus, I don't need to lie down! Again, I know exactly what he's thinking. That I'm completely off my trolley.

'Please believe me, the photos were left here on my pillow.' I point to the pillow for emphasis, but he shakes his head.

'OK, OK, calm down. Maybe they'll turn up. But I do think you need to rest. Dr Cousins thinks you're putting yourself under a lot of strain, and that it's affecting your mental health.'

'Dr Cousins? You've spoken to her? She said that?'

I'm confused. And mad with my shrink. Again. Every time I give Dr Cousins the benefit of the doubt, she goes and does something to piss me off. She's not supposed to discuss me, or anything I've said to her, with anyone. Even the police, unless I confess to murder or something. It's a patent breach of patient/doctor confidentiality. So what is she playing at?

'Yes. She called me while you were on your way here. Said she was concerned for your state of mind.'

Sneaky bitch. How could she? 'Well, she shouldn't have done. That's a clear breach of trust.'

'Yes, maybe, but she was worried you might be delusional.'

'Delusional? Why?'

'Well, the dress, for one.'

I can't believe she's doing this. It makes no sense and it's so unfair. 'DI Phillips, you saw the dress for yourself. I didn't imagine it.'

'Yes, I saw it.'

'And then there's the note, the email.'

'Yes.'

I look at him, and again I realize what he's thinking. He's wondering whether I might have written the note and email myself. But for what purpose? To gain attention? To get the case reopened? It also dawns on me that in this day and age it would be perfectly possible to get hold of a replica dress on the internet and stain it to make it look like Heidi's. But the idea I would go to such lengths is ridiculous.

I just can't believe Dr Cousins: pretending to care, assuring me I could confide in her when she's been talking about me behind my back and making up stories that aren't true. Practically implying all this is some sort of elaborate attention-seeking ploy of mine.

Well, it's not, for pity's sake! Someone else sent all those things, someone who's trying to set me up, make me look crazy. And now I'm wondering if my psychiatrist is involved somehow. And maybe Miranda? After all, it was Miranda who first introduced Dr Cousins to Janine. Miranda who tried to warn Greg off me, and no doubt wants me out of the picture. *But does she know my secret?* If she does – although I don't want to admit it – it makes her actions more justifiable.

'She also says,' DI Phillips goes on, 'as have others we've questioned – namely your husband, your children and your friend, Janine – that you drink quite a lot, and we all know how alcohol can play with a person's mind.'

This is insane. I study DI Phillips' face and see that he's deadly serious. I feel like I'm about to burst with fury and humiliation. 'I like a glass of wine, yes, but I am not an alcoholic and I haven't made all this up under some alcohol/drug-infused stupor. I am perfectly sane, OK?'

'But when your husband found you on the kitchen floor with the note, it was clear from the used wine glass on the sideboard next to you that you'd been drinking. Correct?'

'Yes, but—'

'Look…' He holds up his palm as a peace offering. 'No one's accusing you…'

'Well, it certainly feels like they are.'

'But maybe you need to cut down on the drinking and the pills, so we can sit down and think clearly about what's happening here.'

He doesn't trust me, I can see it in his eyes. There's no point in telling him about Miranda now. He won't believe me. I want him out of here, so I can be alone and try and gain some sort of perspective on the situation. I'm hurt, confused and angry; I can't get over the fact that Janine told him I drink too much. That hurts the most. Her betrayal. I know she's an honest person, but it feels hugely disloyal, not like her at all, and I wonder why she'd want to paint me in such a bad light.

Five minutes later, I close the door on DI Phillips. I badly want a drink, but I resist. I can't give him any more leverage over me.

But then something happens which weakens my resolve and has me reaching for the bottle.

A text from a number I don't recognize. There's an attachment, and when I open it my knees nearly buckle with shock.

It's a photo of Ella kissing another woman.

And she looks exactly like Dr Cousins.

Chapter Sixty-Four

Greg

Now

I'm on the Tube heading for St John's Wood, hoping to catch you at home, Chrissy. After I threw up at Dan's, I made tracks fast. Just said I must have eaten something dodgy but didn't want to chance passing anything on to him. I realize how odd my behaviour must have seemed, even for a supposedly sick person. But I had no choice. I had to get out of there; the realization that I've been screwing our son's fiancée for the last six months filling me with disgust.

Dan is so madly in love with this woman, finding out – after she's just gone and dumped him – that his father's been sleeping with her too; no, make that fucking her brains out, is going to kill him. Even though I had no idea who Amber really was, I hate myself for what I've done, and I feel helpless, adrift, simply because there's nothing I can do to change the situation, to make it better. Which is why I couldn't look Dan in the eye when I emerged from his bathroom. I feel unfit to be his father and I honestly don't know how I'll ever be able to face him again.

As I stand gripping the rail in the crowded Tube carriage, all I can think about is Amber/Freya/Dr Cousins and what the hell she is up to. Was it pure chance she crashed into Miranda's car that day? Or was it premeditated? Why has she targeted Dan, you and me? Have we done something unforgiveable to her or her family without realizing it? Does she bear a grudge against us for some reason that, right now, eludes me? Or is it part of some sick psychological experiment she's conducting?

Is she mad herself?

Is she even a real psychiatrist?

There's something sinister going on here, and I wonder if it's connected to the messages we've received from Heidi's alleged kidnapper. One way or another, I intend to find out.

And then, just as the Tube comes to a stop, another thought occurs to me. One that makes me shiver, despite the carriage being hot and airless.

Janine introduced Dr Cousins to you, and she caught Amber (or rather the back of her) with me in Deco's, when I had no idea that Dr Cousins and Amber were one and the same person. But now that all this is happening, I'm suddenly thinking more clearly and remembering things that should have occurred to me at the time. Should have set alarm bells ringing in my head. Deco's is so named being adorned in the Art Deco style. From its lighting to its crockery to its furniture, to its *mirrors*. And that's when a startling realization hits me. Was it really just the back of Amber – or rather, Dr Cousins – Janine saw? Because now I remember, as clear as day, that hanging on the wall at the back of the room, where I'd deliberately chosen to sit, was a whopping great mirror. Big enough, as Janine held eye contact with me, for her to have glimpsed Dr Cousins' face in it. And so, assuming she did, assuming she saw her holding hands with me, gazing into my eyes, why then, did she behave as if they were two different people? Why didn't she tell you that I was cheating on her with her psychiatrist? Why in God's name did she keep quiet about that?

I need to talk to you, Chrissy. And I pray that you'll believe me when I tell you I never intended to steal Dan's girlfriend from him, and that, somehow, we can put our heads together on this and figure out what the hell is going on. But first, as soon as I get off this Tube, I'm calling Miranda. I texted her the other night, while I was waiting for Ella to arrive at the restaurant, to tell her that Dan's been dating Dr Cousins, but never got a reply. It makes me wonder why. I'd expected her to respond instantly. But she didn't. Which makes me wonder if she already knew?

The fact is, she brought Dr Cousins into our lives and I need to know if the story of how they met is really the truth.

Chapter Sixty-Five

Miranda

Now

I feel like such a fool. So humiliated. What's worse, is that my humiliation is all of my own making. I should have known not to have trusted a man. Should have known that they're basically all the same. Selfish arseholes ruled by their penises. Why on earth was I stupid enough to think Greg was different. Why?!

The really perverse part of all this is that I don't even regret making those crank calls, sending those bogus typed notes, claiming to have information about Heidi in the initial months after she went missing. I enjoyed doing what I did because I enjoyed messing with your mind, Chrissy. It gave me a real kick. And the irony is, the day Heidi went missing, it was, in fact, my plan to take her myself. Hearing you yell at her over the phone, having just suffered my third miscarriage and learning that Duncan was cheating on me (suspecting it might be with you because of the way he used to eye you up, but later down the road learning it was actually with his fucking PA!) I couldn't tolerate any more. I felt this burning urge to take something from you. To make you feel the pain I felt. But just as I was about to walk into Peter Jones, I got a call. My father had had a serious heart attack. And although he was a bastard, and we'd never been close, I was still in shock – the moment to abduct Heidi passed. I could no longer focus on hurting you, and even now, I take some comfort from that. Some solace that I am not completely callous. Little did I know then that someone else would do the job for me. Be that a total stranger with no connection to you, or someone who resented you as much as I did, we're all still none the wiser.

I've never been a church goer, but that first week Heidi went missing and Father was in the hospital, I found myself visiting a church nearby, trying to clear my mind and find some peace. You rang me twice while I was there, asked me where I was because it seemed so quiet at my end. I said I was by my father's side, that it was a quiet ward. I'm not sure you believed me, but I didn't want to tell you where I really was because I couldn't stand you thinking I was weak.

After a time, when the novelty of messing with you wore off (it was wrong of me, I know, but I got a buzz out of it like I said, plus, I've always been a letter-of-the-law person, so it felt wild, freeing, to do something so bad) it distressed me to see Greg so upset, and it was my hope that eventually Heidi would be found. But as time went by, and it became clear that Heidi was never coming back, I'd sometimes cry myself to sleep, pray for the poor mite's safe return. At one stage, I even regretted enjoying your suffering. But then, as more time passed, and Duncan and I drifted further and further apart, I saw how you treated Greg, treated those closest to you. Pushing them away, failing to comfort them when they needed to be comforted as much as you did. Once again putting your own needs above everyone else's. And again, more than ever, I became determined to win Greg back; convinced that some day, if I remained patient, if I was there for him, he'd return to me. And I was so close. Or, at least, I thought I was. Until I found out Greg's no better than the rest of them. Screwing some blonde bimbo. And so now, as I see his name pop up on my caller ID, I think twice about answering.

But I can't resist the temptation. I can never resist him. I pick up the phone, swipe to answer, hold it against my ear.

'Hello, Greg.' My voice is cool. Gone is the warmth I normally greet him with.

'You sound upset. What's wrong?' he almost snaps. 'I assume you got my text the other night, about Dr Cousins being Dan's fiancée?'

He knows me so well. Better, it seems, than I know him. But his tone riles me. I did get his text and was about to respond when Janine called and told me about his affair. After that, Dr Cousins being Dan's fiancée was the least of my worries. Rather than respond to Greg, I felt like deleting his number from my phone forever.

I can't hold it in any longer. 'How could you, Greg?' I say. 'How could you stoop so low?'

I hear him swallow hard. Guilt consuming him. He knows exactly what I'm talking about.

'Miranda, it wasn't intentional. You know me...'

'I thought I did.'

'Jesus, Miranda, listen, will you? You know what it's been like, all this time, living with Chrissy. The more I tried to reach her, comfort her, the more she pushed me away. She's not been a proper wife to me for years.'

'So, you saw picking up a girl half your age as the solution? Rather sad, don't you think? I expected more from you.'

'That's always been your problem, Miranda, you always expect more from me, you always put me on a fucking pedestal, but the fact is, I'm human. I can be weak, gullible.'

I hadn't expected this admission. He sounds really upset. Like something dreadful's happened to make him regret his affair. I ask him what it is. He tells me, and after he's finished speaking, I'm dumbstruck.

'Miranda, be honest with me—' Greg's voice is snappish again '—did you pay this Dr Cousins to mess with me and my family, all to get back at me for rejecting you, to get back at Chrissy for taking me from you? Did you send the note, the email, the dress? If so, you need to tell me now, or I swear I'm calling the police.'

Once again, I'm speechless. For him to actually think I'd be capable of such a warped plan is beyond belief. I mean, I was all for splitting him and you up, but I would never in a million years mess with Ella and Daniel's lives. I would never dream of causing them pain. And I certainly wouldn't have paid some stranger to sleep with him. I mean, why the hell would I have had a go at him for screwing this woman if I was behind it all? I tell him this.

He doesn't respond at first.

'Greg, it's the truth, I never put Dr Cousins up to anything. She bumped into my car and that's how we met. It was total and utter chance. Fate.'

I'm too scared to tell him about the crank calls and messages at this point. But I will, at some stage. There can be no more secrets. Even if it means losing him.

More silence. Then Greg says, 'Or was it?'

I'm confused. 'How do you mean?'

'What I mean is, what if it wasn't fate? What if she had every intention of crashing into you that day?'

It seems incredible, but what if he's right? Thinking about it, I never braked that hard at the traffic lights. What if she played me too?

'Give me a couple of hours,' I say. 'I'm on pretty good terms with an officer at Newcastle police. He can do a background check on Freya Cousins for me.'

'Thanks,' Greg says, his voice softer. 'I'm on my way to see Chrissy now, I have to warn her she could be in danger. Call me as soon as you hear anything.'

Greg rings off and I am suddenly imbued with a renewed energy. I forget about the bad things I've done, about wanting to make you suffer, about Greg's affair. My entire focus is centred on getting to the bottom of this woman's abhorrent deception of us all.

Chapter Sixty-Six

Ella

Now

I feel jittery. Mum's coming over. Something she never does, and I can't help wondering if she's on to us, Robyn. She didn't say a lot on the phone, just that she needs to speak to me urgently about something, and that it has to be in person and can't wait. It pissed me off because she's got no right to make demands of me. But there's little I can do to stop her. If I say she isn't welcome, or make myself scarce before she gets here, she'll only track me down and think I'm hiding something.

I sent you a text to warn you she's on her way here, but you haven't responded. I still haven't been able to get hold of you, and I'm worried something bad's happened. Every time I call your mobile, it goes to voicemail. I don't understand why you've gone silent on me. You know I love you, plus I've done everything you asked of me, so what the fuck are you playing at?

I'm looking out for Mum through the living-room window when I get a text. It's from Dan. What the hell does he want now?

Dad's just been over. He asked to see a pic of Freya, and after I showed him one he started acting strange. Vomited in my bathroom, then took off. Said he'd eaten something bad, but he seemed fine before I showed him the pic. Can you think what's up? Does he know Freya from somewhere? Really confused. D

That's odd. I know for sure that Dad's never met Dr Cousins because he told me so, and I guess it's understandable he was interested to see a photo of her. But why would he react like that after seeing one? Unless he was already feeling iffy but trying his best not to show it, and therefore it was just a coincidence?

All of a sudden I'm worried about him – he's the only one I care about in my messed-up family – but I'll wait to call him until after Mum's been round. I don't want her turning up while I'm on the phone to him.

And there she is, speak of the Devil. Walking up the street, looking as miserable as ever. Although I'm nervous, I'm also intrigued as to what she wants.

Guess I'll find out shortly.

Chapter Sixty-Seven

Greg

Now

Bugger. You're not in. You're almost always in at this time, Chrissy, so why the hell aren't you in now? Today of all days.

I let myself inside, at the same time wondering if Miranda's contact will be able to come up with any information on Dr Cousins. I'm glad I asked her outright if she was involved. My heart told me she wasn't, but I had to be sure.

The house is unusually cold. It's unlike you not to have cranked up the heating in winter. It's as if you've been too preoccupied with bigger things to think about it. I switch on the hall light, then go upstairs just to make sure you've not passed out drunk on your bed. You're not there, but I do notice a bottle of pills on the bedside table. Jesus, Chrissy, pills as well as booze? But then it occurs to me that Dr Cousins may have prescribed them. My mistress, Amber, who's been playing us. Again, I wonder if she's even a qualified shrink? Is she really Amber or Dr Freya Cousins, or is she neither of these women and a complete imposter – who the hell knows? The certificate on her wall could be fake.

I fish out my phone and call you, but you don't pick up. Perhaps you're underground, or your phone is on silent. It's frustrating, and I can't just sit here waiting. If I can't speak to you right now, I'll go and see Janine; see if she can answer my questions, ask her why she kept silent about Amber being your psychiatrist.

I send you a text. It's not ideal, I wanted to tell you in person, but it can't wait. If you've gone to see Dr Cousins/Amber, you could be in danger.

> Chrissy, I need to speak to you urgently. I just found out that the woman I've been seeing is Dr Cousins, but I swear I didn't know that until today. I don't think she's right in the head. She's playing some kind of game with us. Miranda's looking into her background for me. Call me as soon as you get this. G

Chapter Sixty-Eight

Daniel

Now

I still don't get why Dad took off like that. It was like he saw a ghost when I showed him your picture, Freya. Almost like he recognized you. But he can't have done, because he's never met you. It makes no sense, and something feels very wrong.

I wish I could talk to you about it. If anyone can help me to make sense of all this, it's you. It's what you're best at. Listening to people, talking them through their problems. Besides, I miss you so much – I miss your face, your body, your conversation – it would be a good excuse to hear your voice.

I pick up the phone and dial your number, but it goes straight to voicemail. Fuck, I need a drink. I go and pour myself a Jack Daniel's, neat – a beer won't cut it – then I go and check my phone again, in case you've texted. But you haven't. Someone else has, though, although I don't recognize the number.

I'm confused, think maybe it's a mistake and I should just ignore it. But I don't. I open it, and immediately regret my decision.

It's a photo of you, naked, straddling a man who's not me.
It's Dad.

Chapter Sixty-Nine

Christine

Now

I look at my daughter, and she might as well be a stranger. We don't even pretend to hug or kiss, we're too far gone for that. Plus, although I feel awful for saying it, right now I don't trust her. She's always been the shrewder of my children, and so I wonder whether she knew the woman she was kissing in the photograph is my psychiatrist and Daniel's fiancée. And, if so, how she could hurt her brother like that?

I long for it not to be true, for her to be innocent of any prior knowledge. But I won't know the truth until I've asked her point blank. Although it's come as a shock, I can handle the fact that my daughter is a lesbian, but I need to know whether she deliberately set out to cause me – and, more importantly, her brother – pain.

'Why are you here, Mum?'

I don't procrastinate a second longer. I pull out my phone and show her the image, at the same time noticing that I have a missed call and a text from Greg. I can't deal with that right now, it'll have to wait.

Ella's jaw drops. For once, she's lost for words. But after a time, she finds her voice. 'Where'd you get that?'

'It was sent to me.'

'By who?'

'I don't know. I don't recognize the number.'

'Show me it.'

'No. First tell me who this is.'

Her tone becomes smug. 'So, now you know, Mum, I like women. That cool with you?'

'That's it?' I scrutinize her face for any sign she might be hiding something, but I can't detect anything.

She arches her brow in surprise. 'What do you mean?'

'Who is this woman? What's her name?'

'Robyn. Her name is Robyn.'

My stomach flips. What's going on? Whoever I've been having therapy with, whoever Dan's been dating, whoever Ella's been kissing, this woman is quite clearly deranged, choosing to play some twisted, elaborate mind game with my family and me.

'And how did you two meet?'

'Quite by chance, as it happens. She came into the store one afternoon to escape the rain. We hit it off, had a drink, realized we had a lot in common, and that was that.'

It's so sad. She looks so pleased with herself, and obviously has no idea that I know her girlfriend.

'And where is she now?'

Ella tenses. Evidently, all is not right in paradise. 'Not sure,' she stammers. 'I've not heard from her for a few days.' She pauses, then says with some emphasis, 'Which is unusual because we're extremely close.'

'She doesn't live here, then?' Of course, I already know the answer to my question.

'Nope. Has her own place.'

'Yes, I know; I think I've been there.'

Ella looks puzzled, opens her mouth to speak, but I don't let her.

'I suspect your brother has too.'

'What?'

Poor foolish girl. I dread telling her the truth, that she's been had, but I must, she needs to know.

285

But before I do, I need to ask her a few more questions. 'You said you had stuff in common. What?'

'Hang on a sec,' she says with the same confused expression. 'Let's go back a bit. So you're not mad that I'm dating a woman? You realize this isn't some little experiment I'm having? I'm a full-on lesbo, Mother dearest.' Her eyes are gleaming, like she's enjoying her moment of glory, like she wants to hurt me badly, like she hates me so much, disappointing me affords her great pleasure.

I despise myself for what I have done to her. Feel ashamed that it has taken all this to happen for me to acknowledge that. She goes on, trying her best to distress me further.

'I like fondling tits, going down on women, women going down on me. And that's what Robyn and I have done. Many, many times. What do you think about that, Mum?'

I'm suddenly woozy, feel short of breath, as a plethora of questions raid my mind. I think of Daniel in bed with this woman, of me, unburdening my darkest secret to her. And I wonder, why is she doing this? To break up my marriage, my entire family? Is she trying to destroy what little there is left of us, and, if so, why? Is she working with the kidnapper? Possibly related to him or her? Again, I think of Miranda, who introduced her to Janine, wondering if she's mixed up in all this. Whether she took Heidi that day, and then... God I hate to think what then.

'Mum!' Ella's shrill voice brings me back to reality and I realize she still hasn't responded to my original question about what she and Robyn have in common.

'I don't care that you like women, Ella,' I say. 'But you haven't answered my question. What stuff do you and Robyn have in common?'

She doesn't respond immediately, seems unsure whether to, no doubt pissed off I'm not reacting badly to her being a lesbian. Then finally, she tells me. 'Her older brother died when he was little. Not the same circumstances as Heidi, because of course we don't know what happened to her, but the point is he died young. But her mum, instead of retreating into a self-pitying shell like you did, devoted herself to Robyn, showered her with love. She didn't treat her like she didn't matter, once her brother was gone.'

Ella's eyes are spilling over with tears, and I feel my own moisten because I know she is right.

I edge closer, try to take her hand in mine, but she backs away. 'I'm sorry I wasn't there for you,' I say. 'I should have been, but I failed you. I know it's no excuse, but I couldn't bear to feel the same pain I felt after losing Heidi should something bad have happened to you or Daniel. Didn't feel I'd be able to survive. It was easier to switch my feelings off.'

Ella gives me a look as if to say, *That's the lamest excuse I've ever heard*, and she's entirely within her rights to do so.

I go on. 'But it wasn't just about losing Heidi; there was something else, something I was so ashamed of – it caused me to shut myself off from everyone, made me feel like I wasn't fit to be a mother. Didn't deserve to be one.'

'You mean your affair with a married man?'

I already knew from Daniel that Greg told Ella about my affair, but now I realize she already knew from someone else. Dr Cousins, aka Robyn.

'Robyn told you about that, I assume?' I say.

Ella frowns, looks uncomfortable, as if she's hiding something. 'No, Dad did,' she says defensively. 'Didn't Dan tell you? Why would you think it was Robyn?'

I stare at her long and hard. 'Don't lie to me, Ella.'

She bites her lip, shrugs her shoulders, says, 'OK. You might as well know, I suppose. Robyn's mum was married to the arsehole you had an affair with. Robyn came here seeking revenge against you. Initially, she wanted to use me to get to you, but then we fell in love and I forgave her. She realized how much you hurt me, and that I wanted you to suffer as much as her mum had suffered. Jesus, Mum, the woman lost a child like you did; how could you have done that to her?'

I don't move, my head still trying to make sense of this latest bombshell. What she says isn't true, so why would Robyn tell her this? And then, a horrifying thought hits me. 'Did you send that note, Ella? Did you send Dad that email?'

Guilt swathes her face. 'Yes.'

'So Heidi's not alive?'

'Fuck knows.' She shrugs her shoulders again. 'We just did it to mess with you.'

'And the dress?'

'Fake.'

All this time I've been living in hope that Heidi might still be alive, when it was just a hoax. I can't hold back. I slap my daughter hard and she doubles back in shock, her eyes wide with horror as she presses her hand to her cheek. My own hand stings, but it's nothing compared to the pain shooting through my chest.

'The postmark for the note was somewhere up North. Who helped you? Is it someone we know? Someone close to us?' This is her time to own up to Miranda's involvement.

Ella's a bright girl. She twigs immediately.

'Are you serious, Mum? You think Miranda put me up to this?'

'It's not an unreasonable question to ask.'

'She didn't, OK.'

'So why was it postmarked Sunderland?'

'Well, I had to make it look authentic, didn't I? Also, it was safer for me to send it from up there. No chance of it being traced back to me. Used gloves, of course. And by the way, the email was encrypted. I sent it from some random internet cafe, using a temporary address which is now defunct.'

I'm flabbergasted by the lengths my daughter has gone to, to cause me pain.

'And what about the photos?'

Still clutching her cheek, Ella looks puzzled. Genuinely puzzled. 'What photos?'

'The photos of me and my lover. The ones you left on my bed.'

'I didn't leave any photos on your bed. Really, I didn't.'

She appears to be telling the truth, but I'm confused, because it can't have been Robyn, because I was with her, aka Dr Cousins, in her office when the photos would have been left. Which only leaves one other possibility.

'Ella, do you know what Robyn's mother's name is? What she looks like?'

'Cynthia. And yes, I've seen a photo, but she lives abroad. She's a decent sort. Forgave her husband for shagging you, gave him another chance when he promised to end things with you.'

A sickening realization is progressively dawning on me, and I feel decidedly unwell. I don't want it to be true, but it's the only explanation I can think of. And now, it's time to tell Ella who Robyn is.

'Sit down, Ella.'

'Why?'

'Do it.'

She does as I ask, and I bring up the image of her and Robyn again, and point to her girlfriend. 'This is my psychiatrist, Dr Freya Cousins, your brother's ex-fiancée.'

My voice is measured, my expression deadpan, but she looks at me and bursts into hysterical laughter. 'Have you gone mad? What the fuck are you saying?'

'I'm saying you've been used. This is Dr Freya Cousins. Or at least, that's what she calls herself to me and your brother.'

Ella's face is suddenly white. 'Stop it, you evil bitch. Stop telling lies. What are you, sick?'

'No, but I think this woman is.'

She gets up, starts pacing the room. 'No, it can't be true. Janine introduced you to Dr Cousins, didn't she? She was her psychiatrist first, wasn't she?'

'Yes,' I say faintly. 'She was.'

Ella stops pacing, looks me straight in the eye. 'So she must be a real shrink and you must be mistaken. Maybe they look alike?'

'I'm not mistaken, this is her – ask Daniel.'

As Ella continues to stare at me, aghast, my phone rings. It's Greg. Probably following up his earlier call and text. I realize it must be urgent.

'Greg?'

From the corner of my eye, I notice that Ella is shaking. I want to comfort her, but for now I listen to Greg.

'Chrissy, why haven't you texted me back? Didn't you read my message?'

'No, I've been too caught up with something. I'm with Ella. Something bad's going on, Greg, and I don't think Dr Cousins can be trusted.'

'I know.'

'You do?' I can't think how he can, but he's obviously about to tell me.

'Yes. Chrissy, I can't bear to tell you this, but Dr Cousins is the woman I've been having an affair with.'

Chapter Seventy

Daniel

Now

Bastard. Bitch.

I want to kill you both. No wonder he didn't show up that day I brought you round for lunch, Freya. But then again, when I think about his reaction to your photo, it really seemed like he didn't realize he'd been screwing my fiancée. Could have all been an act, of course. Jesus, I don't know what to think.

I'm so confused, so fucking miserable. My dad's dick has been inside you, and I feel like I want to die. I wonder, did *you* know? Did you know I was his son? Can it be chance? Are you just some slut who likes to shag around and happened to be shagging a father and son without knowing it? Even this – the best-case scenario – doesn't make me feel any better. Or – worst case – is it part of some sick psychological experiment you're conducting at our expense? I know Janine introduced you to Mum, but I wonder if she knows you're a worthless whore. I dial your number again but get nothing.

Then I try calling Mum and Ella, but they're not picking up either. Everyone's abandoned me, and I feel like I'm at breaking point.

I know what I'm going to do. I'm going to find Dad, and when I do, I'm going to smash his face in. But not yet. Right now, I need to stop feeling this pain. Just for a bit at least.

I go to my bedroom and find the special batch I keep for emergencies. I've not got high in ages, you got me off that stuff, you were my high. But now that I know it was all a lie, I can't stop myself.

I prepare my fix like an old pro, only a bit more than the usual amount, but I don't care, I need it, and as I plunge the needle into my vein, all the pain, all the hurt you've inflicted on me swiftly dissolves. And I get the most divine sense of relief as I leave this world and the unceasing misery it has caused me.

Chapter Seventy-One

Christine

Now

This cannot be happening. This nightmare I am living cannot possibly have got worse. It just can't.

'Chrissy, are you there?' I vaguely hear Greg's voice on the line.

I remain rooted to the spot, my ears plugged with cotton wool.

And then I hear Ella saying, 'Mum, what's wrong, tell me, what's Dad saying?'

It's the ultimate humiliation. All this time I've been laying myself bare before Dr Cousins she was tricking me, laughing at me behind my back. Seducing my husband, son and daughter with sex, seducing me into confessing my sins. But why? Who is she? Why does she have a problem with me?

'Chrissy!' Greg repeats.

'Greg, I'm with Ella. She knows Dr Cousins too. Or rather, she knows her as Robyn.' I glance at Ella, who looks pale.

'What?' Greg says weakly. 'How does she know her?'

'They've been seeing one another.'

Silence. I picture Greg trying to digest this information. Not just the fact that this woman has got her claws into our daughter too, but that Ella is gay.

'She's been seeing a woman?' Greg says. 'Ella's a lesbian?'

I glance over at Ella, who's watching me intently, then put Greg on speaker for her benefit.

'I… I'm not entirely sure. You're on speaker now.' I glance at Ella. 'But whoever this woman is – whatever her real name is – she seems to have cast a spell over Ella, the same way she's cast a spell over the rest of us.'

Ella shakes her head. She's in denial, doesn't want to believe it, the fact that she's been used the way we all have.

'Why, what the hell has she got against us?' Greg asks, his voice full of fury.

'I'm not sure. She told Ella that her father had an affair with me, and that our affair broke her mother's heart, and she wanted to get her revenge against me. But I swear I didn't know Dr Cousins' father, Greg. He wasn't my lover, that was someone else. Even worse, she made Ella send you that email, and me the note and the dress, a very convincing fake apparently. Even the police judged it to be authentic. But she didn't send me the photos.'

'What photos?'

I realize I haven't told Greg about the photos left on our bed, so I fill him in, including the fact that they've gone missing, and that DI Phillips thinks I'm delusional.

'So someone's been in the house? Do you think it was her?'

'It can't have been, because I was with her at the time. At first I thought Miranda might be involved, but now I'm pretty certain she's not.'

'I also had my suspicions, but not any more. Miranda's doing some digging for me.' Greg pauses, then says, 'So, someone else is helping her. Ella, you have a key. Did you leave them? Be honest.'

'No, Dad, I know nothing about any photos,' Ella insists. She still looks pale, shell-shocked by what's happened. It's understandable; we all are. Just like Daniel, she's besotted with this woman and she must feel devastated by her betrayal.

'Are you sure there were no other men, Chrissy?' I can hear the doubt in Greg's voice, and it's no surprise. After all, I hid my affair from him all these years. But it's the truth, and I need him to believe me.

'Yes, Greg, I swear I only ever cheated on you with one man. I really have no idea who this woman's father is, but clearly she's got the wrong end of the stick.' I pause, then ask, 'Does Daniel know you've been seeing his fiancée?'

'What?!' Ella exclaims, placing her hand over her mouth. I realize she didn't hear the first part of my conversation with Greg before I put him on speaker, and I watch her double back in shock, nearly falling onto the staircase, but somehow managing to steady herself on the bottom stair.

'Ella, Christ, I'm sorry; take her off speaker, Chrissy.'

'She has to hear this, Greg. She needs to know what kind of person we're dealing with.'

I hear Greg sigh. 'OK. Ella, the woman I told you I was seeing is Robyn, although she told me her name was Amber. I had no idea until I asked Daniel to show me a photo of Freya. She lied to us all.'

'What are you implying?' Ella says. 'That she's some kind of sociopath?' Tears flood her eyes.

'I don't know, Ella,' Greg replies, 'but she's clearly not well.'

'But why hurt you, me and Dan? She seemed certain that Mum had an affair with her dad. But why hurt us?'

Ella looks at me with desperate eyes. Desperate to believe her girlfriend is innocent, that there's a simple, rational explanation behind it all. All I can think is that by hurting them, she was hurting me.

I am hurt, in so many ways. Including by Ella's cruel deception, by the fact that she deliberately led Greg and me to believe that Heidi might still be alive.

'How could you, Ella?' I can't stop myself from saying. 'How could you give me and your father false hope? How *could* you?'

My eyes are heavy with tears as I think of the rekindled hope that filled my heart. The chance of discovering, after all these years, that Heidi is alive and well, the chance of being reunited with her. But it was all just a cruel prank, in which my other daughter played a key role.

'How could I? How could I?' she mimics, her face like thunder. 'Have I still not got it through your thick skull? Well, allow me to elaborate. Because you were a shitty mother. How I would have killed for you to give me one tenth of the affection you still poured Heidi's way. How do you think Dan and I felt seeing you pine for her day after day, year after year? We were here, alive and well. But it was like we didn't exist. It made us feel worthless, unwanted, a burden on your time. And later, when I was growing up, going through all kinds of changes, I needed you more than ever. But you didn't want to know when I got picked on at school, you told me to grow a spine, get tough, because you have to be tough to survive in this world.'

'She's right, Chrissy,' Greg says unhelpfully. Although, who am I to judge? 'I'm sorry, Ells.' I can hear the choke in his voice. 'I'm so sorry I wasn't around more.'

Ella is literally bawling now. And before long, I am too. I always knew I'd been a terrible mother, but somehow, I'd pushed the thought to the back of my mind, swallowed my shame, my guilt, because neither Ella nor Daniel had ever confronted me about it, the way Ella just did. But now it's out in the open, now she's bared her soul, I realize just how badly I've let her down. If I'd been there for her, she would probably have turned out very different. We could have been so close, but instead she hates me, and I hardly know my own daughter. I have made her hard and vicious. And vengeful. And now I understand why she wanted to hurt me. Reasons which Dr Cousins took advantage of. Ella may act tough, but she's vulnerable inside and desperate for love, and Dr Cousins manipulated that to get what she wanted.

But *why*, I ask myself again? What could I have possibly done to harm her when I know I didn't sleep with her father? And why did Janine…

Again, the unthinkable occurs to me, and it's like being hit by a bullet. But I don't say anything to Greg or Ella yet, in case I'm wrong. I desperately want to be wrong, because the truth is too hideous to contemplate, but it's the only thing that makes sense. The only explanation for what's happening to us all.

For now, I put it to one side and ask Greg again if Daniel knows.

'Christ, no.' His voice is frail, and I can detect gentle sobbing. Like me, he's telling himself he's being punished for his infidelity. But unlike me, he is not at fault. I pushed Greg away, I drove him into *her* arms. I – and only I – am to blame.

'I couldn't even look him in the eye when I realized who she was,' he carries on. 'But I'm pretty sure he suspects something's wrong because of my reaction.'

'He does,' Ella says. 'He sent me a text, saying as much.'

'Shit,' Greg sighs. 'But how the hell can I tell him I've been sleeping with his girlfriend, Chrissy? If he finds out, I'm not sure he'll ever recover. I think it could tip him over the edge.'

He's referring to Daniel's drug habit, of course, which once caused him to end up in A&E. He seemed to have put all that behind him with Freya. In fact, when he came round for lunch, I couldn't ever remember seeing him looking so well. I was so thankful to her for saving him. He'd finally found a woman he loved and trusted. But now, just like me, she's let him down. Her ending things hit him badly enough, but like Greg, I can't see how he'd ever recover from learning the truth about his father's relationship with her.

'Greg, where are you?'

'On my way to Janine's.'

I freeze. 'Janine's? Why?'

Ella and I lock eyes. She doesn't know what I'm thinking. I take Greg off speaker. 'Greg, go back home. Don't go to Janine's.'

'What? Why?' Greg proceeds to tell me about the mirrors in Deco's. And once again, the unthinkable is suddenly looking more plausible. 'Assuming I'm right and Janine saw her face,' he continues, 'why didn't she tell you that Amber was Dr Cousins? That's odd, don't you think, and warrants an explanation?'

'Yes, I agree. But I'm the one who should confront her, not you. She's my best friend, not yours. So it has to be me, do you hear me, Greg?'

After a brief silence, I receive a grudging, 'Yes, OK. But let me know what she's got to say for herself as soon as you can.'

'OK, I will.'

'Promise.'

'I promise. Now go home and wait for my call.'

'Be careful.'

'Don't worry, I will.' I don't give him the chance to say anything more and hang up.

I glance over at Ella, who doesn't look well. I go to her, kneel and place my hand on hers. I expect her to yank it away but to my surprise she doesn't, and I take comfort from this. I put my face up to hers, kiss her forehead and whisper, 'I'm so sorry, Ella.' Then again try to rationalise my behaviour even though I know in my heart there is no excuse.

She's still crying, and I wipe away her tears with my fingertips.

'But that's so stupid, Mum – all those years wasted.'

'I know,' I nod. 'I know I've fucked everything up. But I want to make up for it now. Please tell me it's not too late.'

She doesn't respond. Just lays her head on my shoulder, brings her arms around my neck and squeezes me hard. It's like she's five years old again, and her embrace feels warm and wonderful.

After a few minutes, she breaks away and I caress her cheeks tenderly and look her straight in the eye. 'Ella, is there anything you can tell me? Anything that might help us have a better understanding of who Robyn is and why she's doing this?'

Ella shakes her head, wipes her nose with the back of her hand. 'No, I mean, I told you. She said that you and her dad had an affair, and that although her mum found out and eventually forgave him, she never really got over it. Robyn said we'd both been hurt by you. Me, because you weren't a good mum, and her, because you hurt her mum. She also said that her dad died six months ago of a heart attack.'

'Did she ever tell you his name?'

'No. Just her mum's. Cynthia, like I told you.'

'OK, thanks, darling. Stay here.'

'Mum, I don't want to be alone. I'm frightened.'

I don't say it out loud, but I'm frightened for her too. Because although I have my suspicions as to who's behind all this, that's all they are right now. Suspicions. There are too many ifs and buts, too many pieces of the puzzle I don't know how to fit together just yet, and all that makes me nervous and unsure of my next move.

'Drive to your brother's,' I say. 'See how he's doing, but don't tell him about your dad and Freya or whatever the hell her name is.'

'He's bound to ask if I know what's up with Dad.'

'Just say you have no idea. Don't mention any of this until I've sorted things out.'

'What are you going to do, Mum?'

'Don't worry about that for now. I'll text or phone when I have something.'

'OK,' she nods. 'Be safe, Mum.'

'Thanks.' I smile, grateful that my daughter no longer appears to despise me. But someone does, and I need to find out for certain who that is.

Chapter Seventy-Two

Greg

Now

Sitting here alone, the house seems so big and empty, and it makes me feel vulnerable, twitchy. I get up and pour myself a whisky, then go and sit back down, switch on the TV, flick through the channels, but quickly switch it off again. My pride is wounded by the way Amber tricked me into believing she cared for me, and I feel nothing but shame knowing that her walking into the bar that day was no coincidence; that she somehow knew how low, how starved of affection I was, and played on this, using her beauty and feminine charms to entrap me. I was a sure thing, and I ate her seduction up like a naive schoolboy.

I am disgusted with myself; a pathetic middle-aged man who should have known better. Of course, I never set out to hurt my son, but how will he ever forgive me if he discovers the truth?

The hardest thing is not knowing why all this is happening. I believed Chrissy to be genuine when she swore she didn't have an affair with Amber's father, but I wonder, how does she know for sure that Amber (or Dr Cousins to her) isn't, in fact, the daughter of the man she had an affair with? Couldn't she be? Couldn't Chrissy be legitimately mistaken? Unless, that is, her former lover is still alive and lives locally, in which case she may know the identity of his children.

I thought she might finally have told me who her lover was while we were on the phone, but she avoided the subject again.

It makes me even more certain it's someone I know or once knew. That's why her guilt is so acute. And Janine's silence still puzzles me. Assuming she saw Dr Cousins' face, she should have been livid with her, stormed her way into her office and demanded to know what the hell she was up to. Surely that would be the reaction of a best friend?

I don't care what Chrissy says, Janine's my friend too, and I can't sit here any longer. I'm going over to her place, and I'm going to ask her myself what the hell's going on. Besides, why should I listen to Chrissy? Her affair is the nub of our children's pain. And even now she refuses to be upfront with me. For once, I'm going to play it my way, and I don't care if that pisses her off.

I get up, make for the hallway, sling on my coat and head out the door.

–

Janine lives in Swiss Cottage, and so I could easily walk there. But it's cold and damp, and I just can't face it, so I hop on the Tube and in no time at all am exiting the station and turning right onto her street. I'm bound to make it there before Chrissy. As I walk I send a quick text to Miranda, **Any joy?** even though I know she would have called the minute she learned anything worthwhile.

When I reach Janine's house my stomach is in knots. I've always felt comfortable around her. She's never been one to put on airs and graces and she's been a consistently loyal friend, protective of Chrissy and our family. So it disturbs me that I should suddenly feel uneasy around her.

I press her buzzer, nerves pricking my insides, and at the same time receive a text from Chrissy, telling me she's on her way to Janine's and checking that I'm at home. I quickly respond, **No, at Janine's**, then put my phone on silent and slip it into my pocket. I expect she'll be livid with me and that she'll try and call, but this way I won't hear her.

Just then, the door opens and Janine is there to greet me. She has this kind of glassy smile on her face, looks so calm, almost like she's on tranquillizers. It unnerves me.

'Janine, are you OK?' I ask as she beckons for me to come inside.

'Never better,' she smiles. 'Would you like some tea? I've just made a cup for myself.'

'No, I'm fine, thanks.'

We sit down next to each other on a sofa in the living room, and I can't hold it in any longer. 'Janine, why didn't you tell Chrissy you saw me with Dr Cousins in Deco's? I mean, thinking back I'm pretty certain you did see her face because of the mirror behind me.' Nothing. 'You told her that you thought I was having an affair, but not who I was with, when you knew very well. Why?'

She's silent, and I feel even more on edge. And angry.

'Janine,' I persist, 'I didn't know the woman I was seeing was Chrissy's psychiatrist. I swear I had no idea. She just came on to me in a bar one evening and told me her name was Amber, and that she worked in PR.'

Still nothing.

'Janine, for the love of God, she seduced both my son and my daughter, and none of us had any idea that we were seeing the same woman. Do you know what she's up to? Speak, for fuck's sake!'

Her silence is driving me crazy. It's like the woman's gone insane; doesn't even register what I'm saying.

'Do you hear what I'm saying?!' I shout.

And then I can't help myself. I grab her shoulders and shake her violently, as if I'm attempting to wake her from a coma. She looks at me blankly, and slowly I release my grip, tell myself to calm down or I'll end up doing something I'll regret.

Then, without saying a word, she gets up from the sofa, goes over to a bureau nestled in the far corner of the room, opens a drawer, removes a large brown envelope and brings it over to me. 'Here,' she says, 'have a look inside.'

I take the envelope from her in something of a trance, wondering what the hell I'm about to see. My heart accelerates as I open the seal and place my fingers around what feels like several large photographs. *Photos of me with Amber?*

But they're not of me and Amber. They're of Chrissy and her lover in some car park. Kissing.

Words cannot describe how I feel when I realize who the bastard was.

Nate. Janine's husband. My best friend.

Chapter Seventy-Three

Janine

Before

It's been such a happy day, and I can't wait for the dancing later. I'm the only one who knows what your and Greg's first dance is (I haven't even told Nate), and that makes me feel so special; important, even. That's how close we are, Chrissy, how strong our friendship is. We're like sisters, you and I, and I don't know what I'd do without you. Before you came into my life, I felt lost. Nothing but a burden on society. My mother was horrid to me. She always wanted a son, so I was a disappointment to her from the beginning, and my father – a spineless womanizer – was equally disinterested. Perhaps his womanizing was another reason my mother was so cruel to me. I was her human punchbag, someone to take her pain out on. But you can't do that to a child, can you? Children can't be expected to suffer for adults' mistakes. That's cruel and unfair, and all it does is mess them up for life.

You look incredible in your wedding gown. Like a model. Not that I'm surprised, because you always look stunning, even in jeans and a baggy jumper with barely any make-up on. I should feel insanely jealous of you because you always overshadow me whenever we walk into a room together. I'm like one of the ugly sisters to your Cinderella. But I don't feel jealous, I feel proud and lucky to have you for my best friend – my one true best friend who loves me for me and who I know will stand by me through thick or thin. It's a wonderful thing to have found a friend like you. Sometimes I can't believe my luck.

I was never popular at school. Never chosen for school plays or sports teams, never had a look-in for head girl or been invited to cool parties by the cool girls. I've always lacked confidence, despite being a gifted writer. I'm plain, although with a bit of make-up I look decent enough. Always been on the portly side, although I'm not fat as such, just lack definition around my waist, plus I have thick legs with little shape to them. Unlike you, who has a great pair of pins, lithe and toned.

There was this girl at school. She was good at everything. At sport, academically, and she had loads of friends, got invited to all the parties, and she was nasty to me because I was the complete opposite of her. Sometimes, I would imagine what it would be like to wipe that smug look off her face. I'd imagine stabbing her through her stony heart, pushing her off a cliff, poisoning her food. Secretly, I once put a heavy dose of laxative solution in her water bottle one lunchtime when she wasn't looking, and she was off sick for two days. It was the day after she embarrassed me in the playground when she said I needed to lose a good ten pounds to even be considered for a place on the netball team. Fuck, it made me so mad, almost drove me crazy with anger, but it was so satisfying to play that trick on her and make her suffer. She got her comeuppance. Since then, I've played similar tricks on others who've hurt me, although I've never taken things too far, despite wanting to. For example, when my ex-boyfriend, Ben, dumped me.

I loved Ben, and I thought he loved me, but he had a roving eye and I found out he was sleeping with this girl at the tennis club he belonged to. You never liked him. You told me repeatedly that I should leave him, and it pissed me off at the time. But turns out you were right. It all worked out for the best because – although I didn't know it then – my dream man was just around the corner, waiting to whisk me off my feet. Ben's cat met a nasty end, though. I never liked the stupid mog, so mowing it down in front of his house didn't cause me to lose too much sleep.

I've been tempted to teach Miranda a lesson too. It's been so hard holding back, but I can't risk being found out and losing your friendship. It maddened me, the way she wormed her way into our lives. She's so fake. Although you always try and see the best in people, I know exactly why she pretends to be your friend. It's because she's obsessed with Greg, despite now being married to that moron, Duncan. It's the only way she can stay close to him. You might not see her for the fraud she is, but I do. I hate people like that. People who pretend to be something they're not. Take today, for instance. She's been gushing about how beautiful you look, about what a wonderful happy day it is, but I know she's seething inside. I know more than anything she wishes it was her in that wedding dress, exchanging vows with Greg, not you. I suppose I shouldn't be quite so critical. I mean, you and I are the lucky ones. We're both loved by very special men, while she's had to settle for second best.

Meeting Nate was a gift from God. I still can't believe he chose to marry me out of all the women he could have picked. It was you who introduced us, another thing I'm thankful to you for. It was sort of a blind date. I was still feeling low after my break-up with Ben, but you insisted that I meet this guy from your work, a good friend of Greg's. I agreed, but wasn't looking forward to it. And when I first saw Nate, he seemed so out of my league, I almost resented you for even daring to try and hook us up. I was also slightly hurt, because I wondered if you were playing some kind of joke on me, wanting to get my hopes up about someone who clearly wasn't on my level, and yet you were supposed to be my best friend. But to my surprise, Nate seemed genuinely interested in me. He was funny and warm, and not in the least bit fake or full of himself as I'd expected.

You and Greg excused yourselves early (not very subtle), leaving me alone with Nate in the restaurant. I felt nervous as hell, but Nate sensed this and made a real effort to put me at ease. He told me he was fed up with beautiful, yet highly superficial City women, who either fawned at his feet because they were shallow, money-grabbing social climbers, or were so consumed by their own careers it made any meaningful relationship impossible. And I guess that's why he was attracted to me. He liked the fact that I wasn't a power-driven career woman, or obsessed with my looks, or with money, or with finding something better. And, deep down, although he'd never say as much out loud, he knew I'd never stand a chance of nailing someone better than him, and therefore he could count on my loyalty.

He loves me because I love him unconditionally; for *him*, and not because of his money or success. He feels safe with me; knows he can trust me to remain true to him for as long as we both shall live.

You were so nervous this morning, and you told me you'd hardly slept for nerves. I wasn't nervous on my wedding day. In fact, I slept like a baby the night before. Nate and I got married in Mexico on the beach, just you, Greg and Nate's brother and parents there to help us celebrate. My parents were dead by then, not that they would have come anyway. It was so relaxed, and the entire affair took very little planning. I think that's why – unlike you – I didn't have any pre-wedding jitters. I was there with the man I adored, along with the people I loved and who loved me most in this world. So what did I have to feel nervous about?

You, on the other hand, have almost single-handedly organized a wedding for 200 guests, and with that has come a myriad of obligations. I cannot begin to imagine how stressful it has been for you, on top of working long hours at your law firm. I offered to help numerous times but you declined, and it was just like you to consider accepting help – even from your best friend – to be an admission of defeat. You've always been a high achiever – dare I say it, a bit of a show-off – and I guess you felt you needed to prove to yourself that you could organise the perfect wedding and wow all your guests on your special day all by yourself. That's the difference between us, I suppose.

I never thought I'd be married before you, certainly not back when we were at uni and you had a string of boyfriends while I went on no more than a handful of fruitless dates. It was a whirlwind romance with Nate, and I thought I was dreaming when he proposed after four months. But I guess people can date forever and then, when they do get married, they're disappointed when it feels no different to how it was before. Nate and I didn't live together before we were married. So I guess there was something new and exciting to look forward to when we did tie the knot. It felt special, incredibly romantic, when he lifted me over the threshold of *our* new home for the first time.

You and Greg have been dating for more than two years now, and I just pray the romance, the desire, is still there for you both like it was for Nate and me. I suspect you were a tad jealous when I told you we were getting married. You're always so competitive; it must have bothered you that I'd got there first. Beaten you at something for once.

Earlier, I made you down a vodka to settle your nerves before you put on your dress. You looked at me with grateful, almost sad, apologetic eyes as I handed you the glass, and when I asked you, 'Why the sad face?' you said that I'm just such a good friend and that you don't deserve me. For someone like you to say that to someone like me was quite something, and it made me feel pretty damn special. Not for the first time, I couldn't believe how different my life has turned out to how I'd expected it to before I met you. You completely transformed it, and I have you to thank for my happiness today.

The ceremony was so beautiful I cried, not caring that my carefully applied make-up was now smudged. And as I watched you and Greg exchange vows, bowled over by how much Greg loves you – it was so obvious from the way he looked at you, almost the same look I gave Nate at our wedding – I locked eyes with Nate, and he gave me a knowing smile, a smile that said, *I love you too. Now we can welcome our good friends to the married couples' club.*

We're now at the top table, and the speeches are drawing to a close with Tom, the best man, at the end of the customary 'embarrass the hell out of the bridegroom' discourse. There have been tears of joy, much laughter (not to mention a look to kill from Miranda I couldn't fail to notice when Greg was professing his love for you), and I expect there's a lot more of that to come. And now the speech is over, and we're giving Tom a rousing round of applause. As the clapping dies down, I notice you whisper something in Greg's ear, then you stand up and announce to those in our immediate vicinity that you need the loo.

I ask you if you need any help, at which point you bend down, lean over to me and whisper, 'Bit of a dicky tummy. I'm going to my room for some privacy. I'll be back as soon as I can.'

Then you smile and kiss me on the head. Worried and sad that you're feeling unwell on your wedding day, I again offer to go with you, but you insist on going alone, and say you'll get word to me if you need me. I don't protest and watch you go off, then get distracted by your father who asks if I'd like a top-up of my champagne. I say, 'Yes please,' and once I'm topped up, he gets sidetracked by another guest and I take the opportunity to look around for Nate. He's been sitting with your and Greg's other close friends whom we've known for some time but is nowhere to be seen.

It occurs to me that he might have gone to the bar, and so I excuse myself to go and investigate. But he's not there either. Feeling frustrated, I realize you've been gone a good twenty minutes, and I'm worried you might be seriously ill. I know you're in Room Thirty at the end of the corridor – a few doors down from our room – so I head up the grand, sweeping staircase to go and find you. But as I turn the corner, I see my husband emerge from the far room, your room. And almost as soon as he does, he swivels back round and I see a hand grasp his neck and pull him back in. The hand is wearing a large emerald-and-diamond engagement ring, along with a diamond-studded platinum wedding band. Beautiful and instantly recognizable.

It's your hand, and they are your rings.

Chapter Seventy-Four

Janine

Now

Oh, Greg, you *poor* man. I look at you. Mute. Every inch of you paralyzed by shock. Exactly the reaction I'd expected.

I get no satisfaction from seeing you suffer like this, although – it has to be said – you've been unforgivably weak all these years. You didn't have to stay with her, you could have left her years ago. Christ, if you felt unable to exist without a woman in your life, you needn't have looked further than Miranda. As much as she irritates me, I can't fault her devotion to you. Granted, I couldn't resist telling her about your affair (just hearing the shock in her voice, imagining the look on her face, was priceless) but she would have been a better mother to your messed-up kids than Chrissy.

But despite Chrissy pushing you away, despite her being a terrible wife and mother, you stayed, and that makes you pathetic in my eyes. A real man wouldn't have stayed. You're a master of your own misery as far as I can tell, and therefore it's hard to have sympathy for you.

I can't tell you how much I've enjoyed watching her suffer all these years. And now my daughter and I have taken her suffering to new heights, although her biggest shock is yet to come.

I wanted to kill myself when I discovered her betrayal. She knew how much I loved Nate. He was my world and I worshipped him. And she knew what a miserable life I'd had before she and I became friends. When she befriended me in the dinner queue at our university halls, she restored my faith in human nature. At eighteen, I'd finally made a best friend. Someone who, unlike me, was stunning, but also funny and warm, and for the first time in my life I was happy, and I finally believed that not all successful, attractive women were stuck-up, manipulative cows. Never for a second could I have imagined that your wife was, in fact, the worst of them; capable of inflicting indescribable pain on those who loved her most. But I was wrong. And when I realized she'd had sex with my husband at your wedding, my heart shattered into a million pieces. The realization that my best friend, whom I trusted completely, was – behind all the smiles and gestures of affection – a compulsive liar; a wicked, disgusting Jezebel who had – without any hesitation or remorse, and for God knows how long – been sleeping with my husband was like a pain akin to grief.

Looking back, I'm not sure how I got through the rest of your wedding celebrations; through the evening reception, your first dance, talking to guests as if everything was fine and agreeing what a wonderful day it had been, and yes, of course, I was so happy for the new Mr and Mrs Donovan. And I don't know how I stopped myself from standing up and announcing to your guests what an evil, cheating whore the bride was, and that your wedding was nothing but a sham. I can only imagine how delighted Miranda would have been. Especially as Duncan – in his usual undiplomatic fashion – had likened her to a goddess in her wedding gown while Miranda was standing right next to him.

But maybe, in my heart of hearts, I do know how I made it through. It wasn't out of respect or sympathy for you, Greg, that I held back. It was purely because I was weak and lacked courage. And, I suppose, too overcome with shock.

I was quiet with Nate when we eventually retired to our room. He asked me what was up – can you imagine that, the unscrupulous bastard?! I remember cringing when he tried to touch me, get frisky with me, utterly repulsed by the idea, knowing that only a few hours ago he'd been inside her. I turned my back on him in our romantic four-poster bed at the luxury hotel you and she had taken over for what was supposed to be the happiest day of your lives; said it had been a long day, I was whacked and needed sleep. I think he was surprised because I rarely spurned his advances unless I was genuinely ill.

But I didn't sleep, of course. All I could think about was him and her having an affair behind my back, behind your back. Fucking each other's brains out. Wondering how long it had been going on, whether it had started before Nate and I were married, whether they'd screwed each other in Mexico on my wedding day. And I wondered how I could have been so naive, so stupid to think that a gorgeous, successful woman like her could have befriended someone like me. And I came to realize that I'd been a kind of pet project for her – some charity case she'd taken on because she'd always liked challenges, and so adopting me as her friend was just another challenge she'd set herself. Another boost to her massively inflated ego. Likewise, I remember thinking, was it really any wonder that a man like Nate – Chrissy's male counterpart in terms of brains and beauty – would desire someone like her? I was nothing compared to her; how naive I had been to think he actually preferred a plain Jane like me over a stunner like Chrissy.

I thought about all the times in the past when pretty, successful women like her had got the better of me. Despite playing a few pranks on them here and there, I had submitted to their domination. But this time, I told myself things would be different because, unlike all the other times, I had truly believed Chrissy was my friend, and therefore her blanket betrayal of our friendship was unforgivable and had to be punished. Although I wasn't sure how, I vowed to myself that I would get my revenge.

–

Of course, I knew how tough it was going to be, pretending to be her friend, acting normally around her and Nate, and you for that matter, plus still being 'friends' with Miranda, as if nothing had happened. But somehow, I found the strength to do so.

I know that she and Nate carried on their affair after you two were married because I hired a private investigator to follow them. He photographed them entering and exiting their shady fuck-fest hotels, snatching a quick passionate exchange in some car park or on a hotel doorstep. And I kept all this ammunition, locked it safely away in a box in my wardrobe, still not knowing how I was going to use it. All I knew was that there was no point throwing the evidence in her face because where would that get me? I wanted her to suffer in a big way and for a long time, and so when, three months later, she told me she was pregnant, not long after I received the devastating news that I couldn't have children of my own and there was a possibility of Nate being sent to Hong Kong at some point in the future, it came to me.

Although it's unfortunate that you, Greg, have had to suffer for her sins, it is what it is, and it couldn't be helped.

As I gave Chrissy a fake hug, congratulating her on her pregnancy – despite seething with jealousy inside knowing that, once again, she had attained something I could never have, and yet craved with all my heart – I hatched the perfect plan that would destroy her charmed life. When the time was right, I would take the one person who was most important to her, as she had taken who was most important to me. And I would raise her as my own.

Her beloved firstborn, Heidi.

Chapter Seventy-Five

Miranda

Now

I end the call with my contact, stunned by what he's told me, appalled by my naivety. Turns out Freya Cousins never attended Imperial College to study medicine, or any other UK university. And she certainly wasn't attending a psychiatry conference at the Hilton Newcastle the day she slammed into the back of my car.

I think back to that time. When she got out of her car, almost in tears, so kind and apologetic, thrusting her fake business card my way, immediately drawing attention to her profession. *What was it she'd said?*

'I'm so sorry, I'm really not a bad driver. It's just that I'm running late for a psychiatry conference at the Hilton, where I'm due to present a seminar on bereavement.'

Of course, when she said this, I forgot about being angry with her for denting my brand-new Audi. Immediately thought what a nice young woman she seemed, felt sorry for her, noticing the tears well up in her sheer blue eyes. In any case, there wasn't much damage, it was no big deal. We'd pulled over onto the kerb on the next road. And that's when she'd suggested we settle the matter privately. 'It's just that I made a huge cock-up with the provider I went with and my policy excess is already pretty steep. I really can't afford for it to go up further if I make a claim for this.'

Thinking back, being a lawyer, I wonder how I could have been so bloody stupid. I mean, I should have spotted something fishy then. Someone in her line of work choosing not to notify her insurers. But she had such a nice way about her I didn't have the heart to say no. Now I know the real reason she didn't want to get the insurers involved is that there'd have been no record of car insurance registered to a Dr Freya Cousins.

She gave me her business card, with the same West Hampstead address she operated her so-called practice from, and told me to send her the invoice for the repairs as soon as I had it. I thanked her, wished her good luck, and we went our separate ways.

That night, Janine called, telling me how depressed she felt, how she didn't feel able to go on with life now that Nate was gone. And that's when I remembered the business card Dr Cousins had handed me and – more specifically – her reference to giving a talk on bereavement. Although I was never one to believe in therapy, meeting Dr Cousins had felt like fate to me. Plus, her website was so impressive. Although now I realize why there was no photo despite thinking little of it at the time. I told Janine all about her and – as luck would have it – that she was only a couple of stops away on the Jubilee Line.

But now I realize our meeting was no accident. No accident that Dr Cousins banged into my car that day. No accident she happened to give me her business card and tell me where she was headed. No accident that she had revealed to me her experience in helping patients cope with their grief.

And – as I realize this – I wonder whether it was also no accident that Janine called me that night, telling me how desperate she felt.

With no time to lose, I call Greg. But frustratingly, he's not answering. So I leave him a voicemail and tell him all I know.

I just hope he picks it up soon.

Chapter Seventy-Six

Greg

Now

Hearing Janine's confession, seeing the smug look on her face, I want to put my hands around her neck and crush the life out of her. But my feet are cemented to the ground, and I feel utterly powerless. The realization that she – your best friend, Chrissy – took our daughter is horrifying enough, but hearing her reasons, hearing that you fucked her husband, one of my best friends at the time, on our wedding day, is akin to a dagger being thrust through my heart. Questions rip through my mind.

When did it start? How long did it go on for? When did you see him? How could Nate have betrayed our friendship like that? Was he the one who convinced Graham Small to give Julia Keel what she wanted, because by then, being a few years older than us, he'd been made a partner and had influence at the firm? What exactly did he say to you on the phone the day Heidi was taken? How could he have gone along with Janine kidnapping Heidi, knowing it was a crime, knowing it would destroy our lives?

I would see him every now and again, for Christ's sake, when he was called back to London for meetings. But he always travelled alone. Claiming Janine was too frightened to travel with Sarah after what happened to Heidi. And we, in our grief, had sympathized. Later, when Sarah was older, less vulnerable, it was never the right moment. Either it was term time, or she was too busy studying. Again, with busy teenagers of our own, we empathized. We received occasional photos, mostly of Sarah in senior school. Photos which must have been of some random child, because now I realize that 'Sarah' is really Heidi. Granted, for a long time you had no inclination to leave the house, let alone fly to Hong Kong. But later, when it seemed you might be coming around to the idea and I secretly broached the subject with Nate, it was never a good time. And now we know why. They couldn't risk it. Because surely we would have recognized our own daughter? Even when Sarah – or rather, Heidi – grew up, they'd say she was travelling or too busy with her friends. And, more recently, too tied up with her high-powered job. But the truth was that they couldn't risk us identifying our missing daughter.

I somehow find my voice, ask, 'How did you get Nate to go along with this? You both committed a serious crime. If you'd been caught back then, you'd have gone to prison for a very long time. He was a lawyer, for goodness' sake, his job was everything to him.'

'I didn't care about that. It was a chance I was willing to take because your bitch of a wife broke my heart. She took what was most precious to me, and getting my revenge was all that kept me going. I made it clear to Nate that if he didn't go along with it, I'd go public with the photos of him and her and ruin not just his career, but hers too, and make a laughing stock out of you. His career – making partner – was everything to him. He loved his work, loved being a big shot, and it would have killed him to lose all that under such disreputable circumstances. And, as you know, at the time he was being transferred to Hong Kong, so it was the ideal opportunity to snatch Heidi and take her with us.'

I am stunned, and yet I find myself asking more questions. 'Is that why he phoned Chrissy that day? To distract her?'

'Yes. The week before I took Heidi, I told him I knew everything. For the first time in my life, I called the shots. I held the power in our relationship. And I can tell you, Greg, it felt fucking fantastic. I followed Chrissy and Heidi that day, watched them from a distance, waited for my chance to pounce the moment she walked away, banking on the fact that she would. And Heidi knew me, of course, so she wasn't afraid, didn't make a fuss at all. I'd done my homework on where the CCTV was. The only thing that had threatened to ruin my plan was bloody Miranda.'

I'm confused. 'Miranda?'

'Yes, I saw her standing at the entrance to Peter Jones – who knows why, perhaps Chrissy had told her she was shopping there, and she'd offered to join her. I was so mad, but then she got a call, and I watched her face fall, before she started running in the opposite direction. I was so relieved. Of course, later we discovered her deadbeat father had had a heart attack which explained her rapid departure. Though, if it were me, I wouldn't have bothered.'

Janine's eyes are glistening as she talks, she seems to be enjoying herself, and although I understand what drove her to it, I realize there is something seriously wrong with her, and that perhaps her unhappy childhood had a more detrimental effect on her mental health than any of us ever imagined. It's clear to me that over time, her grief and her obsession with getting revenge against you have soared to dangerous levels.

'How did you get her to Hong Kong? The police circulated her photo everywhere.'

She hesitates, as if thinking how best to answer, then says, 'Back then, before 9/11, before the rise of ISIS and other extremist cells, border control was slacker, and it was much easier to get away with a fake passport. And so I got one off the black market for Heidi, using a different name and gender. For two months I hid her in our house because, well, I couldn't take off immediately, could I? What best friend would do that? I had to be there for you and Chrissy in your time of need. Especially as I knew Miranda would be.'

I remember going over to Janine and Nate's during that time, when we were still searching for Heidi. But all along she was right under our noses, upstairs in their house, alone and no doubt drugged to her eyeballs to ensure she wouldn't cry. My heart aches with such pain, I almost can't breathe. Again, I remember Janine slapping me across the face when I had a go at you for losing our child. Who'd have believed she was such a good actress?

Janine continues. 'Then, when it was time for us to leave for the Far East I cut her hair, dressed her up in boys' clothes, and she and I took the ferry from Portsmouth to France, then drove to Italy. Nate flew out separately, telling people over there I had a few last-minute things to sort out. From there, we took a night flight from Rome to Hong Kong, where Nate was waiting for us.' She pauses, smiles. A sickly-sweet smile that makes me cringe. 'She was such a good child, no problem at all. She didn't cry or ask for Mama, and so I realized she felt safer with me than she did with *her*. I was more of a mother to her than Chrissy ever was, because I devoted myself to her 100 per cent. I wasn't off shagging another woman's husband.'

Hearing what she has to say, seeing the triumphant look on her face, I am consumed with hatred for this woman – for what she put our daughter through – but even so, I need more answers.

'And when you got there, how did you explain her to everyone?'

'Heidi never left the house for the first couple of years. I had a trusted maid who watched her when I needed to go out. We paid her more money than she could dream of to keep quiet and not ask questions.'

It occurs to me that two years went by before Janine and Nate told us they'd adopted a child, having found out they were unable to have children of their own.

'You kept her a prisoner?' I'm so horrified by this I almost start hyperventilating. I imagine my poor child, imprisoned in a strange house, thousands of miles from home, being denied the normal childhood all kids deserve.

Janine carries on. 'Once the hoo-ha surrounding Heidi's disappearance had died down, and I was sure that no one would recognize her, I started taking her out once a day, to the park, the local shops, small playgroups. We told the locals that she was our adopted daughter, just as we told everyone back in England, including you and Chrissy. And no one questioned it.' Another pause, then, 'Rest assured, Greg, she was a very happy child. I was devoted to her, as if she were my own.'

'Did she go to school? I mean, you used to send us school photographs of your so-called adopted daughter, Sarah, but I'm assuming there was no Sarah, and that the photos weren't of Heidi?'

'No, they weren't, that's right. I couldn't take the chance you wouldn't recognize her, could I? The photos you received were of Heidi's tutor's daughter. Anyway, in answer to your first question, Heidi was home-schooled by Mrs Bates up to the age of eleven, at which point we decided it would benefit her to attend a normal secondary school. Neither Mrs Bates nor I was enough for her by then. She needed friends her own age.'

'How gracious of you,' I say sarcastically. 'Did you tell her she was adopted?'

'I did more than that. I told her the truth once she was old enough to hear it. When she turned thirteen.'

I'm aghast. 'Why?'

'Because I thought she had a right to know, and I wanted to prepare her for my future plans.'

'What did you tell her? What lies did you concoct?'

'There were no lies, Greg. I simply told her who and what her real mother was. A lying, cheating, two-faced tramp who never wanted her. Who, instead of shedding tears of joy when she found out she was pregnant, shed tears of despair and wanted an abortion. And that the only thing that stopped her was you finding the test in the bathroom bin.'

That's a blatant lie on Janine's part. I never found the test, you told me of your own volition. 'Why, you...!' I exclaim.

I'm teetering on the brink of getting physical with her, but somehow I manage to hold back. And yes, it's true that you weren't as happy as you might have been when you found out you were pregnant, but all that changed the moment Heidi was born. You may have lied to me, cheated on me, but I know what I saw the day Heidi came into this world was real. You loved her with all your heart, and I believe you when you say you haven't stopped regretting your affair since the day Heidi was taken.

'You bitch,' I say, 'you liar! You've twisted the truth, warped Heidi's impression of Chrissy, led her to believe she didn't love her. But you know that's not true!'

'Oh, really? Tell me, Greg, what kind of mother carries on an affair with a married man when she has a newborn – and later, a toddler – to look after? Tell me that.'

I don't respond. I don't want to think about it right now because something else has occurred to me. 'You still haven't told me what part Dr Cousins has played in all this. Who is she? Something tells me it was no coincidence she bumped into Miranda's car that day. Does she know Heidi? I need to know, Janine. Where's Heidi? I need to know how I can find my daughter. I have a right to see her.'

'You already found her, Greg.'

'What do you mean?' I stare at Janine, confused. She's wearing that same mad look, and it makes me nervous.

As we continue to lock eyes, I wonder if you know the truth. You can't, unless you've managed to speak to Dr Cousins and somehow got some answers out of her.

Janine still doesn't answer, even though my gaze is drilling through her, and it's frustrating beyond belief not knowing what she meant when she said I'd already found Heidi. I have a feeling I'm about to find out when she opens her mouth and says, 'Well—'

But then a knock on the front door stops her mid-flow and I'm guessing it's you, Chrissy.

Chapter Seventy-Seven

Ella

Now

I bang on Dan's door, but he's not answering. Driving over, I nearly had an accident, my mind only half focusing on the road, occupied by thoughts of how you deceived me and my family, Robyn. How you fooled me into believing you loved me when all along you were using me, lying to me, only telling me half-truths, giving me some sob story about a drowned brother, seducing me the way you seduced all of us.

But why? Even if Mum did have an affair with your dad (which she still claims she didn't, and I have to say I'm starting to believe her), how is it fair that you should choose to punish the rest of us? What have Dan, Dad and I done to you? Or is it simply that punishing us is a way of punishing Mum, pushing her guilt to new extremes, to the point where she can no longer live with herself and what she has done?

No, I think there's something bigger motivating you, but I can't think what else could have driven you to such lengths.

I open Dan's letterbox, put my mouth up close to the gap and shout his name several times, but there's still no response. I fear the worst, especially as I missed three calls from him when Mum was at my flat. My shouting draws attention from a neighbour who, thankfully, shows concern rather than hostility. I'm relieved to hear they're on friendly terms, and that Dan gave him a spare key for emergencies. He dashes back into his flat to retrieve it, and as I continue to call out Dan's name I feel increasingly anxious.

The man returns with the key and I ask him to open the door and come with me. I don't want to be alone when my worst fears are confirmed.

As we walk in, we're greeted by silence. Something tells me to head straight for Dan's bedroom, and that's where I find him, lying on the floor, a syringe stuck in his arm, his face deathly white.

Chapter Seventy-Eight

Christine

Now

After I left Ella's, I didn't head straight for Janine's. I first went to Dr Cousins' flat, intending to give her hell for what she and Janine have done to my family. But she wasn't there. Although I didn't tell Ella or Greg my theory, I'm almost certain that Janine is behind all this. I was already suspicious when I turned up at Ella's, but when Ella told me that Robyn's mother's name was Cynthia, I knew for sure. Cynthia was Janine's mother's name, the woman she hated with a passion, but whom she now seems to be emulating.

When you weigh up all the facts – not just the name, but her deliberate failure to tell me who Greg's lover was – it fits. Plus, she's the only one who could have put those photos of Nate and me on my bed. And later, removed them. There was no sign of a break-in and, aside from Greg, Miranda and the kids, she's the only one with a key to our house.

But I still need to get to the bottom of Dr Cousins' involvement. My instinct tells me she's Janine and Nate's adopted daughter, Sarah, which is why she's helping Janine. I'm guessing Janine told her all sorts of vicious lies about me and got her to make contact with Miranda by banging into her car so we'd never suspect any prior connection between them. But I still need to ask the question to her face.

I don't know how Janine found out about Nate and me – we were always so careful – but somehow she did, and is trying to get her revenge. Leading me to believe that you might still be alive – with the note, email and dress – and, in the process, hurting not only me, but those closest to me.

But why did she wait all this time, pretend to be my friend all these years before acting? All I can assume is that she only found out recently, because surely if she'd discovered the truth years ago, she would have confronted me then, rather than keep it bottled up and pretend nothing had changed between us. That being said, I'm still puzzled as to how she came across the photos. Someone must have sent them to her. But who, and when, and what is their role in all of this?

I brought this on myself. I should have come clean years ago. But I was too much of a coward. I couldn't bear to lose Janine's friendship. It was a form of salvation I clung to after you disappeared. Although she went to live abroad, I would always look forward to her fortnightly letters and occasional phone calls, and, later, her emails. Looking back, I realize how selfish that was of me, because I didn't deserve them and what I did with her husband behind her back was inexcusable. But I intend to tell her this when she lets me inside; how much I regret my actions, even though I know it probably won't make a difference to the hatred she must feel for me.

But despite my blame in all this, there is no excuse for the pain Janine has caused my family. Only a very sick mind would use her daughter the way she has, and I can't help feeling that there's something I'm overlooking here, some major piece of the puzzle I've yet to slot in.

And that's why, as I stand on Janine's doorstep, waiting to be let in, wondering what she's told Greg, I'm going to ask her straight:

What am I missing here, Janine?

Chapter Seventy-Nine

Greg

Now

I catch your eye, Chrissy, as soon as Janine opens the door to you, her back to me as I hover behind in the hallway. A signal to say, *I know your secret; I know who your lover was.* You swallow hard, your eyes full of shame and regret, and then my gaze fleetingly shifts to Janine, another signal, this time to tell you that all is far from right with this woman. The best friend you betrayed without any thought to the consequences.

'Hello, Janine,' you say. You sound calm, but I can tell it's an effort for you. You're not easily afraid, but I sense your fear. All you've said is hello, and so it's clear to me that you don't know the whole story yet. All you think is that Janine's been playing games with you, leading you to believe Heidi is alive when she really has no clue, just to torture you.

But if you knew the truth, you wouldn't be this calm; you'd have beaten down the door with your own two fists, you'd be shouting, screaming at Janine, demanding to know where our daughter is.

Nevertheless, you are afraid of what you're about to hear, and you have every reason to be.

'Hello, Chrissy. Come in.'

We move to the living room but don't sit down. It's like the lull before the storm, and the tension is a killer. I want to ask you how you could have done such a thing; how you could have lived with yourself all these years – knowing what you did to me was the ultimate betrayal, knowing that you lied to me repeatedly. But I say nothing for now. I have a sense Janine is going to do the talking for me.

You look at her, and I see the distress on your face. A face that was once so lovely but is now old before its time. Creased with lines, sallow and drawn with years of heartache and near starvation. Only now do I fully understand why you pushed your body to the limit. You weren't just punishing yourself for losing Heidi. You were punishing yourself for sleeping with your best friend's husband, one of my closest friends at the time, an affair you believe contributed to us losing our child.

You speak. 'I'm sorry, Jani. I'm sorry for having an affair with Nate. For never telling you, for lying to you all these years. What we did was wrong, unforgivable, and I don't expect you to forgive me. But what you're doing to my family is wrong. They've done nothing to hurt you, they're innocent in all of this. To punish Greg, to lead him to believe that Heidi is alive, to seduce him, Ella and Daniel through Dr Cousins, who I assume is your adopted daughter, that's just plain cruel. All you needed to do was have it out with me to my face – why conduct this sick charade? Where has it got us all?'

Janine's brow creases in disbelief. 'How dare you talk to me about what's fair, what's cruel, what's sick, when you are guilty of all three?! You are a liar and a hypocrite, and you deserve to burn in hell. I thought you were my friend. You know how tough I had it at home and at school. Although I didn't dare to believe it at first, when we met, when you became my best friend, it restored my faith in human nature, made me realize that it was possible to have a pretty friend who was also kind, who I could rely on to always be there for me. So you can just imagine how I felt when I saw Nate emerge from your wedding suite, hours after you'd promised to be faithful to Greg. I wanted to die.'

Her eyes are brimming with tears, as are mine. And as I catch your stunned expression – perhaps you are shocked to learn how long Janine has known the truth, how she found out, I don't know – I can tell that you want the ground to swallow you up.

'You hurt me more than anyone has ever hurt me,' Janine continues. 'I loved Nate, you know how much I loved him, but you took him from me, cruelly and selfishly without an ounce of remorse, when you already had a good man who adored you.'

Your eyes are streaming tears now. You are beside yourself with guilt and shame. 'It wasn't love, Janine,' you say. 'It was lust, pure and simple, and I know that's no excuse—' you look at me with heartfelt eyes, but you must know that your explanation doesn't make it any easier to bear; if anything, I feel worse '—and that it doesn't lessen the pain for you, but it didn't mean anything. He did love you, Janine, and I loved you, Greg.'

Again, you look at me imploringly, but all I can do is look away.

'So that makes it OK then, does it?' Janine snarls, her eyes full of hate, her tone icy. 'You were just fuck buddies, no biggy.'

'It's a lame excuse, I know that.'

I can't hold it in any longer. 'How could you have carried on after Heidi was born, Chrissy? Leaving her with me, with my mother, with your mother, while you and Nate were off screwing each other? What kind of a mother does that?'

'Exactly,' Janine cuts in. 'You know, I gave you the benefit of the doubt, Chrissy. I waited – waited to see if you would stop after you were married. Hoped it was a one-off, or one last fuck for the road. But you didn't.'

'How do you know?'

'Because I hired a private detective.'

'He took the photos?'

'Yes. And not only did you carry on after you were married, you carried on after you got pregnant and beyond. After Heidi was born. And I knew then that this was never going to stop, that you were beyond the realms of forgiveness.'

'Is that why you and Nate left? Did he ask to be transferred to Hong Kong?'

'No. That was just coincidence, decided sometime before. But it turned out to be my lucky break. Meant I wouldn't have to see your face any more. And you wouldn't be able to carry on fucking my husband.'

'But why wait all this time to punish me? Why didn't you just have it out with me back then? All of this could have been avoided.'

You're wondering if Janine felt sorry for you when Heidi was abducted. Whether – despite what you did to her – the soft side of her couldn't bring herself to have it out with you when your child had been taken. But you are wrong, so wrong.

'I did punish you back then,' she replies, her eyes twinkling with delight. 'In fact, I've been punishing you for the last twenty-three years.'

'What are you talking about? I don't understand.' You look at me, and I guess my face says it all, because then the penny drops. 'You took Heidi?' you gasp.

'Yes.'

The colour drains from your face.

Like me, never in your wildest imagination could you have believed it was Janine who took Heidi. All this time, when she pretended to be our friend, pretended to care, it was her who stole our daughter from us.

I watch you eye the nearest seat, your legs about to fold. But before you can move, Janine says mockingly, 'Surprised?'

I don't know where it comes from, but a surge of adrenaline appears to shoot through you and I watch you launch yourself at her. I intervene just in time, before you have the chance to do something you might regret, pulling you away even though you fight back and try to release yourself from my grip. But your twig-like frame is no match for me, and you soon relent and allow me to sit you down on the sofa.

I can almost hear your heart pounding as you ask, 'Why? How? There were other, less drastic ways to punish me. How could you take a child from its mother? What kind of a monster does that?'

330

'You made me into a monster, Chrissy. You brought all this on yourself. Hurting you in the worst possible way was what kept me going. I wanted to die when I found out about you and Nate, but taking Heidi – seeing you fall into the depths of despair – sustained me.'

'And Nate agreed?'

'Yes. After I confronted him, threatened to expose him and ruin his career, his pristine reputation, if he refused to help me.'

'So his call that day was all a ruse? To distract me?' you ask.

'Yes, and you were so predictable. Leaving Heidi in her buggy to take his call, not thinking about her safety, because your needs took precedence. You weren't – you aren't – fit to be a mother. You proved that with Heidi, and you proved it with Ella and Daniel. You had a second chance with them, but your guilt ate you up, drove them away, made them hate you. And now you've fucked them up for life.'

Again, I get the urge to put my hands around Janine's neck and crush her windpipe until her eyes bulge from their sockets, but then I look at you and it's as if the cold, hard truth has finally hit you. You see that Janine is right.

'You see it now, don't you?' Janine says sanctimoniously. 'You see that I saved Heidi from you. She was better off with me. I devoted myself to her, and so did Nate. He was a good father, I'll give him that.'

You glance at me, and I can tell that you are sorry for what you've put me through. But it's too late for that. And now I need to know what Janine meant when she said I'd already found Heidi.

I ask her this very question, whereupon you give me a puzzled look, then turn to Janine, hoping for an explanation.

'What did you mean by that?' I repeat.

Without saying a word, Janine leaves the room. You and I exchange looks, wondering what we're in for now. And then, as we hear her call out, 'Darling, it's time, you can come down now,' we realize we're about to see our daughter for the first time since she disappeared from our lives all those years ago.

Chapter Eighty

Heidi

Now

Ever since Janine, my adoptive mother, told me the truth, I've found myself fascinated by the human mind. Our brains are incredibly complex, but what's always intrigued me is the way our social and cultural settings can profoundly affect the way we think, behave and live our lives. For example, my life would have been quite different if you hadn't abandoned me that day, Christine. I would have been raised by different parents, in a different house, in a different country, mixing with different people, going to a different school and so on. Although I was born with certain traits, I know from my reading that nurture has played a crucial role in the way I think and behave, and the same goes for my half-siblings. Your lack of love and attention has scarred them for life. Both have trust and commitment issues, both have mean, selfish streaks, even though Ella can't see that and always thinks she's the one who's hard done by, more selfless than Daniel. But that's just her head telling her that; her own conceitedness. She doesn't see what the rest of us see, even though she willingly helped me harass you by sending the note and the email. And the dress, of course. Which, incidentally, was my original dress (I fucked up a bit there, I'll admit it, when I referred to the stain before you mentioned it), but she didn't know that, of course.

Ella has your genes. She is self-centred, twisted and a liar, and just as fucked up as our brother, Daniel. The truth is, above all else, we human beings are needy. We crave love and attention, praise and respect. They got none of those from you. But they got them from me. I made them feel wanted, special, adored, just as I made Greg feel wanted, special, adored.

I have no regrets in helping Janine (whom I consider to be my real mother) with her plan because you never wanted me (despite what you might claim when you are lying on my couch) and because you nearly destroyed the woman – your supposed best friend – who did want to be a mother to me. Our intention was always to turn Greg and your children against you for good. And it's worked as far as I can tell. We've exposed your lies, and they'll be turning their backs on you forever. You are finished. You are dead to them, as you are dead to me.

I know that makes me as messed up in the head as Ella and Daniel, because – let's face it – who in their right mind agrees to sleep with their own siblings? But I don't care. I have no emotional attachment to them, and I was prepared to do whatever it took to destroy you. After all, it's not as if I slept with my father, which would be far worse. I'm not Greg's child. I'm Nate's, which only makes Daniel and Ella my half-brother and sister. Greg is nothing to me, nothing at all. Just a desperate, middle-aged man more than twice my age, who was flattered by my attention.

You've had so many chances to confess to my mother – even recently, when you finally told her you had an affair but not who your lover was – but time after time you looked her in the eye knowing you had betrayed her and said nothing. And you were even too gutless to tell me who he was when I was being Dr Cousins.

You are a coward, and I am ashamed to have your blood running through my veins.

I'm not a real psychiatrist (I couldn't possibly be at the age of twenty-five despite you and Dan believing me to be older) although I do have a degree in psychology, and have worked on and off as a school counsellor at a British international school in Hong Kong. The website we set up for Dr Freya Cousins, the degree on my wall, the business cards, are all fake. As were the framed photos of my 'family' and me on my desk. Photoshopped snaps of me with random people plucked off the internet. I have to say, I quite enjoyed playing different roles. It helps that I've always been on the mature side, capable of looking and acting older than I am. Sometimes I almost believed I was those characters, I got so into them and the stories that came with them; like the one you and Dan fell for about Freya's mother dying of cancer, and Ella naively believing poor Robyn had not only lost a sibling in tragic circumstances but also been dumped by her dickhead boyfriend. And, of course, the photo I showed her of Robyn's mother was of some woman I pulled off the web. It was a challenge I thrived on, and at times highly risky, like when I came round for lunch that Sunday with Daniel. Naturally, I checked that morning with Greg that he wouldn't be able to make it, but it was still a risk, because there was always a chance he'd show up, and that would have put paid to our plan before it had reached its zenith.

I also enjoyed playing that irritant Miranda for a fool. Of course, we didn't need to use Miranda. Janine could just as easily have recommended me to you without bringing her into the equation. But that wouldn't have been as much fun. And it also meant you were less likely to suspect our previous connection. Janine has never liked Miranda, and she enjoyed toying with her. It added to the fun stirring trouble between you, making you wonder if her intentions had been honourable. Even more gratifying is that Miranda will be mortified with herself for bringing 'Dr Cousins' into your lives once she knows the truth and the damage it's caused your family. And knowing this gave Janine added satisfaction, considering what a contemptible hanger-on Miranda's been towards you and Greg all these years. She deserved to be disgraced. I won't lie, though, it was quite nerve-racking at the time, deliberately running my car into hers. I mean, what if she'd refused to go private? That would have made life tricky. But thankfully she fell for it hook, line and sinker, just like the rest of you.

But best of all, I enjoyed fooling you. Because you were always the target.

You trusted Janine (just as she had trusted you), and you took the bait. The medication I gave you was real, though. It was my medication, actually. Lithium. Commonly used for the treatment of bipolar disorder and major depressive disorder, both of which I suffer from because of you. Although, if you take too strong a dose – which is what I gave you – it can have some very unpleasant side effects, especially when taken with alcohol, as you found out only too well.

–

I've been hiding at the top of the stairs, listening to all that's been said, first when it was just Greg and Mother and, more recently, between the three of you.

But now it's time to make my grand entrance. Mother's just called for me to come down and show myself, and as I descend the stairs my heart pumps with adrenaline, knowing that I'm about to give you the biggest shock of your life. Greg, too, although I won't allow him to think he's committed incest for too long. That would be too cruel, and he doesn't deserve that. Not like you.

Calmly, I approach the living room, gently push the door open and walk in.

All eyes are on me. Yours and Greg's are wide with shock, while my mother's are gleaming with triumph.

But I hold my gaze on you and you alone, and say, 'Hello, Mother.'

Chapter Eighty-One

Christine

Now

My chest feels so tight, I can scarcely breathe, and it's as if all the oxygen has been sucked out of the room.

It can't be true, it can't. They're just messing with me again – they have to be. I try to stay calm and think rationally, tell myself this is all part of the same malicious game Dr Cousins and Janine have been playing with Greg, Ella, Daniel and me for the past six months.

'You're lying,' I say, searching Dr Cousins' face (noticing that her eyes aren't electric blue any more, they're brown), then Janine's, willing them both to say, 'Yes, OK, we're lying, but we had you fooled there, didn't we, ha ha.' But they don't.

I glance at Greg, whose face is deathly pale, like he's about to be sick. I know what he's thinking. He's thinking he's slept with his own daughter. I should tell him now, the other secret I kept from him. I lied to him before because at that point neither of us had any idea that Dr Cousins and Amber were one and the same person, and I couldn't bear to hurt him any more. Not when he'd just found out about my affair. That was bad enough. But something stops me from speaking up now. I'm still in disbelief, I guess. Too busy studying Dr Cousins' face.

How can my own daughter have fooled me all this time? How did I not recognize her? Surely a mother knows her own child, despite the passage of time? Is this yet another failing of mine?

Her expression is steadfast. 'I am your daughter, Heidi. The daughter you had with your lover, Nate, my mother's husband, your husband's friend...'

My eyes flit to Greg, who should of course feel relieved. As should I, knowing that he no longer thinks he's slept with his own child. But the flip side to this is that I've hurt him even more. He's realized I've told him another lie. Led him to believe he was Heidi's father all this time, when he wasn't. Led him to mourn someone who wasn't his own flesh and blood. Heidi is Nate's, that's what the DNA sample proved. And that's how we justified carrying on our affair: we were bound to one another through Heidi. That's what we told each other.

I look at Freya. Could she really be Heidi?

She is still talking. '...the one whose phone call you prioritized over making sure I was safe. The one you fucked at your own wedding, in the same room where you slept with your new husband.'

She is blonde, but back then, Heidi had dark curly hair, darker than Nate's. She reads my mind, touches her hair, says, 'Dyed, can't you tell?'

'Your eyes,' I murmur.

'I wore contact lenses for you and Daniel.' She looks at Greg. 'Au naturel for you and Ella, though.'

'How do I know you're telling me the truth?' I say.

She looks at me and grins. If this is my child, she's been primed to hate me. 'You know it's me. You're my mother, of course you know your own child when you see her.'

I take a step closer, try to reach out and touch her, but she pulls away.

'Back off, Christine. We may have the same blood running through our veins, but as far as I'm concerned, *she's* my real mother.'

She and Janine exchange arrogant smiles, and then Janine speaks. 'You should be so proud, knowing what a beautiful, smart woman your daughter has turned into. You know, she had a bit of a wobble recently, was finding our project a bit tough going, but I calmed her down, made her believe in herself, the way only a mother can.'

'How can you say all that? You've brainwashed her into hating me, you've turned her against me.'

'No, you did that yourself.'

'How could Nate have gone along with this? Is that why he killed himself? The guilt ate him up?' I study Janine's body language and see no hint of remorse for her husband's suicide. Her quest for revenge must have driven him to it, but if this bothers her, she shows no sign of it.

'Who knows?' she shrugs. 'Yes, maybe it was the guilt. Guilt for having an affair with you, the reason why I took Heidi in the first place. Deep down, he knew it was all his and your doing. And the lying bastard couldn't deal with that.'

I see no trace of the woman who once worshipped the ground Nate walked on.

'Tell me, Janine, did you even shed a tear when he died?'

I watch her closely, but if she did cry, she doesn't want anyone else to know. Chin up, she says defiantly, 'To be honest, it was a relief to be rid of him. That way, there was no chance of him interfering with the next stage of my plan.'

'So taking Heidi, watching me suffer all these years, was just the tip of the iceberg? Tell me, did you always plan to bring her home one day? Once she was grown and brainwashed into hating me enough to want to destroy me and my family forever? Is she even a psychiatrist?'

'Yes, that was always my plan. Nate knew that, and so did Heidi. And what better time than the year she turned twenty-five? But Heidi understood. I didn't force her. She wanted the same. Didn't you, darling?'

'Yes,' Heidi says. 'And no, I'm not a psychiatrist – bit young for that – but I am very interested in the human mind.' She pauses, then looks at Greg. 'I knew you'd snoop around in my study if I told you it was out of bounds. That was always the plan, and you were so predictable.'

Greg looks crestfallen, and I shiver at her deception, at what my daughter has become. Although it's a futile exercise, I have to at least try and make her believe how much I loved her back then. That I'd have done anything to get her back – that if there'd been any indication at all that she was still alive I'd have given my life to have her returned to us safe and sound. I say all this, tell her how much I loved her from the moment she was born, just as I did when I thought she was Dr Cousins. But it makes no difference. Janine has had the advantage of years spent grooming her for this day, while I haven't set eyes on my child since she was a toddler. I am nothing to her, I realize that now, and nothing I say is going to change that.

'And you used Miranda to get to us? Why?'

Heidi and Janine share another chilling grin. Then I listen in horror as my daughter explains what I already suspected.

'You won't get away with this,' Greg, who's been quiet since learning he's not Heidi's father, suddenly pipes up. 'I'm calling the police, Janine. You're going to prison.'

'Do what you must. But just hear me out: if you have me arrested, everything will come out in the press. Chrissy's affair, your affair with Heidi, your children's incestuous affairs with their half-sibling. It'll all come out, and think what that will do to Ella and Daniel. They won't be able to leave the house for shame. Their lives will be destroyed, I'll make sure of that.'

Greg looks fit to burst. His face is red and taut, and I worry he's on the verge of having a heart attack. We lock eyes, and I know he hates me, but right now he's also feeling what I'm feeling. Torn. The last thing we want is to inflict more damage on our children. And not for one second do I doubt Janine's threat to make their sex lives public.

Just then, at the mention of my other children, I realize I've not checked my messages to see if Ella's OK, and how things went at Daniel's. I retrieve my phone from my handbag and am shocked to find I have six texts and two voicemails from Ella. I look at Greg and he reads my mind. My hand is shaking as I open the first text.

Dan's overdosed. I've called for an ambulance.

I can't help myself; I scream, 'No!' suddenly seeing stars.

'What is it, Chrissy?' I vaguely hear Greg say as he comes rushing over.

I tell him.

'Jesus Christ, no,' he cries, glaring at Heidi and Janine who, for the first time, look rattled. 'Which hospital?'

'UCH.'

'I'm going over, now.'

'Wait!' I say, going through Ella's texts. I daren't listen to her voicemails, I can't bear to hear my daughter's tortured voice. 'I haven't read her latest text.'

I get to the last one, and this time my knees do cave and I fall to the floor.

'Chrissy?' I hear Greg say.

I can barely get the words out. 'Dan's in a coma. Ella says the doctors don't expect him to recover.'

Chapter Eighty-Two

Ella

Now

I sit at your bedside, Dan, holding your hand, but I might as well be holding a plank of wood. It doesn't reciprocate, just hangs there limply, as unresponsive as the rest of you. Your face is uncharacteristically peaceful, though. As if you've already left this world for a far better one.

Mum just told me everything, and I thank God you never learned the truth. She and Dad rushed over here as soon as they read my texts. First, they wanted to know what had happened. I explained how I'd found you unconscious with a syringe hanging from your arm, and then seen your phone lying on the floor beside you, a photo of Dad and Robyn (I still can't help calling her that) having sex displayed on the screen. Of course, you didn't know she was your half-sister, just as I had no idea she was mine. You simply thought that the love of your life was sleeping with our dad – that Dad had betrayed you, let you down, just as Mum had let you down.

And their betrayal has brought you to this point; brought us all to this point.

I want to be strong, but I'm not sure I can live with what I've done. I was fucked up before I met Robyn, but stupidly I'd thought she'd gone a long way to fixing me. But I was wrong. So fucking wrong. She tricked me, and I bought into her lies like a lamb to the slaughter. I had sex with my own sister. OK, so she might be my half-sister, but it's still gross, perverse.

I can't live with this on my conscience. Life was bad enough before, but this is too much to handle. Mum and Dad have gone to get coffees, but by the time they get back it'll be too late. I'm drifting off now, I can feel myself leaving my body and never coming back. All the pain and misery will soon be over, and I won't have to think any more. I'll see you soon, brother; whether in heaven or in hell remains to be seen.

Chapter Eighty-Three

Christine

Now

I spot you with your head resting on your brother's chest, Ella, and it touches my soul. I thank God that at this moment of crisis, you are there for him. I know you two haven't always got on – again, that's my fault – but when it comes down to it, we're family, and now, more than ever, we need to help each other through this. Seeing this gesture of affection, I am suddenly filled with hope. Hope that Daniel will emerge from his coma, and I can try and make up for all those lost years.

As much as I am loath to admit it, we can't turn Janine in. If we do, our personal lives will be splashed all over the press, and I don't think any of us are strong enough to withstand that. Greg is fuming. He says her getting away with what she's done is a crime in itself, and I know that he's right. But I don't doubt Janine's appetite for revenge. She'll do and say whatever it takes to justify her actions, whatever the cost to her and Heidi, and that's not going to help you or Daniel. There will be no more notes, emails or packages, and so, with time, with no more leads to go on, the case will be closed once again. Miranda – who I just spoke to, and whose voicemail Greg listened to as we raced here – agrees with me. She feels equally humiliated but agreed that you and Daniel have suffered enough, that we must try and put all this behind us if the two of you are to have any hope of a peaceful future.

As for Heidi, I need to let go of her. I thought being reunited with her would be the happiest day of my life, that it would make everything right for all of us. But Janine has inflicted such damage on my little girl – made her hate me so ferociously – there is no hope for us ever having a relationship. She is alive, but she might as well be dead, and I need to accept that. My priority now is to be here for you and Daniel, as I should have been from the day you were born. I just pray it's not too late for me to salvage my relationship with both of you.

Greg is barely talking to me. It's understandable, and I expect he'll divorce me eventually. Seeing Daniel in such a vulnerable state is too much for him right now. He blames himself even though he couldn't have known Heidi was playing them both. For now, he's sitting in the hospital waiting room, wanting to be close by if Daniel wakes up.

I edge closer to Daniel's bed, say, 'Are you asleep, Ella?' just because you are so still, and I can't even detect the rise and fall of your breathing.

Nothing. You must have dozed off. Which isn't surprising. No doubt you're shattered, and anyhow, it's pushing midnight.

Closer still, and I place my hand on your shoulder, then your head, and stroke your hair softly. No reaction. I go around the other side of the bed to see if your eyes are closed, which they are. It's as if you're locked in as deep a sleep as Daniel. I'm amazed because, even if you are tired, I would expect your sleep to be patchy, fretful, what with everything that's gone on. Something feels wrong. I reach out with my left arm across the bed and gently shake your shoulder, but you don't even stir. My heart accelerates and nausea overcomes me as I shake you once again, only this time more aggressively as I shout, 'Ella, Ella, wake up!'

But you don't wake up, and as I come back round and roll you onto your back, you fall into my arms like a rag doll, and I see that your lips are blue and when I touch your cheeks they are cold. I feel for a pulse, but can't make one out, and now I am panicking like crazy. I dash out into the corridor and scream, 'Someone help me, my daughter's not breathing!' at the top of my lungs, a feeling of helplessness, despair and desperation taking hold of me.

And then the room is suddenly a thoroughfare of doctors and nurses working to save your life, as I prop myself up against the wall, weak-legged and alone, wishing I could turn back time and do it all again.

Chapter Eighty-Four

Greg

Now

I will never forgive you for this, Chrissy, never. Even if our children recover, whatever was left of our relationship is over. There is no way back for us. You've inflicted so much pain on so many people; the person I met all those years ago, the person I thought you were, is dead to me. In fact, I'm not sure that person ever existed. Miranda was right about you all along.

Ella took an almost lethal overdose of heroin, and experienced seizures and near respiratory collapse. We think she must have pocketed it from Daniel's stash, along with a syringe, while waiting for the ambulance to arrive, perhaps out of desperation, or possibly a spur-of-the-moment thing when she wasn't thinking straight, and then later, after hearing the full story from you, injected a dangerous amount into her bloodstream, for the same reason Daniel did. Because the person she loved had turned out to be a liar; because she felt like a fool and life for her had become unbearable. She's lucky not to be in a coma like her brother; although it was a close call, she's been fitted with an artificial airway connected to a respirator to maintain her breathing and circulation. Thankfully, the doctors managed to administer an antidote called naloxone in time, which reverses the effects of the overdose. It remains to be seen whether she'll suffer any long-term damage.

Although the consultant looking after Daniel says there's always hope he'll wake up – you hear of these one-in-a-million stories – my gut tells me my boy is dead and never coming back. Even if he does wake up, there's every chance he'll be severely handicapped, and I don't want that for him. He certainly wouldn't want it. I love my boy with all my heart, and I can't help feeling responsible for his situation, even though I know it's not my fault. I'd swap places with him in a heartbeat – my inclination to live is waning fast. I keep thinking, if I hadn't been weak, if I hadn't, like you, been driven by lust, I'd never have started an affair with Heidi, the biggest mistake of my life, and one which has led Daniel to be in this state. How can I live with myself, with this guilt, day after day?

But then I look at Ella, and I realize I need to be there for her when she wakes up. She needs me. I can't trust you to be there for her, and I can't lose all three of my children, I just can't.

Chapter Eighty-Five

Christine

Now

September 2019

We turned Daniel's machine off yesterday. Within hours he was gone. Just like that. Although I resigned myself a while ago to the fact that he was lost to us, it didn't make it any easier, and the finality of it all was almost too much to bear. Ella and I sat by his bedside, clinging to one another for support as Greg hovered in the background, barely able to look, poor man. And that was it. We'd lost another child, and our hearts were a bit more broken.

Last week, Greg filed for divorce. I'd expected him to and I won't contest it. There is no way back for us and he's entitled to be rid of me after all the lies I have told. I pray, for his sake, that it's not too late for him to find love, or at least companionship with someone kind and loyal. I don't think he'll find it with Miranda, though. She confessed to making prank calls and sending hoax messages to the police in the initial months of Heidi's disappearance. I wanted to be angry with her, but to be honest I didn't have the energy. Greg is refusing to speak to her, though. I can't say I blame him. I wouldn't blame him if he never trusted another woman in his life again.

For myself, all I want is to work on my relationship with Ella and try and be the best mother I can to her now, even though I know it won't make up for the past.

The house is up for sale. Greg was happy for me to stay in it, but I need a fresh start. It holds too many memories and I don't feel comfortable in it any more. I intend to move away from London, to the outskirts. I need to escape Janine, who's got away with her crimes scot-free. I know I should hate her and that she should be made to pay for what she's done, but I almost feel I don't have the right to. She already had issues from her childhood, but my actions – my betrayal – turned her into the monster she is now, and I must face up to that. I just hope she can live with herself.

And that she is a good mother to Heidi.

Chapter Eighty-Six

Heidi

Now

November 2019

It's been nine months since you learned the truth, Christine, and last week Mother and I moved back to Hong Kong. We achieved our goal, and although we're almost certain you and Greg won't turn us in, we feel more secure here. Hong Kong was our home for so many years, and it feels right to return, where we have permanent residency. I love my mother, but I am too used to my own space now, and so I am renting an apartment five minutes' drive from her place.

Although we never meant for Daniel to do something so drastic, we don't regret what we did. When I met him, he was already severely troubled because you'd been such a terrible mother to him, and he was always going to have issues, with or without me. I feel no guilt for sending him the photo of me having sex with his dad (I set up a camera in the hotel room where we used to meet regularly) because you are to blame for the way things have turned out. That's what I tell myself, anyway. That's what my mother tells me constantly.

Right now, I'm at Mother's. She's not well. Got a nasty cold, and I've come round to see if she needs anything. Her eyes are streaming, her nose is congested, and she has a bit of a temperature. I watch her blow into a hankie, which looks sodden with gunk, then notice that she doesn't seem quite with it. Like she's spaced out.

'Mother, are you OK?' I ask. 'Can I get you anything?'

She's lying on the sofa, weak and feeble, but still manages a faint smile in my direction. 'A clean hankie would be good. Can you go and fetch one from my underwear drawer, dear? Chest of drawers next to the wardrobe.'

'Sure,' I smile.

Up in Mother's room, I'm not sure which drawer she keeps her hankies in, so I start at the top and work my way down. Mother's a very methodical person, so I'm not surprised to find her underwear sorted into neat compartments. Pants and bras at the top, socks and tights in the middle, and then – bingo – hankies and slips at the bottom. Hankies to the left, slips to the right. But as I pull out a hankie from a pile of twenty or so, I notice something hidden under the pile. It's a crumpled envelope, and the seal is broken. But the real surprise is that it's addressed to me.

I recognize the handwriting instantly. It's my father Nate's handwriting, and it just says, *Heidi*.

I feel my pulse speed up, and I can't resist pulling out the note, feeling slightly angry, but more confused as to why my mother chose to open the envelope and hide its contents from me. But then I tell myself to give her the benefit of the doubt. That perhaps it discloses something terrible she wanted to protect me from, and therefore she only had my best interests at heart.

But as I begin to read, my anger takes over, and not for the first time, I feel like my entire life has been based on lies.

Chapter Eighty-Seven

Nate

Before

My darling child,

By the time you read this, I'll be gone. Please know that I am sorry for putting you through this, for not having the courage to tell you the truth years ago. I am not a brave man. I lack the strength to face up to the consequences of my actions, and I have always put my own needs first. Although I know I will go to hell for my sins, I can at least die with a clear conscience, knowing I have done all I can to put things right before it's too late.

When Janine blackmailed me into going along with her plan to take Chrissy's child, I should have said no. But I was too scared and too selfish to do that. I loved my work, I loved the kudos and power that came with it, and I feared that my career would be ruined if our affair was exposed, and that I wouldn't be able to withstand that. My work was what drove me every day. I also knew it would humiliate Greg and ruin his and Chrissy's marriage. I didn't want that. Greg's a good man and he didn't deserve that.

But ever since that day, the day Janine took Chrissy's child, my child, I've been racked with guilt. Not just because I went along with her plan to kidnap Heidi and make Chrissy suffer, but because I helped my deranged wife cover up another crime. A crime far more repugnant than kidnapping.

Janine never brought my biological daughter to Hong Kong. She suffocated her with a pillow a few hours after she took her, then stripped her naked and set fire to her body in the woods. She couldn't live with the fact that I'd fathered a child with her best friend, and she therefore hated Heidi with an intensity that knew no bounds; her hatred amplified by the fact that she couldn't have children of her own. I honestly had no idea that she planned on killing Heidi – she was my daughter, for heaven's sake – and I nearly committed murder myself when I found out what she'd done.

If I'd known, I swear I would never have made that call to distract Chrissy or been a part of Janine's heinous plan. I honestly thought that the plan was to kidnap her, then raise her as our own. I know I should have turned Janine in then, that you must think me a monster for not calling the police straight away. That any decent father wouldn't have been able to live with the knowledge and pain of his daughter's murder, would have done anything to bring her killer to justice in order to have some peace of mind. But the truth is, I was a coward. I knew I'd be treated as an accomplice, and at the time I couldn't face going to prison, losing everything. And, while I'm being honest, I'll also admit that Janine frightened the hell out of me. I knew she'd make sure the entire world knew about my and Chrissy's affair, and I couldn't bear the consequences of that. The humiliation and hurt it would cause Greg who, since the day he met her, worshipped the ground Chrissy walked on. And so, somehow, I lived with Heidi's murder, told myself that moving to Hong Kong would help me to put it behind me. That a new life, a new environment, where I could bury myself in my work, would solve things.

But killing Heidi wasn't enough for Janine; even though I didn't know it at the time. So utterly consumed by revenge, her plan was to take things further. It became a kind of project for her, one she could focus on and bring to fruition at some point in the future. She wanted Chrissy to suffer for the rest of her days, until she took her dying breath, and concocted a plan so warped – one I didn't find out about until much later – I truly didn't believe her capable of going through with it. Which is why I never took steps to stop it. Until now.

We adopted you, Freya, (yes, that is your real name, the name your birth parents gave you) not long after moving to Hong Kong. You looked a bit like Heidi. Same dark hair, petite nose, big brown eyes, and I loved you like you were my flesh and blood from the first moment I set eyes on you. Janine kept you in the house because later she needed you to believe that you were Chrissy's child, whom she had kidnapped and couldn't risk being recognized. She told me at the time it was because she wanted to keep you safe from harm. She told the same to Mrs Bates. I didn't argue with her, even though I thought it was unhealthy to keep you locked inside the house like a prisoner.

You became the only silver lining to the black cloud my life had become. I could almost imagine you were Heidi, almost convince myself that what happened to her wasn't real. Little did I know then, that Janine still wasn't done.

When you turned thirteen, she told you about Chrissy. I had no idea she was going to do this, and I was shocked when she told me afterwards. She told you that you were Chrissy's and my biological daughter – the product of our illicit affair – and that Chrissy had never wanted you, had hated you from the moment we conceived you, and that this was why she lost you in a department store one day. She told you that Chrissy didn't care about you, that you were a hindrance to her life. She made you hate a woman who had no connection to you whatsoever, and she brainwashed you into helping her destroy Chrissy and her family for good.

I couldn't believe she could do this to you, our adopted daughter, whom I thought she loved like her own. But, like I always feared, she said she'd implicate me in Heidi's murder if I told you the truth. I had no choice but to keep quiet, even though I know that was gutless of me. But it killed me to see her twist your mind and turn you into a clone of herself. I know you never looked at me the same way after that day, and I can't even begin to tell you how much that hurt. Your love, the way you used to look at me, hug me, adore me, was the tonic that kept me going despite what I had done, but when Janine poisoned your love for me, I gradually lost interest in life. In fact, I'm not entirely sure how I've lasted this long.

I should never have cheated on Janine with Chrissy. I know it's by no means an excuse, but all I can say is that we were irresistibly attracted to each other, and we were too weak to repel that attraction. Looking back, I should never have married Janine. She idolized me from the first, and this fed my ego. After several failed relationships with various attractive, ambitious women, I knew she would be the devoted, loyal wife I needed, but I failed to reciprocate her love and devotion in the way she deserved. I took her love for granted, and my actions backfired on me in the worst possible way, and with tragic consequences. I also misjudged what a deeply troubled woman she is, although she did well to hide it. Her miserable home and school life seriously affected her, made her bitter, suspicious, but when Chrissy became her friend, and later I her husband, she believed things had finally come right for her. And so, when she realized we had betrayed her trust in the cruellest way possible, it drove her to the depths of despair and lunacy.

My life has been a series of mistakes and tragedies, but since Heidi's death you, Freya, are the one good thing I've had. You were never a mistake. Please believe that. And I know, in her own way, Janine loves you, even though she should never have lied to you about who you really are.

I am sorry for not telling you all this before, Freya. I was weak, and that is why I can no longer live with myself.

I know what you and Janine are planning, I'm not stupid, but I pray that now you know the truth, you won't go through with it. It's not right that Chrissy's family should suffer for her and my mistakes. None of this is their fault, and you have no real cause to hate her. Because it wasn't you she took her eye off and lost.

I hope you receive this before it's too late. Please forgive me. Please stop Janine from going through with her plan.

Dad.

Chapter Eighty-Eight

Freya

Now

I feel broken from head to toe. I might as well shatter into a million pieces and cease to exist. And who would care? No one, as far as I can tell.

My whole life has been a sham. First, I found out I wasn't Janine's real daughter, but Christine's. Now, I discover I'm not Christine's either, and I don't, in fact, have any idea who my real mother and father are. And I have done the most reprehensible things at the behest of a bitter, depraved, manipulative woman.

Everything I am, everything I've done, has been based on lies, and I only have one person to blame for that. The twisted woman lying downstairs on the sofa. The woman who has lied to me all my life for the sake of her own sick fixation with getting revenge against the woman she both worshipped and envied.

I feel numb. I'm not even sure I feel human. I slept with Daniel and Ella, thinking we were related. It should be a relief to know we aren't, but I'm suddenly disgusted with myself for being OK with it at the time. Just as I am disgusted with myself for sleeping with their father, another innocent. One blameless young man is dead because of me, and his sister could so easily have gone the same way. I just hope she can recover and make some sort of life for herself.

But I cannot blame myself. I blame her downstairs. She brainwashed me, made me hate a woman I had no connection to, and she used that hate to her advantage. A hate that can blind you to what's right and wrong, impede your ability to separate reason from madness.

I don't know who I am or what I stand for. I serve no purpose, and I feel incapable of forming relationships going forward. How can I be a wife or a mother to another human being, when my view of what it means to be those things is so distorted?

I take the note downstairs with me and lay it on the kitchen table, where I am hoping someone will find it, and the truth will be exposed. Christine deserves to know the truth. And so does what's left of her family.

Then I walk back into the living room and see her still reclined on the sofa, waiting for me to return with her hankie. Good little Freya. Her servant. Her stooge. How can she lie there, knowing that she deceived me, knowing that I am not Heidi and yet continuing to pretend that I am?

She turns and smiles at me, but quickly reads the look on my face and realizes her mistake in sending me upstairs. She knows that look. She's seen it in the mirror countless times before. It is the look of revenge.

'Look, don't be dramatic, I can explain.'

Just the sound of her voice makes me sick. Before she has a chance to fight back – she's too weak, in any event – I grab the nearest cushion and, with all the force I can muster, press it hard against her face, just as she did to poor little Heidi. And I keep it there. My entire being filled with hurt, regret, pain and rage at all the lies she's told, and all the terrible things I've done at her command.

I press down harder still with all my might as she kicks and thrashes in vain, until finally, she kicks no more.

I remove the cushion, satisfied that this woman is dead and can do no more harm, then pick up the phone and dial emergency services, give them the address and say, 'Come quickly. Two women are dead.'

And then I go to the kitchen and find the almost full bottle of lithium my mother keeps in the top cupboard and swallow its entire contents.

Wait for peace to embrace me in death, the way it never did in life.

A letter from A.A. Chaudhuri

Dear Reader, I hope you are keeping well. Firstly, I wanted to thank you for reading my novel. This is my debut psychological thriller with Hera Books and therefore it feels that extra bit special. Having invested so much time in the book, as well as my heart and soul, it really means the world that you have chosen to read it, and it also makes the hours of graft worth it and all the more rewarding.

I began writing this book in April 2017 and once the idea came to me, I very quickly became immersed in Christine's story which, granted, wasn't an easy one to tell. Being a mother of two young boys, it was difficult to write at various points, but at the same time, I hope this helped me to convey the sheer horror and incomparable pain of Christine's, as well as her husband Greg's, loss. Of course, there is more to this story than the loss of a child, and I hope you found the premise, twists and turns compelling, as well as the characterisation, bearing in mind the story is told through different viewpoints. I very much enjoyed creating each of the characters, with their own distinct idiosyncrasies, as well as getting inside their minds and skins (bearing in mind their gender and age differences) in order to try and see things from their unique perspectives – the how and the why, the backstories/life events that made them the people they are today, and which motivated them to act and think in the way they did. The human mind is a complex thing; none of us, as imperfect human beings, are immune to the feelings, inner turmoil, not to mention uglier, more destructive emotions and desires my characters experience, and I hope this therefore made the book all the more engaging for you.

The story and characters are completely fictional, although the references to law and North London/the City stem from my time living and working in London as a student and a lawyer for thirteen years.

All that being said, if you enjoyed *SHE'S MINE*, I would be over-the-moon to hear your thoughts via a review, and which I hope might encourage other readers to read it. It's so rewarding seeing reader reviews; they are inspiring and hugely appreciated, and give me encouragement to keep writing, keep honing and perfecting my craft going forward to the next book and beyond. Incidentally, if you enjoyed this book, I'd love for you to read my next psychological thriller with Hera, due out in the early part of 2022.

Again, thank you for your support on my writing journey and I hope you'll continue to follow me as I work on new titles.

You can get in touch on my social media pages: Twitter, Facebook, Instagram, Linked In. Also, please visit my website for further information on my books, and latest news/blog posts. I'd love to hear from you if you'd like to talk about this book, or anything else for that matter. Readers' support is the lifeblood of an author's work, the tonic that keeps them going. I hope you know how grateful I am for your time and trouble.

Best wishes and happy reading.

Alex x

https://www.facebook.com/AAChaudhuri/
https://twitter.com/AAChaudhuri/
https://www.instagram.com/A.A.Chaudhuri/
https://www.linkedin.com/in/a-a-chaudhuri-55a83524/
https://aachaudhuri.com/

Acknowledgments

It goes without saying that writing a book is no easy feat. It takes hours and hours of hard work on the part of the author to bring it to the point of publication. But that point would not be reached without the help and support of others. First and foremost, it is a collective effort, and that being so, there are certain people I would like to thank from the bottom of my heart:

My publishers, Keshini Naidoo and Lindsey Mooney, for taking this book on. When I first learned how much they loved my novel, and wanted to publish it, I was literally dancing around the room. To work with Keshini and Lindsey, two of the most respected, talented, not to mention nicest, people in the industry, who together, have forged such a unique cutting-edge and successful publishing house with Hera Books, is truly a dream come true. It goes without saying that I would not be writing this page without them. My heartfelt thanks to Keshini for her phenomenal editing advice and vision to make this book as compelling as possible. I feel very privileged to have had the benefit of her expertise and can't thank her enough for her kindness and patience with me throughout the editing process. Just on this note, I must also thank the copy editor, Jon Appleton, whose comments were invaluable, along with the proof-reader, Andrew Bridgmont, for helping to make it as error-free as possible. Thank you also to Head Design for creating such an evocative cover and one that perfectly captures the sense of foreboding and dark, sinister atmosphere of the novel.

My agent, Annette Crossland, for taking me on, always believing in me, always encouraging me to keep going through thick or thin and who loved this book from the first. Again, I wouldn't be writing this page without her. She is not just a fabulous agent – always there to listen and advise and champion my writing, to tell me to "hold on, we'll get there, it's just a matter of time," – but also a one-in-a-million friend who makes me laugh.

Kirstie Long of A for Authors for taking the time to read my book in its infancy, for offering me her advice, as well as being a constant source of support, encouragement and friendship.

Awais Khan, author of *No Honour* and *In The Company of Strangers*, not just a supremely talented author but who, since we launched our debuts together, has been a true friend, always there to support and encourage me, pick me up and make me laugh when I need it.

Sabine Edwards of Pendleton Events for her support, encouragement and tireless efforts in promoting my work.

Ayo Onatade, for her support and encouragement with my writing, and generally being so gracious and kind.

Chika Ripley, one of the best friends a girl could ask for. I am so grateful to her for reading an early draft despite her crazy work schedule, for always being so supportive, as well as the voice of reason. She really is a Supermum!

To another Supermum, Danielle Price, not only an exceptionally talented blogger, but a great friend, and someone who has selflessly championed my books since I have known her, while inspiring authors like me every day.

To my fellow A for Authors authors for being such a kind, fun and supportive bunch who I can have a laugh with. Being able to see the lighter side of things is so important and their support means the world.

To all the amazing book bloggers out there, with a special mention to the very kind and generous Surjit Parekh, without whom authors would be lost. So many of them have supported my writing journey from the start, and I am just so grateful to them for that. Their love of reading and selfless support is immensely appreciated. Also, the CWA, Capital Crime and radio show Crime Fiction Addiction hosted by the inimitable Jacky Collins, who've been immensely supportive, giving me opportunities to talk about and promote my work to a wider audience. The writing community is such a welcoming, supportive one, and I feel very lucky to be a part of it.

Friends and family, of both the writer and non-writer variety, who have supported and encouraged me from the start, and been happy for me. With a special mention to Zoe Gale for reading an early draft.

Last but by no means least, I want to thank my Mum and Dad, my husband, Chris, and my two gorgeous boys, Adam and Henry, for being there for me every step of the way; for their unflinching support, love and belief in me and my dream, and for giving me the time and space to make this book the best version of itself. Collectively, you are my rock, and I feel so lucky to have you in my life and by my side.